CURSE OF THE SPELLMANS

CURSE OF THE SPELLMANS

Lisa Lutz

WINDSOR
PARAGON

First published 2009
by Simon & Schuster
This Large Print edition published 2009
by BBC Audiobooks Ltd
by arrangement with
Simon & Schuster UK Ltd

Hardcover ISBN: 978 1 408 43085 9
Softcover   ISBN: 978 1 408 43086 6

British Library Cataloguing in Publication Data available

Printed and bound in Great Britain by
CPI Antony Rowe, Chippenham and Eastbourne

For Stephanie Kip Rostan
& Marysue Rucci

IN THE MIDDLE . . .

Saturday, April 22,
1900 hrs

'Hello?'
'Hi, Mom.'
'Who is this?'
'Isabel, and don't ask me again.'
'Who?'
'Mom, it's really not funny when you do it.'
'Seriously, who is this?'
'I don't have time for your games right now.'
'Neither do I,' said Mom, finally dropping the amnesia act. 'I'll call you in a few days.'
'Don't hang up!!!' I shouted into the receiver.
'Isabel, calm down.'
'Just don't hang up.'
'Why not?'
'Because . . . I only get one phone call.'

1

ARREST #2 (OR #4)
[Depends on whether you count #2 and #3
—I don't.]

That statement was, in fact, untrue. I used it purely for dramatic effect. According to the California Penal Code, Section 851.5, California grants arrestees the right to three telephone calls to the following individuals: 1.) an attorney, 2.) a bail bondsman, and 3.) a relative or other person. The code isn't clear on whether the three calls must be made to each of the above or if you can double or triple up on any one.

Regardless, my mother was not my first choice. Before Mom, I tried my brother, David (no answer), and Mort Schilling, an old ['Old' refers to the age of the friend, not the length of our friendship.] friend of mine who used to be a defense attorney. As of this arrest, I had not yet acquired the services of a regular bail bondsman. After searching through my internal Rolodex and running the list by my new friends, Scarlet and Lacey (also in lockup but for different offenses), they both agreed that I should call my mother.

'If your own mother won't bail you out of jail, who will?' Lacey asked.

Her reasoning was sound, but I called my mom because I thought she owed me after arrest #1.5? (or #3, depending on how you're counting). The rest of the conversation went like this:

MOM: Not again, Isabel. Please explain this to me.

ME: I'll explain as soon as you pick me up.

2

MOM: We're already on the road, dear. I'm not canceling our disappearance ['Disappearance' means 'vacation' in the Spellman household. I will explain the origin of this later.] to bail you out of jail.

ME: Oh, I forgot about the disappearance.

MOM: You're on your own, sweetie.

ME: No, Mom! You've got to call someone to get me out of here. I don't want to spend the night in this place.

MOM: That might be a good idea. Remember Scared Straight!?

ME: Of course I remember it. You made me watch it at least ten times in high school.

MOM: A lot of good it did.

ME: Listen, call Morty again. Call until he picks up the phone. He's home. He just can't hear it.

MOM: I don't think he should be driving at night.

ME: Mom, please.

MOM: Or during the day for that matter.

Officer Lindley: Spellman, can you hurry this up?

ME: I got to go. Just make sure someone gets me out of here.

MOM: I'll do my best. See you on Monday, Isabel.

ME: Have a nice disappearance.

*   *   *

Three hours later, Officer Lindley banged his nightstick on the cage and said, 'Spellman, you're out.' After retrieving my personal effects from the clerk, I was led into the waiting room, which I scanned for a familiar face.

Morty was slumped over, asleep, in one of the green vinyl chairs. His wild, thinning hair drooped

3

over his square Coke-bottle glasses. There was a crumpled lunch bag on his lap. His snoring alternated between kitchen blender and energy-efficient dishwasher.

'Wake up, Morty,' I said, gently shaking his shoulder.

Morty woke with a start, then turned to me and smiled. 'How's my favorite delinquent?' he asked.

'I've been better,' I replied.

'What's this, arrest number four?'

'Do you think it's fair to count two and three?'

'We don't have to count them if you don't want. I thought you might be hungry, so I brought you a sandwich,' Morty said, and then handed me the abused paper bag. 'It's your favorite. Pastrami on rye.'

'No, Morty, it's your favorite, which would account for why there's only half a sandwich left.'

'I had to wait over an hour,' Morty said in his own defense.

I put my arm around my pint-sized octogenarian friend and kissed him on the cheek. 'I knew you wouldn't let me rot in there.'

'Let's talk business for a minute,' Morty said.

'Shoot,' I said, knowing it wouldn't be good news.

'Your arraignment is on Monday. I don't think I can get this charge dropped. Four arrests in under two months. They're getting tired of seeing your mug around here. You violated a TRO. [Temporary restraining order.] Izzila, [Morty likes to Yiddishify my name.] what were you thinking?'

'Arrests two and three don't count, Morty. As for the other two, I think we can defend against those charges, although I need more evidence.'

4

'Gathering evidence is what got you in trouble in the first place. You got to stop that. Besides, your mother wanted me to tell you that you're grounded.'

'I'm thirty years old. She can't ground me.'

'She can fire you,' Morty replied. 'And then what are you going to do?'

Morty had a point. But I was convinced that once I solved my primary mystery, all my troubles would vanish. But first, I had to stay out of jail, which meant staging a defense.

*   *   *

At 9:00 A.M. the following Monday morning I was arraigned in Courtroom Four of the San Francisco criminal court building. Morty predicted correctly: these charges would not be dropped. My preliminary hearing was set for the following Monday, which gave Morty and me a full week to stage my defense. We returned to Morty's office later that morning to go over the details of my case.

THE 'LAW OFFICES' OF
MORT SCHILLING

Monday, April 24
1000 hrs

Morty punched holes on my arrest sheet and secured it in his brand-new file on Isabel Spellman, or Spellman, Isabel (case #2 [Notice the case number. The only other case Morty had this year was his nephew's traffic violation.]). Me.

'We should be able to keep the second and third arrests out of any court hearing. I can argue that they're not related.'

'Good.'

'What?'

'Good!'

'During our lunches [Morty and I have a standing lunch date every week. I will explain how we met and the nature of our relationship in due time.] you've told me bits and pieces about this case, but I need the whole picture to figure out the best way to paint your story in court.'

'Do you really think this is going to court?'

'What? Speak up.'

'Do you think this will go to—Morty, put in your hearing aid.'

Morty reached into his desk drawer, stuck in his hearing aid, and adjusted the volume.

'This thing drives me crazy. What were you saying?'

'Do you think this will even go to court? I mean, we can explain the evidence to the district attorney

6

and maybe they'll finally investigate this guy.'

'Isabel, first things first. Let's get your story down and then we'll figure out how to deal with the DA. Right now I want you to tell me the whole story, and don't leave anything out. I like the details and I've got all day. And I've got tomorrow and the next day, God willing.'

'But I've already figured out my defense.'

'Enlighten me,' Morty replied.

'I'm innocent,' I said.

'But you acknowledge you violated a TRO?'

'I acknowledge that.'

'Then how can you be innocent?'

'Because the person who filed the restraining order is not who he says he is. Therefore the TRO is invalid.'

'Why don't we start at the beginning, Isabel.'

Part I

Beginnings

SUBJECT MOVES INTO
1797 CLAY STREET . . .

Sunday, January 8
1100 hrs

I have trouble with beginnings. For one thing, I don't find stories all that interesting when you start at the beginning. If you ask me, you only know there is a story when you get to the middle. And besides, beginnings are hard to determine. One could argue that the true beginning to all stories is the beginning of time. But Morty is already eighty-two years old, so given our time constraints, I'll begin this story on the date I met, or more specifically, first laid eyes on 'John Brown' (hereafter referred to as 'Subject' or by some variation of his alias, 'John Brown').

I remember the day that Subject moved in next door to my parents like it was yesterday. He was taking over the second-story apartment of a triplex, previously occupied by Mr. Rafter, whose tenancy lasted close to thirty years. David knew Mr. Rafter better than I since his bedroom was six feet from Rafter's den and their windows were level enough to provide each a fishbowl view of the other. Since Rafter spent most of his time watching television in the den and David spent most of his time studying in his bedroom, the two men got to know each other in their respective comfortable silences (minus the sounds of the television, that is).

But I digress. As I said, I remember the day

11

Subject moved in next door like it was yesterday. And I suppose the reason I remember it so vividly is because of the events that transpired earlier that day, the events that caused me to be at my family's home at the precise moment Subject's moving truck double-parked out front. So, I'm thinking I should probably start earlier that day and mention the aforementioned events.

0900 hrs

I woke in my bed, or, more precisely, the bed in the home of Bernie Peterson, a retired SFPD lieutenant who I sublet from. My illegal residence in the Richmond district is exactly 2.8 miles and one giant hill away from my parents' home, but I'm always just a phone call away.

The phone rang, like it always does, before I'd had enough coffee to face the day.

'Hello.'

'Isabel, it's mom.'

'Who?'

'I'm not in the mood for this today.'

'Not ringing a bell. When did we meet?'

'Listen to me very carefully; I don't want to repeat myself. I need you to pick up Rae from the hospital.'

'Is she all right?' I asked, concern altering the tone in my voice. [In case you're wondering, I know when to give up the shtick.]

'She's fine. But Henry [*Inspector Henry Stone. I'll explain all about him later.*] isn't.'

'What happened?'

'She ran him over.'

'How?'

12

'With a car, Isabel.'

'I got that part, Mom.'

'Izzy, I'm in the middle of a job. I have to go. Please get all the details of what went down. As usual, record everything. Call me when you get home.'

San Francisco General Hospital
1000 hrs

The woman at the reception desk told me that only immediate family would be allowed in Henry's room. I flashed my quarter-carat engagement ring and asked if fiancées qualified.

A nurse directed me toward room 873 and explained that he was in a serious, but stable, condition.

'Can you tell me what happened?' I asked the nurse.

'Your daughter is with him now. I'll let her explain.'

'My daughter?'

*   *   *

I found my sister, Rae, sitting by Inspector Henry Stone's bedside staring at the electronic device monitoring his vitals.

Henry's nurse tried to smile over her annoyance at Rae's hypervigilant announcements.

'Seventy-two. His heart rate went up by five beats,' Rae said as I entered.

My sister's eyes were bloodshot and her flushed cheeks showed signs of recent crying. The nurse looked relieved when she saw me and said to Rae,

13

'Oh, good. Your mother's here.'

'Eew,' I said, offended. 'I'm not her mother. Do I look old enough to be the mother of a fifteen-year-old girl?'

'I hadn't thought about it,' she replied.

'I'm his fiancée,' I clarified to the nurse, and then turned to the inspector.

Henry Stone was lying in the hospital bed with an assortment of tubes and monitors attached to his body, wearing the standard-issue hospital gown. Minus the unfortunate outfit and the single gauze bandage stuck to his left temple, he looked pretty much the same as he always does: well groomed, slightly underweight, and handsome in a way that's very easy to ignore. His usually short-cropped salt-and-pepper hair had grown out more in the past few weeks, which had the added benefit of making him appear younger than his forty-four years. Although, at that moment, the dark circles under his eyes and his patently agitated expression had offset that benefit.

'How is he?' I asked the nurse, trying to emote the appropriate shade of concern.

'There's some bruising on the legs just below the knee, but nothing's broken. The main concern is the concussion. He lost consciousness for five minutes and is experiencing nausea. We did a CT and everything looks fine, but we need to keep him under observation for forty-eight hours.'

'Will he have permanent brain damage?' Rae asked.

Henry grabbed my wrist. Hard. 'I need to speak to you in private,' he said.

I turned to Rae. 'Leave the room.'

'No,' she replied. I never thought a single syllable

14

could possess such heartbreaking desperation.

'Get out,' Henry demanded, unmoved by her wells of emotion.

'Are you ever going to forgive me?' she said to him.

'It's only been two hours since you ran me over,' he replied.

'Accidentally!' she shouted.

Then Henry shot her a look that seemed to have more power than any lecture, punishment, or curfew my parents ever unleashed on Rae.

'Two and a half hours,' Rae mumbled as she soberly exited the room.

Henry gripped my arm even tighter after Rae was out of earshot.

'That kind of hurts, Henry.'

'Don't talk to me about pain.'

'Right. Sorry.'

'I need you to do me a favor.'

'Shoot.'

'Keep her away from me.'

'For how long?'

'A couple weeks.'

'Dream on.'

'Isabel, please. I need a break.'

'I'll do what I can, but—'

'Your sister almost killed me today—'

'Accidentally!' shouted Rae from the other side of the door.

'I need a Rae vacation. [In this instance the word 'vacation' is being used in its traditional sense.] Please. Help me.'

THE 'LAW OFFICES' OF MORT SCHILLING

Monday, April 24
1015 hrs

'When did you and Inspector Stone get engaged?'

'We're not engaged. We're "engaged,"' I said, using finger quotes.

'You're not wearing an engagement ring.'

'I don't need to wear it anymore.'

'Run that by me again.'

'It's a really long story. Are you sure you want to hear it?'

'I want to hear any story that will help explain the evidence that has been amassed against you.'

'That might take a while.'

Morty shrugged his shoulders. Retirement hadn't been his cup of tea. Anything that kept him busy was.

Like I said, beginnings are impossible to define. For my story and my defense to make complete sense, I need to provide details from long before my troubles with 'John Brown' began.

A BRIEF HISTORY OF ME

I am the second child of Albert and Olivia Spellman. Since the age of twelve I have worked for the family business, Spellman Investigations, a private investigative firm located inside the Spellman family residence in San Francisco, California. My brother, David, is two years my senior and my sister, Rae, fourteen-plus years my junior.

I was, unequivocally, the difficult child (and adolescent and young adult). My reign of terror over the Spellman household lasted almost twenty years. I have often theorized that my bad seed MO arose out of having a sibling (David) whose perfection, both physical and intellectual, could not be matched. Because I could not compete with my brother, I responded by slumming in imperfection, leaving a wake of vandalism and truancy everywhere I went. David often tried to temper my exploits by sweeping whatever he could under the rug, but eventually even he grew tired of compensating for me. Now David is a lawyer married to my best friend, Petra. [Who happened to be my partner in crime during most of my delinquent years.] His primary connection to the family business is throwing work our way.

My sister, Rae, age fifteen (and a half), barely looks a day over thirteen. She inherited her small frame from our mother, but the dirty-blond hair and freckles mimic no one else in the family. My sister's grand loyalty to the family, and especially the family business, has set her apart from me and

David. Rae began working for Spellman Investigations when she was six years old and seemed to believe that she led the perfect life. For her, maybe it was true; it appeared that she was born into precisely the right family.

In my mid-twenties, I eventually came to realize that my behavior was the formative example to an impressionable pre-teen; because of this and a few other mitigating factors, I grew up. My transformation was quick and sudden. To the untrained eye it would appear that I fell asleep a delinquent and woke up as a somewhat responsible member of society.

It was then that my family experienced its longest spate of normalcy, which lasted approximately four years. Then two years ago, after my Uncle Ray [I'll get to him in five pages or so.] moved into the Spellman home, battles began to simmer between me, my parents, my sister, my uncle Ray, my brother, and Petra, my best friend. And then we went to war.

The war began when I started dating a dentist behind my mother's back. My mother hates dentists, you see. Or she did, back when the wounds were fresh from her undercover work in a sexual assault case. I still say Mom and Dad fired the first shots. They hired my sister Rae (fourteen at the time) to follow me. That's how they discovered I was dating Daniel Castillo, DDS (Ex-Boyfriend #9—see appendix). After a humiliating meeting between Ex #9 and my family, I decided that I had to get out of the family business.

That is when our war escalated. My parents commenced twenty-four-hour surveillance on me (using my sister as their primary operative), and just when we thought this game of cat and mouse couldn't get any worse, my sister disappeared.

It was later discovered that Rae kidnapped herself in a preemptive strike to end the war. And she got exactly what she wanted: the war ended and my family returned to its previous state of normalcy. Although my sister's dramatic play did not go unpunished.

It was during Rae's six month probation that she began visiting Henry Stone—the primary officer on her own missing person case. What began as weekly visits to the oddly well-groomed, highly ethical inspector in the San Francisco Police Department's Bryant Street headquarters, would end eighteen months later when my sister almost murdered him with his own car.

SAN FRANCISCO
GENERAL HOSPITAL

Sunday, January 8
1005 hrs

My mother would have murdered me if she knew how long I had been in the hospital room without turning on the tape recorder. Before another word was uttered, I slipped my hand into my pocket and switched on my palm-sized digital recorder.

The transcript reads as follows:

[Rae reenters the room as Nurse Stinson finishes filling out Inspector Stone's medical

19

chart. The nurse smiles professionally and goes to the door.]

NURSE: If you need anything, Inspector, please use the call button. [She turns to me and Rae.]

NURSE: Ladies, visiting hours will be over in two hours.

HENRY: I'm very tired. I think they should leave now.

ISABEL: We'll leave in a few minutes.

HENRY: No. Leave now. Please. Nurse?

RAE: His pulse just went up by two beats. Now it's seventy-four.

NURSE: He's fine. I'll check on you in an hour. [Nurse Stinson exits the room.]

ISABEL: Henry, we'll be out of here in a minute. But Mom wants a complete rundown of the events, which means she needs to hear it from you. Oh, and I'm recording this. Tell me exactly what happened.

HENRY: Your sister ran me over—

RAE: Accidentally!

ISABEL: The 'accidental' is implied, Rae. What I'd like to know is how. You have a learner's permit, not a license. You're not supposed to be in the driver's seat of a car without a licensed driver with you at all times. If you ran Henry over, clearly he was *OUTSIDE OF THE CAR*.

HENRY: Please keep it down. My head hurts.

ISABEL: Sorry. [to Rae] Talk.

RAE: We were leaving the police station for my driving lesson.

HENRY: I hope you enjoyed it, because that was the *last* driving lesson I will ever give you.

RAE: I think that's the head injury talking.

HENRY: Mark my words.

20

ISABEL: Can we get on with the story?

RAE: Henry was carrying a box and then he stopped to talk to that guy who smells like fish.

HENRY: Captain Greely.

ISABEL: Why does he smell like fish?

RAE: I have *no* idea.

ISABEL: So he just smells like fish all the time?

RAE: Every time I've smelled him he's smelled like fish.

HENRY: [snappishly] He takes fish oil supplements for his heart. Can we get on with this?

ISABEL: Right. Okay, then what happened?

RAE: I ran ahead to the car, got in the driver's seat, and waited for Henry. But he was still holding the box and talking to the fish guy.

HENRY: Captain Greely.

RAE: [snotty] Captain Greely.

HENRY: Young lady, on the day you run me over—

RAE: Accidentally!

HENRY: —you don't get to talk to me like that.

RAE: I think you need to calm down. Your heart rate is up to eighty beats per minute.

HENRY: Isabel, I want you to get her out of here.

ISABEL: In a minute. I promise. Can I please hear the end of the story? Rae, hurry up and talk.

RAE: So he had this heavy box and he was talking to the—Captain Greely, and I just thought if I drove the car twenty feet that wouldn't be a big deal and he wouldn't have to carry the box to the car. I was *trying* to be nice. So I turned on the engine and started to drive and then I saw Henry and he looked so mad and he stepped out in front of the car and shouted for me to stop

21

and I got scared and I meant to hit the brakes, but I hit the gas.

[Tears of guilt have formed in Rae's eyes.]

ISABEL: Are you crying?

RAE: I almost accidentally murdered my best friend today.

HENRY AND ISABEL: Stop saying that!

* * *

Although Morty had not interrupted my story for further exposition on the bizarre relationship between my fifteen-and-a-half-year-old sister and the forty-four-year-old inspector, I think further background information would help illuminate this moment in the hospital room and many of the events that will follow.

A BRIEF HISTORY
OF HENRY AND RAE

Remember the wars I mentioned earlier? They were not exclusive to me and my parents. My sister, Rae, was a party in her own conflict against Uncle Ray. Uncle Ray was my father's older brother. Almost seventeen years ago, within the span of six months, he got cancer, his wife left him, he almost died, and then he recovered. The once clean-living/responsible/much-admired police inspector uncle then became a slovenly shadow of his former well-scrubbed self. New Uncle Ray would often disappear on benders that my family dubbed 'Lost Weekends.' Every time he

22

disappeared, we would retrieve him, pay off his gambling debts, sober him up enough to maintain civilized grooming standards, and keep as watchful an eye on him as we could until the next Lost Weekend.

My sister's age and high work ethic made her initial relationship with her namesake hostile at best, but eventually, when Rae realized that her uncle was not a selfish old fool but a lonely man who got dealt a hand of cards that he didn't know how to play, she softened her opinion of him and they eventually made peace.

However, as soon as my sister had grown accustomed to her regular television-watching/sugar-consuming/card-playing companion, Uncle Ray passed out in a bathtub in a casino hotel in Reno, Nevada, after a long day of poker losses and binge drinking.

My sister took Uncle Ray's death harder than anyone, and soon her bimonthly visits to Henry Stone turned into biweekly drop-ins to his station office. Henry tried to turn her away, but she came back again and again, despite his repeated requests for her to make friends her own age. Eventually Stone would reluctantly accept my sister as a constant in his life, and I suspect he decided that if he couldn't get rid of her, at least he could make her do her homework.

At first I considered the casting of the clean-living, buttoned-up inspector as an Uncle Ray surrogate quite odd. But my mother explained that he was the perfect replacement. He was like Uncle Ray before he was broken. Uncle Ray would pass out in the bathtub; Henry Stone would find the body.

23

My sister's early visits to the inspector (which commenced approximately two years ago) typically involved her sitting in the leather chair across from his desk doing homework. The dialogue that would pass between them would fill no more than five minutes, but the time they shared in the same room could be hours. Since my mother has very few official sightings of Rae actually doing homework, Mom in no way discouraged these visits, even after Henry called her and pled his own case. My mom, in turn, responded that so long as Rae made it home by curfew, she could not justify grounding her for visiting a friend, especially when that friend worked in a place as safe as a police precinct.

I, on the other hand, was not without some sympathy for the hassled inspector and would often pick Rae up from his office when he called. Unfortunately for Henry, depending on the job I was working, he'd often have to wait hours for her removal.

The primary conflict between Henry and my sister was how they should go about defining their relationship—not to each other, but to other people. The first time this problem arose was when Henry's boss, Lieutenant Osborn, entered Stone's office shortly after Rae's arrival.

'Henry,' the lieutenant said pleasantly, 'is this nice young lady an informant?'

To which Rae, genuinely flattered, replied, 'No. We're just good friends.'

The lieutenant gave Inspector Stone a double-take, handed him a case file, and left the office with a cordial nod of the head.

'In the future, Rae, it's probably best if you don't refer to me as your friend.'

'But we are friends, right?'

'I guess so,' Stone reluctantly replied, unable to come up with another definition. 'But just don't say it out loud.'

*   *   *

Approximately six months after Rae's office visits commenced, my sister decided to take their relationship to a different level. She asked Henry for a ride home from school after a two-hour detention, in the midst of a violent downpour. She called Stone's cell phone number, which he gave to her in a moment of weakness, I suspect. After three messages and a series of negotiations, [Will briefly explain Rae's negotiation habit shortly.] Henry agreed to pick Rae up from school. Stone arrived in Rae's homeroom forty-five minutes later, carrying an extra police-issued raincoat.

'Finally,' Rae said as she haphazardly tossed her belongings into her schoolbag.

Mrs. Collins, Rae's homeroom instructor, English teacher, and punisher, approached the odd pair, her curiosity and suspicion genuinely piqued.

'Rae, introduce me to this nice young man who was kind enough to pick you up from school.'

'This is my . . . colleague, Henry Stone.'

Henry smiled uncomfortably and shook Mrs. Collins's hand.

'We're not colleagues, Rae.'

'Associates?' my sister asked.

'No.'

'Then we're friends, like I said before.'

'I'm a friend of the family,' Stone said to Mrs. Collins, sensing her suspicion. 'Inspector Henry Stone.'

'A new friend?' the older woman asked, her eyes narrowing.

'I guess so,' Stone replied, and then turned to my sister. 'Are you ready?'

'Let's blow this joint,' Rae said, heading for the door.

'Don't say that,' Henry cautioned as he waved to Mrs. Collins and followed Rae to his car.

HOW I BECAME
HENRY STONE'S 'FIANCÉE'

Mrs. Collins's radar went up the moment she met the inspector. A non-family member of the opposite sex picking up an impressionable adolescent girl was like a flashlight in a blackout for the seasoned educator. However, as Rae's English teacher, she had further evidence to fuel her wariness. Mrs. Collins had recently assigned her students a five-page essay on a person whom they admired. Rae predictably wrote about Henry Stone. That in itself was not incriminating, but the fact that she referred to this man as her best friend did. Shortly after Rae turned in that essay, Mrs. Collins came upon Henry and Rae in the parking lot when he was picking her up yet again from school. Rae was introducing the inspector to a few of her classmates as her 'uncle Henry.'

What Mrs. Collins didn't hear was the argument that ensued on the car ride home, which went something like this:

'Why did you call me your uncle? I'm not your uncle.'

'You already said I can't call you my colleague, associate, or friend. So what's left?'

'Just say I'm a friend of the family.'

'But you're more my friend than my family's friend.'

'Rae, most people would find a forty-four-year-old man being friends with a fifteen-year-old girl inappropriate.'

'So what? I mean if Mom and Dad don't care, what difference does it make?'

Henry chose not to pursue this line of conversation with Rae. Instead, he dropped Rae off at the Spellman house and pursued it with my mom. There he got precisely the same response.

'If I'm comfortable with you and Albert's comfortable, then I don't care what anybody else thinks,' said my mother.

Unfortunately what other people thought mattered. Mrs. Collins called Mom and Dad to the school for a parent-teacher conference the following week. My mother, always on guard with school administrators, recorded the entire conversation.

The transcripts read as follows:

MRS. COLLINS: I've asked you here, Mr. and Mrs. Spellman, to discuss your daughter's unusual relationship w ith an older gentleman

27

named Henry Stone.

OLIVIA: Inspector Henry Stone.

ALBERT: What about it?

MRS. COLLINS: I think you might want to rethink the company you allow your daughter to keep.

OLIVIA: Excuse me?

MRS. COLLINS: I have on more than one occasion overheard Rae refer to Inspector Stone as her quote-unquote best friend. I find their relationship highly inappropriate.

OLIVIA: Respectfully, Mrs. Collins, if anything inappropriate were going on, I would know about it long before you. I assure you, Henry Stone is not a predator.

MRS. COLLINS: So you approve of their relationship?

OLIVIA: He's clearly a good influence on my daughter.

ALBERT: Undeniably.

MRS. COLLINS: How so?

OLIVIA: I can't even remember the last time Rae asked me if I was on crack. It has to be at least three months ago.

ALBERT: More like six.

MRS. COLLINS: She treats him as her equal. I consider their relationship highly unorthodox.

OLIVIA: Do you have my daughter's transcripts in front of you?

MRS. COLLINS: Yes, I do.

OLIVIA: What was Rae's GPA two years ago?

[Mrs. Collins consults her file.]

MRS. COLLINS: It was two-point-seven.

OLIVIA: What was her GPA last semester?

MRS. COLLINS: Three-point-four.

28

OLIVIA: Mrs. Collins, I raised two children before Rae, neither of whom have fallen victim to a child predator. I assure you I know the signs and I know what's best for my daughter. I appreciate your concern, but I hope this is the last I hear on this topic.
[End of tape.]

* * *

This was, in fact, not the last my mother heard on the topic. Two weeks later, Mom received an at-home visit from a social worker. Mrs. Collins, unconvinced after my parents' meeting, had filed a report with Child Protective Services and requested a full investigation.

My mother, cornered by state authority and concerned that the investigation would cast suspicion on Henry Stone's reputation, promptly brought their meeting to a close with the following statement.

'Henry Stone is engaged to my older daughter, Isabel, who happens to be thirty years old. I don't know what Mrs. Collins's problem is, but Henry is like a son to me and soon enough he will be my son. And if my future son-in-law is willing to pick up his future sister-in-law from school now and again and help her with her homework, I think that is the epitome of family values, don't you?'

The social worker checked her file, perplexed.

'I'm sorry,' she said. 'There's nothing in here about Henry Stone being engaged to your oldest daughter. That's very curious. Well, I apologize for the inconvenience. We may have to do a follow-up visit. It's procedure. But otherwise, I think we can put this matter to rest.'

'Thank you,' my mother replied. 'And I might add that I'd like a tiny complaint to go in the file against Mrs. Collins. She could have destroyed a man's career and reputation with her ungrounded accusations.'

Mom told this story over dinner with a shorter than usual guest list—Henry, Dad, and me. Rae was sent to David and Petra's house under the ruse of helping them erase their hard drive. [Rae would later express bafflement over this request.]

Henry and I were on guard from the start, the limited guest list lending itself to suspicion. I recorded the proceedings.

The transcript reads as follows:

OLIVIA: You're probably wondering why I brought us all together.
ALBERT: I assumed it was to eat dinner. Pass the steak.
OLIVIA: No, Al. Start with the salad like a civilized person.
ALBERT: In France, they eat the salad last.
OLIVIA: When you're fluent in French, you can save the salad for dessert. Until then—
ALBERT: Henry, pass the steak.
OLIVIA: Henry, don't pass the steak.
  [Henry obeys my mother. Albert serves himself salad and passes the bowl around the table.]
OLIVIA: Before I was interrupted by cholesterol number two hundred and twenty-seven—
ALBERT: Two hundred and twenty-three.
OLIVIA: That's something to be proud of?
ISABEL: Mom, Dad. It's one thing to do this in

30

front of family members, but maybe Henry doesn't need to listen to a two-decade-old argument.

OLIVIA: Thank you. Now there's a reason I brought us all together. I—um—had a situation with Rae's English teacher. Mrs. Collins. I believe you've met her, Henry.

HENRY: Yes, I have.

OLIVIA: Well, Mrs. Collins had an issue with Rae's growing attachment to you. I explained to her that this was not a concern to me or Albert and that it shouldn't be her concern. But that stupid bitch—

ALBERT: Take it easy, Olivia—

OLIVIA: That woman did not trust my judgment and filed a complaint with Child Protective Services.

HENRY: She filed a complaint about me?

OLIVIA: Well, she was concerned about Rae being so close to a non-family member of the opposite sex in your age range. Anyway, I received a visit from a social worker—

HENRY: Olivia, this could become a problem.

OLIVIA: Yes, Henry. I know. But I took care of it.

ISABEL: How?

OLIVIA: [nervously] Well, I explained that Henry was a member of our family.

HENRY: They can check that out, you know.

OLIVIA: I anticipated that problem, so you're not a blood relative.

HENRY: I don't understand.

ALBERT: Olivia, it's like ripping off a bandage. Do it quickly and it will hurt less.

OLIVIA: [very quickly] I said you were engaged to my older daughter Isabel.

ISABEL: Are you on crack?!

OLIVIA: It really was the only option.

HENRY: No. I think there were a few other options.

ALBERT: Henry, you don't have to actually marry Isabel. All you have to do is *pretend* you're going to marry her.

ISABEL: What if I get engaged to somebody else?

OLIVIA: Who?

ISABEL: I don't know. It's just a hypothetical.

OLIVIA: You only have to do this for two and a half years, until Rae turns eighteen. I hardly think you're going to get engaged before then. I mean, honestly, Isabel. You're not even dating anyone right now.

ISABEL: Stop laughing, Dad!

HENRY: I'm not comfortable solving this problem with deception.

OLIVIA: I said it quickly and without much forethought. But after I told the lie, I thought, I am a genius. I mean, this really solves the problem. It won't hurt anyone. And it will keep Child Protective Services off our back, and considering your position with the SFPD, I think that's the best thing for your career.

[Mom hands me a tiny velvet box.]

OLIVIA: Isabel, you can wear my old engagement ring.

ISABEL: Is anybody interested in my opinion?

ALBERT: No, sweetie.

HENRY: Listen, Al and Olivia. It might be time now to put an end to Rae's visits.

OLIVIA: You can try that, Henry. But if it doesn't work, we'll do it my way.

THE STONE AND
SPELLMAN SHOW

Approximately six months ago, sometime between Mrs. Collins's first meeting with my parents and the visit from the social worker, my mother began recording random conversations she was privy to between Henry and Rae. Initially her reasoning behind the privacy invasion was to provide evidence of the nature of Henry and Rae's relationship should Mrs. Collins or any other official 'busybody' decide to follow up more enthusiastically. My mother is excellent at anticipating the behavior of bureaucrats.

However, eventually the Henry and Rae tapes were made for pure entertainment value. Mom told Dad that if you listened to them while eating a sandwich, it was the equivalent of dinner and a show. My mother saw the recordings as an auditory photo album and would diligently title and label each recording. If a stranger were to come upon the collection, he would assume these tapes were a long lost radio show.

THE STONE AND
SPELLMAN SHOW—EPISODE 1

'NO-NEGOTIATION'

Background: When my sister was eight years old, my brother, in the interest of explaining his legal career to Rae, taught her how to negotiate. It was a lesson he and the rest of us would soon regret. Rae took from this lesson that everything—from simple acts of grooming, to household chores, to homework—could be negotiated to her end.

Setting: After dropping Rae home from school, Stone agrees to drive Olivia to the auto shop to pick up her car. Rae comes along for the ride.

The transcript reads as follows:

RAE: Shotgun!

HENRY: Rae, let your mother sit up front.

RAE: Did Mom call shotgun when I was temporarily deaf?

HENRY: What did I tell you about sarcasm?

RAE: That it's the lowest form of humor. But you're wrong. The saying is 'The pun is the lowest form of humor.'

HENRY: A pun requires some element of cleverness. Sarcasm simply requires an annoying tone.

[Henry opens the back door for Rae.]

HENRY: You're sitting in the backseat.

RAE: I'm willing to negotiate. I'll sit in the

34

backseat if you give me two driving lessons.

HENRY: Rae, you can get in the backseat or you can stay home. Those are your two options.

[Rae gets in the backseat, Olivia the passenger seat.]

OLIVIA: That was very impressive. I always get sucked into the negotiation.

HENRY: I have a strict policy not to negotiate with Rae.

OLIVIA: Really? I'm in awe.

RAE: Turn on the radio, Henry.

HENRY: Excuse me?

RAE: Please.

HENRY: Thank you.

RAE: You are so prehistoric.

[Henry laughs.]

HENRY: What did you call me?

RAE: You heard.

*   *   *

Henry Stone does not laugh. Later my mother would claim that *The Stone and Spellman Show* was archival evidence of the mutually beneficial nature of Henry and Rae's relationship. What this moment confirmed for my mother was that the inclusion of Henry Stone in our lives was not coerced or cruel (an assumption my father had made); it was not just Henry who was a good influence on Rae, but perhaps the other way around. Whatever prior reservations my mother had regarding the manner in which Rae infiltrated Henry's life vanished. She decided that Inspector Stone was a grown man and if he wanted Rae out of his life, he could take care of it himself.

35

And this is how Henry Stone came to be an honorary member of the Spellman family. Which brings me back to the beginning of my story—the one about 'John Brown.'

SUBJECT MOVES INTO
1797 CLAY STREET . . .

Sunday, January 8
1100 hrs

Fifteen minutes after we left Henry at the hospital, Rae and I pulled into my parents' driveway at 1799 Clay Street just as Subject's moving truck double-parked in front of the triplex next door.

Rae and I both registered the vehicle in our peripheral vision, but our attention was otherwise occupied.

'Get out of the car,' I said, unlocking the doors.

'No,' Rae replied stoically.

'Are you planning on sitting in the car all day?'

'No. I'm planning on taking the bus back to the hospital.'

Rae remained still, but I knew she was about to make a run for it. I picked up my cell and dialed the house.

My father answered. 'Hello.'

'Dad, we have a situation.'

'Where are you?'

'In the driveway. I think I'm going to need backup.'

Just as my sentence was complete, Rae hopped out of the car and jetted down the block. She would have made it too. She would have found a way to the hospital before we could stop her. She would have returned to Henry Stone's room and I would have broken my promise.

But our new neighbor, unwittingly, gave Henry a twelve-hour reprieve. Just as Rae was jetting along the sidewalk in front of his new residence, the still unknown male stepped out of his U-Haul truck, carrying two file boxes, and blocked her path. It happened in an instant. The human crash. Bodies flew to the ground, boxes tipped over, files scattered like a deck of cards, and a few individual papers floated in the air.

My father and mother exited the house in time to witness only the aftermath.

'What happened?' my mother asked, turning to me.

'She ran him over,' I replied, 'literally.'

'Not again.'

There were no serious injuries visible to the naked eye. Subject, who had yet to introduce himself, took the brunt of the impact. Rae kind of bounced off the side of the file boxes like a cartoon character and fell smack on her behind. She quickly jumped to her feet and dusted herself off. My first opinion of the unknown male as he lay on the ground, woozy from apparently the second head injury Rae had inflicted that day, was that our new neighbor had a certain something, enough of a something for me to contemplate Ex-boyfriend possibilities. Not that he was really my neighbor. I didn't live at home anymore, but perhaps it was time for more regular visits.

I estimated the age of Subject, who was splayed on the sidewalk, to be approximately thirty. He was about six feet even, with sandy blond hair, blue eyes, and an easy tan, the kind I myself have never been able to attain. What the still-unknown male did next I found curious. No, I found it suspicious.

He didn't check his body for cuts or bruises. He didn't look to his attacker (Rae) for an explanation. His eyes darted around noting only the papers encircling him. He grabbed at them as if they were stock certificates or hundred-dollar notes and quickly returned all loose items to the boxes and shut the lids. Only after he performed several three-hundred-and-sixty degree scans of his immediate circumference, and satisfied himself that he'd caught all the loose pages did he turn to my family and acknowledge our existence.

He first cast his eyes on Rae. The prior focus during his minute-ago treasure hunt softened, and a smile formed on his face.

'What's the hurry?' he said to my sister.

'I have to get back to the hospital.'

'Why?' Subject asked. Unfortunately.

Rae, unable to respond to any question without the precise answer, said, 'Today I almost accidentally murdered my best friend.'

'I wasn't aware you could accidentally murder someone. I thought the accidental causing of death was called manslaughter.'

'Thank you,' my mother said pleasantly. She's all for other people educating her children, as you've probably figured out by now.

'Well then I almost accidentally manslaughtered my best friend today and I want to get back to the hospital to see him.'

'That's redundant, Rae,' said my dad.

'But he doesn't want to see her,' I said to

38

Subject, who was appearing more and more perplexed.

'You don't know that,' my sister replied snappishly.

'I do,' I said. 'He asked me to keep you away.'

'We'll see about that,' Rae said, and I could tell from the way her eyes darted about that she was planning another escape.

My father noted Rae's body language out of the corner of his eye and put his arm around her, holding her in place. Then Dad broke the tension with the stranger by finally making introductions.

'Hi, it seems we are your new neighbors. I'm Albert Spellman, this is my wife, Olivia, my oldest daughter, Isabel, and this one here, trying to make her getaway, is Rae.'

'Nice to meet you. I'm John Brown.'

*   *   *

If the obsessive paper-gathering wasn't enough, my suspicion grew the moment I heard Subject's name. John Brown. It was so common, too common, conveniently common. For the private investigator the common name is the kiss of death. Unless we have a social security number or a date and location of birth, it might be impossible to acquire any true background information on an individual with a name such as that.

John. Brown. According the 1990 census, 'John' is the second most common male name in the United States and 'Brown' is the fifth most common surname. The only thing worse would be if he were named James Smith. But as I've said before, I find everyone suspicious. And, once again, I get ahead of myself. On Sunday, January 8, John Brown was far down the list of things demanding my attention. My mother, my sister, my father, and my best friend's strange behavior were all in the lead.

SUSPICIOUS BEHAVIOR REPORTS

I keep lists. They're kind of like to-do lists, but I've already done them. They can document habits, crimes, or relationships (see appendix for complete list of ex-boyfriends). I had always found that the simple list form worked for me. It was clear, concise, and easily folded up into a single-page reference sheet. However, recently I had discovered the need to document suspicious behavior. My habit was to jot down notes shortly before bed or when thoughts came to me in the middle of the night. Unfortunately, the next morning, I would often find cryptic Post-its blanketing my nightstand.

Dad. REAFO #3?
Mother. Wrench in car.
Rae. Phone call. Why?
Subject. Bags of dirt.

You get the point. My suspicious behavior notes required reports. So I purchased a notebook and took the time to elaborate on my subjects, who happened to be, for the most part, family members. I wrote my first complete suspicious behavior report the night after I met the neighbor

40

Subject—John Brown—although that particular report had nothing to do with Subject.

*   *   *

After dropping my sister off in the afternoon, I returned to the Spellman house that evening for the recently implemented Sunday night dinners. These began shortly after David's wedding to my long-time best friend, Petra. The wedding occurred a year ago (from the date of Arrest #2 or #4) after four months of sneaking around behind my back and three months of open dating. Apparently David didn't think I would approve. I didn't back then. In fact, I thought Petra could do better than my freakishly attractive, intellectually superior, and all-round charming brother. Anyway, I got over it and grew to fully appreciate that family gatherings include my vandalism buddy from years past. See, Petra was as much a delinquent as I was. Now she's a hairstylist, married to a respectable lawyer, and sometimes she seems almost respectable herself.

That evening, suspicious behavior must have been in the air, because I also noticed it from every single family member.

*   *   *

I'll begin with Petra. In case the suspicious element isn't obvious to you, I've put an asterisk next to the behavior in question with a brief explanation.

When Petra entered the house with my brother, she looked me over and said, 'When's the last time

41

I saw you?'

'I think it's been about two weeks.'

'I can't believe I let it get so bad,' she said, referring to my hair.

'Relax, it's just hair.'

'Don't belittle my profession.'

'Sorry.'

Petra excused us to administer my quarterly haircut. When she removed her sweater I noticed a new tattoo of a rose (how original) where Puff the Magic Dragon used to reside before he was disappeared with a laser last year. In fact, Petra disappeared several of her tattoos when she and my brother began dating. The arrival of a new tattoo is asterisk worthy.

'What is that?' I asked.

'It's called a tattoo,' Petra replied with the tone of a kindergarten teacher.

'But you just had a bunch of them removed.'

'And your point is?'

'If I were your skin, I'd stage a revolt,' I said.

'The space just looked empty.'

'What does David think?' I asked.

'It doesn't matter what he thinks,' Petra replied snappishly. 'It's my skin.'* [No argument from me on that point, but the response seemed more hostile than necessary.]

'Since I've got you alone,' Petra said, changing the subject, 'let me ask you something.'

'Shoot.'

'Are David and your mother in a fight?'

'Why do you ask?'

'Because she doesn't call as much as she used to, and the last time she called, it sounded like they were having an argument, and then David hung up on her, or at least it sounded like he did.'* [David and my mother do not fight. David does not hang up on my mother. I cannot recall the last conflict that they've had.]

'That was a mistake.'

'So you haven't heard about any conflict?'

'No, but I'll look into it for you.'

* * *

Over dinner, I spotted the next subject of my report: Dad. He arrived late with a yoga mat* under his arm, sat down at the table, and asked David to pass the salad.* All eyes were on Dad, since this suspicious behavior was the most suspicious of all.

'Honey, were you just at a yoga class?' my mom asked.

'Yes,' Dad replied.

My mother, too stunned and pleased that my father was—even for a single day—considering his health, opted against any further discussion for fear of discouraging him.

What followed was a brief discussion about Rae's almost manslaughter, but I drew that conversation to a close since, frankly, I was sick of it.

'We've decided to take a couple of disappearances this year,' my mother casually said over an incredibly bland turkey loaf. 'Aunt Grace left us some money that she wanted used specifically for leisure activities.' [Aunt Grace was on my father's side. The Spellmans are notorious micromanagers. Even bequests must be used according to the deceased person's bidding.]

'You've never mentioned that before,' David interjected.

'We don't tell you everything, David. Just as you don't tell us everything,' my mother replied sharply.* [There was clearly a hostile subtext here that I was not privy to. Further investigation would be required.]

This might be a good time to explain how 'disappearance' came to mean 'vacation' in the Spellman household.

Disappearance (dis-e-'pir-an(+)s) n: A vacation or otherwise restful escape.

Almost two years ago to the date of this dinner, my sister went missing. As I explained before, it was a dramatic yet somewhat effective move to bring the family together again. It was also a terrifying ordeal that left every Spellman physically and emotionally drained and somewhat bitter toward my younger sibling. Rae, sensing the quiet hostility and wanting it to simply go away, began referring to this disturbing event as her 'vacation.' She'd casually exchange the two words in the following manner:

'When is the last time you went to the dentist, Rae?'

'Uh, I think it was a couple weeks after my vacation.'

My parents attempted to disabuse her of this word exchange, but Rae refused in a feeble attempt to rewrite history. My parents' response to this was to exchange the word 'vacation' for 'disappearance' so that Rae would never forget. Hence, if Rae uses the word 'vacation' she is often

44

referring to her five day absence during winter almost two years ago. If my parents use the word 'disappearance' they are most likely referring to taking a vacation [Word used in its traditional sense.] of their own.

*   *   *

Over a dessert of fresh fruit for my dad and ice cream for the rest, the main point of discussion was whether Rae would be allowed to stay home alone at the Clay Street house during my parents' disappearances. What followed was a brief discussion of taking Rae along with them on a summer cruise, but when Rae said she'd take a vacation [Her revisionist definition.] to get out of the disappearance, my parents backed down.

The final suspicious behavior of the night was when Rae's cell phone rang. She picked up on the first ring and said hello. She then turned to Mom and asked to be excused.

After she left the table, my dad said, 'We might need to implement some telephone etiquette with her. She's becoming a regular phone hound.'

'Who's she talking to?' I asked.

'She has some friends* now,' my mother replied. [To date my sister has had only a few acquaintances, who she would see on rare occasions for study and even rarer occasions for a birthday party or movie. But actual friends with whom she might enjoy a casual conversation over the phone were an extremely rare occurrence.]

The evening ended with Rae on the phone, ignoring the family; my father sipping herbal tea; my mother sending David off with a cool 'good

45

night'; and Petra bidding an uncomfortable adieu after being oddly silent during dinner.* [I made a note to ask her about this at a later date.]

A BROKEN PROMISE

Monday, January 9
0930 hrs

I'm a late sleeper. Unless the alarm clock wakes me for an early job, I can usually crash until late morning. In fact, to feel rested, I need to crash until mid-morning. But at 9:30 a.m. the following morning, I was awakened by the phone ringing.

'Hello,' I said, which sounded more like 'nahlow.'

'You promised,' said the sad voice on the other end of the line.

I had no idea whom I was speaking to, but I often have to apologize for something or other, so I just did.

'I'm sorry,' I said. 'I'm so sorry.'

'Get her out of here.'

'Who?' I said, although if I had been more awake, I would have figured it out right away.

'*Rae!*' Henry Stone shouted into the receiver, which had the stimulating effect of at least one cup of coffee.

Then it all came back to me. The promise to keep my sister away from him for two weeks. I'm not sure why I made the promise to begin with— probably because he was gripping my wrist really hard and it hurt. I shouldn't have made the promise. It was an impossible one to keep. But I was not unsympathetic. Henry had been put through more than any non-family member had the right to be put through. I could hear it in his voice. And I knew the feeling.

'I'll be right there,' I said.

San Francisco General Hospital
1030 hrs

I flashed my quarter-carat engagement ring at the desk nurse and entered Henry's room. He was reading the *San Francisco Chronicle.* Rae was nowhere in sight.

'Where is she?' I asked.

'I don't know,' Henry replied. 'But she'll be back, so you're going to wait here until she returns and then you're going to take her away for good.'

'I'm sorry about this, Henry. But you know that unless we lock her up in her room, which I think Child Protective Services would really frown upon, we can't stop her from visiting you.'

'Why isn't she grounded?' he asked.

'She is. She's grounded for five years, which—yes—I know doesn't make any sense since she's almost sixteen, but it doesn't matter to her.'

A new nurse opened the door to his room and stared at me.

'Who are you?' she asked.

'I'm Henry's fiancée,' I replied, circling the bedside and taking his hand.

'Oh,' she said, looking me up and down with a decided scowl. 'I'll be back later to check your vitals,' she said to Henry.

'Why does she hate me?' I asked.

'Because you're a lousy fiancée.'

'What did I do?'

'She's been here since last night and this is the first time she's seen you. Plus, you didn't bring me anything.'

'I'm sorry.'

'What happened to your hair?' Henry asked after staring at me a second too long.

'I got a haircut.'

'Oh. I liked it better before.'

'You prefer it sloppy?'

'Yes.'

'Why?'

'It's more you.'

I realized I was still holding Henry's hand. His warm fingers loosely gripped mine. I let go just as Rae entered the room, carrying a motley assortment of bags. I reached into my pocket and turned on my digital recorder. Mom later dubbed the following episode a classic.

THE STONE AND SPELLMAN SHOW—EPISODE 27

'GET-WELL-SOON'

The transcript reads as follows:

[Rae enters the room and places her new purchases on Henry's stomach.]

RAE: [to me] What are you doing here?
ISABEL: I've come to take you home.

48

[Rae ignores me and begins unloading her goods.]

RAE: I got you some gifts to take your mind off of the incident.

HENRY: Stop calling it 'the incident.' You ran me over. Call it what it is.

RAE: Okay. Here are some gifts to say I'm sorry I ran you over.

[Rae rifles through the bag.]

RAE: I got you some candy. I know you don't eat candy, but I figured that you might make an exception when you're in the hospital. M&M's, Skittles, and Raisinettes. There are actual raisins in there, so you get some fruit. Anyway, it's mostly non-messy candy, because I know you don't like the messy stuff.

HENRY: Thank you, but I don't want the candy.

[Rae opens the bag of Skittles for herself.]

RAE: I could use a snack.

ISABEL: Pass the M&M's. I didn't have breakfast.

HENRY: Ladies, there's a cafeteria downstairs.

RAE: Wait, there's more stuff. I got you magazines. *The New Yorker*—I've seen it at your house, so I know you read it—*The Atlantic Monthly,* which looks boring, so I figured you'd like it, and *Playboy,* because men like *Playboy,* right? Also, I wanted to see if the store on the corner of Twenty-first and Potrero would sell me porn. I wrote down their address for you, in case you want to bust them. Oh, and I went to the corner store on Fifteenth and Market the other day, and I tried to buy beer, but they wouldn't sell it to me. So you can mark them off your list.

HENRY: Would you please stop trying to buy beer

49

and porn? I don't work vice. I don't care who's selling it. I'll read the other magazines. You take the *Playboy*. I don't need the nurses thinking I'm a perv.

ISABEL: I don't think reading *Playboy* qualifies someone as a perv. They've got some good interviews.

HENRY: I'm really very tired now and could use some rest.

ISABEL: It's time to go, Rae.

RAE: I'm not done. I also bought a deck of cards. I thought you could teach me how to play poker.

HENRY: You can't play poker with two people.

RAE: Isabel's here and I saw a bunch of nurses outside who look bored.

HENRY: Isabel!

ISABEL: Rae, if I have to, I will pick you up and carry you out of here.

[Rae gathered the candy and *Playboy* magazine.]

RAE: Okay, okay. I can take a hint.

[No, actually, she cannot.]

RAE: I'll see you tomorrow, Henry.

[End of tape.]

SUBJECT IS OBSERVED TAKING OUT THE TRASH . . .

Monday, January 9
1120 hrs

When Rae and I returned home from the hospital we spotted Subject—John Brown—putting four pillow-sized clear plastic bags into the recycling bin in front of his building. The contents of the bags were light and fluffy. Bags of shredded paper are mostly bags of air, a waste of space in the recycling bins, which is why my parents keep two extra green receptacles around at all times. We need the space since we shred everything. And I mean *Everything.* At the time I noted the bags, but it wasn't until a month later that I put that detail into my suspicious behavior report on Subject.

As Rae and I exited the car, our new neighbor waved and approached us. This time I noticed he shared a vague resemblance to Joseph Cotten, my all-time favorite classic film actor. According to my calculations, I've watched *Shadow of a Doubt* at least twelve times and I will always argue its superiority over *Vertigo* and *Rear Window.*

Subject smiled at Rae and said, 'How's your friend?'

Rae, refusing to keep the conversation light and neighborly, responded with 'He might have permanent brain damage.'

I pinched Rae really hard on her arm, which lately is code for *'Whatever you're doing, stop doing it.'*

51

'He's fine,' I replied. 'Just a concussion.'

'Glad to hear it,' Subject said, tipping back and forth on his heels and toes. I got the feeling there was something he wanted to say. Then Rae ruined the moment.

'If you were in the hospital, what would be the one thing you would want the most?' my sister asked.

'To be out of the hospital,' Subject quickly replied.

'Thanks, that was helpful,' Rae responded rudely. She was looking for real info—a list of items to bring Henry Stone. This was not helping her.

'I'm going inside,' Rae said, darting for the front door.

'I should probably go,' I said slowly, turning around and following after Rae.

'I like your hair,' Subject said.

'Thanks,' I replied, and it was then that I thought for real, *Could this be Ex-boyfriend #11?*

THE 'LAW OFFICES' OF MORT SCHILLING

Monday, April 24
1035 hrs

'So far, he sounds like a mensch,' [mensch or mensh (mensh) n: pl. mensch•es or mensch•en (men'shen) Informal A person having admirable characteristics, such as fortitude and firmness of purpose.] said Morty.

'But I've just started,' I replied.

'He makes conversation with the girl who ran him over, he compliments your hair, he's well groomed. I'm not getting *'evil'* from your description so far, Izzilla.'

'Give me time. The story has just begun.'

'I hope you didn't date this man.'

'Why?'

'Because if you dated him and then he filed a TRO . . . that does not look good.'

'I see.'

'You dated him, didn't you?'

'Briefly,' I said.

'So what happened?'

'All the pieces came together and I realized he was evil.'

'What is he doing that is so evil?'

'I haven't worked that out yet, but I will.'

'As your lawyer, Izz, I must caution you against any further investigations.'

Morty's wife, Ruth, entered the office, carrying a cardigan sweater. I should mention that Morty's 'office' is in his garage. Please note that I did not write 'converted garage.'

'I thought you might be chilly,' Ruth said.

'If I'm chilly I can get my own sweater.'

'The last thing we need right now is for you to catch pneumonia.'

'Ruthy, I'm conducting business in here.'

'Hello, Izzy, how are you doing? Can I get you something to eat?'

'No, thank you.'

'Drink?'

'No thank you.'

'Coffee? Tea?'

'No, I'm fine,' I said.

Then Morty continued with the beverage list. 'Hot cocoa, orange juice, tomato juice, prune juice.'

'No, thanks. I'm fine.'

'She'd like a cocoa,' Morty said to Ruth, apparently placing his own secret order.

'Give me a holler if you need anything,' Ruth said pleasantly. 'Good seeing you, Isabel. Morty, put on the sweater.'

'I'll put it on if I get cold. Now, please, we have lots of work to do.'

Ruth returned to the main house. Morty eyed the sweater, but didn't put it on just yet. He consulted his notes and contemplated his next question.

Morty and Me

This might be a good time to explain how Morty and I met. It was approximately a year and a half prior to the date of this meeting. I was on a surveillance job, which brought me to Hayes Valley. The subject (at the time, not the current one) entered one of the very few Jewish delis in the city. Moishe's Pippic. I had never been inside the establishment before and would soon discover that it was both quite small and, as an aside, a shrine to the fine city of Chicago. Aside from being small, it was also empty, which made my presence there all the more obvious. Had I left the deli immediately after entrance, I would have been made. If I sat down at one of the fake-wood-topped tables and ordered lunch, I would have been exposed. I suspected Deli Subject was onto me and I had just a moment to make a decision.

I spotted an elderly man with oversized glasses and wildly unkempt, thinning gray-and-black hair at a table in the corner. I approached casually and sat down across from him.

'Mind if I join you?' I whispered.

'What?' he said.

Deli subject turned around. He looked directly at me, which meant further surveillance was out of the question. However, he didn't know I was on his tail. If I could come off as a customer then the surveillance could continue with another investigator.

I leaned over the table and kissed the strange old man on the cheek.

'Hi, Grandpa, how are you doing?' I said, rather loudly, and then quickly wrote down on a piece of paper, PLAY ALONG. I'M A PI FOLLOWING MAN IN DELI. PLEASE HELP!

*   *   *

It took Morty a good thirty seconds to register my request. At first I thought it was my look of desperation that convinced him to play along with my charade, but later I would discover that the boredom of retirement made Morty game for anything. My new friend slid the menu in my direction and said, 'You're late.'

I called for backup over lunch and Mom got another investigator on Deli Subject's tail. I ordered a turkey on rye and handed Morty my card.

'I owe you,' I said, and two weeks later Morty suggested I repay the debt by having lunch with him again. On that second lunch I learned that Morty had a long and lucrative career as well-respected defense attorney in the city. He had finally retired ten years ago, when his wife of fifty years gave him one final ultimatum. Though eighty-two years old, Morty remained current on the law and was an excellent source whenever we had a criminal related investigation on our hands.

By the time of Arrest #4, when I realized that my legal troubles would not go away, I turned to Morty before anyone else, mostly because he knows his business, but also because he works for me pro bono. And he always springs for lunch.

*   *   *

'Tell me about the next time you had any contact with Mr. Brown,' Morty said. Then he picked up his sweater and put it on. 'Chilly in here, isn't it?'

My story is stuck in mid-January, a few short days before my first date with Subject. The following event, which on first glance seemed simply annoying, would spur a chain of events that led me back to my parents' home and into the perfect seat to witness an assortment of odd behavior. I should mention that Subject's collection of inconsistencies was not my only concern. Inconsistencies abounded.

But I get ahead of myself. It's time I talked about Bernie.

THE DAY BERNIE PETERSON MOVED IN WITH ME

Wednesday, January 11
2300 hrs

Bernie used to work and play with my Uncle Ray. They shared a common love of booze, poker, and loose women. When Bernie decided to get engaged to his ex-Vegas-showgirl sweetheart, Daisy Doolittle, [Yes, a stage name.] Bernie offered his apartment to me as a sublet, which he admitted was because he wasn't sure the November-December relationship would last. He packed his things and moved to Carson City. I wrote Bernie a check for eight hundred dollars a month and Bernie wrote his landlord a check for seven hundred. Our entire relationship consisted of rare telephone calls during which I would inform him that something in the apartment was not working, and then he would pass the information on to the landlord and I would make myself scarce as repairs were made.

I hadn't laid eyes on the retired lieutenant for

two years. That's when he'd handed me a set of keys and said, 'I hope you get as lucky in here as I did.' It never occurred to me that Bernie had kept a set of those same keys. But he had.

It was eleven P.M. when I heard someone fumbling outside my door and the sound of a key entering my lock. I looked through the peephole and caught the top of a bald head—not a bald head I immediately recognized. Just as the deadbolt unlocked, I locked it. A moment later the deadbolt was unlocked again and I locked it, this time running for the phone before I landed back by the door to lock it again. I was about to dial 911 when Bernie figured out that someone was on the other side of the lock.

'Isabel, is that you?' he asked in a sloppy drunk slur.

'Bernie?' I replied.

'Open up,' he said, lightly smacking the door with the palm of his hand.

I looked through the peephole, just to be sure. It was Bernie all right, but an aged, bloated, ruddy-faced version of his former self. Not that his former self was anything to write home about—on the contrary. I reluctantly unlocked the door, knowing for certain that my life (or at least my immediate future) had taken a turn for the worse. I knew, even before Bernie took one step into the apartment, that he was moving in with me. I knew that my one-bedroom, eight-hundred-dollar-a-month apartment [In San Francisco this is an unbelievable deal.] was no more.

Bernie stumbled inside, leaving two suitcases in the foyer. See? This did not look good. Then it got worse. He threw his arms around me and pulled

58

me into a tight bear hug.

'Isabel, am I glad to see you.'

'Bernie? What are you doing here?' I said, trying to twist out of the embrace. On any normal occasion I would have been unhappy to see Bernie. But on this night I was especially unhappy. You see, I had spent the previous two evenings on a stakeout, clocking in maybe five hours of sleep total. This kind of overtime goes against Spellman Investigations's policies, but we were low on manpower and, needing the cash, I volunteered. My point is that I needed to sleep in a bad way. I didn't need to be consoling Bernie Peterson.

My intruder took me by the shoulders and looked me in the eye.

'She broke my heart,' he said with a kind of soap opera, over-the-top delivery.

'What happened?' I asked, out of politeness, not genuine curiosity.

'I caught her with the gardener.'

'You're kidding, right?'

'Well, he wasn't the gardener. He was my best friend. We used to play poker and go to the track together.'

'So why'd you say he was the gardener?' I asked, now curious.

'He had an electric lawn mower. Sometimes he'd just come by and mow the lawn for us. But Donnie wasn't doing me any favors. And he wasn't mowing the lawn, either. 'The grass grows fast in the desert,' my ass.'

Bernie continued rambling on. I had a hard time following him. I think in that last sentence, Bernie was quoting his cuckolder, but I can't be sure.

'Where were you when Donnie was doing

Daisy?' [I said it before I realized how it sounded.]

'Carson City is just outside of the strip. I was at a casino, the track, what difference does it make? You got anything to drink?'

'There's beer in the fridge,' I said.

Bernie took off his coat, grabbed a beer, walked over to the couch, and pulled up the cushions.

'I can't remember. Does this thing open up?' he asked.

'No,' I replied, and only then did it really sink in that Bernie was staying the night (and many nights thereafter).

'I'm going to go to bed,' I said, not only because I was exhausted but because I knew I had to stake my claim.

'Go ahead. Make yourself at home. [Huh?] I'll be just fine,' Bernie replied, trying to gain my pity and perhaps my ear.

I grabbed some blankets and towels from the closet, left them out for Bernie, and locked myself in the bedroom.

The lock prevented Bernie's entrance into my room for a midnight chat. It did not lock out the parade of noises over the next eight hours that made even a moment of REM sleep impossible. First there was the AMC Western, starring Jimmy Stewart and John Wayne, [*The Man Who Shot Liberty Valance.*] played at full volume, not because Bernie is hard of hearing, but I suspect to drown out the sounds of his sobbing. The second track on the Bernie playlist was sobbing, as a solo act, muffled as if he was crying into a pillow. (If you think I'm insensitive, let me explain something: If I offered a shoulder for Bernie to cry on, he'd cry on my shoulder, then cop a feel. I don't know this

60

man well, but I know him well enough.) Third on the Bernie playlist was forty-five minutes of nose-blowing and mumbling encouraging words to himself: 'You can handle this. You're a tough guy. You'll find another broad in no time.' I paid attention to this part, since it provided the exact script to comfort Bernie in future, daylight hours. Certainly the words one says to comfort oneself are most likely the precise words one wants to hear in one's time of need. The fourth track on the album could have used some editing. It was four hours of snoring. And the closing number? The clanking of pots and pans and the sizzling of bacon grease.

When seven A.M. rolled around, I had not slept for even the briefest moment, which brought me to approximately eighty hours of being awake versus five hours of being asleep in the past three days. I put on my bathrobe and entered the living/dining room.

'Morning, roomie,' Bernie said, looking up at me with a theatrical look that read like I'm-broken-hearted-but-I'm-not-going- to-let-it-show. It all felt like a desperate plea for attention.

My complexion must have whitened over my final sleepless night.

'You didn't sleep well, either?' Bernie asked sympathetically, as if here was yet another thing we had in common. I stumbled into the kitchen chair and demanded coffee. Thankfully Bernie was in a serving mood, so I refrained from telling him all the violent fantasies I'd had about him during my previous sleepless night.

Unable to find the will to do anything, I drank Bernie's coffee (weak), ate his eggs (runny), bacon (undercooked), and toast (burnt), listened to what I hoped would be the final track of the Bernie album. The breakup story was told in excruciating detail. I have yet to discover a single individual who can relay the events that facilitated the end of a relationship without getting into the minutiae. Why can't people keep it simple (see appendix)?

Since repeating the minutiae to complain about the minutiae would seem silly, really, I'll simply provide you with a brief excerpt from Bernie's saga:

'On our second date, I took her to the Red Lobster. I said, 'Order anything on the menu.' And she did. She ordered the lobster. That was the kind of woman she was. And she ordered two cocktails. First a Manhattan and then a gin and tonic, and then we shared a bottle of wine. I said, you know, maybe you shouldn't mix your drinks. But she could handle it. Yeah, she could drink me under the table . . . Then when dessert rolled around we agreed to split it . . .'

What I'm trying to convey is that I was in hell, or at least the closest to hell that my everyday life had yet to take me (since Rae's 'vacation,' that is). I managed to extricate myself from Bernie's needy conversation and drove to my parents' house/office to try to get some work done.

My dad was alone in the office when I arrived. 'What happened to you?' he asked.

'Bernie,' I replied, unable to summon the energy to form a complete sentence.

'Care to elaborate?' Dad said.

'No. Where's Mom?'

'At the dentist.' [Ex-boyfriend #9—Daniel Castillo, DDS.]

62

'Huh,' I said, and then sat down behind my desk. I stared at a stack of papers in front of me and thought they looked soft, like a pillow. I rested my head and closed my eyes.

'The hard-drive crashed last night,' Dad said, interrupting what might have become a very nice nap.

'Well, that's why you have backups.'

'Everything is backed up except yesterday's work. You need to retype the Wilson surveillance report.'

*   *   *

Three hours later, I had completed two pages of the thirty page report, in between involuntary catnaps. My mother entered the office just as my head was about to hit the desk again.

'Isabel, are you hungover?' Mom asked. 'You were supposed to go home and straight to bed last night.'

'I'm not hungover,' I said, suddenly aware that my head seemed to weigh more than it used to.

'What's wrong with you?' she said, when she finally got a look at my face.

'Bernie's back. He watches Westerns, he cries, he snores, he thinks we're roommates.'

'Go take a nap in the guest room.'

'I need to finish typing this. Unless you want to type it for me?'

'I can't read your writing, Izzy. I'm sorry. And the report is due today. Go outside, get some sun, and I'll make you some strong coffee.'

I don't have any recollection of walking outside, sitting down on the porch, and going to sleep in a patch of sun on the concrete, but that must have been what happened since I woke up to find Subject, John Brown, sitting by my side.

'Isabel? Isabel? Are you okay?' Subject was gently shaking my shoulder. I slowly sat up and shook off my dizziness.

'I'm fine. Just seriously deep sleprived.'

Then David pulled his brand-new Mercedes into the driveway and got out of the car, looking like a movie star, as he always does. Having not previously met our new neighbor, David looked at us quizzically.

'Hi,' David said, taking in the full effect of my drowsiness. 'Everything all right?'

Subject got to his feet and held out his hand. 'Hi, I'm John. I just moved in next door.'

'I'm David, Izzy's brother.'

'I—uh—just saw Isabel out cold on the front porch. I wanted to make sure she was okay.'

'If I had a dime for every time I found her that way, I could buy you a steak.'

Subject simply stared at my brother, not understanding the jab.

'More like a cappuccino,' I said, sounding sloppy drunk.

'Right,' David replied. 'Is Mom home?'

'She's in the office.'

David waved at our new neighbor and smacked me on the head as he went through the door.

'Nice guy,' Subject said, politely.

'Total asshole,' I responded.

Ten seconds of awkward silence followed, during which time I started to fall asleep again and leaned my head on Subject's shoulder.

'Sorry,' I said, waking up.

'It's okay,' he replied, and smiled. Yes, Joseph

Cotten in *Shadow of a Doubt*. Although I was too exhausted to really consider any doubts at the moment. I was simply blinded by Subject's considerable attractiveness.

'You seem nice,' I said.

'I am nice,' he replied.

'I think you should cook me dinner sometime.'

The previous statement was along the same lines as drunken misconduct, which sleep deprivation often mimics. It never could have occurred under sober circumstances. However, at that very moment I was briefly thankful to Bernie. John Brown responded without hesitation.

'Okay,' he said, and to be sure I didn't ruin the moment, I got up and went directly inside.

*   *   *

In a month's time I would be wholly ensconced in my primary obsession: investigation of John Brown. But as I mentioned earlier, suspicious behavior must have been in the air. That afternoon I drew up my second report.

SUSPICIOUS BEHAVIOR REPORT #2

'Olivia Spellman'

I entered the Spellman house a few minutes after my brother. To the left of the foyer is the living room, your standard middle-class fare, with a brown couch, a television, and a slightly worn easy chair (a relic from my Uncle Ray). The living room leads to the dining room, which consists of a large mahogany table and chairs and a credenza. The dining room leads to a somewhat cramped kitchen with an even more cramped dining nook. On the right side of the foyer is the door to the office, which has another door that leads downstairs to the basement, where my father used to interrogate me for my crimes in my youth. Upon entry, the main staircase confronts you, which takes you to the main bedrooms and the attic apartment (my old home), now the guest room. Although I can't remember the last time my family had any guests.

From the foyer, I could vaguely overhear my brother talking to our mother in the kitchen. Even from a distance I could hear that their voices were filled with tension. Eavesdropping is a great skill all the Spellmans possess, but especially the second generation. From the foyer of the house, I can tell you where any sound emanates from. I climbed the stairs to the second landing and listened in on their private conversation.

'I know you're following me,' David said to my mother.

'I don't know what you're talking about, David.'

'Mom, I saw you last night.'

'You're just paranoid, sweetie,' my mother replied, not sounding pleasant at all.

'It's an invasion of privacy, Mom. Would you like it if I started following you around?'

'I can't imagine you'd have the time, David. But if you did, I wouldn't mind. Although I'd suggest we have lunch more often, since it would be so convenient.'

'I'm not doing what you think I'm doing.'

66

'Really,' replied my mother. 'Then why are you always looking over your shoulder?'

'It's going to stop, *now,*' David said, in a tone more hostile than anything I ever mustered in my wayward youth. I briefly feared for his safety.

'Don't ever talk to me like that again,' Mom coldly replied.

Then David stormed out of the house. I'd like to mention that in most households a thirty-four-year-old son getting into a spat with his mother would not be that unheard of. However, until the previous night's dinner, I had never witnessed a serious conflict between those two. So, obviously, I wanted all the dirt. I picked my sleep-deprived body off the stairs and headed into the kitchen.

'Hey, Mom,' I said.

Mom poured me a cup of coffee like it was medicine and said, 'Drink this.'

I drank the unusually strong brew and asked the obvious question: 'You sure there's just coffee in here, Mom?'

'Would I drug my own child?'

'With Ritalin, you might.'

Mom shrugged her shoulders, not disagreeing with me.

'What's up with you and David?' I asked while I was still awake and had the chance.

'Nothing.'

'I just heard you fighting, Mom.'

'Isabel, it's none of your business.'

'Come on. Spill it. David was always your favorite.'

'No, Rae has always been my favorite. But good news, sweetie, you're now in second place.'

Mom patted me on the head and darted out of

the room before I had a chance to respond or continue the discussion. I would have to learn the truth through some other method besides talking.

Later that afternoon, after I dredged through the surveillance report, Henry Stone called with his usual request. After two days in the hospital, he had been released with a clean bill of health. He had recovered at home for a few more days, refusing to answer his door when Rae showed up. But now that he was back at work, she was impossible to escape.

'Hello?'

'Isabel, it's Henry. Please get her out of here.'

'Are you calling for a Rae extraction?'

'Yes.'

'I'll be there in fifteen minutes.'

'Thank you?' Henry replied, taken aback by my easy response. My usual MO involves some kind of stalling tactic.

I entered Henry's office to find Rae in her usual spot—the brown leather chair across from his desk. She was holding up the picture side of her Spanish language flashcards.

As much as I found the unusual behavior around me intriguing, it was nice to know that some things stayed precisely the same.

THE STONE AND SPELLMAN SHOW—EPISODE 32

'ENGLISH-AS-A FIRST-LANGUAGE'

Setting: Henry Stone's office. Rae sits in the usual brown leather chair across from his desk. She holds the picture side of Spanish language flashcards for Henry to view. I enter the office, sit down in the chair next to Rae, and turn on my digital recorder.

The transcript reads as follows:

HENRY: Okay, Rae, it's time to go.
RAE: We're not done.
HENRY: No, we're done.
ISABEL: I just need to rest here for a moment. Those stairs were much harder today. [Only two flights, but need I remind you again how exhausted I was?]
RAE: What is this? [referring to the flashcard]
HENRY: I'm not playing anymore, Rae.
RAE: This isn't a game. It's about your health.
HENRY: How many times do I have to tell you: I didn't have a lobotomy; I had a concussion and I'm fine now, no thanks to you.
RAE: Just answer the question and then we can move on.
[Henry glances at the flashcard.]
HENRY: It's a boat.
RAE: What color boat?
HENRY: A yellow boat.

[Rae moves on to the next flashcard.]
RAE: What's this?
HENRY: Scissors. Isabel, wake up.
   [Apparently I had fallen asleep.]
ISABEL: Oh, sorry. Rae, we got to go.
RAE: We're not done.
   [Rae moves on to the next card.]
HENRY: Yes, we're done.
ISABEL: What are you doing, Rae?
RAE: I'm making sure Henry doesn't have
   permanent brain damage.
ISABEL: Huh?
HENRY: I'm not playing anymore.
RAE: Then I'm not leaving. What is this?
   [referring to flashcard]
HENRY: [angry] A dog.
RAE: And this?
HENRY: A tree. Are we done yet?
   [The mixture of this being very funny and
   exhaustion caused me to begin laughing
   hysterically. I simply could not stop.]
HENRY: After three hours, it's not so funny.
   [This caused me to laugh even harder.]
RAE: Are you drunk?
ISABEL: No.
RAE: Be quiet. You're interrupting.
ISABEL: We have to go. [still laughing]
RAE: What's this?
HENRY: I'm done, Rae. You're leaving now.
RAE: Just answer this last one and then I'll go.
HENRY: I'm not falling for that again.
ISABEL: [still laughing] I'm sorry. I can't stop.
HENRY: Rae, can you leave me alone with your
   sister for a few minutes?
RAE: Why?

70

HENRY: Because I want to talk to her in private.

RAE: About what?

[Henry walks over to Rae and gently takes her arm, leading her to the door of his office.]

HENRY: [quietly] Have you conveniently forgotten that a week ago you almost killed me?

RAE: Accidentally.

HENRY: Have you forgotten?

RAE: I'll never forget that. Never.

HENRY: I don't ask that much of you, Rae. But when I say 'Leave my office,' I want you to leave my office.

RAE: But then we'd never hang out.

HENRY: Once again, you almost killed me.

RAE: I'll be right outside.

[Henry shuts the door.]

HENRY: Isabel, stop laughing.

[I stop. Sort of.]

ISABEL: Sorry.

HENRY: What's wrong with you?

ISABEL: I haven't slept in forty-eight hours. No, more than that, because you have to count the whole day before the first night of missed sleep. So more like fifty-six hours, or maybe sixty; I'll have to get back to you on that.

HENRY: Is it insomnia?

ISABEL: I wish.

HENRY: Were you on the job?

ISABEL: The first two nights, yes. Then it was John Wayne, Jimmy Stewart, sobbing, snoring, and sizzling.

HENRY: Do I need to call Rae back in here with the flashcards?

ISABEL: No. We're leaving.

[As I got to my feet, I stumbled and Henry put

71

his arm around my waist to steady me. He felt the tape recorder in my pocket and pulled it out.]
HENRY: Are you recording me again?
ISABEL: Sorry.
[End of tape.]

The tape ended, but the conversation didn't.
'I wish you all would stop doing that.'
'We can't help ourselves. Besides, Mom gets really mad at me if I forget.'
'Look at me, Isabel.'
I was feeling a little dizzy and had some trouble focusing. Henry steadied my chin in his hand and held up a finger that floated from side to side.
'Follow my finger,' he said.
'I'm fine,' I said, trying to focus.
'No. You're not. You can't drive like this.'
'Henry, don't be such a cop.'
'Let's go. I'll take you and Rae home. You can get your car tomorrow.'

*   *   *

Rae called shotgun, so I fell asleep in the backseat. When we got to my parents' house, Henry briefly reprimanded my mom for letting me drive. It occurred to me that I had never seen anyone reprimand my mother and get away with it, including my father. But there was something about Henry that my mother could not resist. Before he left, Henry tried to have another discussion with Rae about giving him some space, but it didn't take. My mom sent me up to my old attic apartment/her current guest room and told

72

me to get some rest. I woke up in the morning, thirteen hours later.

SUBJECT IS OBSERVED DIGGING A HOLE . . .

Saturday, January 14
0830 hrs

Whenever one wakes up in a different place than usual, the obvious question arises: How did I get here? Thirteen hours of sleep provided me with much-needed rest, but I woke up in a panic, seriously unable to place myself. You see, while I had lived in this attic apartment for close to nine years, it was fully redecorated into an uncluttered, hotel-like guest room once I had vacated. Having spent so few (if any) hours in there since, I truly had no idea where I was.

I got out of bed, my heart thumping in confusion. The drapes were drawn and the room was unusually dark. Darker than Bernie's—no! *my—* place. I ran to the window, opened the curtains, and looked outside. As my slow-moving brain and newly revived senses were putting the puzzle together, I noticed Subject in the backyard of the adjacent residence digging a hole in the ground.

I climbed halfway out the window and straddled the sill to get a better view. Subject spotted me and looked up.

'Good morning. I didn't know you lived there.'

'I don't,' I said, now that I knew where I was.

'Oh,' he replied, not sure what to say.

'Someone is staying in my apartment,' I said, thinking an explanation was required.

'Oh,' he replied. Clearly, I was confusing him even more.

'Someone who snores,' I added.

'I see,' Subject said, with a bit more inflection. But I got the feeling he was still confused.

'And cries,' I added, because, frankly, I hadn't had any caffeine yet.

'Is this person all right?' Subject asked.

'He caught his wife with another man.'

Then Subject simply stared at me, as if he was thinking of what to say next.

'What are you doing?' I asked.

'Gardening,' Subject replied.

'That explains the digging,' I said.

Subject seemed to think the previous statement was a joke and laughed. It was not a joke.

'Do you want to come over for breakfast?' Subject asked.

'Now?'

'In about fifteen minutes,' Subject said. 'I'm almost done here.'

'Uh, okay,' I said as I noticed I was wearing my father's XXL pajamas. [Can't wear Mom's clothes; she's a size 2.] 'I just have to find my clothes.'

My clothes were washed and folded and left in a laundry basket outside my (no longer my) door. I brushed my teeth, washed my face, and dressed in under five minutes. When I looked out the window the second time, I spotted Subject in his kitchen making coffee.

Instead of taking the stairs and going out the front door and perhaps being required to explain my destination to any family member, I crawled out the window and took the fire escape [There is absolutely no logical reason why this exit should be used exclusively in case of fire.] to the ground level. Subject observed my unusual method of exit and shouted, 'What are you doing?'

'Shhh,' I replied and then motioned that I was going to use the back entrance to his apartment.

*   *   *

As Subject beat eggs and prepped the skillet for omelets, [Score! The only thing on the Spellman menu that morning was lower-Dad's-cholesterol-oatmeal.] I very briefly explained that I didn't quite understand the big deal about doors. I casually mentioned my habit of window entry and exit as a throwback from my rebellious youth, but also as a rejection of the absoluteness of doors being the only socially acceptable mode of entry and exit.

I'm not sure I convinced Subject to give windows a try himself. He stared at me a second too long and said, 'Well, that's another way to look at it.'

Over breakfast Subject and I attempted to get each other's vital statistics.

'So what do you do?' I asked.

'I run a landscaping business.'

'Oh, that explains the gardening.'

'Does gardening need explaining?'

'I think so.'

'And you?'

'I haven't gardened in years. Thirty to be exact.'

'You should try it sometime. Some people find it relaxing.'

'What kind of people?'

'I'm changing the subject,' Subject said.

'Good omelets.'

'So what do you do?' he asked.

'And good coffee.'

'For a living.'

I've run into this problem before. I don't want to tip my hand too soon, since my job makes some people uncomfortable. But if I lie and claim to be, say, a schoolteacher, then for the next few months I've got to run around in pencil skirts and sweater sets pretending to be a teacher. Then, what usually happens [Based on one anecdotal piece of evidence. See previous document—*The Spellman Files* (now available in paperback!)—for a full explanation.] is the person I've lied to becomes very angry and doesn't want to see me again. On this occasion I went with a new approach.

'I'm an information technologist.'

'So you work with computers?'

'Yes. And people, and the occasional dog or cat.'

'You're being vague.'

'I talk about work every day. Sometimes I need a break.'

'Fair enough.'

Subject then suggested that perhaps gardening was what I needed to get my mind off of information technology. After breakfast we retired to the backyard and transplanted potted hydrangeas into the ground. Subject explained that the plants survive better through winter [The temperature in San Francisco in winter rarely dips below freezing. While I'm on the subject of San Francisco weather, anyone with the urge to quote Mark Twain should think twice (see appendix).] in the soil, and so we prepped the soil with compost

76

and laid the perennials into the ground. Surprisingly, I was enjoying myself, until my father spotted me through his bedroom window.

'Izzy, I've been looking for you.'

'Congratulations. You found me.'

'What are you doing?'

'What does it look like?'

'Gardening.'

'Bingo.'

'Wait there. I need to talk to you,' my dad said, and then disappeared from his window.

I got to my feet and dusted off the wet soil from my hands.

'You stall my dad,' I said to Subject. 'I'm going to make a run for it.'

This time I was joking. My dad showed up a minute later. Dad shook Subject's hand and made some form of genuine pleasantry. Subject explained to Dad our morning activity and my dad replied with 'I'm just glad to see Izzy spend her leisure time doing something other than drinking.'

Subject laughed. I glared. Dad quickly changed the subject.

'Have you been by Mrs. Chandler's place?'

'I have no idea what you're talking about,' I said. This was a knee-jerk reaction to any mention of Mrs. Chandler. Will explain shortly, but suffice it to say, I really had no idea what he was talking about.

'Have you seen her dog?'

'No,' I said, growing suspicious.

'I'd like you to go by her place before she has a chance to give her dog a bath.'

Subject was confused, but I chose not to enlighten him. I held out my soiled hand and said,

77

'Thanks, it's been fun. See you later.'

CRIMES AGAINST
MRS. CHANDLER

I drove by the Chandler residence and parked in front. Upon exiting the car, I caught sight of her miniature poodle, barking by the fence to the backyard. It was kind of hard to miss since its coat was dyed hot pink. The second I saw her dog, I rushed back into my car and drove away to avoid being spotted. You see, ten years ago, my first crime against the twenty-year widow was dying her miniature poodle cobalt blue. But that was only the first of many crimes against the woman.

Constance 'Connie' [To her friends; I was not her friend, so I always called her Mrs. Chandler.] Chandler has lived three blocks away on Pacific Avenue as long as I can remember anything. She was a high school art teacher by trade, a hippie by all appearances, and a millionaire by her checkbook. At the age of forty she was widowed by her financier husband. Their marriage was the most striking example of opposites attract that I have ever seen. Some years after her husband's death, budget cuts in the San Francisco school district (and, I suspect, knowledge of her flush financial situation) led to her early retirement. This happened about twenty years ago. Soon after that Mrs. Chandler's holiday enthusiasm took a turn for the worse (or better, depending on whom you ask).

'Art' or *'eyesore'* was how most of the

78

neighborhood split on their reaction to Mrs. Chandler's holiday decorations. Shortly after retirement, the widow began channeling all her 'artistic' energy into seasonal installations in the front of her house. Her attempts to cover every major and minor event, from Christmas nativity scenes to Valentine's Day cupid landscapes, simply screamed 'Vandalize me!' At least Petra and I heard the scream.

* * *

1992 was the year Petra and I began editing Mrs. Chandler's elaborate decorations. Having cased the widow's residence for two years, we were able to predict her decorating style and plan our capers accordingly. The following is a complete list of the crimes Petra and I committed against Mrs. Chandler during the 1992–93 season. We began with Thanksgiving.

Adjustments to Mrs. Chandler's Holiday Tableau

Thanksgiving
Mrs. Chandler presented a peaceful banquet scene between the Native Americans and the recently landed British. [While it is true that Petra's and my academic interests were limited, at best, we always perked up in history class when Mr. Jackson went on tangents regarding the many crimes of our founding fathers.] Mrs. Chandler, an incorrigible optimist, presented a world that she wished existed. In her world, the white devils and the Native Americans joined hands in unity and each partook of the other's delicacies. The 'authentic'

menu on Mrs. Chandler's table included wild turkey, fish, maize, nuts, squash, beans, and dried fruit (since none was actually in season). To make the picture more realistic, Petra and I threw US Army blankets around the Native Americans, painted pox marks on their faces, and placed empty whiskey bottles by their side. [Ironically Petra and I performed actual library research to determine our alterations to Mrs. Chandler's lawn. In fact, we probably learned more history from our attempts at sabotage than we ever did in school.]

Christmas
Christmas was, of course, Mrs. Chandler's raison d'etre. Her nativity scene was as fine a piece of amateur secular art as there ever was. Portraying Jesus as a sixties-era hippie (in Birkenstocks and hemp clothing, and wearing a hard-to-miss peace sign around his neck) was Chandler's personal touch in the exhibit. Plus, she burned patchouli incense instead of myrrh. Petra and I wanted to respect her efforts but simply provide a more universal [And, some might argue, historically accurate.] appeal. Using stage makeup, we painted all the mannequins chocolate brown. Then we smoked some pot and came up with an addendum to that idea. We returned a few hours later with Afro wigs and NBA headbands and placed them on the three kings.

New Year's Day
Mrs. Chandler, I suspect, could find no political message in New Year's, so she did nothing. Petra and I, in turn, left her alone—mostly because we were just too hungover to bother.

Groundhog Day

When this half-holiday rolled around and Mrs. Chandler's lawn remained untouched, Petra and I decided (partly based on our love of the recently released Bill Murray film) that we had to honor this day on our own. Grass of any legal variety is in short supply in San Francisco. Sometimes you'll find a small patch of wild lawn behind a Victorian row house, but in front it's extremely rare. Mrs. Chandler's residence is one of those exceptions. Years ago, she dug out the cement driveway in front of her home, replaced it with a plot of lawn approximately six feet by eight feet, and wrapped a picket fence around it. It looks completely ridiculous but provides for her the main stage for her outrageous decorations.

Petra's and my ode to Groundhog Day was a no-brainer. We simply dug up 'rodent holes' in her grass.

Valentine's Day

It was hard to explain an old hippie's fondness for a Hallmark holiday, but we later learned that Mr. Chandler was a traditional romantic sort who pulled out all the stops on February fourteenth—flowers, candy, candlelit dinners, violins, etc. Mrs. Chandler resorted to mythology and styled her yard with winged and diapered cupids, along with hearts and arrows suspended in midair. According to Petra's and my research she was mixing genres, so we added another genre to her mix: horror film.

We toppled Mrs. Chandler's cupids on their side. We dismembered some and split the cloth guts of the others. We sprayed red food dye in a crime-scene pattern and left the murder weapons—

plastic knives from the costume shop—at the scene. We wiped all smooth items for prints and discarded our tainted clothes at the dump. We called it the Valentine's Day Massacre.

St. Patrick's Day

Chandler's husband was Irish and so the widow could not neglect this 'holiday.' We transformed a lively green scene of leprechauns, pots of gold, and a rainbow into the aftermath of a drunken wake. We toppled the leprechauns on their side and strew at least fifty empty cans of Guinness [And we drank every last one of them.] on the lawn. We titled it 'The Morning After.'

Easter

Mrs. Chandler's motif was the traditional pastel violet landscape of an Easter egg hunt, with baskets of painstakingly decorated hand-painted eggs. The only Chandleresque touch was that the eggs all had peace signs on them. Petra and I brainstormed for hours on how to adjust this particular installation, and then it came to me. We swapped the pastel-colored eggs in the giant white-painted straw basket for eight-balls. If you think painting Easter eggs is time consuming, try acquiring two dozen eight-balls [There was also the drug-reference subtext.] without actually paying for them. [Years later, my father would say that this one was his favorite because of its 'sheer simplicity.']

Independence Day

By the time the fourth of July rolled around, word on the street was that Petra and I were the saboteurs of these elaborate decorations. And yet, Mrs. Chandler appeared to be taking no measures to stop us. One day, when we were casing her yard for our next attack, trying to figure out how we could violate a collection of peace-loving mannequins in a sit-in, Mrs. Chandler exited her home and approached us.

'Hello, ladies,' she said. 'I think it's time to make a formal introduction. I'm Constance Chandler; my friends call me Connie. And you are?'

Petra and I mumbled our names while we tried to figure out a speedy but non-guilty-looking escape.

'We're not so different, you and me,' she said, making direct eye contact.

Petra and I looked askance at each other and waited for her to continue.

'I'm all for personal expression. That's why I do my art,' she continued, sweeping her hand over to her latest installation. 'And I understand the need for sabotage. But I ask you to consider the statement you're making. There was a political undercurrent to your Thanksgiving and Christmas designs. Although I do think you could have done without the NBA headbands and Afros. Unnecessary, and it diminished the point you were making. But lately, I think you're slipping,' she said.

Petra and I were slowly backing away, but Mrs. Chandler, believing us to be a captive audience, didn't stop.

'Groundhog Day? A Valentine's Day murder

scene? St. Patrick's Day? Ladies, that's just juvenile vandalism. If you're going to attack my art, I ask you to think about what you're doing. I ask you to take a position.'

'I have no idea what you're talking about,' I said. 'But have a nice evening.'

Petra and I turned on our heels and made a quick exit. As we briskly headed up the hill, Mrs. Chandler shouted after us, 'And I hope that was all-natural food coloring you put on my dog!'

A few minutes passed in silence as Petra and I reflected on our recent encounter.

'We're done here,' Petra said, marking a finite end to our 'adjustments.'

'You heard her. She's not going to turn us in. She just wants us to take a more political slant,' I said.

'First of all, Izzy, it's no fun if we're adjusting our adjustments to make our victim happy; second of all, I think the neighborhood watch committee wants to take action. Even if Mrs. Chandler doesn't mind, they do. Lastly, I'd like to stay on that woman's good side.'

'Why?'

'Couldn't you tell? She was totally stoned. We're gonna need another source in case Justin's [Petra's boyfriend at the time.] connection dries up.'

As it was we never used Mrs. Chandler as a drug source, but we did end our attacks on her decorations. That night Petra and I made a pact that we would never admit our crimes, to ensure that we could never be punished or turned against each other. When any reference to our previous crimes was made, we both spoke the same exact refrain: 'I have no idea what you're talking about.'

THE 'LAW OFFICES' OF MORT SCHILLING

Monday, April 24
1050 hrs

Mort's overgrown eyebrow rose about an inch as he jotted down notes on my petty criminal past.

'Do you have a record,' Morty asked, 'besides your current one?'

'It's sealed,' I replied.

'Juvi?'

'Yes, Morty. It was a long time ago. People make mistakes in their youth.'

'Izz, you're thirty years old and you've been arrested four times in the last two months.'

'Two don't count!'

'But what about the other two?'

'I'll be vindicated as soon as I can get some real dirt on Subject.'

'My point, Izzy, is you're getting a reputation, and your line of work is all about the reputation.'

'No. My line of work is about getting to the truth.'

ISABEL SPELLMAN, LICENSED PI

The truth isn't my primary goal. My job is about discovering answers for specific questions asked of me. For instance, if I am providing a background check on a recent hire for a major corporation, the question they want answered is whether the individual is who he says he is and also whether that individual might become a danger to the already vested employees.

First I run a criminal check on the potential employee to be certain there are no felonies in his wake, then I make sure he is exactly who he says he is. If Potential Employee claims to reside at 12 Lombard Street, I run a credit header and cross-check the addresses. Most of my job is cut-and-dry. If a wife wants to know if her husband is cheating, I follow him for a week or two until he does or doesn't. Usually, what we want to know about someone can be discovered quite easily, but the problem with my work is that I've grown accustomed to having answers at my finger tips. I expect a brief stab of curiosity to be sated by five minutes at a computer or five hours behind the wheel of my car.

My job requires me to be curious and insists that I be naturally suspicious. But there are many occasions when I simply cannot provide an explanation for the facts presented to me. On those occasions I may cross some ethical boundaries to reach my goal, simply to get answers to questions that won't go away. I have many flaws, but I suppose the only one that truly damages my life is that I believe all questions have answers and I believe that I am entitled to those answers.

I say all this because I hope it will explain all the events that have transpired. If you have enough unanswered questions, you have a certifiable mystery, and those are impossible to resist.

MILFOS AND REAFOS

MILFO ('mil-foe) n: 1. Acronym for mid-life freak-out; 2. Something resembling a mid-life crisis, but occurring more than once.

REAFO ('re-foe) n: 1. Acronym for retirement-age freak-out; 2. Something resembling a mid-life crisis, but occurring more than once and later than it's supposed to.

After breakfast with Subject, I returned to the Spellman offices to finish up a series of background checks for our biggest client, Xylor Corp. Since Mom and Dad took on the giant conglomerate, there have been no more cash flow problems, although the work has gotten decidedly duller. Backgrounds are almost exclusively desk work—database research with a couple phone calls thrown in. Anytime I'm stuck in the office means more quality time with the family.

Since it was Saturday, Rae was home and bored. She strolled into the office to disrupt my already lagging work ethic, plopped down in an old vinyl chair, rolled herself over to me, and put her feet up on my desk.

'Dad's definitely having a REAFO,' Rae said.

'One yoga class does not a REAFO make,' I replied.

'I've been watching him,' Rae said. 'He's taking showers outside of the house, which can only mean one thing.'

'Oh my god,' I replied, other factors weighing in on my response. 'He's going to the gym, isn't he? I thought he'd lost some weight.'

'He goes at least three times a week and to that yoga class. But the part I don't get,' Rae said, 'is that he tries to keep it from Mom.'

'That doesn't make any sense,' I said. 'She's the one who's been nagging him to do that for years.'

'He sneaks out when she's not around. It's really weird.'

'Maybe that's just a coincidence.'

'I doubt it,' Rae said. 'But I'll take this REAFO over MILFO number three any day,' Rae replied, spinning around in the chair.

'Can't argue with you there.'

'So this is REAFO number two, right?' she asked.

'According to my calculations.'

MILFO #1—'Mirror Man'

Dad's first MILFO began in his forty-eighth [A bit late for mid-life crisis to begin, but he makes up for it, as you will see.] year. At the time we referred to it as a mid-life crisis, since it so completely resembled one of those. In Dad's case it took the form of vanity. He purchased sharper clothes, dyed his hair, and checked himself in the mirror with the regularity of a cuckoo clock. He would even solicit fashion advice and ask random family members to go shopping with him. He started wearing bracelets and using expensive moisturizers. Although the origin of this first MILFO was never scientifically proven, Rae and I surmised that it was a direct product of attending Mom's twentieth high school reunion. My father is a large man—six foot three, in the mid-two-hundred-pound range, with slightly oafish features. The reunion reminded Dad that he married a woman both far better looking and ten years younger than him, which we believe contributed to his insecurity. The MILFO lasted approximately a month. However, my father, not being a naturally vain man, soon lost interest in his looks when he realized my mother had not.

The MILFO acronym was coined when Dad had his next flip-out. Rae and I were under the impression that a mid-life crisis was supposed to happen once in a man's life. We decided that if Dad wanted more than one, they needed a new name. MILFO #2 occurred approximately four years later. We would eventually discover that MILFOs and REAFOs recurred with the frequency of a leap year. Not on the dot, but close enough.

MILFO #2—'Space Detective'

Spellman Investigations was going through some financial difficulties at the time. Dad picked up the Arts & Leisure section of the *San Francisco Chronicle* one morning and read an article about a screenwriter who penned the latest Bruce Willis vehicle and earned two million dollars in the process. Dad then decided that he had a screenplay in him. Over the next two weeks he purchased Syd Field's book on how to write a screenplay, worked on his pitch, and eventually concocted a story about a detective who accidentally [No matter how many times I asked, Dad always failed to come up with a plausible explanation for how this happened.] ends up on the space shuttle and discovers the body of a murdered astronaut. In the strict confines of the gravity-free shuttle, Detective Jack Spaceman [Note: this was not a comedy.] had to solve the crime before all the 'real astronauts' were killed and there was no one left to bring the shuttle back to earth.

One of the major problems with Dad's screenplay, other than the characters and plot, was that he didn't actually want to write it, he just wanted to practice his pitch on family members. I was a teenager at the time and put up with it just once. David was a bit more patient and offered feedback maybe two or three times before he pled his too-much-homework case. Mom, after hearing the title, refused to listen to a single word. Uncle Ray had the best excuse of all: 'Movies ain't my thing,' he'd say, and run off to the bar.

Unfortunately, only one family member remained—Rae, who was eight at the time. Dad would tuck her into bed, night after night, reworking his screenplay pitch as a bedtime story. On day seven, Rae went screaming into Mom and Dad's bedroom, crying hysterically to Mom, begging for a new bedtime story. Mom told Dad that making Rae listen to his screenplay pitch was tantamount to child abuse. She suggested Dad write the screenplay and stop talking about it, which brought MILFO #2 to an end.

MILFO #3 'The Learning Annex'

Three and a half years later, Dad decided his worldview was limited, and MILFO #3 began. Dad first took a class at the Learning Annex called 'Two Thousand Years of World History in Two Days.' Then he moved on to 'How to Speak to Anyone about Anything,' 'Conversational Latin,' and then the bizarrely inappropriate 'Knitting 101.' These classes would have been fine if Dad could have kept them to himself, but he felt the need to share, and Rae, as the youngest and the least able to defend herself, usually got the brunt of Dad's regurgitation of information.

Being a curious and intelligent child, Rae didn't mind the condensed history lesson that Dad provided, although we would later learn that his grasp of the Civil War and the American Revolution was sketchy at best, with a number of comingling facts. However, Rae's brief lesson on Latin greetings got the cold shoulder, since my six-year-old sister had only recently gotten the hang of English.

What really got under Rae's skin was the knitting lesson. She protested loudly for a full evening until my father left five spools of yarn in her bedroom and told her to think about it. Rae, realizing that you can't knit yarn if it's chopped up into a bunch of tiny little pieces, woke up early the next morning and began dicing the spools up in two-to-three-inch strands with a pair of safety scissors from her art supply box. My mother came upon the crime scene the next morning, finding my sister's room carpeted in a motley assortment of yarn. They spent the next hour cleaning up the mess. When my father finally got out of bed, Mom informed him that MILFO #3 was over.

By the time MILFO #4 rolled around, Rae pointed out that Dad was no longer middle-aged. We both concurred that the MILFOs needed to be renamed and came up with the much superior acronym REAFO. Which brings me to REAFO #1.

REAFO #1—'Wood Shop'

After building a flower box in class, Dad decided he was ready for a more ambitious project. Soon after Dad's three-week class came to an end, he began construction on a loft bed in Rae's room, with a study annex underneath. David was at college at the time, so Rae slept in his room for the two months Dad worked on this project. What I remember from those months was a great deal of swearing and yelps of pain coming from upstairs. I recall Dad's fingers covered in makeshift bandages, blood seeping from an assortment of wounds. But my father's dedication was tireless. When his project was completed, he placed a large sheet over the construction and invited the family into the room for a formal unveiling.

My mother eyed the primitive-looking structure with a great deal of skepticism. Rae ran for the ladder, eager to climb her new, exciting piece of furniture. But my mother pulled her off the bottom rung and turned to me.

'Isabel, would you mind testing this out first?'

'Oh, right. Sacrifice me,' I said, giving my mom a

look of mock betrayal. 'This is just like *Sophie's Choice.*'

I approached the construction. The ladder creaked beneath my weight until I reached the top of the bed. I threw myself on top of the mattress, expecting (and half hoping) that the structure would crumble beneath me. [His guilt would come in handy for years to come, I thought to myself.] Sadly, the loft bed merely swayed back and forth, creaking like the stairs of an abandoned building after years of decay. There would never be any dramatic collapse. My mother instructed my father to disassemble the bed immediately. Rae cried all afternoon and REAFO #1 came to an end.

REAFO #2 OR SUSPICIOUS BEHAVIOR REPORT #3?

'Albert Spellman'

Rae departed after our MILFO REAFO chat to make a phone call. As I ran a criminal check on Martha Baumgartner, executive assistant applicant, secretly hoping that she had been arrested at least one time in her forty-five years, Dad entered the office, hair still slightly damp— from his gym shower, I presume. Dad said hello, patted me on the head, and sat down behind his desk. Fifteen minutes passed in silence, until I noticed my father glancing in my direction more often than can be reasonably justified.

'Take a picture. It'll last longer,' I said.

'With all that charm it's a crime you're not yet

married,' Dad mumbled sarcastically, and returned to his work.

Five minutes later, I caught him looking at me again. I narrowed my eyes and stared back at him.

'Can I ask you a question?' Dad asked.

'I'd rather you didn't,' I replied.

Long pause.

'Are you happy?' he asked sincerely.

'I'd be happier if you gave me a raise.'

'I'm not talking about money.'

'No, but I am.'

'Change. Of. Subject,' my father said in the tone of a demand.

'Fine,' I replied.

'Is this what you want to do with your life?' my dad asked. 'Is this enough for you?'

'What are you getting at?'

'I've been thinking lately,' he replied.

'A by-product of the new REAFO, I don't doubt.'

'I'm a complicated man, Isabel.'

'So you say.'

'It's not too late for you,' Dad said, a little too seriously.

'Oh, good.'

'I mean, it's not too late to do something different.'

'Like what?'

'Anything. You're still young. You could go to medical school—'

'Dad, if you're gunning to have a doctor in the family, you better work on Rae. Or David. He could be one of those total high-achieving freaks who earn both an MD and a JD. You know, I think I'd have more in common with a career bank robber than a doctor-slash-lawyer.'

My dad picked up a stack of papers from his desk and gave me a disappointed stare.

'I know you're very proud of your truly spectacular defense mechanisms, but I swear sometimes it's impossible to have a simple conversation with you.'

Dad walked out of the room, in a moderate huff. REAFOs (and MILFOs) had never typically taken the form of hostility. This might have been something else entirely.

EX-BOYFRIEND #9

Monday, January 16
1300 hrs

Daniel Castillo, DDS, phoned the Spellman offices just as I began to tackle a two-foot stack of papers left on my desk to file.

'My three o'clock cancelled and you're overdue for a cleaning. I'll see you then,' he said, and then quickly hung up the phone. Daniel has learned that waiting for a response from me can only result in further conversation and negotiations. He discovered the wait-for-no-answer tactic sometime after our breakup and has been using it ever since. The key to his success is that once he hangs up, he won't pick up his cell phone or accept any calls from me, rendering all communication impossible.

I like to reward innovation, and so I arrived at my appointment at 3 P.M. sharp. [Just a figure of speech. I never arrive at anything sharp. It was around 3:15 p.m.]

95

'You're late,' Daniel said.

'You never asked if I could make it on time.'

'Sit down.'

I sat down in the chair. Daniel put the paper bib on me and said, 'Open up.'

'That's it? No small talk? Don't you want to ask me 'What's new?' first?'

'All right,' Daniel said, reluctantly, 'what's new?'

'Well, Rae almost vehicular-manslaughtered her best friend, and I briefly had a sixty-five-year-old roommate, but now have temporarily moved back in with my parents. I think my Dad might be having his second REAFO, provisionally titled 'Gym REAFO.' And something's up with my mom, but I can't put my finger on it.'

'Speaking of your mother,' Daniel said, unmoved by my headline news, 'tell her she's overdue for a cleaning.'

'She was just in here a few days ago.'

'No, she wasn't. I assure you, I remember when your mother visits.' [Forty pages ago, Dad said Mom was at the dentist. Remember?]

'Interesting. I'll have to put that in my report.'

'Open up.'

'No. Now I say, 'What's new with you, Daniel?' '

'I'm engaged,' Daniel replied. 'Open wide.'

Daniel mistook my gawk for acquiescence and promptly stuck the scaler and mirror in my mouth.

'Aat? En id at appen?'

'I proposed three weeks ago,' Daniel replied. He's fluent in consonant-free cleaning speak.

'Onrayuashons.'

'Thank you.'

'Aaa oes eee ooo?'

'She's a neurosurgeon. Rinse.'

96

I rinsed and said, 'You're kidding, right?'

'How is that funny?' Daniel replied, and stuck his fingers back in my mouth.

'Ard ooo splain.'

'Are you flossing regularly?'

'Uh huuhhh.'

'Was that a yes or no?'

'Esss!'

'Liar!' Daniel shouted, then modified his tone. 'Rinse.'

I rinsed and said, 'So what else can you tell me about her?'

'She's a Latina, so my mother is thrilled. She's an excellent tennis player, gourmet cook. What do you want to know?'

'Did she model to put herself through medical school?' I said sarcastically, which Daniel didn't pick up on.

'Not that I'm aware of. Open up.'

'Ank odd.'

'But she was in the Olympics,' Daniel said, twisting the knife into my gut.

THE PHILOSOPHER'S CLUB

After my teeth cleaning and reminder of my all-around mediocrity, I needed a stiff drink. I knew my bartender (yes, *my* bartender) would lend a sympathetic ear, so I headed over to the Philosopher's Club.

'Do you want to be a neurosurgeon?' Milo asked, unsympathetically.

'*No.*'

'So what's the problem?'

'Forget it.'

'You want to be in the Olympics, that's it?'

'I said forget it.'

'Forgotten,' Milo replied, gladly. 'Oh, your sister came back here the other day.'

'When?'

'A couple of weeks ago. Forgot to mention it.'

'Why didn't you call me?'

'She came in, ordered a drink, I told her to leave, and she phoned a cop to pick her up.'

'Henry?'

'I think that's his name. Stiff-looking fellow. Doesn't smile.'

'That's the guy.'

'And then yesterday, he came into the bar by himself. He was asking about you. When you came in and stuff.'

'What did you tell him?'

'I said you weren't on a schedule. I figured I better be cagey, a cop coming in here asking questions.'

'I appreciate your concern, but relax. I'm not in trouble with the law.' [Not yet.]

THE PETERSON PROBLEM

For the five days following Bernie's reentry into my life, I remained in the Spellman house, but I did not give up hope that soon my apartment would be mine again. The most direct approach I considered was reuniting Bernie and Daisy. On day three of my Bernie eviction, I phoned Daisy and suggested a reconciliation, citing that Bernie was devastated by their breakup. Daisy then told her side of the story, which involved her husband of eighteen months clocking in close to thirty hours a week at the local strip club. She hung up on me when I recommended marriage counseling.

Shortly after my drink at Milo's, I drove back to my apartment, thinking I might try a night at the address on my phone bill, as a change of pace. I cast aside the tie on the doorknob and unlocked the deadbolt. I opened the door to a vision that I still cannot erase from my memory no matter how many bourbons I drink: Bernie, half naked, chasing Letty, a fifty-something woman with a bouffant hairdo and blue-eye-shadowed raccoon eyes, also half-naked, around the apartment, which in the last week had turned into a disaster zone.

I stared at the couple in utter disbelief.

'What the hell is going on, Bernie?'

'I'm entertaining a friend,' Bernie said, not even trying to cover up. 'Didn't you see the tie on the door?'

'Yes,' I replied, averting my gaze from . . .*everything*.

'What did you think it meant?'

'I thought it meant you were a slob.'

'In the future, roomie, the tie on the door means—'

'We have no future,' I replied, grabbing a suitcase out of the closet and heading into the bedroom. 'I'm not coming back until you're gone.'

I packed another suitcase and a backpack of clothes and told Bernie to call me when he was planning to vacate. He managed to even look sad as I slammed the door on my way out. In San

Francisco a rent-controlled apartment is a goldmine and I had just lost my treasure. I accepted defeat in the moment but planned a series of far more drastic measures to win back my home.

SUSPICIOUS BEHAVIOR REPORTS #4 AND #5

'Olivia Spellman'

As I was driving up the block to the Clay Street house, with the clock on my dashboard reading 11:15 P.M., I saw my mother pulling her car out of the driveway. I knew she wasn't on the job and could come up with no reasonable explanation for her late-night venture, so I decided to tail her.

I stayed at least one car back the entire drive. Mom, in her nondescript Honda, was traveling at a leisurely just-above-the-speed-limit pace. She was clearly not tailing anyone, nor was she aware of being tailed. She took Gough to Market Street and Dolores Street over the hill into Noe Valley. She parked in an illegal corner spot and got out of her car. I double-parked, thinking Mom wasn't planning a lengthy visit, and followed her down the block, scaling shrubbery the entire way.

From about twenty feet back, I saw my mother kneel down in front of a motorbike, unscrew the air caps on the tires, stick a pin inside, and let out all the air. She looked around nervously as she was accomplishing this simple act of vandalism and then quickly got up and walked briskly, but confidently, back to her car. I remained in the bushes watching her as she drove away.

'Henry Stone'

When you witness your mother vandalizing a motorbike for no apparent reason, there aren't a whole lot of people you can discuss it with. I jotted down the address where the motorbike was parked and then returned to my car. It was too late to phone Petra, so I went to Milo's, even though the last time I went to Milo's his ear wasn't as sympathetic as it used to be.

When I entered Henry was sitting at the bar, nursing a whiskey neat, and staring down at the counter. I nodded at Milo, who pulled a Guinness for me. I had begun ordering those lately because they take a really long time to serve and it annoys Milo. I also like the rich, soupy flavor, but that's secondary. I sat down next to the unexpected patron and asked the obvious question.

'What are you doing in *my* bar, Henry?'

'It's a free country,' he replied, sounding almost drunk.

Henry Stone's expressionless face was impossible to read. All communication with him happened through words and he chose them very carefully. But there had to be a reason he was in my bar at close to midnight, maybe intoxicated.

'Are you drunk?' I asked, hoping he'd say yes, hoping that I had finally caught him with his guard down.

Then he did the oddest thing. He reached over to me and put his hands in my jacket pockets, then slid them down over my hips and thighs.

101

I smacked his hand away. 'You're buying my drink now.'

'Sorry. I wanted to make sure you weren't recording me,' he said by way of explanation.

'I only do that when Rae's around,' I replied.

Henry then returned his focus to the bottom of his drink. Milo slid the Guinness in front of me. I pointed at Henry.

'He's buying.'

Henry reached into his wallet and bought me my drink. Usually Henry's eye contact had a way of unnerving you, making you feel like he knows exactly what you're thinking and is disappointed that you're thinking it. But Henry wasn't looking anyone in the eye. I had never seen him appear so . . . weak.

'I'm going to ask you if there's something on your mind, Henry, because clearly there's something on your mind. Please don't deny it. It will just insult me. So, if you want to tell me what it is, I promise, I'll be quiet and listen.'

Henry finished his drink and pointed at his glass for Milo to pour him another.

As Milo was refilling Henry's whiskey, Milo turned to me and said, 'Still upset about not making the Olympics?'

'You've changed,' I snapped back at Milo.

Milo chuckled to himself and turned to Henry. 'You doing okay there, son?'

'I'm fine,' Henry replied politely.

'How many has he had?' I asked Milo, and then finally Henry made eye contact. His loaded glance at *my* bartender was a clear warning to respect his privacy. Milo nodded back to him in understanding and turned to me.

'Mind your own business. That's between me, my customer, and the cab driver.'

I flashed my ring for Milo and said, 'Can you leave me alone to talk to my fiancée in private?'

Milo rolled his eyes and walked away.

'There are over three hundred bars in San Francisco, give or take. There has to be a reason why you came into *my* bar,' I said.

Henry finished his drink and continued to ignore me.

'Let me drive you home,' I said.

'No, I'll take a cab.'

'Why? I'll drive you. Come on, let's go.'

Henry took my left hand in his and pulled off my mother's ring. He then stuck it in my pocket and got to his feet.

'You shouldn't wear it all the time. Makes them think you're taken. Then you attract the wrong kind of guy,' Henry said.

'I attract the wrong kind all on my own,' I said. 'But I find if I wear the rock [Albeit a flawed quarter-carat diamond.] I get much better customer service. Give me your keys, Henry.'

Henry looked like he was thinking about it. I didn't want an argument. I just wanted the keys, so I reached into his pocket and took them.

'Let's go,' I said, exiting the bar and waving to Milo.

Henry took his time following me to the car, like he was making a point, although the point was lost on me.

Henry buckled up his seat belt and said, 'You people have taken over my life.' There was a flash of genuine hostility in the delivery that rendered me speechless.

In all my car rides with cops in squad cars, none were as tense as this one. The silence was that eerie cricket kind, as if breaking it would disrupt nature. I had ten minutes to consider what we had done to this man, and it was true. Somehow we did take over his life. But I suppose we had been mistakenly convinced that he didn't really mind.

As I pulled up in front of Henry's apartment, he prepared to shoot out of the car. I locked the door from the control panel and held on to his arm.

'Is my family the source of your troubles?' I asked point-blank.

'No,' he replied. 'But I need some space to think.'

'About what?'

'That's not giving me space.'

'Got it,' I said, and unlocked the door.

DISAPPEARANCE #1:
THE NOT-SO-GRAND CANYON

Four days later, still not wanting to bunk with Bernie, I returned to my parents' home to retire for the night. I found my mother and father packing for their disappearance. The next morning they were departing at 8 A.M. sharp on their road trip to the Grand Canyon. Mom was packing with an attention to detail usually reserved for brain surgery. The last time my parents had taken a disappearance was fifteen years earlier, and the only traveling they had done since were weekend PI conferences—on subjects as far ranging as 'A PI's Best Friend: The Latest in Gadgetry' and 'The

Post-Pellicano PI'—where one never leaves the hotel.

In the morning, Mom, Dad, Rae, and I had breakfast together. My parents' edginess regarding an activity most people look forward to was cause for concern. As my dad and Rae loaded the car with their suitcases, Mom hugged me good-bye.

'I'm glad we don't have to experiment with leaving Rae alone just yet,' she whispered to me, and smiled just as Rae walked by carrying a piece of luggage.

'I'm almost sixteen,' Rae said. 'I can stay home alone without a responsible adult keeping tabs on me.'

'Dear, Isabel's not that responsible,' was my mother's reply.

'Whatever,' Rae said, and continued on to the car.

I ignored their previous exchange and focused my attention on the more serious matter at hand: 'Disappearances are supposed to be fun, Mom. Why do you look so nervous?'

'Your father and I haven't had this much quality time since our honeymoon.'

'So?' I replied.

'What if we can't stand each other?'

HOME ALONE

CHAPTER-1

Saturday, January 21

My parents departed without incident. As Rae and I cleared up the breakfast dishes, I asked her what her plans were for the day.

'I'm going to see if I can talk Henry into giving me another driving lesson,' she replied and that is when I gave my sister the Space Talk.

I kept it simple because Rae prefers bullet points to essays, especially when the lesson is in the form of a lecture.

- If you don't give someone enough space, they become sick of you.
- If they become sick of you, you might lose them forever.
- Therefore, sometimes you can keep a relationship going longer if you completely ignore someone for a while.

I played the expert on this subject even though everyone in my family knows I'm not an expert. Rae asked for a specific time line for how long she should leave Henry Stone alone. I suggested six months. We negotiated down to one. We'd cross that bridge when we came to it. In the meantime I gave Rae driving lessons to distract her from her absent best friend. My parents had made it clear a while back that they didn't want me instructing

Rae on the rules of the road, but they were gone and I had to sidetrack her somehow.

An hour later, as Rae practiced backing the car into the driveway, Subject exited his apartment carrying two bags of topsoil. After he placed them on the truck bed, he approached our car.

'Not bad,' he said to Rae, impressed with her reverse driving skills.

As Rae exited the vehicle, she said, 'My best friend taught me.'

'The one that was in the hospital?'

'Yes,' Rae replied. Behind her back I was trying to signal Subject to get off the subject, but he simply eyed me quizzically and continued on.

'How is he?' Subject asked.

'He's fine. I guess. I'm trying to give him his space.'

I sliced my finger across my throat and mouthed to our neighbor to change the subject. Subject did, quickly.

'So I ran into your parents this morning. They said they're going on a road trip, although they called it something strange.'

'A disappearance,' Rae said.

'That was it.'

'I have to pee. Good-bye,' Rae said, apparently giving our neighbor some space.

I stood in the front yard awkwardly, hoping that perhaps he'd ask me out again, but as you will soon discover I'm extremely impatient.

'So, uh, thanks for breakfast the other day.'

'You're welcome.'

'Maybe you'd like to cook me another kind of meal just so I can see where your true talent lies.'

'Maybe I would.'

'When do you think you would like to do that?'

'Maybe at 6 P.M. tonight. You can bring your sister.'

'Maybe not.'

*   *   *

As I made Rae a sandwich for dinner (not because she can't make her own sandwich, but because I thought if I made it she'd be more likely to eat that than a bowl of Froot Loops for dinner) she quizzed me about my upcoming date.

'Do you like this guy?'

'I don't know him, but I think he's cute.'

'I think he's too young for you,' Rae said.

'He's about my age.'

'But Mom says you should go out with someone more mature so that you grow up.'

'I'm grown up enough,' I replied.

'That's not what Mom says.'

SUSPICIOUS BEHAVIOR REPORT #6

'Subject'

When I arrived at Subject's residence, he put on his coat and said we had to go for a ride to pick up a few extra ingredients for dinner. Instead of driving to the store, Subject took me to a community garden in the Mission District. There was a padlock securing the fence, which Subject had the key for. We entered the garden and

Subject found a four-by-six-foot patch of soil that was growing an assortment of winter vegetables. Subject grabbed some carrots, kale, and squash and placed them in a paper bag.

On the way back to Clay Street, Subject explained that the plot in the garden was his friend's. Subject was taking care of it while he was out of town and was therefore entitled to its crop.

While I found the garden side of Subject interesting, I had a few more practical questions up my sleeve. I tackled these interrogations while Subject was cooking. I've discovered that people are often more forthright when they are double-tasking.

'Where are you from?' I asked.

'St. Louis,' he replied.

'Were you born there?' [Place of birth makes collecting background information much easier.]

Pause. 'Yes.'

'Why'd you move here?'

'Change of pace. So do you like your job?' Subject asked, trying to steer the topic away from him.

'Eh,' I replied, trying to avoid any follow-up questions.

'Still don't want to talk about work?' Subject asked.

'Nope,' I replied.

'I'm going to serve dinner now.'

'Excellent idea.'

Subject could certainly cook and drink, two things in a man I am quite fond of. We touched on many subjects over the ninety-minute meal, but none of them provided any real personal information, which, for the time being, was fine with me. But Subject was still fishing, even after we finished our meal.

'Got any hobbies?' he asked.

'Not that I'm aware of,' I replied.

'How about special skills?'

As it turns out, I am something of an expert on the classic sitcom *Get Smart,* which aired between 1965 and 1970, plus a few unremarkable TV movies some years later. I decided to mention my encyclopedic knowledge of the show's 138 episodes. Subject claimed to have never seen an episode of *Get Smart.* I, of course, asked him if he had been raised by wolves. Subject then explained that he simply didn't watch much television growing up. I gave Subject the appropriate amount of sympathy and then excused myself to grab my DVD collection from my parents' house (a bootlegged set 'borrowed' from Ex-boyfriend #9). Over the next two hours I forced Subject to watch what I firmly believe are the top three episodes of this classic TV series.

'The Not-So-Great Escape'

CONTROL [An international spy organization—the good guys.] agents start vanishing from the airport. Max [Maxwell Smart, Agent 86.] and the Chief go to the airport to investigate and The Chief disappears as well. Eventually Max discovers that the all the CONTROL agents are being held at a KAOS [The International Organization of Evil.] prisoner-of-war camp, somewhere in New Jersey. Max returns to the airport to get himself kidnapped and is also sent to the prison camp. After several failed attempts at escaping, The

CONTROL prisoners decide to dig their way out. Max loses his sense of direction underground and ends up digging back into the prisoners' barracks. Fortuitously he cuts a power line in the process, which sends the fire and police departments to the camp. KAOS [Ibid.] agents flee for fear of being caught, freeing the CONTROL agents. I am of the opinion that any *Get Smart* episode that features Ludwig Von Siegfried (charmingly over-acted by Bernie Kopell [Best known for his role on The Love Boat.]) is a classic.

'Ship of Spies'

Max and Agent 99 board a ship carrying only four other passengers (five if you count the unstable Agent 44; [He's actually a very good agent, but he has a crying problem.] six if you count Agent 44 and the murdered passenger they discover). They're looking for the plans for the Nuclear Amphibian Battleship. Their only clue is that the 'plans are not plans' and they're searching for someone who makes a clip-clop noise when he/she walks. Unfortunately all their fellow passengers make clip-clop noises.

'The Little Black Book'

Max's old army buddy, Sid (played by the borderline-psychotic Don Rickles), comes for a visit. Sid borrows what he thinks is Max's little black book but is in fact a list of KAOS agents, left to Max by an agent trying to defect. [There is an amusing lack of follow-through in the defecting agent's story. She is shot but still alive, and yet Max never seems to call an ambulance for her.] Sid inadvertently returns the book to KAOS. When Max tries to explain to Sid that he's a spy, Sid thinks he's crazy and sabotages Max's attempts to get the book back. Finally Max convinces Sid that he's a secret government agent and they work together to find the book, only to get arrested for playing patty-cake. I'm completely serious. Max and Sid just shot three guys, but get arrested for 'the old patty-cake trick,' [If you are unfamiliar with the old patty-cake trick: This is where two men (usually) pretend to play patty-cake and then surprise their would-be attackers by punching them.] (which originated, I believe, during the Bob Hope/Bing Crosby *Road* pictures). This two-parter episode of *Get Smart* defies logic more than usual for this show, but the Adams/Rickles chemistry is priceless.

After two hours of *Get Smart* and 1.5 bottles of wine, Subject still had not offered to give me a tour of his apartment. I decided to give myself a tour.

'Where's your bathroom?' I asked while Subject was doing the dishes. [*Yes*, I offered to help, but he said no.]

'At the end of the hall on the right.'

It's easy to forget the descriptive words in directions. Plus, I'd had at least $^{3}/_{4}$ of a bottle of wine, so I opened all four doors that I came upon.

Door #1
The bedroom: Spare and uncluttered. Not the clean lines and empty counters of a neat freak, but the unclutteredness that comes with simply not having that many belongings.

Door #2

Hall closet: Contained coats and shoes. Nothing suspicious to speak of, unless you find the wearing of Hush Puppies suspicious.

Door #3

The bathroom: Clean enough. Passes my inspection. Although it probably wouldn't pass everyone's inspection.

Door #4

Locked. Highly suspicious.

So suspicious, in fact, that I didn't notice that the water had stopped running and Subject was watching from the other end of the hall as I tried to open Door #4.

'It's the other door,' Subject said, growing some suspicion of his own. You see, the bathroom door was open and in plain sight.

'Oh, right,' I said, playing drunk, although it would have taken at least another full bottle of wine to get me to the point where I couldn't recognize a bathroom in plain sight.

When I returned to the kitchen, I internally debated whether I should ask Subject about the door. I'll let you figure out which side won.

'More wine or coffee?' Subject asked.

'Wine, please.'

'Good.'

'So what's up with the door?' I asked.

'What door?'

'The locked door.'

'It's my office.'

'Why do you lock the door?'

'It's messy.'

'Normally people just close a door to a messy room, they don't usually lock it.'

'I have important files in there.'

'Did you think I might steal them?' I asked, and as soon as I finished the sentence, I knew I had gone too far.

'Why don't you forget about the door?' Subject said with a note of finality.

I let the topic drop for now. But I did not by any means forget about it. [This was yet another bullet point in my suspicious behavior report on Subject.]

SUSPICIOUS BEHAVIOR REPORT
#7

Rae Spellman
[While it had been previously established that Rae now had friends, witnessing it still seemed out of the ordinary and worthy of a report.]

When I arrived home, Rae was talking on the telephone and eating chocolate-chip cookie dough—the store-bought kind in a roll, not from scratch.

'Did I tell you about Mr. Peabody? Okay, so we're in math class and he blows his nose. Not just like a little bit, but a lot, like he's got a bad cold or serious allergies. He folds up the tissue and, instead of putting it in the trash, he sticks it in the top-right drawer of his desk. Now, it's not like the tissue was half used and he's trying not to be wasteful. Based on the sound of things, there was a lot of snot involved. *You think it's gross hearing*

114

about it? Try being a direct witness. Where was I? . . . Okay, so then on the way out of class, he's standing by the door, passing out the homework assignment. I decide to see what else he's got in the drawer and guess what I find? No, not porn. No, not lipstick. Do you want to know or what? So I open the drawer and all there is inside are like dozens of used-up tissues. There had to be at least three full ounces of snot in that drawer.'

Rae starts laughing hysterically. 'I swear. It was the most disgusting thing I ever saw . . . Wait, I might have to think about that.'

Rae spots me entering the kitchen and turns around so her back is facing me.

'I better go,' Rae said. 'Isabel just got home. Got to hear about her date.'

Rae hangs up the phone and spins back around.

'Who was that?' I asked.

'A friend,' Rae replied.

'From where?'

'From school.'

'How old is she?'

'My age.'

'What's her name?'

'Ashley Pierce. If you want her social security number, it'll have to wait until I've had a chance to search her residence.'

I picked up the log of cookie dough off the table, rewrapped it, and returned it to the refrigerator. Rae then opened the freezer and pulled out a pint of ice cream.

'It's a miracle you're not fat,' I said.

'David says it's only a matter of time,' Rae (all of ninety-five pounds) replied.

'Want some?' she asked.

115

*   *   *

As Rae and I finished off the ice cream, we contemplated the Mysterious Door.

'If you lived alone, why would you lock a door in your own home?' I asked.

'Clearly he locked it to keep you from snooping,' Rae replied.

'Until tonight he had no idea that snooping was one of my many fine traits.'

'He still doesn't know you're a PI?'

'Nope.'

'You didn't tell him you were a schoolteacher, did you?' Rae asked, referring to the lie I told Daniel Castillo, DDS, when we first began dating.

'No. I said I was in information technology.'

'That could mean anything,' Rae replied.

'My thoughts precisely.'

'What does he do?' Rae asked.

'Landscaper.'

'Fancy gardener?'

'Yep.'

THE 'LAW OFFICES' OF MORT SCHILLING

Monday, April 24
1115 hrs

'I blame it all on the door. My two arrests—'

'Four,' my lawyer interjected.

'I don't count the other ones.'

116

'So, having a record doesn't bother you?'

'Of course it does. I could lose my PI license.'

'Yes, you could.'

'But I think once I find out what I need to find out and can prove what John Brown has been doing—'

'So far the only thing you have accused this man of is locking a door, Isabel.'

'And there was that suspicious thing he did with the papers when Rae knocked him over, and then he's got that name that's all wrong, and then there's that gardening business, which is highly suspicious, but that part comes much later. I'm presenting the facts as they unfold, Morty. If you want me to jump ahead and just give you the bullet points, then fine. But I assure you, he has done other things. But the door . . . the door was what started it all. The door was my point of no return.'

Part II

Disappearances and More Suspicious Behavior Reports

DISAPPEARANCE
DISPATCH #1

Sunday, January 22

Rae and I often refer to our parents as the Unit, and while they present a united front when conflicts arise, in their day-to-day existence, they are unique and separate individuals. Within twenty-four hours of my parents' week-long road trip, we received our first set of road trip dispatches. I entered the office as Rae was checking her e-mails.

'Got something from Mom and Dad,' Rae said.

I pulled up a chair and read the e-mails over her shoulder.

From: Albert Spellman
Sent: January 22
To: Isabel Spellman, Rae Spellman
Subject: Disappearance, so far

It's a miracle we've made it this far with your mother driving. I'm thinking of taking up religion if we actually make it back to the city. The Grand Canyon is indeed grand, but you can only stare at a giant abyss for so long.

This might be our last disappearance for a while.

Love,
Dad

From: Olivia Spellman
Sent: January 22
To: Isabel Spellman; Rae Spellman
Subject: Greetings from a giant crater

I do hope you both are staying out of trouble and giving Henry his space. Rae, just because I'm gone doesn't mean you can eat junk food all day. Isabel, please set an example.

Your father drives like an old man. No more than ten miles over the speed limit at all times. What's that about? I'm not sure a combined twenty hours in a car was the best thing for our marriage.

Today we woke up at 4:30 A.M. to view the sunset. Eh. I would have preferred sleeping in. All this driving and staring into space just isn't for me.
Love,
Mom

Rae stared at the computer screen, studying the e-mail messages.

'This does not bode well,' she said, shaking her head. 'I'm going to have to take action,' she continued, and hit the *Reply* button.

From: Rae Spellman
Sent: January 22
To: Olivia Spellman
Subject: Re: Greetings from a giant crater

Mom, it sounds like Dad is having a really good time. Maybe you need to suck it up and try to enjoy yourself for the sake of your marriage.

Everything is cool here. Izzy and I ate some broccoli yesterday.
Love, Rae

From: Rae Spellman
Sent: January 22
To: Albert Spellman
Subject: Re: Disappearance, so far
Dad, Mom really seems to be enjoying her vacation. I think she really needed a break from the city. Maybe you guys should sleep in more. Mom looked pretty tired before she left. Don't tell her you're not having fun. She needs this, Dad.
Love, Rae

'I can't believe you just did that,' I said, commenting on my sister's diabolical e-mail replies.

'I had to,' she said earnestly. 'Otherwise they'll never go out of town, and one of these days I'd like this house all to myself.'

Rae needing space from her parents was a new development in her adolescence. I couldn't help but recognize that she was finally growing up.

By the afternoon of day two of my parents' disappearance, Rae had already shredded the four-foot stack of papers in the Spellman office (the one job Mom insisted be complete by her return), cleaned her room (i.e. stuffed all visible items into the closet and under her bed), completed all her homework assignments (although I suspect not with the vigor she showed under Stone's watch), and made two batches of

123

Rice Krispies Treats.

After she consumed her third square of marshmallow and puffed rice, she began roaming the house aimlessly.

'I'm bored,' Rae said, demanding my attention away from the newspaper.

Had this been an ordinary weekend, there would have been some surveillance activity that I could have used to distract Rae. However, in the last few weeks there had been an unusual lull in business, and we found ourselves with an overwhelming amount of leisure time. As my parents' e-mails might indicate, leisure is not something the Spellmans are all that familiar or comfortable with.

'Do you want to go to a movie?' I asked.

'No,' Rae replied.

'Why don't you call your new friend and see if she wants to hang out?'

'I did. She has to visit some sick aunt in Pleasanton.'

'Are there any other friends you could call?' [This was a question with an anticipated answer of 'no.' Asked just to be sure.]

'Yeah, but they're busy.'

'You have friends in the plural now?' I asked.

'Yes, but they all have things to do today and I'm bored.'

'You could go visit David and see how much money you can extort out of him.' [Until eighteen months prior, Rae's weekly visits—A.K.A. shakedowns—with David had resulted in an income of almost $100 a month. My parents put the kibosh on that when they found a hollowed-out algebra book with almost two grand inside.]

124

'No. He's been weird lately.'

'Weird how?'

'Nervous and stuff. Short tempered.'

'Do you know why?' I asked, my curiosity piqued. Rae often has insight into family matters that somehow escapes me. I attribute this to her short stature and ability to disappear into the walls a little better than me.

'No, I don't know. Do you think I can call Henry yet?'

'It's only been ten days, Rae.'

'Ten whole days of space,' Rae said, shaking her head in disbelief.

'It's not enough time. You're going to have to trust me on this.'

Whether my judgment was sound or not, I decided to distract my sister with a simple but necessary caper. Since my date two nights prior, that locked door had been nagging at me. I had a simple question that I wanted answered. Was the door locked for my benefit or was it locked all the time?

OPERATION LOCKED DOOR

Rae hid in the backseat of the car under a blanket. I pulled my 1996 Buick out of the garage and drove three blocks away.

'Are you ready?' I asked Rae.

'I'm ready.'

'Leave on your cell and call me as soon as you're done. In and out, Rae. Nothing fancy. You got me?'

'I got it,' Rae said, rolling her eyes as she walked back toward 1799 Clay Street.

Two minutes later, Rae was knocking on the door of the Spellman home. She shouted my name (for show, of course). She peered through windows, she even tried to jimmy some open. She paced nervously and looked around. She hopped up and down. She made a call on her cell phone to me.

'Phase two in action,' she said, and then hung up her phone.

Rae buzzed 1797 Clay Street, apartment two. She pressed the buzzer frantically until she was buzzed in. She ran up the single flight of stairs and met Subject as he opened the door into the hallway.

'Rae, what are you doing here?' Subject said pleasantly.

'Isabel's out. I lost my keys and I have to pee,' Rae said, hopping up and down. 'Really, really badly. Can I use your bathroom?'

'Of course,' Subject said, and allowed Rae's entry. Rae ran down to the end of the hall and into the bathroom. She waited thirty seconds, flushed the toilet, turned on the faucet, and then peered outside the door. Subject was not in sight. Rae crossed the hall and tried the mysterious door—I had drawn a very clear diagram—and it was locked. She tried again, just to be certain, and then walked down the hall to the kitchen.

'Thanks so much,' Rae said, when she met Subject in the kitchen. 'I really don't like peeing in the backyard.'

'No problem,' Subject replied.

'Do you want to come over for dinner?' Rae

asked without a moment of hesitation.

'When?'

'Tonight.'

'Are you sure it's all right with your sister?'

'I'm sure. How does seven o'clock sound?'

'Okay,' said Subject. 'Should I bring anything?'

'You could bring dinner,' Rae said, not entirely joking. 'No, we'll have dinner,' she said after a long pause. 'And dessert. The dinner won't be the best dinner you ever had, but the dessert will be pretty good.'

'Okay. I look forward to it.'

*   *   *

During Rae's debriefing ten minutes later at the house, I asked the obvious question.

'Why'd you invite him over for dinner?'

'Because we need to get a DOB on him before we can do a background check and I could not figure out how to transition from 'Can I use your bathroom?' to 'What's your birthday?' without sounding like a weirdo. If we invite him over for dinner, we can bring it up casually in conversation. We can also take his coat, and there's a chance he keeps his wallet in his coat pocket.'

'Who said I want to investigate anyone, Rae?'

'The door was locked,' Rae replied. 'Who is he locking it from, himself? Besides,' she continued, and I wished she hadn't, 'you always investigate your dates.'

Besides having to 'cook,' there was another unfortunate side-effect of inviting Subject over for dinner: cleaning. In my parents' absence Rae and I had reverted to our natural slothfulness. As we entered the foyer, we kicked off our shoes and threw our coats over the side of the couch, each day a new pair of shoes and a different coat—it adds up after a few days. Our habit was to fill the sink with dishes until no clean dishes remained, and then we would load them into the dishwasher. We lied to each other that this was a more time-efficient strategy. We had the same system with mail. We let it pile up on the table in stacks, grabbing only the most promising-looking items (magazines, checks, anything in a box).

The living room, dining room, and kitchen (all on the main floor) took the brunt of our sloppiness. Imagine a garden of used glasses, footwear, coats, dirty dishes, and schoolbooks sprouting in the living room. The dining room table was fighting off an invasion of paper products and the kitchen had already lost its battle with dirty dishes and an overflowing trash can. I am not proud of this unfortunate tendency of mine; I simply present you with the facts.

That said, I like to keep my vicious untidiness a secret, and so Rae and I spent the rest of the afternoon cleaning or hiding the evidence.

There was one final cover-up that had to be handled before Subject's arrival. On the front porch of the Spellman household there are four separate mailboxes: one is for the family and the other three are for the family business. They read: Spellman Investigations; Marcus Godfrey; [Dad's long-lived undercover name.] and Grayson Enterprises. [A dummy business name that our firm uses for cases that require an extra element of privacy.] Rather than remove three of the mailboxes, Rae and I simply relabeled all of them with individual family members' names. While it would seem unusual that each Spellman required his or her own mailbox, it would not give away the family business.

OPERATION: DOB

Subject arrived at the previously agreed-upon time. He brought a bottle of red wine, which I said would go well with the pasta. [päs-ta n: 1. Unleavened dough, made of what flour, water, and sometimes eggs, that is molded into any of a variety of shapes and boiled. 2. A prepared dish containing pasta as its main ingredient. 3. Spaghettios, Raviolios, or any other canned dish containing a semolina flour product and red sauce.] Subject did inquire about the mailboxes, as I suspected he would, but Rae explained (without prompting) that the Spellmans really liked their privacy. Even from each other.

Rae politely asked to take Subject's coat, disappeared to the coat room (we don't have a coat room), and rifled through his pockets. It was determined that Subject either arrived without his wallet or Subject keeps his wallet in his back pocket. Since I had only been on 1.5 dates with Subject, I didn't see any way of getting into his pockets. A DOB would have to be determined the other way: we'd ask.

It would have been easy to guide the conversation onto the topic of astrology, hence birth months, hence birth dates, but Subject had an investigation of his own. He wanted to find out the origin of the horrendous slop he was being asked to consume.

'Who cooked?' Subject asked.

'I did,' said Rae.

'Where did you get the recipe?' Subject asked, after he took his first bite.

Rae stared at him, not sure of what to say. 'It's a secret,' she replied.

And then I took my first bite . . . and last. I cleared the table before any more of the grub could be politely ingested.

'Rae, did you raid the emergency supplies for dinner?'

'What's the big deal?'

'Did you check the expiration date?'

'Cans don't have expiration dates.'

'Yes, they do,' I said, and quickly turned to our guest. 'Sorry about this, John. Um, what do you say we order pizza?' [My mother had left one dining rule upon her departure: no pizza. Rae was apparently losing interest in all other main courses and my mother wanted to cut her off cold turkey. She even went so far as to call most of the regular pizzerias in the neighborhood and convince them to refuse us service in her absence.]

Rae shouted, 'Victory,' and I realized I had been played.

We had Subject order the food from his cell phone and pick it up at his front door, since he was not on any *Do Not Serve* lists. Dinner arrived shortly thereafter.

*　　　*　　　*

130

Sometime after my second slice of pizza and third glass of wine, but before Rae served the Rice Krispies Treats dessert, I made eye contact with my sister and pointed to my watch, which was simple code for 'It's time.'

'What's your sign?' Rae asked Subject.

'Excuse me?' Subject responded, choking on his wine. I guess it came out kind of weird.

'You seem like a Pisces,' Rae said.

'He's sooo not a Pisces,' I interjected. 'More like a Gemini.' [I've discovered that astrology talk is really the best way to get a DOB out of someone. Unfortunately I know very little on the subject. However, I know much more than my sister.]

'Are you on crack?' Rae asked me. [Four days away from Henry and she's off the wagon.]

'No. But I think you are. A Pisces?'

'He's totally a Pisces. Or maybe . . . uh . . .the one with the scales or the . . . um . . . the one that looks like a bull?' [Rae was choking. I told her to study the zodiac, but she didn't think it was necessary.]

'You mean a Taurus?' I said.

'Right,' Rae replied. 'Slipped my mind. I had an Alzheimer's moment.'

'Rae, only old people should say that. It sounds stupid when you do.'

'Don't tell me what I can and can't say,' Rae replied. 'My point is: He's definitely not a Pisces. Definitely not.'

'Thanks for your input, Rain Man. This debate can be solved easily enough,' I said, finally cutting to the chase. 'What's your birth date?'

'December twenty-sixth,' Subject replied.

'So that makes you what?' Rae asked. [Yes, Rae was very disappointing in this charade. If this were her own investigation, I guarantee she would have prepared better.]

'A Capricorn,' Subject replied suspiciously.

'A Capricorn,' I said. 'I never would have guessed that. Huh.'

'December twenty-sixth?' Rae repeated, just to make sure it was lodged in her memory. 'That must suck having a birthday so close to Christmas. I think I'd kill myself.'

Subject wasn't sure if he should laugh or be concerned with Rae's hyperbolic response.

'Hey, Izzy, where's that Chinese New Year book?'

Subject, after cross-checking his year of birth against the twelve-year Chinese zodiac, informed us that he was a Rat.

*   *   *

Mission Accomplished: John Brown, DOB 12/26/72.

THE 'LAW OFFICES' OF MORT SCHILLING

Monday, April 24
1135 hrs

'After John left that night, Rae and I spent two hours in the office trying to run a background check on him,' I explained to Morty.

'Do you always do this, Izz?'

'What?'

132

'Investigate your dates.'

'I've been trying to cut back.'

'Unsuccessfully, I see.'

'Don't judge me, Morty.'

'You know I have a son. Well, two sons. But one is about to get divorced.'

'What's your point?'

'He's a doctor. A surgeon.'

'I don't need surgery.'

'I can vouch for him. No criminal record. Nothing. You could skip the investigation and everything.'

'He's your son?'

'Yes.'

'How old is he?'

'Fifty-two.'

'I'm thirty, Morty. He's too old for me.'

'I've got a grandson for you. Only twenty-five.'

'Too young, Morty.'

'Ah, I guess you're right. When you get to be my age, everyone's a kid.'

'Let's get back to my case. Okay?'

'Whatever you say. But when you're on the market again, let me know. I have many acquaintances.'

'Where was I?' I asked, hoping to finally get Morty off the subject.

'You and your sister had just gotten a DOB on John Brown.'

'We started with the DOB database. As you know, it goes by state. Subject told me he was from Missouri. So, I guessed that he was born there. Well, there were two John Browns born on that date in Missouri. One of them is dead and the other one still lives there and runs an Audi dealership.'

'So he was raised in Missouri, but was born in a different state.'

'I asked him and he confirmed that he was born and raised in Missouri.'

'Are you sure all your questions weren't making him suspicious?'

'At the time, they weren't.'

'He still didn't know your occupation?'

'I didn't lie about what I did. I just didn't give him that information.'

'What happened next?'

'I didn't see Subject for the rest of the week, then parents returned from their disappearance and blew my cover.'

SUBJECT HELPS DAD
WITH LUGGAGE . . .

Saturday, January 28
1700 hrs

Rae and I saw our parents pull up in the driveway a full two hours before their ETA. There was still some evidence that we needed to dispose of— pizza boxes, a bag of licorice, and the dirty dishes from the previous night—before their entrance. As Rae and I scrambled to return the house to Mom's idea of order, Subject was exiting his residence and offered to help my dad with the bags. Dad once read a study that explained that when you allow a person to do a favor for you, that person (doing the favor) will later feel more indebted to you.

134

Therefore, Dad almost never turned down an offer of help.

Rae and I were unprepared for our parents' arrival because Mom deliberately fudged their ETA. She's a huge fan of the element of surprise. She called the house when they were one hour away and said to expect them by dinnertime (approximately five hours from phone call). She planned it so well that she had mapped out the town they would approximately have been in if they did have five hours left on the road. Mom entered the house to the clanging of dishes, the rustling of garbage, and the double-checking of closets. [Where we had stuffed some items in our previous night's cleaning effort.] I grabbed the bag of trash and passed my mother on her way into the kitchen.

'Mom! You're four hours early. Did your car learn to fly?' I kissed her on the cheek and headed for the door. 'I was just taking out the trash. You'll have to tell me all about your trip.'

As I exited the house, Dad and Subject were on their way in. I caught a short clip from their small-talk.

'It's good to be back,' said my dad, 'even if it means back to work.'

'I've been meaning to ask you . . .' Subject said.

This is where I tried to make eye contact with my dad indicating that he should not divulge any information. But Dad merely patted me on the head as we crossed paths. Subject said hello and continued his sentence.

'. . . what do you do for a living?'

'We're private investigators. I would have thought Izzy might have mentioned this.'

Damn!

'Isabel, what's up with the mailboxes?'

*   *   *

After a diplomatic debriefing by my parents regarding their road trip, which they gushed about in each other's presence, I noticed something different about my father.

'Dad, you look like you lost more weight.'

'Maybe a few pounds,' Dad replied dismissively.

'More like ten,' I said. 'Although it's hard to tell on a frame as large as yours.'

'At what age are your manners going to kick in?' Dad responded.

My mother looked at my father suspiciously. 'Now that you mention it, he does look thinner. It's hard to tell when you're with someone every day. How odd,' she continued, 'since you always claimed to be running off to the buffets.'

But then Dad distracted Mom by mentioning how much he enjoyed their daily hikes.

Later that night, I had the opportunity to compile Suspicious Behavior Report #7: Rae Spellman.

My mother was in the office, checking her e-mail, when I entered.

'Mom, were you aware of the fact that Rae appears to have friends now?'

'Yes, dear,' my mother replied without looking up.

'Friends her own age,' I clarified.

'I know,' Mom said, without a hint of genuine shock.

'I even have a name on one. First and last.'

136

'I know all about Rae's friends, dear.'

'How long has this been going on?' I asked.

'At least six months.'

'How did I miss it?'

'You miss a lot of things, Izzy. Always obsessing with one angle, you often fail to see the big picture.'

'Whatever, Mom. Next question: Why does she have friends now?'

'Henry told her she couldn't hang out with him anymore unless she started making friends her own age.'

'And that worked?' I asked.

'Yes.'

'Wow. He is, like, raising your child for you,' I said.

'It takes a village,' my mom said.

'I'm not sure she meant have your local police inspector co-parent.'

'Let me tell you something about teenagers,' Mom said. 'Even the best ones turn on their parents, and then they turn to someone else. Well, if the person Rae turns to is Henry Stone, then I've got nothing to worry about. And, frankly, you did me in with worry. I don't want to go through that again.'

SUSPICIOUS BEHAVIOR REPORT #8

'Olivia Spellman'

At two-thirty a.m. the morning after my parents returned from their disappearance, I heard a noise downstairs. I awoke and exited the attic apartment. I tiptoed down the stairs and saw my mother, wearing pajamas and an overcoat, exit the house.

I ran up to my apartment, slipped on a pair of sneakers, and grabbed my jacket and keys. I climbed out the fire escape and circled the house to my car. Mom had just pulled out of the driveway and was heading down the block. I got into my car and followed her.

She had approximately a four-block lead. However, at that time of night, she was practically the only car on the road. I could see her left-turn signal as she approached Gough Street and I felt fairly confident that she was returning to the same Noe Valley location where I had previously discovered her. Trusting my gut, [Which has a 75 percent accuracy rate.] I used a different route to the residence to avoid detection. I parked a block away and stealthily moved along the shrubbery until I had a visual on my mother. She was kneeling in front of the same motorbike, but this time, she had a hose and a pump and was siphoning gas out of the tank. Huh? I could have approached my mother in that very moment and asked her what the hell she was doing, but I didn't.

138

She was clearly being covert for a reason and I wanted her to think she had this secret a little longer.

I went directly home, hoping to return my car to the same parking space, in case my mother had noticed it when she left. I decided that I should probably get some more sleep during the day so I could keep up with my mother at night.

However, my mother was not the only unpaid case I was working. There was also Subject, and he still did not have an identity.

GROUNDHOG DAY

Thursday, February 2

On the morning of February 2, I happened to be driving by Mrs. Chandler's home and saw that her lawn had about half a dozen holes resembling the tunnels dug by groundhogs—almost an exact replica of my long-lost caper. Fearing that Mrs. Chandler would assume I was back to my old ways, I took a proactive measure, in part out of guilt, but also to prevent any accusations.

I returned to Subject's residence and asked him if he could repair her lawn. I opted against relaying my interest in the crime. I played it off as a neighborly good deed, which Subject bought without question.

Later that afternoon, I drove by the Chandler residence to find her lawn restored to some semblance of decency. I returned to the Spellman home and decided to drop by Subject's residence and thank him.

Just as I was about to ring the buzzer, Subject exited his building carrying two large bags of shredded recycling. *For a gardener, he sure shreds a lot of paper,* I thought to myself.

'Thanks,' I said. 'I just drove by Mrs. Chandler's place.'

'It was a Groundhog Day prank,' Subject said, as if it weren't obvious to the naked eye.

'I know,' I replied, trailing Subject as he placed the pillows of paper into the green receptacle.

'She said it's happened before,' Subject then said, looking me straight in the eye.

'I have no idea what you're talking about,' I replied, according to script. 'So, can I buy you a drink later?'

SUBJECT ARRIVES AT THE PHILOSOPHER'S CLUB . . .

'Remember,' I said to Milo a moment before Subject sat down in the adjacent bar stool, 'you don't know me.'

'Whatever,' Milo said, scowling.

'What are you drinking?' I asked Subject.

'What have you got on tap?' Subject asked.

Milo pointed to a board with a list of domestic beers.

'Anchor Steam,' Subject said.

'Can I see some ID?' asked Milo.

'Oh, uh, sure,' Subject replied, reaching for his wallet. In the dim lighting of the bar, I could only make out that his driver's license was not issued in

140

California.

Milo checked the license as I instructed him to. He pretended he couldn't see and moved over to the light. [I made that suggestion so he could have more time to memorize the details.]

'Thank you,' Milo said, handing back the ID. Then he turned to me. 'ID, please.'

'But you already served me.'

'It slipped my mind. Hand it over, sweetheart.'

I scowled at Milo's use of the word 'sweetheart' (a first, as far as I can recall) and handed him my ID.

My bartender studied my driver's license for a moment and began chuckling to himself.

'What's so funny?' I asked.

'A hundred and twenty pounds?' he said, handing me back my card.

I shot him one final hostile glance and then he served Subject his beer. Milo retired to the end of the bar and Subject asked the question he had refrained from asking for over a week.

'So you're a private investigator.'

'Uh-huh.'

'Did you investigate me?'

'No.'

'Are you sure about that?'

'I'm positive.'

'Because that little performance with you and your sister and the eastern/western zodiac quiz, well, it sure seemed like you were trying to get my date of birth.'

'We're just really into astrology.'

'Is that so,' Subject said, looking me right in the eye. Then he leaned in and whispered in my ear.

'I'm going to let you in on a secret,' Subject said.

141

'I'm not a rat.'

'Then what are you?' I asked.

'A snake,' Subject replied, giving me the chills.

My mother used to say that if you can't verify a man's existence, you probably shouldn't go home with him. [For a partial list of Mom's criteria for men, see appendix.] However, based on my most recent observations of Mom, she was hardly the spokesperson for sound judgment. Two hours later, I was on my second whiskey in John Brown's apartment.

I stayed off the subject of birthdays and employment histories, just to throw Subject off balance. Instead, I let the topic of discussion float over to me for a while, since clearly he did not want to talk about himself. I told Subject about Ex-boyfriends #4 and #9 (because that is the normal thing people do on dates, discuss past relationships) and then we had an hour-long conversation about Bernie and my rent-controlled apartment. Subject seemed to believe that I should fight for the space. Watching Subject speak on this matter, I noted that his interest was purely for show. It was a magician's sleight of hand. He thought he had redirected my attention from his nonexistence and locked doors to my own upscale homelessness.

But I am not so easily handled. I excused myself to use the restroom because 1) I had to pee, and 2) I wanted another crack at that door. After 1 was completed, I exited the restroom and reached for the mysterious door. Still locked, but I came prepared. I pulled a picking tool out of my pocket and knelt in front of the keyhole. I knew there wasn't much time. Even if I got the door open, I'd

142

only have a chance to look inside for a second before I'd have to close it again.

But Subject was on guard. He knew better than to leave me unaccompanied in any part of his home. I was still working on the lock as I heard his footsteps turn the corner. There were two ways I could play it: A cover-up, or the direct approach.

'Can I help you with anything?' Subject asked as I was still working on the lock.

'If you don't mind, I could use a minute alone with your door,' I replied.

'Isabel.' It was said as a warning.

'Just one more minute,' I said, not budging, 'and I'll be right with you.'

Subject approached me, looking very stern, and cornered me in front of the door.

'What is it with you and that door? I'm starting to get a little jealous.'

'You *have* to let me inside that room.'

'I don't *have* to do anything.'

'Let me rephrase,' I said. 'It would be in your best interest to let me see what's in there.'

Subject slid his arm around my waist and pulled me close. He whispered in my ear, which was both sexy and creepy.

'It would be in your best interest to forget about the fucking door. Can you do that?'

I looked Subject in the eye and ignored the half of my brain that was telling me to run.

'For now,' I said, because the other half really wanted to stay.

Subject kissed me, or I him (the details are now a blur). What I remember about the kiss was the absence of the internal monologue that often accompanies first kisses. I'm usually preoccupied

143

with what the guy's hands are doing, concerned that the kiss will ruin everything. Because sometimes you don't really know how you feel about someone until he actually kisses you. The thing about Subject was that his kiss made me forget everything. My mind went blank. My suspicion went away.

It came back, however, in the middle of the night. At three A.M., I made one more valiant attempt at cracking the mystery room, but I was caught and reprimanded with 'If you can't behave yourself, maybe you should go home,' and I did. But mostly because I preferred not having my parents know that I spent the night with our new neighbor, even if they did think he was harmless and pleasant.

The following morning I called Milo for the scoop on the previous night's intelligence gathering.

'Hold on a second,' Milo said. 'I have that scrap of paper around here somewhere.'

'What state was the driver's license from?' I asked.

'Hold your horses. I wrote it down.'

'You don't even remember that?' I asked.

'Is this how you talk to someone who is doing you a favor?'

'All I'm saying is that maybe you should see a doctor.'

'I don't need to see a friggin' doctor. Okay, I found it. It was a Washington state license.'

'What was the name on it?'

'John Brown.'

'How about the birthday?'

'March 7, 1971.'

'Really?'
'Yep.'
'Are you sure?'
'Yep.'
'Positive?'
'I'm gonna hang up now,' Milo said.
'No, don't. Sorry. Do you have any other info?'
'Nope.'
'You didn't write down his address?'
'I think it would have been suspicious if I took out a pen and paper and started copying down everything on his license, don't you?'
'Do you remember what city?'
'I'm pretty sure it was Olympia.'
'How sure?'
'Pretty sure.'
'Is that like ninety percent or sixty?'
'Good-bye, Izzy,' Milo said and hung up the phone.

*   *   *

Subject was neither a rat nor a snake, according to the license issued by Washington state. He was a Pisces pig, which made him older than he appeared. Also, Subject claimed to have been born and raised in St. Louis. At no point did he mention having lived in Washington. It occurred to me that the St. Louis backstory was used purely to throw me off the scent. I ran a DOB database search for Washington state and came upon two John Browns born on March 7, 1971. One was currently a CPA in Seattle and the other died five years ago. Who was I kidding? I didn't need Subject's driver's license, I needed his whole wallet. I was banking on the fact that he might keep his social security card in there. With a common name and no verifiable birth date, I needed a social security number. I leaned back in my office chair and tried to come up with another plan.

THE VALENTINE'S DAY MASSACRE

Tuesday, February 14

Over the next two weeks I remained at my parents' house, making the occasional phone call to Bernie, praying that reconciliation with Daisy was imminent. Bernie repeatedly invited me to move back in with him and explained that he was already back on the market. Reconciliation was out of the question.

I continued to garden with Subject, always hoping that I'd catch him with his guard down and he'd reveal at least one piece of identifying information about himself. No matter how hard I tried, I couldn't get my hands on his wallet. I was growing more impatient and suspicious with each flower bed and tomato plant I watered.

In the early [I played early-riser, hoping to get more information. This almost killed me.] morning of February 14, Subject and I were returning from one of his community garden projects when his cell phone rang. He picked up on the first ring.

'Hello? Oh, hi. Yes, I got your message. Are you sure? Okay. I can't talk right now; I'm driving. Meet me Thursday, ten A.M., at the Ashby Community Garden in Berkeley. I'll see you then.'

146

'Who was that?' I asked Subject, hoping the question sounded more casual than it was.

'I'm meeting a potential client,' Subject replied, and then changed the subject. 'I think I'd like to swing by Mrs. Chandler's residence and see how her grass is doing.'

Five minutes later, Subject and I were at the scene of the crime. Had these been real cherubs and real knives, Mrs. Chandler would have been the prime suspect, since she was standing over the bodies, her hands covered in 'blood,' although it was obvious to me that she was simply cleaning up the mess. When Subject and I approached, Chandler gazed at me with a look of genuine bafflement. She *knew* it was me back then and chose not to punish me. The fact that the crime was an exact replica of the original seemed to make me the guilty party once again, but I'm sure she could find no logical explanation why a thirty-year-old woman would be repeating the crimes of her adolescence. I couldn't help but feel sympathy this time around. I was indirectly responsible; I just couldn't figure out how. I believed the tableaus were tasteless monstrosities; I still believe that. But they were her monstrosities, and she took pride in them. Subject and I helped her clean up the debris and then quickly parted ways.

ASHBY COMMUNITY GARDEN

Thursday, February 16
0900 hrs

I departed from the Spellman residence at nine A.M. Thursday morning and crossed the bridge. I parked approximately five blocks away from the garden, found a spot under an oak tree that provided a perfect visual of the grounds, sipped coffee, and waited, binoculars in hand, for Subject to arrive at his rendezvous point.

Shortly before the hour, Subject parked his truck next to the fenced-in patch and entered the gardens. Five minutes later, a woman, approximately thirty years of age, with long brown hair, wearing jeans and a sweatshirt, approached Subject hesitantly. Subject and female spoke for approximately five minutes. Then female handed Subject an envelope and Subject handed female a brown paper bag. They spoke for a few more minutes. Based purely on their body language, there was nothing light and friendly about the conversation. Both parties shook hands and left the grounds separately. Neither did any gardening. [Another detail that went into my report on Subject.]

THE CHANDLER JOB

CHAPTER-1

Saturday, February 18

A few days later, as I sat at my desk and contemplated different methods of acquiring Subject's true identity, my mother interrupted me with a new job.

'We have a new case I'm going to put you on. Mostly surveillance. It'll get you out of the office.'

'What's the job?' I asked.

'Mrs. Chandler. Her yard is getting vandalized again. She says she's tired of just sitting back and taking it. She's willing to pay to make it stop.'

'Mrs. Chandler?' I repeated.

'Yes,' my mother replied. 'I thought it was poetic justice that her first vandal should investigate the next generation.'

'I have no idea what you're talking about,' I replied, per my usual script.

'Of course not,' said my mother, nonchalantly.

'Mom, I'd rather not take this job.'

'Too bad,' Mom replied. 'She asked for you specifically, Isabel. And she's paying very well. I told her you'd be by this morning at eleven A.M. Sharp. Do not be late. She's a very prompt woman.'

*   *   *

'It's a labor of love,' Mrs. Chandler said of her

holiday tableaus. 'I know it's not for everyone, but it makes me happy and I think it brightens up the neighborhood. Don't you agree?'

Yes, eyesores often brighten things up, I thought to myself. Then I said, 'I admire your dedication.'

'Each installment can take from ten to thirty hours of labor. I do it all myself. I hang every streamer, I dye every egg and sew every item of clothing. As you know, I've been doing this for fifteen years.'

'I have a vague recollection of when you began.'

Mrs. Chandler's calm expression shifted slightly. 'Let's cut the bullshit, Isabel. I let your little pranks slide all those years ago because clearly you had to get something out of your system. You needed to express yourself just as I did. But this time it's different. There's no expression in copying a piece of work. What is happening now is a base prank and I want it to end. You know, it was Groundhog Day that always got under my skin. There is nothing creative about it; it's just an excuse for vandalism.'

As awkward as this situation was, I was glad to be on the job. Someone out there was copying Petra's and my pranks down to a T. This was a case I had to solve.

'Mrs. Chandler, I am terribly sorry for the inconvenience this has caused you. I assure you I will give this job top priority and find out exactly who is behind it.'

Mrs. Chandler followed me to the door.

'I forgive you, Isabel,' she said as I turned around to shake her hand.

'I'm sorry. I have no idea what you're talking about,' I replied, and made a quick departure.

Mrs. Chandler and I shook hands and I drove directly to Petra and David's house to confer with my ex–partner in crime.

SUSPICIOUS BEHAVIOR REPORT #9

'David Spellman'

It was Saturday and David's car was parked in the driveway, so I assumed he was home. However, by my fifth ring of the doorbell, there was still no answer. David really frowns upon unannounced visits, [By me. Have not yet established whether this is a universal stance.] so I thought he might be trying to ignore me in the hopes that I'd go away. But that never works. I began banging my fist on the door and shouting his name like Marlon Brando screamed 'Stella' in *Streetcar*.

The door swung open soon after. David was wearing pajama bottoms, a stained white T-shirt (a first), mismatched socks, and a bathrobe.

'Hi, is David home?' I asked.

'Very funny.'

David left the door ajar and walked back into his house. I followed after him, hoping for some form of explanation.

'Rough night?' I queried.

'Unggh,' or something that sounded like it, was his only response.

'English, please.'

'What do you want, Isabel?' David suddenly snapped.

'I need to see Petra about something.'

'She's not here.'

'Where is she?'

'She's visiting her mother in Arizona.'

'She hates Arizona . . .and her mother.'

'Then she's having an awful time.'

'Why is she visiting her mother?'

'You never stop with the goddamn questions.'

'Just tell me what's going on and I'll get out of here.'

David stumbled over to his liquor cabinet, grabbed a bottle of scotch, and poured himself a drink.

'David, it's only noon.'

'You want a drink?' he asked me.

'Is that single-malt scotch?'

'Uh-huh.'

'Okay.'

Three hours and four drinks later, after I had shared all the details of my recent dates with Subject, chronicled the Henry Stone Saga, and mentioned Mom's inexplicable vandalism habit and Dad's shrinking waistline, I knew it was time to get David to do the talking.

'David, did Petra leave you?'

David stared down at his drink. 'Not exactly.'

'Then be more precise.'

'Don't tell Mom.'

'Give me something not to tell her.'

'I'm begging you, Isabel. Just leave this alone.'

'You slept with somebody else, didn't you?'

David wouldn't look me in the eye.

'I don't want to talk about it anymore.'

'You did, didn't you?'

'*No.* This is none of your business. And don't tell

Mom anything. If you do, I will give up every piece of evidence I have ever amassed against you.'

'Why didn't Petra call me? She used to always call me.'

'It's not what you think, Isabel. It's better if you stay out of this.'

'You are an asshole. Just so you know, she gets custody of me in the divorce,' I said as I got up to leave. I could hear David pouring himself another drink as I exited his home.

* * *

I was too drunk to drive, so I took the bus back to the house. Mom saw me stumbling up the walk and asked where I had been. She then forced me to reenact my visit with David at least a dozen times. Her police-level interview rendered no revelatory information beyond his three-day-old beard, his stained T-shirt, and Petra's mysterious vacation. [Spellman definition applies here: disappearance.] By the sixth time I mentioned that David served me single-malt scotch, my mother barked, 'Yes, Izzy, I got that already.' It was only when I started asking for a pack of cigarettes and a lawyer that my mom brought the interrogation to a halt.

'You're useless,' she said, and I went to my old apartment to nap off my afternoon booze.

1700 hrs

I phoned Petra on her cell phone when I woke up and left a message.

'I know,' I said. 'He told me. I'm sorry. Please

153

call me back.'

STONE AND SPELLMAN . . .
TOGETHER AGAIN

Tuesday, February 21,
1610 hrs

I could hear my mother talking to an unrecognizable voice in the living room, so I went downstairs to check it out.

Mrs. Schroeder from Child Protective Services was politely sipping tea as my mother played her a few tracks from Stone and Spellman's Greatest Hits. It turns out that Rae's chronic discussion of her almost-murder of Henry Stone prompted yet another teacher to file an anonymous report with Child Protective Services. When Mrs. Schroeder arrived, my mother phoned Henry, requesting his presence. She then went into the kitchen, called my cell phone (even thought I was upstairs), and told me to put on my ring and meet them in the living room. I had since stopped wearing the ring on a regular basis, but found it in Mom's jewelry box in her bedroom. As I arrived downstairs, my mother was pulling her collection of tapes to share with her inquisitor.

'This is one of my favorites,' she said.

THE STONE AND SPELLMAN SHOW—EPISODE 18

'SAT-PREP'

Setting: Henry Stone's apartment. Rae rode her bike over and got a flat tire. Mom has just arrived to pick her up and she stays for a cup of coffee.

The transcript reads as follows:

HENRY: Get your book out, Rae.

RAE: I don't feel like it.

HENRY: We had a deal. I made you pancakes; now we do some SAT work.

RAE: He made buckwheat pancakes. Mom, have you ever had buckwheat pancakes?

OLIVIA: Not that I recall.

RAE: Well, they're not the same.

HENRY: Get your book.
  [Rae goes into the other room to grab the SAT prep book.]

OLIVIA: Why is the SAT book here?

HENRY: It's an extra one. I found it at a used-book store and thought I should keep it around for these unannounced visits.

OLIVIA: We don't deserve you, Henry.

HENRY: By the way, how did Rae get my address?

OLIVIA: I don't know. Every time I ask her about it she's very cagey.
  [Rae hands Henry the SAT book and then opens one of the cabinets in the kitchen.]

RAE: What happened to my candy?

155

HENRY: I got rid of it.

RAE: Why?

HENRY: I think you should *abstain* from junk food for a while.

RAE: But it's the weekend. [My parents' rule is that Rae can eat junk food on the weekends only.]

HENRY: 'Absolution.' Definition first, then use it in a sentence.

RAE: Absolution. Forgiveness. I . . . uh . . . give you absolution for throwing out my candy.

HENRY: Good. 'Hamper.'

RAE: What you throw dirty clothes in.

HENRY: I'm looking for another definition.

RAE: I don't know.

HENRY: To hinder or obstruct. Use it in a sentence.

RAE: You're hampering my fun.

HENRY: You're hampering my weekend.

RAE: What were you going to do, anyway?

HENRY: Work.

RAE: You're so abstemious.

OLIVIA: Good word. Not that I think you are abstemious, Henry.

RAE: Me neither. Isabel called you that.

HENRY: I didn't think Isabel knew words that big.

RAE: She doesn't. She got it out of the book when she was helping me study.

HENRY: So you have been studying?

RAE: I told you I was.

HENRY: Olivia, you're not recording this, are you?

OLIVIA: Yes, I am.

HENRY: Please, stop.

[End of tape.]

156

The doorbell rang just as the tape was complete. I ran into the foyer and answered it. Subject was standing there holding a pair of boots.

'You left these at my house,' he said.

'I knew I had forgotten something.'

My mother and presumably Mrs. Schroeder could overhear our conversation. Mom shot me a severe glance that said *'Don't blow our cover.'* [The subtext of this glance was 'If you ruin this, I will make your life a living hell.'] I took my boots and Subject back outside.

'Mom's having a very important meeting inside.'

'Didn't mean to interrupt,' Subject said.

'No problem.'

'Free for dinner tonight?'

'Your place?' I asked.

'Nah, I'd like to keep you away from that door, if you don't mind.'

Out of the corner of my eye, I could see Henry Stone parking his car across the street. His impossible-to-read expression was as cold as usual.

'Sure. Where?' I said, trying to not appear too distracted.

'Delfino's.'

'What time?'

'I'll pick you up at seven.'

'See you then.'

I waited for Stone on the walkway to give him a quick debriefing. 'The social worker has been in there about an hour already. She probably just wants to say a quick hello and then she'll close the case for good.'

'Who's your friend?' Stone asked, nodding at Subject, who was entering the adjacent residence.

'I don't know,' I said. 'That's the problem.'

My mother tried buttering up the social worker with baked goods, but Mrs. Schroeder would not be bought. This visit was less a product of concern over the nature of Henry and Rae's relationship than an interest in my sister's reference to the almost-murder. Mom suggested that Mrs. Schroeder speak directly to Henry on this matter and kept Rae out of the room, explaining that my sister's tendency toward hyperbole might interfere with the facts. Henry, in a calm and straightforward manner, relayed the events of that fateful day and further explained that Rae's actions did not go unpunished. She would receive no more driving lessons from him.

Mrs. Schroeder appeared satisfied that there was nothing untoward in Henry and Rae's relationship, although she seemed highly skeptical of Henry's and my 'engagement.' Perhaps it was the eighteen inches of distance we kept between ourselves, the complete absence of eye contact, and then there was that awkward moment when I offered Henry a cookie and he said, 'I don't eat that stuff.'

And my response was, 'Oh, right.'

My mother's disappointment in our lousy performance manifested itself primarily in hostility toward me after the social worker's departure.

'Well, that was Oscar worthy,' Mom said sarcastically. 'What the hell is going on with you and the neighbor?'

'Nothing,' I said.

'Men don't have to return your footwear if nothing is going on.'

'We were gardening,' I said.

'I hope that's not a euphemism,' my mom replied.

'Eew, Mom.'

'You're supposed to be engaged to Henry,' said my mom. 'And yet the social worker sees some random male returning your footwear. I'm sure she thinks you're a slut now.'

'He could be a cobbler for all she knows,' I replied.

Rae raced down the stairs (I'm sure the moment she saw Mrs. Schroeder's car pull out of the driveway) and then she quickly slowed her pace at the bottom of the landing, as if she was trying to appear casual.

She sat down across from Henry and smiled politely.

'Hi, Henry.'

'Hi, Rae.' Henry smiled back at her. It was an open and warm smile. A smile that seemed absolutely foreign to the man I knew. It occurred to me that whatever coldness I sensed from him was not a generic anti-Spellman hostility, it was anti-Isabel. Or so it seemed.

'Have you had enough space?' Rae asked.

'What are you talking about?'

'Isabel told me I had to leave you alone because you needed your space and if I didn't give you your space, you would hate me.'

Henry then shot me the meanest look I've ever seen.

'I'm not ever going to hate you, Rae. I just needed some time to clear my head. That's all.'

My mother looked like she was falling in love.

'So I've been giving you space for forty-six days

when I didn't have to?' Rae said, and then turned to me with an expression of loathing I had seen only a handful of times.

'You're not recording this, are you, Olivia?' Henry asked.

'Oh, I forgot. Dammit.'

'No,' Henry said. 'I don't want to be recorded. Do you mind if Rae and I go for a walk? I want to have a little chat with her about space and stuff,' he said, and then shot me a glare.

Henry and Rae exited the house. My mother studied the inspector from the living room window.

'Something is wrong with him,' my mother said.

'What?'

'I don't know. He looks depressed.'

'He looks the same as he always does.'

'No. Something is different,' insisted my mother.

Whatever conversation occurred between Rae and Henry on their walk put a spring in my sister's step.

When she returned she announced, 'I'm not giving Henry any more space. Although when he asks me to go home I'm going to heed his request.' She said the last line as if it were pulled from a script.

'Mom, I'm going to go over to Ashley's house and do some homework. Is that okay?' she then asked.

'Just leave her phone number on the counter and have a good time. Call me if you need a ride home.'

Rae grabbed her belongings and shot out of the house.

'I just can't get used to Rae having friends,' I

said.

'And none of them are delinquents,' Mom said, making a jab at the backstory of most of my adolescent acquaintances.

Dad returned home shortly after Rae's departure, his hair wet from recent showering and his face flushed from recent physical activity.

'Hi, honey,' Mom said casually to Dad, as he aimed for the stairs.

'Were you at the gym?' I asked.

'Uh—yes,' Dad said dismissively, and quickly headed upstairs.

When Dad was out of earshot, Mom said, 'Your father's definitely having a MILFO, although he seems to be trying to keep it on the down low. Doesn't make any sense. In the past every time he went to the gym or ate broccoli he sent out a press release. Either way, this is one MILFO I can get behind.'

'Mom, they're called REAFOs now, not MILFOs,' I said.

'What's a REAFO?'

'Retirement-age freak-out. Dad was getting too old for a MILFO.'

'When did this happen?'

'We changed it about four years ago. Didn't you get the memo?'[There was, indeed, a memo (see appendix).]

As I was heading back to the attic, my cell phone rang. I picked up.

'Hello?'

'Izzy, it's your roomie calling.'

'Who?'

'Bernie.'

'We're not roomies.'

161

'Sure we are.'

'Why are you calling, Bernie?'

'I got a message for you. Petra returned your call.'

'What did she say?'

'Nothing. She just said to tell you she was returning your call.'

'If she calls again, tell her I'm not staying there and give her my cell number.'

'Give me that number again,' Bernie asked.

'You just dialed it,' I said, and hung up.

I phoned Petra again and left a message, reminding her that I had moved out of Bernie's place. I asked her to return my call yet again.

MY ALMOST FAKE MUGGING

1630 hrs

In preparation for my date that night, I decided to visit my actor friends Len and Christopher. I met them for coffee in between rehearsals at the American Conservatory Theatre. Both men were enrolled in the graduate program. Len and Charles are handsome thirty-something black men, with keen senses of fashion. Len's sartorial style leans toward urban chic, in direct contrast to Charles's nod to Old England. Charles had recently taken to wearing ascots with his starched white shirts and well-tailored pants. He manages to pull off his pretentious garb by possessing the accent to accompany it. He is, in fact, British.

I have a dubious history with Len: In high school

I had the means to destroy his reputation and didn't. Ever since, Len has thought he owes me. Almost two years ago, I cashed in on that debt and had Len and his lover, Christopher, help me stage a fake drug deal as a retaliatory measure against my parents' room bugging. They had always been uneasy about their participation in the ruse, but actors can rarely turn down a job. That's why there's always someone out there who will do a hemorrhoid commercial.

*   *   *

I sprang for Len and Christopher's nonfat lattes, which immediately put Len on guard. I decided small talk was required to butter up my actors for their next roles, and so I talked about what actors like to talk about most: themselves.

'Len is playing Othello this fall,' said Christopher.

'Congratulations,' I replied. 'That's fantastic.'

'And Christopher won the part of Walter Lee in *A Raisin in the Sun*,' said Len.

'The accents are killing us,' moaned Len.

'Murder,' echoed Christopher.

I almost suggested that they should swap parts, what with Len being an American and Christopher a Brit, but you have to watch what you say around actors, so I remained mum.

I wondered how my friends would take to a more avant garde production.

'I have a job for you guys, if you're interested.'

'What?' they both chimed suspiciously.

'Street thugs. I want you to fake-rob my date. Just get his wallet and run. You can use an unloaded gun. Or a knife. Maybe you can borrow something from the prop department. I'm sure those are totally safe.'

'Will your date be in on this performance?'

'No. What would be the point of that?'

'What if he decides to fight us instead of just handing over his wallet?'

'He won't. At least I don't think he will. Are you in?'

'Absolutely not,' said Christopher.

'Why not?' I asked, although I knew why.

'Because it's the most insane idea you've ever had, Isabel.'

'Probably not the *most* insane,' I replied, and then tried to come up with another plan. 'I have a better idea,' I said.

'Can't wait to hear it,' said Christopher.

'Okay. This is good. I take my date to a crowded bar and you guys perform one of those two-person pickpocket scams. Christopher, you spill your drink, and while you're drying him off, Len gets his wallet. You've done it before, Len. Don't pretend like you haven't.'

'It seems to me,' said Christopher, 'that if you're dating the chap you ought to be able to get his wallet yourself.'

'Nah, he's onto me,' I said. 'I've tried. There's just no way.'

'I'm going to say no,' said Len.

'Me too,' replied Christopher. 'It's just too risky.'

Without Len and Christopher to aid me in a more subtle investigation, I had to resort to a direct inquest.

SUBJECT LOSES HIS PATIENCE . . .

It was not my plan to end my relationship with Subject that night. But weeks had gone by without any solid answers to my questions and my patience was coming to an end. I decided it was time to get to the truth, no matter what the outcome.

Unfortunately, Subject decided to turn my interrogation back on me. I recorded the conversation, just in case the wine clouded my memory.

The transcript reads as follows:

ISABEL: So, how long did you live in St. Louis?
SUBJECT: Fourteen years. Have you always lived in San Francisco?
ISABEL: Yes. Was that your first fourteen years?
SUBJECT: Yes. Tell me about your parents.
ISABEL: Average. They're totally average parents. Too boring to discuss.
SUBJECT: Your mother keeps odd hours.
ISABEL: She has insomnia. Sometimes driving relaxes her.
SUBJECT: So that's why she's always wearing her pajamas when she goes out in the middle of the night. I found that very curious.
ISABEL: Mystery solved. So, after St. Louis, where did you go?
SUBJECT: Iowa.
ISABEL: Why?
SUBJECT: Because that's where my father got a teaching job.

ISABEL: So he's a professor?

SUBJECT: Was. He died four years ago.

ISABEL: Sorry about that. So, what did he teach?

SUBJECT: Mathematics. One night, when I couldn't sleep, I saw your mother go out for one of her midnight drives and then shortly thereafter I saw you leave as well. Was that a coincidence or were you following her?

ISABEL: How often do you have insomnia?

SUBJECT: Often.

ISABEL: Why is that?

SUBJECT: I've got a lot on my mind.

ISABEL: What exactly?

SUBJECT: Why were you following your mother?

ISABEL: I wanted to know what she was up to.

SUBJECT: Why didn't you just ask her?

ISABEL: Because she would have lied.

SUBJECT: Your folks just don't seem all that boring anymore.

ISABEL: I find them dull. So how long were you in Iowa?

SUBJECT: Three or four years.

ISABEL: Which one, three or four?

SUBJECT: I don't remember.

ISABEL: Are you hiding from someone?

SUBJECT: Where'd you get that idea?

ISABEL: I don't think John Brown is your real name.

SUBJECT: Are you always this suspicious?

ISABEL: Yes. Don't take it personally.

SUBJECT: Is there any chance you're going to get off this subject?

ISABEL: Unlikely.

SUBJECT: Why is that?

ISABEL: Because I can come up with very few

166

good reasons why someone would be using an alias.

SUBJECT: My name is John Brown.

ISABEL: Let's say you were in the witness protection program. That's possible, I suppose, but I was always under the impression that the Feds were good at creating legitimate backstories for individuals in their custody. I mean, if a lowly PI can prove someone's not legit, what chance do they have?

SUBJECT: My patience is nearing its end.

ISABEL: So is mine. Who are you?

SUBJECT: I've already told you my name.

ISABEL: How about your real name?

SUBJECT: John Brown is my real name.

ISABEL: Who was that woman you met at the community garden the other day?

SUBJECT: How did you know I met with a woman?

[Silence.]

SUBJECT: Check, please.

[End of date.]

*   *   *

My date and I drove back to our respective residences in almost complete silence. He pulled his car into his driveway and unlocked the door.

'Good-bye,' Subject said, and it was the most final farewell I had ever heard.

'I'm onto you,' was my only reply.

Those were the last polite words we said to each other.

167

THE 'LAW OFFICES' OF MORT SCHILLING

Monday, April 24
1155 hrs

Morty continued jotting notes down on his legal pad.

'You look worried,' I said.

'You're going to look like a stalker, Isabel. You begin harassing him after he rejects you.'

'I was harassing him long before he rejected me.'

'Why were you so suspicious?' Morty asked.

'Would you like to see the complete list?' I asked.

'One thing at a time,' Morty replied. [Morty was trying to drag this out as long as he could, I realized.] 'Just tell me what you knew at this point in the game.'

'I knew that Subject gave me a phony DOB and maybe a fake name. He swapped packages with a woman at a community garden. Who knows what was in those paper bags. And then all that gardening. Something about it wasn't right.'

'When was the next time you had contact with Mr. Brown?'

'A few weeks later.'

'Why so long?'

'I wasn't sure how to proceed. It's hard to investigate someone when you can't even figure out who he really is. Besides, there were other matters occupying my immediate attention.'

SUSPICIOUS BEHAVIOR REPORT #10

'ALBERT-SPELLMAN'

Tuesday, February 21

I returned home that night to find my mother 'out on a job' and my father on the internet planning their next disappearance.

'What are you doing, Dad?'

'Your mom and I are thinking of taking a cruise,' Dad said coldly, 'because that's what people do when they get old.'

'Are you okay?'

'I'm fine,' Dad replied abruptly, having decided I was not the kind of person with whom one could have a serious conversation.

'Would you like to talk to me about anything?'

'Nope.'

'Are you sure?'

'Yep.'

'Because the other day I was off my game.'

'No, you were just being yourself.'

'What does that mean?'

'Nothing. Just that you were doing what comes naturally to you.'

'I think that was an insult, Dad. But in the spirit of self-improvement, I'd like to try that conversation over again.'

Dead silence.

'Please,' I said.

'Forget it.'

'I'd really like a do-over.'

Dad cleared his throat, deciding whether to give me a second chance, which he did.

'I asked you if you were happy doing what you're doing. Are you?' he asked.

'Why are you asking?'

'Why can't you just answer the question?'

'Why can't you tell me why you're asking the question?'

My dad sighed and put his feet on his desk, I'm sure regretting the above-mentioned decision.

'Your mother and I are redoing our wills.'

'Why?'

'Because we haven't changed them in ten years, I'm over sixty, and we're planning another disappearance or two. We need to have our affairs in order.'

'I see,' I replied.

'Is this what you want from your life?' my dad said, letting his hand sweep over the office. He'd picked an unfortunate day to draw my attention to our cramped work environment. The Spellman office is one large room with four desks and mismatched office furniture. The carpet needed vacuuming, the file cabinets needed dusting, and the paper-shredder needed emptying.

'I'd prefer it in a brighter color,' I replied.

'Isabel, just answer the fucking [As a former cop, Dad's use of the f-word was loose and frequent. But as a father he discovered that by moderating its use, he could use it as a warning sign to his children.] question. I'm losing my patience with you.'

'Spell it out, Dad.'

'Do you want me to leave you the business in our

170

will? We can give part-ownership to David and Rae, but since we're hoping Rae goes to college, you'd have to run the business by yourself in case something happens to me or Mom.'

'Oh,' I said, my head starting to throb. I wasn't expecting the conversation to be quite so serious. 'I don't know,' I replied.

'Is this what you want out of life?'

'I don't know. Do I have to answer this question right now?'

'No,' Dad replied. 'But you need to start thinking about it.'

'I need a drink,' I said, and made a beeline for the refrigerator.

SUSPICIOUS BEHAVIOR REPORT #11

'Olivia Spellman'

Mom entered the kitchen after I uncapped a bottle of beer.

'How's the Chandler case going?' she asked.

'Huh?' I replied, my head still in the other room with Dad.

'Have you made any progress, or do we have drunken leprechauns in our not-too-distant future?'

'I'm still working on my game plan.'

My mother silently turned on the teakettle and sat down across from me.

'Where were you?' I asked.

'Nowhere.'

'Really? Could you give me directions? Because sometimes I'd like to go there.'

'I apologize. I was being vague,' Mom said. 'The appropriate response would be "Nowhere of interest to you."'

'Are you sure about that?'

'I'm positive,' my mother replied, making the kind of direct eye contact she only makes when she's trying to stare me down.

'So you weren't vandalizing some poor sap's motorbike?' I asked, and I could tell from her expression that that was exactly where she was.

Mom quickly got up from the table. 'If you know what's good for you, Isabel, you'll keep your mouth shut.'

Some people threaten without any force behind their words. My mother is not one of those people. If I wanted to learn the truth about her increasingly erratic behavior, I would have to be extremely careful. In the meantime, I had another kind of vandal to worry about.

THE CHANDLER JOB

CHAPTER-2

Wednesday, February 22
0900 hrs

The next morning I began working the case by interviewing all those who witnessed the original vandalisms almost thirteen years ago.

Interview #1—Spellman, Albert

The transcript reads as follows:

ISABEL: Dad, do you recall the string of adjustments to Mrs. Chandler's life-size tableaus during the 1992–1993 school year?
ALBERT: Adjustments. Nice word choice.
ISABEL: Please answer the question.
ALBERT: Yes, I do recall the adjustments.
ISABEL: Do you recall them in great detail?
ALBERT: I do.
ISABEL: Do you recall telling anyone about them?
ALBERT: I do.
ISABEL: Approximately how many people?
ALBERT: Has to be at forty or fifty.
ISABEL: Are you out of your mind? Didn't you have anything else to talk about?
ALBERT: Excuse me, Isabel, but I was getting tired of listening to my colleagues rave about their daughters' straight A's or swim team

victories, science fair ribbons and Ivy League educations. These were the only bragging rights I had on you and I enjoyed it. I didn't relish you being a vandal, but the 'adjustments,' as you call them, were downright brilliant.

ISABEL: I have no idea what you're talking about.

ALBERT: Give me a break.

ISABEL: Of the fifty or so people that you told about this, did you tell any of them in great detail? What I'm trying to determine is who would know the details. I mean all the details. If you've noticed, the scenes to date on Mrs. Chandler's yard are exact replicas of the '92–'93 season.

ALBERT: A good twenty or so had enough info to duplicate the . . . adjustments if they really wanted. But then you're forgetting about your Uncle Ray. He used to take pictures. I think he even made a photo album—and would take it to the bars with him and stuff. Was a big hit there, he told me. Your suspect pool, Izzy, it's huge. Huge. The only way you're going to solve this case is by good old-fashioned surveillance.

ISABEL: That's what I was afraid of.

[End of tape.]

Notes on Surveillance

Because it often takes hours and sometimes days or weeks to catch a person in an illegal/suspicious/immoral act, and because surveillance costs at least $50 (and up to $75) an hour per investigator, [The investigator will bring in anywhere from $15 up. My going rate is $25/hr on surveillance; $20/hr for investigative work; $15/hr for administrative (which I try to keep to a minimum).] Surveillance can be the bread and butter of the business. But surveillance isn't fun. It used to be fun when I was an adolescent and protected by child labor laws. It used to be fun when I first got my license and never worked a job solo. However, the very first time I spent eight hours [The last four thinking about how badly I wanted to pee.] in my car alone, listening to late-night radio, I was cured of any affection I had for shadowing folk.

Rae, until very recently, had a serious recreational surveillance habit. We had been unable to cure her of this vice until Henry Stone pointed out that surveillance is in fact very dull and we were encouraging Rae by giving her jobs that were far more compelling than your average surveillance. Over a two-month period, my parents had Rae clock in over forty hours of traditional, boring surveillance, forty hours of Rae sitting in a car with an adult ignoring her, [Henry explained that if we engaged her in conversation, the time would pass. The goal was for time to feel endless.] sans snack food, with limited bathroom breaks. This simple behavior modification trimmed Rae's recreational surveillance habit by 80 percent. We would never wipe it out completely, but now that Rae had Henry Stone, school chums, and Mr. Peabody's mucous mystery, there really wasn't much time left on her schedule.

THE 'LAW OFFICES' OF MORT SCHILLING

Monday, April 24
1205 hrs

Morty was distracted—no, fascinated—by my mysterious case of the copycat vandals.

'It has to be an inside job,' he said, forming his fingers into a pyramid and looking at me askance as if he were a detective in a drawing-room mystery.

'Inside what?' I asked.

'Inside your family.'

'You think my mom and dad have time to ransack an old lady's front yard?'

'If your mother is finding the time to sabotage a random kid's motorbike, I'm not sure where that line would be drawn.'

'Look, I've checked into everyone in my family. Mrs. Chandler had very specific dates for when her lawn was hit. Mom, Dad, and Rae all have direct alibis for most of those dates. Besides, it's not their MO. It's not even my MO, anymore. The person or persons who are doing this are connected to me somehow, but they're not related to me.'

'If I were you, I'd spend more time thinking about those lawn hits than that neighbor of yours.'

'Thanks. But I'm more in the market for legal advice.'

'Let's get back to the TRO,' Mort says. 'As far as your story goes, Mr. Brown had not yet filed it.'

'Correct,' I replied.

'After he broke up with you, when was the next time you had contact with Mr. Brown?'

'I don't think *he* broke up with *me*. It was mutual, I think.'

'Izzila, just answer the question.'

'About two weeks after our final date.'

DISAPPEARANCE #2
SHIPS-AHOY!

Wednesday, March 8

Since I still had a few plots brewing to drive Bernie out of my apartment, I remained steadfast in my refusal to look for another place to live. My parents decided to make the best of my unforeseen arrival and make a departure of their own. Dad found a two-week Caribbean cruise discounted by 60 percent online for a last-minute booking. Apparently this particular ship (*Princess Leia*—christened by Carrie Fisher herself) had been involved in a recent hijacking (yes, hijacking a boat is quite impressive) and reservations had dipped to a ten-year low. Dad jumped at the bargain and started packing.

Mom later explained that she and my father shared their own reservations about leaving Rae home alone, even though they both agreed she knew precisely what to do in an emergency. Dad says I jaded them; I took away their trust forever. In my opinion, Rae was the baby and it was impossible for either of my parents to imagine her old enough to be left alone.

My mother left the following list of rules and instructions on the refrigerator the night before their departure.

Things To Do and Not Do During our Disappearance
DO take out the trash
DO brush your teeth and maintain adequate grooming standards
DO make sure Rae goes to school
DO NOT leave flames unattended
DO NOT order pizza more than 1x per week (or there will be a $200 fine)

* * *

After I saw the list I reminded my mother that I was not twelve, Oscar Madison, or mildly retarded, and she responded with 'I know that, sweetie, but you've always had an undercurrent of laziness and destruction in you, and I just wanted to make sure that it doesn't rub off on Rae during what I hope will be a wonderful bonding time for my two daughters.'

'There's no way you can enforce the pizza fine,' I said, looking at my mother like she was crazy.

Mom returned the incredulous stare and said, 'I'll just dock your pay. How hard is that? Have a good time, and if you guys run into any trouble, call Henry.'

'Wouldn't it make more sense to call David, what with him being our brother and, well, a lawyer?'

'If you want to call David, call David. But I personally think Henry's more reliable,' Mom coldly replied, apparently still holding a grudge against my brother.

Mom, Dad, Rae, and I said our farewells. I watched their cab disappear in the distance. Rae departed for school, after which I called David's office. His secretary said he had been out sick for the last three days. I phoned his house. He didn't answer, as I predicted, so I decided to drive to his house and gather more evidence.

SUSPICIOUS BEHAVIOR REPORT #12

'David Spellman'

David's car was parked in his driveway, but there was no answer at the door. I could tell by the papers piled up by his doorstep that he probably hadn't even opened the front door in the last four days. It was a Wednesday.

David lives in a renovated Victorian not unlike the Spellman home, just fancier. Through the back staircase, I had access to the window of his pantry. I grabbed a flathead screwdriver out of my car. I keep it there for emergencies and when I have to smash in taillights. I quietly jimmied open the window and ungracefully heaved myself through the narrow opening. I rested on the top of the clothes dryer and then crawled, head-first, to the floor. I landed with a thump on my side and slowly got to my feet.

I followed the sound of the television and found my brother in the 'entertainment room' equipped with a fifty-six-inch plasma TV, leather couch, bar, and state-of-the-art stereo system. The room was dark, the shades were drawn, and David was lying on the couch in his pajamas. I sat down next to my brother, who barely turned his head to acknowledge my presence.

'Don't break into my house anymore,' David said, still staring at that offensive TV.

'Wow,' I said. 'You must have really fucked up to wallow on this level.'

'You don't know anything, Isabel.'

'Why don't you just tell me what you've done and maybe I can help you fix it. You might be able to get her back.'

'Go away.'

'I've been calling Petra for three weeks now. I can't even get her on the phone. She's my best friend, David. I want her back, even if you don't. Tell me what happened.'

'I'm not talking about this anymore.'

'Were we ever talking about it?'

'Have your drink and leave. And don't come back here again until I invite you. Got it?'

'David, I just broke into your home. Clearly I don't respect boundaries. Do you really think a verbal request is going to put a dent in any of my plans?'

David grabbed my arm and pulled me out of the chair. He's bigger than me, so if he feels like being a bully, he can. [That is, unless I decide to fight dirty. Stay tuned . . . sibling brawl to come.] After guiding me to his front door and shoving me outside, he gave me as pointed a glare as his drunken eyes could muster.

'I'm not joking, Isabel . . . just . . .'

David didn't complete that thought. He simply

180

slammed the door in my face.

As I strode back to my car, I racked my brain for hints of trouble in David and Petra's relationship. I had nothing. For two years everything is fine, then Petra gets a tattoo and skips town, David stops bathing and leaving his house, and no one will tell me what's going on.

HOME ALONE

CHAPTER-2

That afternoon, when I returned to the Spellman house, Rae was on the telephone. My sister watched me carefully as she was listening to whoever was on the other end of the line. Her responses suddenly became vague and self-conscious.

'Yeah, it's going all right . . . I'm not sure about that . . . I'll let you know when I know . . . Uh-huh . . . I heard you the first time . . . Yeah . . . We need that. I'll buy it. Yeah . . . Isabel's home so, you know.'

'Who was that?' I asked when Rae hung up the phone.

'A friend.'

'Same friend or a different friend?'

'Different.'

'What's her name?'

'Jason.'

'Funny name for a girl.'

'Not a girl.'

'I picked up on that.'

'Any more questions?'

'Is he your boyfriend?'

'You are so prehistoric,' Rae said as she jumped off the counter. 'There's a message for you on the office line,' she continued, and then went to her room.

*　　　*　　　*

I found the saved message after entering the security code.

'Hi, Izzy, it's Petra. I'm in Arizona visiting my mom. I'll be back in a few weeks. Talk to you then.'

I phoned her cell the second I heard the message and it went directly to voice mail.

'Hi, Petra. Izzy here. I'm having some trouble understanding your recent behavior. I have a cell phone. The number is programmed into your cell phone. I know that because I programmed it. Now if you dropped your cell phone into a river I might understand why you called me on the office line, but since we have caller ID and I can see what number you dialed from, you have no excuse. Call me back on my cell phone. I want to know what is going on. Please.'

Ding and Ditch

My plan for the evening was a night-long stakeout in front of the Chandler home. The widow had installed her decorations early, hoping to catch the vandals before the holiday actually arrived. This was my suggestion, in the hopes that I could catch the culprits sooner than later and be done with this case for good. Perhaps it was the reminder of my youthful indiscretion that prompted my repeat of another youthful indiscretion. But at 11:59 P.M., I parked my car down the block from my old apartment, rang the doorbell, and then slipped into the foyer of the adjacent building as I waited for Bernie to press the buzzer. Ten minutes later, I rang my doorbell again and once again slipped into the foyer of the adjacent building. Ten minutes after that I rang the doorbell, returned to my car, and parked in front of Mrs. Chandler's home.

Thursday, March 9
0100 hrs

The leprechauns were sober and upright when I arrived. The pots of gold and crepe-paper rainbows were not yet sullied by a sea of Guinness cans and vegetable-soup vomit. The Copycat Vandals would strike sometime between now and St. Patrick's Day, according to my calculations, which were based exclusively on anecdotal evidence. [90 percent of which was based on my own behavior.]

Unless they struck early, I was looking forward to a long night and then perhaps another long night and then another. But then I had a change of plans.

I made the decision in an instant, the choice between the mystery assigned to me and the mystery I preferred solving. It was just a lucky (or unlucky, depending on who's looking at it) coincidence that I saw Subject's VW Jetta drive past my surveillance vehicle in the early hours of Thursday morning. I didn't immediately recognize it by the license number, but his car has a sharp dent on the driver's-side door, with a stretch of stripped-off paint.

I turned on the ignition and followed him. I could only hope that the leprechauns would abstain from imbibing in my absence.

Subject's vehicle veered left on Van Ness Avenue and continued past Market Street. The problem with late-night pursuits is that empty roads make a close tail obvious, especially if you're prone to looking in your rearview mirror. My guess is that a man who keeps a room locked at all times and adopts fake identities is probably that kind of guy. The only thing I had going for me was that the glare of his taillights was uneven. Often this happens when one is replaced before or after the other.

I hung back as far as I could, trying to keep at least one car between us at all times. Subject drove south on Mission Street for another ten or fifteen minutes, past Cesar Chavez and the highway, and into the Excelsior district. He made a left turn onto a residential street, the name of which I did not catch. It was lined with single-family stucco homes, in various states of repair and disrepair. My pursuit was getting dangerously close and I couldn't risk detection, so I turned off my headlights [Do not try this at home.] and continued weaving along the side streets in Subject's wake.

Subject parked in front of a dilapidated house with a collection of garage sale rejects on the front lawn. The paint job had to have been at least twenty years old, judging by what was left of it. Not a single light shone from inside. But that is all irrelevant. I was looking at the wrong house. Three doors down, a blonde woman in pajamas and a ratty San Francisco Giants sweatshirt exited another stucco single-family home, this one in fine condition other than its less urgent need for a paint job. This residence was also completely unlit.

The blonde woman opened the door and sat in the passenger side of Subject's vehicle for approximately ten minutes. The lights were out and I couldn't risk moving any closer, so it was impossible to see what they were doing. The woman then exited the vehicle, holding something in her hands that was not previously there—it might have been a paper bag, but it was impossible to tell.

Subject started his engine and took off. I followed him a short distance until it became obvious that he was going home. I then took a different route back to Mrs. Chandler's home and parked, once again, out front. In my absence the leprechauns had remained sober.

Three hours later, as dawn broke, I returned home to sleep.

MY ALMOST FAKE DRUG DEAL #2

I awoke in the afternoon with a plan. A plan that arose out of my nagging suspicion that the secret Subject was hiding was that he was a drug dealer. It would explain the cagey behavior, the locked door, and the post-midnight exchange of goods that I witnessed.

After I dressed and downed two cups of coffee, I

searched for Rae to make sure she was accounted for and discovered her in the Spellman office Googling variations on the phrase 'Why would you save your own snot?' The question, as of recent days, had become a constant refrain in our house, like the chorus of a song, always said with a powerful, almost emotional delivery. *'Why? Why* would you save your own snot?'

I answered, as I always did, 'I have no idea.'

I got into my car and drove across the bridge, arriving at the familiar Oakland warehouse shortly thereafter.

Len and Christopher were on guard from the start. They knew I didn't drop by just for tea and cookies (although that was a perk).

Len cut to the chase. 'Spill it, Spellman.'

'I have another acting job for you.'

'What?' said Christopher, nonplussed.

'I'd like you to resurrect your roles as drug dealers.'

'Who is the target?'

'That guy I was seeing. He lives next door. I think he might be a drug dealer.'

'What makes you think that?' Christopher asked.

'For one thing,' I replied, 'I've seen him swap packages at least twice. Once in the middle of the night. Another thing, he's really into gardening, if you know what I mean.'

The look on Christopher's face suggested he did not.

'Well, if he's a drug dealer,' said Len, 'then he probably has his own supply.'

'Okay, then. Try to *buy* drugs from him.'

Len, having once been a drug dealer himself, still had some loyalty to his former occupation. 'Isabel, that's called entrapment.'

'No,' I said. 'I think it's called acting.'

'I'm going to say no,' said Christopher.

I sighed, trying to come up with another plan.

'I also think we should mention that we don't like being typecast,' he continued.

'Ditto,' said Len.

'Huh?' I said.

'We've already played drug dealers for you; the other day you asked us to be armed robbers, then pickpockets. Today you're back to the drug dealers. What's next? Pimps?'

'Sorry, guys. But in my line of work, I don't have much use for dukes and earls. I'm trying to catch people doing bad things, and generally you need someone living in the world of vice to draw them into it. Forgive me.'

'She has a point,' conceded Christopher.

'So, there's no way I can convince you?' I asked.

'Sorry, luv,' said Christopher. 'We're just more Denzel than Tupac. Now would you like some more tea?'

EX-BOYFRIEND #10

Name: Greg Larson
Age: 36
Occupation: Sheriff with the Marin County Sheriff's Department
Hobbies: Target practice and beer drinking
Duration: 6 weeks
Last Words: 'Nope.'

I met Sheriff Larson during the Spellman Wars I mentioned earlier. He was a person of interest in my 'unsolvable' missing person case. I found Larson suspicious the moment I met him. He rarely spoke in complete sentences, preferring simple one- or two-word responses to almost all inquiries. However, when the case was complete and I realized how mistaken I had been about the man—keep in mind, I was fairly certain he was guilty of covering up a murder or was a murderer himself—he grew on me.

After I discovered the truth—which I won't get into here [See previous document if you would like all the details—*The Spellman Files*, now in paperback!]—and the sheriff was exonerated of any foul play, [Sorry, had to give up that one detail.] I thought I owed Greg an apology. Somehow that apology turned into a very brief relationship, one that can best be reduced to our final exchange of words, which, interestingly enough, was the most verbose the sheriff had ever been:

SHERIFF: Enough with the questions.
ISABEL: Enough with the ignoring of the questions.
SHERIFF: Do you ever stop?
ISABEL: Eventually.
SHERIFF: When? And I'd like an exact date.
ISABEL: When I have all the information I need.
SHERIFF: Your brain might be in this, but your heart isn't.
ISABEL: No, my heart simply requires more facts than other hearts.
SHERIFF: Is this working for you?

ISABEL: Not really. You?
SHERIFF: Nope.

It had been a year since I had seen the sheriff. I figured it was ample time to cash in on whatever indebtedness a mediocre six-week relationship entitled me to. Larson gave me a friendly smile and kicked his boots onto his desk when I entered his office.

'Spellman,' he said. 'To what do I owe the pleasure?'

I sat down on the edge of his desk and said, 'I need a favor.'

'I knew it,' he said. 'You had that look in your eye.'

'I left you alone for a whole year. Give me some credit.'

'I wouldn't have minded seeing you now and again, but then you start in with all those questions.'

'I'll keep this brief,' I said, handing Larson a slip of paper with every scrap of information I had on Subject.

'I'm not sure if this is his name,' I continued, 'but assuming it is, I can't find a record on him in St. Louis, Washington, Iowa—all states he's claimed to have lived in. What you can get, that I can't, is whether there's a police file on him. Like, maybe a complaint. Some record that wouldn't be in any database. Can you do that for me?'

Larson picked up the piece of paper. 'Who is this guy?'

'He lives next door to my parents. Something about him isn't right.' [Notice how I am being vague and not offering any further details on

Subject's and my relationship.]

Larson pocketed the paper and said, 'I'll look into it.'

The favor phase of the conversation was now at an end and we moved on to the small-talk phase. One of the things I did really like about Larson was that he had little use for small-talk, so I knew our meeting would end shortly.

'So how have you been?' I asked.

'Can't complain. You?'

'I actually can complain, but I know how you hate that, so I won't.'

Then I made the mistake of noticing a framed picture of a woman on his desk.

'Who's that?' I asked.

'My fiancée,' he replied, and even though jealousy was the farthest thing from my mind, I still felt something vague and unpleasant. I got up to leave.

'Is she a neurosurgeon?' I asked.

'No,' Larson replied, chuckling.

'Was she in the Olympics?'

He gave me an incredulous stare. 'How did you know that?'

THE PHILOSOPHER'S CLUB

Milo continued with his unsympathetic stance.

'You know it's never too late to train for the Olympics. I mean, you're too old for track and field, gymnastics, figure skating, volleyball, basketball, all the good sports, but some of those other 'sports'—he used the generally frowned-upon finger quotes—you might have a shot at if you start now and train really, really hard. Like hurling. You've heard of it, right? It's like shuffle board on ice, using stones. There are those people who crouch down and sweep the ice before the stone passes. You could be one of those sweepers. I got a broom in back if you want to practice. I'd be happy to chip in for hurling outfits. They'd, of course, have to say 'The Philosopher's Club' on them. We could use the advertising.'

'Milo, the sport you're thinking of is called "curling".'

'I could've sworn there was a sport called "hurling."'

'There is,' I replied. 'It's played mostly in Ireland. It's like field hockey, only much faster.' [You think I wouldn't know the details of a sport called 'hurling'?]

'Sounds like you have to be in shape for that sport. So, curling it is,' Milo said. 'Even better, if you ask me. I was beginning to worry about a bar sponsoring an event called 'hurling.' I'm not sure if that's the kind of advertisement I need.'

'What happened to you, Milo? You used to be nicer.'

191

'I'm old, my feet hurt me more, I got a prostate problem, and I'm just getting plain cranky. Listening to you complain about your mediocrity because you were not in the Olympics, is stupid. The only sport you ever practiced was amateur vandalism.'

'I'm sorry about your prostate,' I said to Milo. 'I'm sure having to pee all the time cannot be pleasant.'

From the look Milo gave me, I knew he regretted his brief moment of honesty.

You see, knowledge is power.

THE CHANDLER JOB

CHAPTER-3

Friday, March 10
1030 hrs

Since the next day was Saturday, I invited Rae to accompany me on the Chandler residence stakeout. At first Rae said no, but when I told her she had free rein on the snack food, she acquiesced. In the middle of the night, in a blacked out car with nothing to do, it's hard to resist Pringles, Milk Duds, and Hot Tamales.

Typically my sister will strike up a conversation on an assortment of topics in a five hour time span, but this night was different. She simply could not get past Mr. Peabody, her schoolteacher.

'Why? Why would you save your own snot?'

Four hours later the snot mystery and the copycat vandal mystery remained unsolved.

Rae and I slept through morning. We awoke, after noon, with a sugar hangover. I forced Rae to make a teeth-cleaning appointment with Daniel and then we made omelets for breakfast.

While I drank coffee and Rae downed two glasses of chocolate milk, we checked our e-mails and found the first set of correspondences from Mom and Dad on their cruise.

From: Albert Spellman
Sent: March 10
To: Isabel Spellman, Rae Spellman
Subject: Cruise Ship Dispatch #1

This is like a floating prison. Sometimes I just want to throw myself overboard so I can have some more space. I don't see the appeal. Plus, your mom's sick as a dog, so I have to roam the deck alone. Everyone on board has been drugged with some awful substance that makes them smile constantly. Crew members are always asking me if they can help me with anything. I'm walking down a hallway and they ask if I need assistance. With what?

I hope you both are behaving yourselves. I'll know if you're not.

Dad.

From: Olivia Spellman
Sent: March 10
To: Isabel Spellman, Rae Spellman
Subject: Greetings from hell

After two days of eating saltines, I finally made it out of the cabin, which is about the size of our Audi. In defense of my cabin, however, no one inside of it wears a thong. And your father is up to something. Every time he says he's going to the buffet, he comes back with wet hair, like he's just taken a shower. When I ask him about it, he says he took a dip in the pool, but he smells like shampoo.

On another note, there's no phone service here. Isabel, I need you to follow up with Ron Howell on something for me. His memory sucks. Call him up and say, 'Ron, don't forget to take care of that thing I told you to take care of.' That's it. Love you. Mom.

Rae sent the following replies:

From: Rae Spellman
Sent: March 11
To: Olivia Spellman
Subject: Re: Greetings from hell

Mom, maybe your next vacation shouldn't be on a boat. Dad really likes 'getting away from it all,' so just suck it up and pretend like you're enjoying yourself. I'll look online for a more suitable escape. Boats just aren't your thing. Onward. Everything's cool here. Don't worry. Love, Rae.

From: Rae Spellman
Sent: March 11
To: Albert Spellman
Subject: Re: Cruise Dispatch #1

Dad, Mom feels really bad that she's so sick.

194

She was really looking forward to spending quality time with you. Your next vacation should be on land, but definitely you guys need to try this again. I hear the buffets are great on board. Go nuts. Treat yourself.

As Rae composed her diabolical e-mail replies, I followed up on my mother's request to contact Ron, one of our regular surveillance guys. Ron picked up on the third ring.

'Hello.'

'Ron, it's Isabel Spellman.'

'What can I do you [Notice the swapping of 'you' and 'for.'] for, Izzy?'

'I hate that.'

'I know. That's why I say it.'

'Mom wanted me to tell you don't forget to take care of that thing she told you to take care of.'

'Uh-huh.'

'Ring any bells, Ron?'

'Yeah, I didn't forget. I was gonna take care of it tonight.'

'Oh, good,' I said, trying to figure out the best way to approach this.

'That all, Spell?'

'Need any help?' I asked.

'Nope. Got it covered.'

'Because I'd be more than happy to help.'

'Izz, this is between me and your mom.'

'Whatever,' I said, and hung up the phone.

That evening, after force-feeding Rae a salad and a broiled chicken breast, insisting that she remain home to complete her homework, and further insisting that my evening plans consisted entirely of keeping watch over Mrs. Chandler's ode to leprechauns, I drove to Ron Howell's apartment in Daley City and parked down the block. Two hours and half a CD of *Spanish for Beginners* later, Ron exited his home and drove directly to Noe Valley. Ron, checking his near vicinity, but not, say, twenty yards behind him, decided that the coast was clear and then slashed the tires on that poor sap's motorbike.

After witnessing my mother's patsy at work, I drove to Mrs. Chandler's and parked out front. The leprechauns were untouched and remained so the rest of the night. But the evening was not a total waste. Sheriff Larson called with some very interesting news.

'What have you got for me?' I said.

'That was one thing I always liked about you, Spellman. You have no need for pleasantries.'

'Wow,' I said. 'I didn't realize you could actually string two sentences together. Bravo,' I replied.

'Be nice,' Larson warned. 'I got something.'

'What?' I said, pulling out paper and a pen.

'I got a friend on the job in Tacoma, Washington. Gave him the details on your guy and he asked around. A missing persons detective that he knows remembered the name. No charges were ever filed against him, but your John Brown was questioned in a missing persons case.'

'Who went missing?'

'Her name was Elizabeth Bartell. I'll fax you all her details. Basically, the husband accused your guy of being involved in his wife's disappearance. The husband said his wife had been seeing Mr. Brown quite a bit in the weeks before she vanished. But they couldn't pin anything on him, so the case went cold.'

'You're sure it's the same John Brown?' I asked.

'Same DOB on the driver's license, and according to the file he's a gardener.'

'Landscaper,' I corrected.

'Fancy gardener.'

'Anything else?' I asked.

'Nope,' said Larson.

'Thank you,' I replied, and hung up the phone.

THE 'LAW OFFICES' OF MORT SCHILLING

Monday, April 24
1235 hrs

'See,' I said, 'that should help my case, right?'

'Wrong,' Morty replied. 'It will be inadmissible. The only thing that matters is that you violated the TRO. Extraneous circumstances wouldn't matter unless you pulled him from a burning building. Besides, you threatened him.'

'I didn't threaten him.'

'He has you on tape saying, quote-unquote, I am going to make you pay for what you've done.'

'I don't mean to nitpick, but doesn't my particular threat rely upon Subject having done something wrong? How can it be a threat if he hasn't done anything?'

'Why aren't you taking this seriously? Your livelihood is at stake. You get that, right?'

'Yes. But two women are missing and they both had direct contact with Subject before they disappeared. I think that's more important than

197

my job. Wouldn't you agree, Morty?'
   But I get ahead of myself once again.

HOME ALONE
CHAPTER-3

Sunday, March 12

Until I received that phone call from Sheriff
Larson on my third night of leprechaun watch, I
had tried to keep my mind off of Subject. At least,
his suspicious behavior had ceased occupying my
everyday thoughts. I had moved on to other topics
like, say, motorbike sabotage, copycat vandalism,
an unfaithful brother, and an AWOL best friend.
   But then Subject earned my attention once
again, and my other mysteries faded into the
periphery.
   I shared my latest dirt on our neighbor with Rae,
who helped me keep a 'round-the-clock vigil on
Subject. We observed nothing unusual in his
routine. He loaded topsoil into his truck and made
the rounds to various gardens in the Bay Area,
planting, weeding, and doing whatever it is that
landscapers do. I saw him speak to a woman for
approximately five minutes and hand her his card.
I saw no further daytime swapping of packages,
but he did return to that Excelsior district home
and pass that same blonde woman another paper
bag. I would have to look into her involvement
with Subject more thoroughly.

GARBOLOGY 101

Thursday, March 16
0900 hrs

After four full days of avid Subject watching, Rae and I were no further along in our investigation. Then we spotted Subject taking out the trash, and Rae and I turned to each other in understanding. [If you are not privy to our sibling ESP, we both decided at the same time that we needed Subject's trash.]

'Five dollars,' I said.

'Twenty,' Rae replied.

'Ten,' I said.

'Twenty-five,' my sister replied.

'Fifteen,' I said.

'Thirty.'

'You're supposed to go down, not up.'

'There are no rules.'

'Ten,' I said.

'Thirty-five.'

'Okay, fine. Twenty,' I said, and pulled a bill from my wallet.

Rae took the money and headed for the door. In my family, if one loses a negotiation, we like to pretend that we have won.

'I would have given you thirty,' I said.

'I would have done it for five,' Rae replied.

*　　　*　　　*

Ten minutes later, Rae and I were in the basement

sorting through two separate bags of trash.

'Did you get his trash or recycling?' I asked.

'One of each,' Rae said, breaking into one of the forty-gallon garbage bags.

'That smells,' I said.

Rae, wearing yellow dishwashing gloves, dug through the refuse like a champ.

'There have to be at least four banana peels in here,' said Rae. 'Now that's suspicious.'

'Some people like bananas, Rae. They call it the perfect snack food, because it comes with its own wrapper.'

'Suzy Franklin eats at least one banana every day. And she is completely insane.'

'Don't judge a person by their produce preference. He sure shreds a lot of paper. Do you have any paper in that bag?'

'Paper towels, but that's it. I think this really is just trash,' Rae said, trying not to breathe through her nose.

'Get rid of it,' I replied.

Rae placed the opened bag inside of another trash bag and headed outside. I watched her through the window as she returned the garbage to Subject's garbage. Then she returned to the house.

'Why did you put his garbage back in his own bin? He might have seen you.'

'Where was I supposed to put it?'

'Uh, inside our trash bin.'

'What if he noticed his trash was missing?' she asked.

'Most people don't keep a tally of their waste.'

'They do if they're keeping sensitive items in it that might incriminate them,' Rae replied.

Sometimes the soundness of her logic trumps the

principle behind it. I let the argument drop. The single bag that remained was a pillow of shredded papers. We spread the contents on the floor to see if there was anything that stood out. My sister and I were looking for anomalies. Most of the confetti in front of us was from plain white paper, but if we could find something different in it, then we could look for the same and match it.

I focused on shards of laminate, thinking it might be possible to gather all the pieces of a shredded identification card. Rae noticed the distinct heading of an e-mail and tried to piece that together.

Three hours later, I could say for certain that an identification card had been shredded, but whose ID, and whether it was a library card or a driver's license or a frequent buyer's club card, I could not say. Rae fared somewhat better. Shortly before she threatened suicide [Garbology on security-savvy (i.e., shred-happy) people is always a painfully dull chore.] if she had to go on, she taped together the following e-mail.

m James
om: Alley Cat [alleycat25@Nora [jj2376
ck box tomorrow. Then call

'Mystery solved,' I said, as I lay back on the floor and shielded my eyes from the unforgiving light.

'Four hours of my life I can't get back,' said Rae. 'What a waste of time.'

'He's shredding his papers and then separating them and throwing them in different trash bags.'

'How could he know we'd do this?' asked Rae.

'He couldn't,' I replied. 'He's taking precautions

because this has happened to him before.'

'Now what?'

'I have to get into that room.'

OPERATION LOCKED DOOR

PART-II

Thursday, March 16

Almost twenty-four hours later, after an uneventful night casing the Chandler residence, I was back in David's old bedroom, keeping watch on Subject's apartment. When Rae came home from school, she joined me. In between text messaging her friends, she made casual conversation.

'Are you going to sit here all night?' she asked.

'No,' I replied. 'I have a plan.'

'Is that why you're wearing black?' Rae asked.

'Yes.'

'Does your plan have anything to do with the ladder that's propped against the back fence?'

'It might.'

'What are you waiting for?'

'Subject needs to leave for me to implement my plan.'

'I see,' Rae said. 'What about the Chandler job? Tomorrow is St. Patrick's Day.'

'They won't strike until after midnight. I've got plenty of time.'

Subject Exits His Apartment . . .
2300 hrs

I put on a black skullcap and grabbed a screwdriver from Dad's tool kit. I put my cell on vibrate and told Rae to call if Subject returned home unexpectedly. I reminded her not to get sloppy. Rae rolled her eyes and I exited our house through the back door.

I extended the painting ladder on the ground and propped it up against Subject's building. It reached approximately two and a half feet below his office window. This might be a stretch, but I was feeling lucky. I climbed to the top of the ladder and then used the wall for balance as I stepped up the last few rungs, until my feet were on the second rung from the top and my hands were clutching Subject's windowpane. I pulled the screwdriver from my back pocket and jimmied open the window.

The office was dark inside; I held a flashlight in my mouth to get a visual on the inside. Several different kinds of printers and computers lined the walls. There was a high-volume paper shredder on the floor and two phones. Just below the window was a file cabinet. I would have to slide myself over it to gain entry. I put the flashlight back in my pocket and the screwdriver on top of the file cabinet. I stepped onto the final rung of the ladder to heave myself inside.

My foot hit the top rung at the wrong angle and the ladder flew out from under me. My grip on the window was purely for balance. The twelve-foot drop happened in an instant.

The wind was knocked out of me and I didn't

come around until maybe five minutes later with Rae standing over me, a look of genuine fear her eyes.

'Should I call 911?' Rae asked.

'No way,' I tried to shout, but the pain dampened my voice. 'I'm fine,' I said, although that fact had yet to be determined.

Slowly getting to my feet, I happily discovered that all my limbs were still in working order. We circled the perimeter and entered the Spellman residence from the back.

'Get rid of the ladder,' I said to Rae before we went inside.

Rae dragged the ladder into the garage, while I checked myself for injury. There was a small cut on the side of my face, and a nasty scrape on my arm, but nothing that would require stitches. That was the good news. The bad news was that every time I took a breath it felt like I was being stabbed, not that I know what being stabbed feels like.

'You might have a broken or cracked rib,' Rae said. 'I'll be right back.'

I took a shot of my dad's whiskey and tried to find a comfortable spot to lie down on the couch. There was no painless position, so I simply chose the most endurable angle.

Approximately fifteen minutes later (the time frame, apparently, required to do ample research on rib injuries on the internet), Rae returned with a medical degree.

'Show me where it hurts,' Rae demanded with an air of professional authority.

I showed her.

'Does it hurt if I touch it?'

'Ouch!!!'

204

'Yes, it hurts.' Rae jotted this down in her notes. 'Does it hurt when you breathe?' Rae asked.

'Yes.'

'Does it hurt when you cough?'

'I don't know. I haven't needed to cough.'

'You don't know how to fake-cough?'

'I assume that it's going to hurt if I fake-cough, so I don't see the point.'

'You should do it just to be sure.'

I fake-coughed just to shut her up. 'It hurts,' I said. Rae jotted that down in her notes.

'Is your breathing rapid and shallow?'

'I don't think so,' I replied. 'Pour me another shot of whiskey.'

'It doesn't say anything about drinking whiskey in my research.'

'Does it say anything about *not* drinking it?'

Rae skimmed her recently printed sheets of paper. 'No.'

I poured myself a shot since Rae was otherwise occupied.

'I need to check your pulse rate and see if it's elevated,' Rae said, and then placed two fingers on my wrist and eyed her watch.

'What's it normally?' she asked.

'I don't know.'

'Then how am I supposed to know if it's elevated?' she said.

'I don't think it's elevated,' I said, finishing my second shot of whiskey. Finally the pain was starting to dull.

'Are you coughing blood?' Rae asked.

'No,' I replied. 'Would you like me to try fake-coughing up blood?'

'You could try.'

After forty-five minutes of Rae's version of triage, I convinced her that I was not in serious danger and a hospital visit was not necessary. I was fairly certain said hospital visit was suggested so that she could practice driving.

I took three Tylenol and attempted sleep. But the pain made that utterly impossible. I watched four hours of late-night television and then clocked approximately two hours of sleep right before dawn. I awoke at seven A.M. sharp when the telephone rang.

'Huh?' I answered.

'Isabel,' said a stern woman's voice.

'Yes?'

'Happy St. Patrick's Day.'

*   *   *

I was too exhausted, weak, and in pain to argue, so I allowed Rae to drive me the two blocks to Mrs. Chandler's residence. She was already in clean-up mode, adding the cans of Guinness to her recycling bin and sobering up her leprechauns. My copycat vandals had struck in the earliest hours of St. Patrick's Day while I was in bed, writhing in pain.

In my pajamas I got out of the car and walked across the lawn to Mrs. Chandler. Her harsh expression softened when she saw the condition I was in.

'What happened to you?'

'I had an accident.'

'A car accident?'

'No,' I said, calculating a response. See, I had to come up with a lie that my mother could not disprove if it was repeated around her.

'I tripped and fell down a flight of stairs.'
'I'm sorry to hear that, dear.'
'You and me both.'
'Go home and back to bed,' she said.
'I'll get them the next time,' I said. 'I promise.'

HOME ALONE

CHAPTER-4

Friday, March 17
0800 hours

Rae heated up a can of chicken soup for my dinner and served it to me in bed. The noodles reminded me of the leprechaun vomit and I lost my appetite.

'How are you feeling?' she asked.

'I'm feeling very hostile toward that ladder, but otherwise I'm in extreme pain.'

'Do you need me to stay home and take care of you?' Rae asked.

'What would you do, serve me more lukewarm soup? No, thanks.'

'So is it all right if I go over to my friend's house?'

'What friend?'

'Ashley Pierce.'

'Your co-sleuth in the mucous case?'

'Yep.'

'Write down all her info and keep your cell phone on.'

Rae scribbled on a piece of paper.

'Is it okay if I sleep over?' she asked. 'Or do you

need me to come home and change your bedpan?'

'You're disgusting. Go to your slumber party. Have fun braiding each other's hair.'

'*That's* disgusting,' said Rae. 'I'll see you in the a.m. If you need anything, call 911.'

Rae departed shortly after seven P.M.

*   *   *

By eleven P.M., I was desperate for sleep and in unbearable pain. I raided Mom's medicine cabinet and grabbed two Vicodin and a sleeping pill. [I know. Not wise.] I remained unconscious until three A.M., when I felt two strong hands on my shoulder.

The room was dark, I was still drugged, and my eyes could only make out the shape of a man standing above me, roughly shaking me.

I remember fear hitting me immediately. I awoke suddenly and gasped for breath. Then I screamed in pain and threw a punch at the unknown male in the room with me.

The man quickly backed away and touched the side of his face.

'That hurt, Isabel.'

The voice sounded familiar, but that didn't necessarily mean I was out of danger. Remember, two Vicodin and a sleeping pill, and just woken from a deep sleep?

'I'm calling the police,' I meant to say, but it came out 'Em police calling.'

Henry Stone flicked on the light.

'What are you doing here?' I asked, still slurring my words, but now putting them in the proper order.

208

'Rae phoned me about forty-five minutes ago from a party. She was barely conscious. She said she tried to call you and David but there was no answer. The call dropped before I could get an address. I've been calling your house and ringing the doorbell for about a half hour now.'

'Really?'

'What are you on, Isabel?'

'Vicodin and sleeping pills. Singular. Just one sleeping pill.'

'Why?'

'I think my rib or ribs are fractured or something.'

'Have you gone to the hospital?'

'No doctors!!'

'We'll deal with this later. Do you know where Rae is?'

'Uh, yeah. She gave me the address of her friend's house.'

I scanned the room and promptly found the slip of paper Rae left before she departed. Henry went to my closet and grabbed a coat and sneakers. While trying to get my arm inside the coat sleeve, I complained about the footwear option.

'I can't wear those shoes.'

'What?' Stone said, annoyed. 'You look like shit, Isabel. Shoes are not going to make a difference.'

'Boy, you're rude. I can't wear them because I can't tie them. I can't reach my feet.'

'Sit down,' Henry ordered.

I sat down on the bed and Henry quickly put the sneakers on my feet and tied the laces.

'Let's go,' he said, and we got into his car and went in search of Rae.

209

We arrived at the aftermath of a party. The image was not unlike the drunken leprechauns sleeping amongst their wasted beer cans. The house was partially lit and through the window one could see lifeless bodies on the floor, the couch, some slouched against the wall.

Stone rang the doorbell at least half a dozen times and then banged on the door violently.

'Police. Open up,' he said, and I then I remembered that he was a cop.

Since 'Police' usually works better as a wake-up call than 'Anybody home?' the door was answered soon after by a grungy-looking fellow with long, sloppy hair. The stoner-dude mellow look on his face quickly shifted to fear when Henry stormed into the house and grabbed him by the collar.

'Where's Rae Spellman?'

'Uh, I dunno.'

Stone backed the sloppy kid into a corner and offered up the most intimidating glare I had ever seen. I was so accustomed to observing Stone cowed by my mother and Rae's outrageous demands that it never occurred to me he was anything but a slightly simmering, mild-mannered inspector.

'Think really fucking hard, because I'm not leaving until I find her.'

'Upstairs, maybe.'

'For your sake, I hope you're right.'

Henry raced up the stairs. I limped after him. He began opening and closing doors, shouting out Rae's name. Then he did the oddest thing. He picked up a half-awake kid on the floor, smacked his face lightly to wake him up, and then when the kid's eyes opened, he said, 'I'm very disappointed in you. You'll be hearing from me again.'

Henry let the young man drop down to the floor and continued along the hallway. There was one final room that we had not checked. Henry tried the door, but it was locked. He banged on it and shouted, 'Open up,' but there was no response. Henry backed away from the door as if he was going to force it open with his shoulder.

'Stop,' I shouted, searching through my coat pockets. 'I can pick the lock.' I found a paper clip and a nail file. I had worn the same jacket the last time I went out with Subject, so I had the appropriate tools to get into that secret room. Henry paced tensely behind. Maybe it was the prescription drugs or the fact that this party scene didn't hold a candle to some of the bashes I attended in my youth, but I wasn't all that concerned.

'Hurry up,' Henry said as I started working on the door.

Two minutes later, we entered the locked room and found Rae, out cold, on the bed. Alone, thankfully. She had locked herself inside just before she passed out. I tried to wake her, but she was too groggy to walk herself to the car.

Henry carried the mostly unconscious Rae out of the war zone. The few stragglers who we managed to wake cautiously cleared out of the way.

I buckled Rae up in the backseat and sat down next to her. Henry got into the car.

'We're going to the hospital.'

'No, Henry.'

'What if she was drugged?' he asked.

'I can smell the beer all over her. She's just very drunk and passed out.'

'Has she ever done this before?' Henry asked.

'No,' I replied. 'But it's about time.'

*   *   *

As Henry pulled his car into the driveway of 1799 Clay Street, Rae woke up and said, 'I think I'm going to barf.' She vomited once on the front lawn and then raced into the bathroom off the kitchen.

'Thank you,' I said to Henry as we stood in the foyer listening to the traveling sound of Rae's guttural hacking in the bathroom.

The early morning activities had distracted me from the pain. With the distraction gone, the pain returned. I grabbed my side and said, 'Don't worry. She'll be fine.'

'What's wrong with you, Isabel?'

'I don't know,' I said, annoyed. 'All sorts of things.'

'No, I mean your side. What did you do to yourself?'

'Nothing.'

Henry then lifted up my shirt. I smacked his hand away. 'Stop that.'

'Let me see.'

'Stop trying to look at my stomach.'

'Stop moving,' Henry said, and then he finally got a look at the black-and-blue mark on my left side.

'You're supposed to ask before you lift up a girl's shirt.'

'I think you need to go to the hospital.'

'No doctors!!!'

212

'Isabel, be reasonable.'

'I'm not coughing blood.'

'What?'

'I can breathe. My pulse rate isn't elevated. At least I don't think it is. We looked it all up on the internet. If my ribs are fractured or bruised, they'll heal themselves.'

Henry leaned against the door and stared down at his feet, shaking his head. Then he took off his jacket and threw it over the couch.

'What are you doing?'

'I'm staying,' Henry said, annoyed.

'Why?'

'Because, if I leave, it would be like abandoning two mentally challenged people in a nuclear waste dump.'

'That's nice, Henry. Excuse me while I attend to Vomit Girl.'

*　　　*　　　*

I took the first shift with my sister, which meant sitting on the bathroom floor watching Rae heave up everything she had consumed in the previous six hours. Henry took the second shift, which involved an almost scientific replenishment of fluids, I would later discover. I slept eight hours that night out of sheer exhaustion and woke, still in pain but somewhat refreshed, at eleven A.M.

THE MORNING AFTER

I entered the kitchen to the smell of pancakes, toast, and eggs (not sizzling, but poaching).

'Can I have bacon too?' Rae asked Henry. Rae, I should mention, was drinking orange juice, appearing not any shade of green or yellow, and sounding almost chipper.

'No,' Henry flatly replied.

'Good morning,' I said, entering the kitchen.

'I'm really sorry about last night, Isabel,' said Rae.

'Okay,' I replied, studying her for signs of irrepressible nausea and incapacitating head-throbbing.

'Why can't I have bacon?'

'Because you woke me up in the middle of the night to remove you from a party you got wasted at. That's why,' Henry replied.

I slipped over to Henry by the stove and whispered subtly, 'Let her have the bacon. It will help her hangover.'

'She's not hungover,' Henry replied.

'How is that possible?' I said, feeling downright hostile.

'Because,' Henry replied. 'She barfed up everything she drank and then I made her consume half a gallon of water, two quarts of Gatorade, and three slices of toast before she went to bed.'

214

'Why did you do that?' I asked, annoyed.

'So she wouldn't have a hangover.'

'She's supposed to have a hangover right now. You,' I said to Rae, 'are supposed to feel sicker than you've felt in your entire life.'

'It's not like I feel one hundred percent,' said Rae.

'What purpose is a hangover going to serve?' Henry asked.

'Cause and effect. She'll realize that drinking too much makes her feel ill and therefore she will hopefully not drink again, or at the very least drink moderately.'

'Really?' Henry replied, returning his attention to the stove. 'How many hangovers did it take you until you learned to moderate?'

'One hundred and seventy-eight,' [Not a true statistic, but probably in that ballpark.] I replied, graciously losing the argument. I poured myself a cup of Stone-brewed coffee [The man knew how to make coffee.] and sat down across from Rae. Henry placed two poached eggs and dry whole-grain toast in front of my sister.

'Are you sure you don't want any pancakes?' Henry asked.

'No, thanks,' Rae replied with a little too much conviction. Then she began dousing her eggs with ketchup.

'Can I have pancakes?' I asked, suspicious that Rae was turning down one of her favorite meals for morning, noon, and night.

'How many?' Stone asked.

'Three,' I replied.

'She'll have one,' said Rae.

'No, I'm hungry. I'll have three.'

'I tried,' Rae mumbled under her breath.

While Stone mixed the pancake batter and poured it into the pan, I decided it was time to interrogate my sister regarding her previous night's activities.

'Why didn't you tell me you were going to a party?'

'Did you always tell Mom and Dad when you were going to a party?'

My lack of credibility was a problem, I realized. I decided to take a different tack.

'How much did you have to drink?' I asked.

'Only five beers,' Rae replied.

'*Only* five?'

'I didn't think it was that much.'

This is when Henry turned around looking disturbed. 'How can you not think five beers is a lot?'

'I saw Isabel drink an entire six-pack during the last Super Bowl.'

Henry shook his head in disappointment. 'First of all,' he said to Rae, 'your sister has had a lot of practice.'

'Hey!'

'Second of all, she weighs almost forty pounds more than you.'

'More like thirty,' I snapped back.

'Do you want to step on a scale?' Stone asked.

As he predicted, I didn't follow through with that argument. However, another one had to be made.

'In my defense, I was drinking Bud Light, and I had like two hundred dollars on that game, and my team was not going to meet the spread.'

'That's your defense?' Henry said.

Rae looked all too pleased to have the attention

deflected. She continued eating her eggs and toast as if nothing unusual had transpired.

But watching Rae scarf down eggs (albeit poached ones) and drink orange juice as if this were just an average morning in the Spellman house, after the dramatic manhunt of the previous night, started to get under my skin. I slipped out of the kitchen, across the hall, and into the Spellman offices, grabbed a digital recorder, and turned it on while dropping it into the pocket of my robe. I wanted to make sure I got her confession on tape.

When I returned, the pancakes were served with a side of fresh fruit and Rae was doing some screwball comedy act, mouthing words at me when Henry wasn't looking.

THE STONE AND SPELLMAN SHOW—EPISODE 32

'DON'T EAT THE PANCAKES AND BINGE- DRINKING CONFESSION'

The transcript reads as follows:

ISABEL: Thank you, Henry.
HENRY: [gumbles] You're welcome.
  [Rae shakes her head back and forth and mouths *'Don't eat the pancakes.'*]
ISABEL: I'm hungry.
HENRY: So eat.
  [Rae performs a pantomime of picking up the pancakes and putting them in her pocket. I

217

would later learn these were instructions for me.]

ISABEL: Harpo, eat your breakfast.

[Rae shakes her head in the 'I told you so' style. I take my first bite of pancakes, which taste nothing like the pancakes I'm used to.]

RAE: No matter what you do, don't spit it out. He really hates it when you spit out food he's made you.

[Henry sits down at the table. I finish my bite of pancake.]

ISABEL: Do we have any syrup?

RAE: You're not allowed to put syrup on the pancakes.

ISABEL: Have you lost your mind?

RAE: [to Henry] You never let me put syrup on the pancakes. Why does Isabel get to?

[I get the bottle of syrup out of the pantry and douse the pancakes in it.]

HENRY: Rae, your sister is a grown woman—in theory—and she can do as she pleases. The situation you are referring to was very different, if you recall. You demanded I make you pancakes. I made the pancakes, then you spit your half-masticated food back on the plate and asked for syrup to make what I can only assume would be pancake soup.

RAE: Are you mad at me?

HENRY: Of course I'm mad at you. What you did last night was 1) illegal, 2) irresponsible, and 3) really dangerous.

RAE: I'm sorry, Henry. I really am. It's just that I've never gotten drunk before and I thought I should just to see what it's like.

[Yes, I have the confession on tape!]

218

HENRY: So, it's not going to happen again?

RAE: Not until I go to college. [[She said this while scratching her nose and avoiding eye contact. According to basic body language interpretation, this was most definitely a lie.]

HENRY: Right. [The lie did not go unnoticed.]

[Long pause.]

RAE: Thanks for coming to get me.

HENRY: You're welcome.

RAE: I knew you wouldn't let me choke on my own vomit.

ISABEL: Some of us are trying to eat.

RAE: Sorry.

[I reach into my pocket to turn off the recorder, since I have all the evidence I need. But Stone catches me out of the corner of his eye.]

STONE: Are you recording?

ISABEL: Yes.

[End of tape.]

*   *   *

Henry spent the next hour trying to get in touch with David, whom he believed should take full responsibility for his wayward sisters. When Henry finally did make contact, his side of the conversation went like this:

'David, this is Henry Stone. I'm fine. How are you? I see. I see. *Where* are you? Really? You're at a yoga retreat. Hmmm. Yes, flexibility is important. Any chance I can convince you to come home? No, it's not exactly an emergency, but I think Isabel has a cracked or broken rib or something. No, she's not coughing blood, but still. Uh-huh. Well, I think somebody should be keeping

219

an eye on your sisters . . . I know Isabel is an adult, but—I see. I understand. Okay. Yes. I'll tell her that. You're welcome. Good-bye.'

'What did he say?'

'He's at a yoga retreat in Northern California. He needs to clear his head.'

'From what?' I asked.

'We didn't get into that. He said you should listen to me and go to the doctor.'

'No doctors!'

'Why do you keep saying that?'

I didn't respond for fear of incriminating myself. Rae translated my silence: 'She doesn't want to go because Mom gets all the insurance documents and she'll want to know how Isabel injured herself.'

'So she knows you fell down a flight of stairs,' Henry said.

Rae rolled her eyes.

'That's not what happened?' Henry asked.

I turned to Rae and glowered. 'If you know what's good for you, you'll keep your mouth shut.'

*   *   *

The doorbell rang. Rae opened the door to two uniformed police officers.

'Is Isabel Spellman home?' Officer Carmichael, who appeared to have a fake tan, asked.

'Let me check,' Rae replied, and then looked to me for further instructions.

Henry grabbed my arm and walked me to the door.

'Hello officers, I'm Inspector Henry Stone and this is Isabel Spellman. Is there a problem?'

220

The second officer, Townsend, whose physical blandness was the only notable thing about him, remained silent while his partner did the talking.

'We received a complaint from your neighbor Mr. John Brown. Apparently someone tried to break into his apartment two nights ago while he was out. Mr. Brown received a call from another neighbor who claims to have seen a woman on a ladder near his office window, and when he checked the office, he found a screwdriver on the floor, which he believes was used to jimmy open the window. Do you know anything about this, Ms. Spellman?'

'No. I'm sorry, I don't. Did Mr. Brown suggest that I was the person who tried to break into his home?'

'Mr. Brown did not suggest that, but he claims the neighbor who notified him believes it was you.'

'Can you tell me who that neighbor was?'

'I'm not at liberty to say,' replied the talking officer.

'Well, I assure you, I had nothing to do with the attempted break-in, but I will be on the lookout for any prowlers from now on. Thank you for the warning.'

'Is that all, officers?' Henry said with an air of authority.

'One more thing. Mr. Brown wanted us to tell you that he would not hesitate to file a restraining order against you if he deems it necessary.'

'I'm sure it won't come to that,' I replied.

Henry and I said a polite good-bye to the officers. The moment I shut the front door, he took me by the shoulders and looked me in the eye.

221

'You fell off a ladder trying to break into that guy's house, didn't you? That's how you hurt yourself?'

'No,' I said, almost convincingly.

'What's going on between you two?'

'Nothing, anymore.'

'So you're not dating him?'

'No.'

'Then why are you trying to break into his home?'

'Because he's evil.'

'How is he evil?'

'I don't know! That's what I'm trying to figure out.'

Henry tried to humble me with his disappointed gaze.

'Get your coat, we're leaving now.'

'I don't think so,' I replied.

Henry walked over to me and gave me an icy stare. 'Do you want me to tell your parents about our visit from the cops?'

'No,' I replied.

'Good. Then the only choice you have to make is whether you're going to arrive at the hospital looking like an escaped mental patient or like a civilized human being. You have ten minutes to dress or not dress. Your choice,' he said, and I went upstairs to attire myself with some dignity.

*　　　*　　　*

Four hours later, after a three-hour wait in San Francisco General Hospital's emergency room, I was X-rayed and found to have a minor rib fracture, prescribed pain pills, and told to take it easy for the next six weeks. Henry was in a crabby mood, so I didn't reiterate on the drive home that we had just lost one sixth of a day and a five-hundred-dollar insurance deductible that we would never get back. My only revenge was recording the next episode of *The Stone and Spellman Show* on the drive home. Rae had perused a number of organ-donor brochures at the hospital. It got her thinking.

THE STONE AND SPELLMAN SHOW—EPISODE 33

'HENRY'S CHOICE'

The transcript reads as follows:

[Rae, Henry, and Isabel exit San Francisco General Hospital.]
RAE: Shotgun!
ISABEL: Whatever.
[We get into the car and pull out of the parking lot. Rae turns on the radio, flicking through the different stations.]
RAE: What happened to my radio stations?
HENRY: What are you talking about?
RAE: I programmed the bottom three buttons to my stations.
HENRY: When?
RAE: A long time ago.
HENRY: I changed them.
RAE: But I left the top three channels for you. That was totally fair. Fifty-fifty.

223

HENRY: Rae, it's my car. All the stations are mine to program.

RAE: You are so prehistoric.

[Henry always laughs at this. I have no idea why.]

HENRY: Stop calling me that!

RAE: I'm going to program the very last station. Try to leave it alone, if you can.

HENRY: No promises.

RAE: Did you read any of that organ-donation material in the hospital?

HENRY: Yes. It's very sad.

RAE: More people need to donate their organs.

HENRY: I agree completely.

RAE: When I die, I'm donating it all.

ISABEL: When you die, Rae, your organs will most likely be too old to do anybody any good.

RAE: That's the problem. You can't donate them when you're alive.

ISABEL: Except a kidney. You can donate a kidney.

[Long pause]

RAE: Henry, if you ever needed a kidney, you could have one of mine.

HENRY: Thanks, but I think you're too young to be donating kidneys.

RAE: So you wouldn't take it?

HENRY: Nope.

RAE: Even if it meant you might die?

HENRY: Yes.

ISABEL: Can I get a kidney?

RAE: Only if Henry doesn't need it.

ISABEL: He just said he wouldn't take a kidney from you.

RAE: How about Isabel? Would you take a kidney

from her?

HENRY: No, I suspect Isabel will need both her kidneys.

ISABEL: You're hilarious.

RAE: So who would you rather take a kidney from, me or Isabel?

ISABEL: Who said I was offering?

RAE: It's a hypothetical.

HENRY: Good word.

RAE: So?

HENRY: So, I wouldn't want to take a kidney from either of you.

RAE: But you have to pick. That's the game.

HENRY: I'm unaware of any such game existing.

RAE: I just made it up. It's called Choose Your Organ Donor.

HENRY: I don't want to play that game.

RAE: Please.

ISABEL: Just answer the question, Henry.

HENRY: Fine. I'd sooner take Isabel's kidney than yours.

RAE: That's an unwise decision.

HENRY: Why?

RAE: Because my kidneys have to be better than Isabel's.

ISABEL: How do you know?

RAE: Because I'm clearly a superior life form to Isabel.

[Henry catches me checking the batteries on the digital recorder in the rearview mirror.]

HENRY: Isabel, are you recording this?

ISABEL: Yep.

HENRY: Turn it off!

THE ETERNAL QUESTION

'Why would somebody save their own snot?' Rae asked Henry as she was clearing the dinner dishes. My sister insisted Henry stay for dinner to be sure I didn't have an allergic reaction to the pain medication. [Purely a manipulative tactic to keep Henry around longer.]

It was the response to that question that finally shed a different light on Rae's unwavering affection for the man.

'You're looking at this too literally, Rae,' Henry said. 'I don't believe he's found a purpose for his used tissues. I believe the storing of it is simply a symptom of some other psychological urge.'

'So he's saving his snot because he's crazy?'

'No,' Henry said to Rae's comment, and then, 'No. You need to rinse that dish more,' to her dish-loading skills. 'Don't look at just the result of what he's doing, a drawer full of used tissues. Look at the act itself.'

'Blowing his nose?' Rae asked. 'So he's got a sinus condition.'

'Think, Rae. What is he doing?'

'He's saving his snot.'

'Right. He's saving something. Now some people collect dolls or stamps or save every postcard they ever got, but haven't you met a person who collected things that maybe were a little unusual?'

'That one time I went to camp, I bunked with a girl who used to bite her fingernails off and save them inside an old Altoid container.'

'Anything else?'

'Mr. Lubovich, who lives around the corner, he saves his newspapers. He must have at least like a couple years' worth inside his house. And he won't recycle them.'

'Let me show you something,' Henry said, as he strode over to the pantry and opened the door.

'How many boxes of Froot Loops, Cocoa Puffs, and Cap'n Crunch are stored in here?'

'Twenty, last time I counted,' said Rae.

'You're only supposed to consume these goods on weekends, correct?'

'Yes?'

'And we can safely assume that you go through no more than one box a weekend, correct?'

'I'm trying to cut back,' Rae replied.

'Therefore, you have an almost five-month supply of cereal in the pantry.'

'What are you getting at?'

'You hoard cereal. Mr. Lubovich hoards newspapers. Mr. Peabody hoards used tissues. The symptom is different, but I'm not sure the impulse is.'

'No! No! No!' Rae shouted in her weak defense. 'Are you equating my cereal collection with storing a week's worth of gooey snot rags in a desk drawer?'

'I liked your use of the word 'equating.' That was good,' Henry replied.

'They're completely different, Henry. What I'm doing is based on survival.'

'How so?'

'Haven't you heard of earthquake preparedness?'

'I have,' Henry replied. 'But if you're so concerned about a natural disaster, why don't you have any bottled water back there?'

Rae stared back at Henry blankly.

'I'd just like you to have an open mind,' he said, ending the conversation once and for all.

'Dammit!' I shouted.

'What's wrong?' Henry asked.

'Batteries are dead on the tape recorder. Mom would have loved that one. Think you can reenact it?'

Henry confiscated the tape recorder.

After dinner and half a pain pill for dessert, I decided to slip out for a little R&R. [Research and reconnaissance.]

'Where are you going?' Henry asked as I gingerly put on my raincoat.

'I'm sorry, Dad. Am I grounded too?' I asked.

'You're not supposed to be driving, Isabel.'

I tossed Henry my car keys. 'Then you drive me.'

'Okay,' Henry said, unexpectedly. 'Let's go.'

'Can I come too?' Rae asked.

'You're grounded,' Stone replied.

'Whatever,' Rae replied, picking up the remote control and plopping herself down on the couch.

GATHERING INTELLIGENCE

'Turn left. Turn right.'

'Up here?'

'That's a driveway. At the next street turn right.'

'Then what?'

'Go straight.'

'Until when?'

'Until I tell you to turn the car. If I had known

228

you were going to be such a nosy chauffeur, I would have driven in pain.'

'Why don't you just tell me where we're going? I might know a shortcut,' Henry said.

'I'm not sure where we're going. I have to retrace my footsteps, so to speak.'

'Perhaps you'd like to tell me why we're going there?'

'Just park, driver.'

Henry pulled the car into a parking space about four houses down from the Excelsior residence I'd followed Subject to two nights earlier.

'Wait here. I'll be right back.'

Henry took hold of my arm before I could get out of the car.

'First tell me what you're doing.'

'I'm just checking an address from a surveillance job the other day. Subject was on the move and it was too dark for me to read the street numbers. I need to put it in the report.' [I'm good, huh?]

Henry released my arm. 'Okay.'

*   *   *

I noted the address as 1341 San Jose Avenue. The house was dim inside, so I thought it would be safe to check the name on the mailbox. I could run a reverse address search, but if the owner of the house was renting, then I wouldn't get the identity of the true occupants.

MR. AND MRS. DAVIS

According to the 1990 US Census, Davis is the sixth most common surname in the United States.

229

I explained this earlier and in my previous document, [Now available in paperback!] so I don't want to keep repeating myself, but the common name makes my job extremely difficult. Instead of reading the mailbox and running, I lingered a bit on the front porch of the Davis (the assumed 'Davis') residence and looked for any further evidence of the resident's identity. I lingered too long, to be blunt, and a man I could only presume to be Mr. Davis opened the front door of the residence.

'Can I help you?' 'Mr. Davis' asked. He was wearing a flannel shirt over a white T-shirt, blue jeans, and slippers. A can of beer dangled from his hand, his eyes appeared bloodshot, and his skin looked sallow, perhaps from lack of sleep or a vitamin deficiency.

'Is Mary [The #1 most popular female name, according to the same source above.] home?'

'My wife's name is Jennifer,' presumably-Mr.-Davis said.

'I think I have the wrong place. You don't have a book club going on back there, do you?'

'Uh, no.'

'Sorry. I must have written the address down wrong.'

'Must have.'

'Have a nice evening,' I said, about to slip away.

'Hey there,' presumably-Mr.-Davis said.

'Yes?' I replied, turning back around.

'Where's your book?'

'What?'

'You were planning on going to a book club. I was just wondering where your book was.'

'Oh, I never read the book,' I said. 'I just go for

230

the free booze. See you.'

*　　*　　*

'Let's go,' I said to Henry once I was back inside his car.

'You made a new friend?'

'Nah. I just got made.'

Stone and I drove home in silence. It had been a long day and what I needed most was one more full night of narcotic-induced rest. If breathing were unnecessary, I would have been pain free. But you know the story.

Henry pulled the car up in front of the Spellman house. Just as I was reaching for the door, I had a flashback from the previous night's adventure.

'Who was that kid, Henry?'

'What kid?'

'From the party. You went right up to that kid and shook him and said something like "'You've disappointed me."'

'I don't remember,' Henry casually replied.

'I was doped up on Vicodin and Ambien and I remember.'

'Another way to look at it,' Henry replied, 'is that your memory is cloudy from prescription drugs.'

'You know that kid. Who was he?'

'I don't know what you're talking about.'

'You're a lousy liar.'

'I haven't had as much practice as you.'

'Who was the kid?'

'Isabel, at this point, I've spent almost twenty straight hours with you.'

'I too have enjoyed our time together.'

'Get out of my car,' Henry said, trying to sound

231

threatening.

I studied Stone's stolid expression to gauge his resolve.

'Okay, good night.'

Then I did the oddest thing. I kissed him on the cheek. Henry flinched slightly when I moved toward him, as if he thought I might injure him.

'Sorry,' I said, feeling my skin flush with embarrassment. 'I have *no* idea why I just did that.'

'Must be the drugs you're on.'

'Must be,' I echoed as I exited the vehicle.

HOME ALONE

CHAPTER-5

I entered the Spellman home and found my sister plopped in front of the television watching some old sci-fi movie on DVD.

'What are you watching?'

'*Dr. Who: The Five Doctors.*'

'Where did it come from?'

'Henry. He has, like, all forty years of *Doctor Who* on DVD. I just want to watch the new series, but he won't let me until I've viewed some of the older stuff. He has so many rules,' Rae said.

'Yes, he does,' I agreed. 'At the party,' I said, changing the subject, 'there was a boy about sixteen, maybe seventeen. Lanky, sandy-brown hair, skater wear all the way. After we busted into the joint, Henry took him by the shoulders and said, " 'You've disappointed me." So?'

'So what?'

'Answer the question.'

'That was not an interrogative.'

'Rae, who was the skater dude?'

'I think his name is Dylan Loomis, although there were a couple of boys there matching your description.'

'Why would Henry say " 'You've disappointed me"?'

'I don't know. Did you ask Henry?'

'Yes.'

'What did he say?' Rae asked, turning to me. Her demeanor had remained casual up until this point. But the answer to this question held some genuine interest for her.

'He said nothing. But there's no reason for him to be disappointed in a random boy at a party you attended. So here's my follow-up question: Is Dylan Loomis your boyfriend's real name or did you supply a fake one to keep me off the scent just a little bit longer? And I know there was an interrogative in that last sentence.'

Rae pressed the Play button and returned her attention to five middle-aged men in lab coats. I had a brief flashback to my own adolescence and thought perhaps if I didn't push, didn't pry, Rae might have a better chance than me. So I let the subject drop. For now.

'You know what? It's none of my business, although you should probably lay off the beer at parties for a while.'

This time Rae pressed the *Pause* button. 'Are you going to tell Mom and Dad?'

'If I don't, Henry will. You got drunk at a party, Rae.'

'No, the other thing.'

233

'They don't know you maybe have a boyfriend?'

'Uh-uh.'

'Why does Henry know and Mom and Dad don't know?'

'Because I tell Henry everything,' Rae said, getting up and scouring the pantry for more snack food. Rae grabbed a bag of potato chips and a can of root beer and sat back down on the couch. 'So you're not going to tell?'

'I don't know. I have to think about it.'

'I have something to offer you in exchange for your silence,' she said in a conspiratorial tone.

'What?'

'If you want to investigate someone in the family, how about choosing a more worthy subject?'

'Who?'

'Dad.'

'What about him?'

'I don't think he's having a REAFO.'

'What are you saying, Rae?'

'Look in the glove compartment of his car.'

SUSPICIOUS BEHAVIOR REPORT #13

'Albert Spellman'

Confidential sources are common in all investigative work, but this was the first time Rae had ever passed on information instead of using it to her own end. It is true I had found my father's behavior suspicious as of late, but I never thought beyond the wet hair, leafy greens, and attempts at heartfelt chats about life and death. I was purely of the school of thought that Dad was going through yet another REAFO. But after opening Dad's glove compartment, I determined that the suspicious behavior report needed an upgrade.

I found three child-proof pill bottles with prescriptions from a Dr. Nate Glasser at the California Pacific Medical Center. I slipped the bottles into my pocket (Mom and Dad weren't due home for another three days) and re-entered the house. I pressed the Pause button on the remote control and asked Rae if she had researched anything on the internet. She said she hadn't; she was afraid of what she might find out. I told her not to worry. I lied and told her I was certain that Dad was fine. It took tremendous discipline for me to avoid researching the prescriptions myself, but I waited until the next afternoon when I met Morty at Moishe's Pippic for lunch. [Our standing lunch date is Thursday, but I didn't want to wait, and Morty, as usual, was free.]

SUNDAY, MARCH 19

1100hrs [Morty likes to eat most of his meals on the early side.]

Morty ordered decaf coffee with his pastrami sandwich. I noted that the coffee-sandwich combo was perhaps one of the great symbols of our generational differences. I can think of few things more unappetizing. Then Morty did what he usually did after being served a cup of coffee. He burned his tongue on the brew and then put an ice cube in his beverage. He then started talking and forgot about his decaf.

'You mentioned on the phone yesterday that you had a favor to ask.'

'I was wondering if you could give me your son's phone number.'

'I thought you said he was too old for you.'

'He is. But I need to ask him about a prescription I found in my Dad's glove compartment.'

Morty wrote down the number, ate a couple of messy bites of his sandwich, and then tasted his coffee. In the interim the beverage had dipped into the lukewarm range and Morty, as usual, called the waitress over.

'Can you heat this up, dear?' he asked with a wink.

The waitress, Gayle, aware of Morty's beverage MO, hid her annoyance behind a fake smile, took the coffee behind the counter, and stuck it in the microwave.

'You are so predictable,' I said to Morty.

'You like lukewarm coffee?'

'Forget it.'

'Forgotten.'

The waitress brought back Morty's beverage and like déjà vu, Morty sipped the beverage, winced in pain, said, 'Too hot,' stuck an ice cube into the brew, talked some more about a recent bridge game, drank two sips of the coffee, and asked the waitress to heat it up again.

THE 'LAW OFFICES' OF MORT SCHILLING

Monday, April 24
1245 hrs

'You exaggerate,' Morty said, commenting on my retelling of his coffee temperature obsession.

'Every time,' I replied.

'Bah,' Morty said, waving his hand dismissively. 'Can we move on?'

'Sure.'

'So, did you talk to my son about your Dad's prescription?'

'Yes. The prescriptions were for lisinopril, Zocor, and Coreg. Your son said that those were the standard regimen for coronary heart disease. I explained my father's recent lifestyle changes and your son surmised that my dad was aggressively trying to avoid heart surgery.'

'Your mother didn't know a thing?'

'Had no idea. She knew he had a bit of a cholesterol problem, but that's it. She thought he had just decided to take care of his health. I mean, he hid the extent of his healthy activities. If he could go to the gym unbeknownst to her, or eat a vegetarian meal without her knowledge, he would. Because she would have known something more serious was up if she witnessed the extent of the turnaround.'

'So what did you do?'

Once again, I get ahead of myself. The case of my dad had priority, but I must admit the case of

John Brown was far more intriguing.

SUBJECT IS UNOBSERVED FOR THREE DAYS . . .

Monday, March 20
1830 hrs

Despite my constant vigil on Subject's residence, John Brown and his vehicle were not observed for three days following the St. Patrick's Day debacle. Without Subject to guide me in some direction, there was no place my investigation could go besides back to its point of origin. Since I had been made at the Excelsior residence as a book club wannabe with bad directions, I could not return for further information without raising a red flag. And so I turned to the only person I knew who was capable and willing to aid in my inquiry.

'What's my cover?' Rae asked.

＊　　　＊　　　＊

I stuck the listening device in my ear and watched from my car—parked approximately half a football field away—as my sister knocked on the door to 1341 San Jose Avenue.

The transcript reads as follows:

[Sound of knocking on door.]
MR. DAVIS: Can I help you?
RAE: Hi, my name is Mary Anne Carmichael. Is

Mrs. Davis home?

MR. DAVIS: No. Can I ask what this is regarding?

RAE: I'm a Girl Scout and I sold her some cookies a few weeks back. I wanted to deliver them and receive payment.

MR. DAVIS: You're not wearing a uniform.

RAE: We don't wear the uniform anymore. We're like nuns that way.

MR. DAVIS: She's not here. I don't know if I have any cash on me.

RAE: Do you know when she'll be back?

MR. DAVIS: No.

RAE: You don't know when your wife will be back?

MR. DAVIS: No.

RAE: I'm sorry. My parents got divorced. It's hard on everyone.

MR. DAVIS: We're not getting divorced.

RAE: Then why don't you know where your wife is?

MR. DAVIS: Because she's missing.

RAE: Have you contacted the police?

MR. DAVIS: Of course.

RAE: How long has she been missing?

MR. DAVIS: About two weeks.

RAE: Is there any evidence of foul play?

I appreciated the thoroughness of Rae's interview, but she was taking it too far. I dialed her cell phone.

RAE: Excuse me. [Rae answers her cell] This is Mary Anne.

ISABEL: Your cover was Girl Scout, not Inspector Poirot. Get out now.

RAE: [into phone] Yes, Mom. Yes, Mom. I heard you the first time. Good-bye. [to Mr. Davis] I'm sorry to hear what's happened to you. I hope things work out. You can have the cookies for free. Sorry to take up any of your time.

[End of tape.]

'Those cookies were like four years old,' I said to Rae as we headed back to the house.

'I know. That's why I gave them to him.'

'How did he look?'

'He looked concerned. He looked like he hadn't been sleeping. From what I could see of the interior of the house, it was a complete mess.'

My mind was racing in different directions. I tried not to connect Subject's meeting with Mrs. Davis and her sudden disappearance, but it was impossible to shake that association. Once again I was brought back to the same conclusion: I had to get into that locked office.

*   *   *

When Rae and I returned home, we checked our e-mails, hoping for an ETA on Mom and Dad's arrival the next day, but there was nothing from either of them. There was, however, a message from Petra.

From: Petra Clark
Sent: March 20
To: Isabel Spellman
Subject: No cell reception

Hey, I know you tried to call me, but I decided to go to a spa out in the Arizona desert here

240

and there's no cell reception. I'll be out of touch for about a week, but I'll call you when I return to civilization.

Not buying a word of Petra's communication, I promptly e-mailed her back.

From: Isabel Spellman
Sent: March 20
To: Petra Clark
Subject: Re: No cell reception
Are you telling me there are no land lines at your mysterious location? I understand that you're avoiding me, but why? I'm on your side. Seriously, Petra, call me back. I'm starting to worry about you . . .

OPERATION LOCKED DOOR
PART-III

Wednesday, March 22
0900 hours

Rae and I prepared for our parents' next day return by giving the house one final going-over. Under normal circumstances Rae and I would have trashed the place once again, but Henry's presence there had modified our usual behavior. He even forced Rae to clean out her closet. My sister and I only needed to tackle the stack of dirty dishes that had accumulated since Henry's departure, which was significant considering how little time had passed. As we scraped the food off

241

the plates and loaded them into the dishwasher, I realized that tonight would be the last time I could investigate (a.k.a. break into) Subject's residence without the watchful eye of the parental unit. There was no telling when they'd plan their next disappearance.

I noticed that in Subject's absence he had forgotten to close the window of his mystery room. In fact, it was the first time I had seen that window wide open. I saw it as an omen, an opportunity I could not waste. I waited until nightfall, put my cell phone on vibrate, and stuck it in my back pocket. I ran downstairs to Rae, who was making one final farewell (until next weekend) batch of Rice Krispies Treats. [I had relaxed the 'sugar only on weekends' rule since there were so many far more serious rules I had broken during my stay.] I dimmed the lights in the living room and guided my sister to the window.

'I don't think he's coming back tonight, but if Subject pulls into his driveway, you call my cell. Don't move from this spot until I tell you to.'

'What are you going to do?' Rae asked suspiciously.

'Don't worry about it; just call my cell if Subject comes home.'

I ran upstairs to David's old bedroom, pushed the east-facing window all the way open, took out the ladder that had failed me the last time, and stretched it across the six-foot divide between Subject's residence and the Spellman home.

The weight of the extended ladder, before it reached Subject's windowsill, almost toppled me over. But I threw my weight onto the end and managed to stretch the ladder out the final two

242

feet to reach Subject's office window, bridging the gap between the residences. By now I hoped the darkness outside would obscure my escapade.

I was conscious that my intended act was a felony, but my conviction in my quest outweighed whatever moral ambiguity remained. Simply, it was okay to break the law if it meant exposing Subject for whatever act he was guilty of.

I'm not afraid of heights, nor am I a thrill seeker (at least not in the bungie-jumping school of thrill seeking) but I was respectfully frightened as I crawled across the ladder that rested some fifteen feet above ground. My passage took no more than forty seconds as the metal rungs dug deep into my shins and knees. Only sheer adrenaline masked the pain that began to surface as I reached Subject's windowsill. I dove into the office head-first and collapsed on the floor, grabbing my legs in pain.

Once inside the forbidden room, I realized that I had forgotten a flashlight. I decided to risk turning on the overhead. The room consisted of an L-shaped desk with a computer atop the main part and two printers and a laminating machine along the side. One of the color printers looked like it could be used for making phony identification cards, although nothing evidencing that fact was in sight. I turned on the computer and as I waited for it to boot up, I tried the drawers on all the file cabinets. Locked. For the next ten minutes I picked the lock on the file cabinet closest to the desk. An envelope with a small stack of fifty-dollar bills, which I estimated to total five hundred [Another detail for the SBR: keeping large sums of cash handy.] dollars, and two credit cards in Subject's 'name' were inside. The bottom drawer of the file cabinet was filled with personal bills and invoices for his landscaping company. There was nothing out of the ordinary. There was also no reason why this room should be locked twenty-four hours a day.

I turned to the computer and looked for files, but Subject appeared to have used a program that wipes away all the files after each use. There had to be a backup hard drive that he worked off of. I assumed he kept the hard drive in one of the other locked cabinets, and so I started working on the lock.

Approximately fifteen minutes after I entered the office, my cell phone buzzed.

'What?'

'Get out now,' Rae said on the other end of the line.

'He's back?' I asked, as my heart started pounding violently inside my chest.

'Hurry,' she said, and hung up the phone.

I scanned the room for evidence of my entry. I turned off the computer, straightened the contents of the file cabinet drawer, and pressed the lock with my thumb. I hadn't anticipated a room so aware of a potential breach. The computer was erased, the file drawers locked, the waste basket empty. I realized as I was heading for the window that my prints were everywhere. I pulled the sleeve of my shirt over my hand and did a fast wipe, hoping to at least smudge all my prints.

Then I climbed out of the window and crawled back onto the ladder and across the makeshift bridge. The dismount of my circus act was a clumsy head-first collapse into David's old room. I was just about to fix my attention on the withdrawal of the ladder when I noticed Henry Stone sitting on the bed, looking positively furious, and Rae by his side, looking downright guilty.

First things first: Get rid of the evidence—other than the direct witnesses. I struggled to pull the ladder back into the room. Henry got up to help me once I yanked the ladder off Subject's windowsill and began losing control against the seesawing weight. He pushed me aside, pulled the ladder into the room, closed the bedroom window, and pulled the blinds.

He stared at me for an awkwardly long time.

'Rae, could you leave me alone with Isabel?'

'No, you snitch. You stay right there,' I said. Rae must have called him the second I defenestrated myself.

'Don't call her a snitch,' Henry snapped.

I turned to my sister. 'Where's your loyalty?' I asked. 'To Henry or me?'

Rae stared at her feet. 'It looked dangerous, really dangerous.'

'Leave her alone,' Stone demanded. 'Rae, give me a minute.'

Rae exited the room, knowing that my retribution would come one way or another. Stone sat down on the bed and took his time formulating his verbal barrage.

'I'm a police inspector and I just witnessed a felony. What am I supposed to do?'

'He's guilty of something, and when I find out what that is, you'll thank me.'

'Can you stop?' he asked. It was much more a sincere question than a directive.

'I don't think so,' I replied, feeling my eyes start to water, my grip on everything slipping. It wasn't a

245

question of my will or my discipline or my understanding of the law. I *couldn't* stop. I knew I wouldn't feel right unless I had the answer. Nothing else mattered besides knowing what John Brown was guilty of.

'Could you be wrong about him, Isabel?'

'Maybe,' I replied. 'I've misread evidence before. But I know what someone looks like when they're hiding something. He's hiding something really big.'

Stone appeared helpless, sensing that my resolve was something even I couldn't control. He got to his feet and headed for the door.

'This is no way to live,' he said.

'No kidding.'

Stone was about to say something else, but he simply shook his head and left.

That night Rae and I ate pizza for dinner and Rice Krispies Treats for dessert. Then we stuffed the pizza boxes into the recycling bin behind the corner store to hide the evidence.

I couldn't bring myself to observe Subject's residence anymore that night, knowing that if I witnessed any unusual behavior I would not be responsible for my own actions. Well, I would be— technically—but it wouldn't feel that way.

ARREST #1

My parents couldn't hide their joy at landing upon Spellman soil. I suspect they mistook each other's enthusiasm as that very simple happy-to-be-home feeling. A feeling I had not experienced in quite some time, what with me not having my own home and all.

My mother threw the suitcases inside the door and began her inspection. Rae [Planning on being late for school.] tailed her every move, asking innocent questions about the cruise, but covertly trying to make sure we hadn't missed anything in our clean-up. I, on the other hand, kept careful watch on Dad. We would have to talk about his secret soon enough. But I decided to give him time to settle.

*   *   *

When the doorbell rang, it was my father who answered it. I heard the initial exchange from the kitchen.

'Is Isabel Spellman here?'

'Can I ask what this is regarding?'

'Is she home?'

'Isabel!'

I walked to the foyer, unaware that I had just missed my last chance to escape. Not that escaping would have been advised.

'I'm Isabel. What's going on?' I said as I noticed

247

two uniformed police officers standing in the doorway.

'We have a warrant for your arrest,' the first officer said.

'Huh?' was my numb response.

My father reviewed the warrant. 'B and E?'

Dad turned to me with a dazed look on his face. I shrugged my shoulders, playing innocent for the time being.

'What kind of evidence do you have for this charge?'

'Foolproof evidence,' the second officer said. 'Mr. Brown had a hidden camera trained on his west-facing window and has a very clear recording of Ms. Spellman climbing through that window and searching the premises.'

My mother entered the room while the officer was outlining my guilt. It had been over twelve years since I committed an actual felony— rephrase, been *caught* committing an actual felony. My mother, unlike during my adolescent years, was unprepared for this moment. She simply gawked in disbelief.

'Is this true?' she asked.

'I can explain,' I replied.

'Stop talking,' my dad said.

Rae heard the commotion from her bedroom and ran downstairs. She watched as that first officer handcuffed me.

'*Oh, no,*' was all she said.

'Isabel Spellman,' the officer spoke in a monotone, 'you have the right to remain silent. Anything you say can and will be used against you in a court of law. You have the right to an attorney . . .'

Part III

Mysteries and More Arrests

ARREST #1

PART-II

Thursday, March 23
0900 hrs.

The last time I was in a holding cell was two years ago, when I 'assaulted' my sister after I found out that she had disappeared herself. Since Rae was unharmed and my motivations were of the sympathetic variety, all pending charges were dropped. I had no record. But if the B&E charges stuck, then I would have a record and I could lose my PI license.

I was arraigned four hours after my arrest and bail was set at five thousand dollars. Mom took another eight hours before arriving at the precinct and posting bail. I used that time to affect a demeanor of unapproachable but not confrontational to my parade of cell mates. In that half day's time, without any reading material to occupy my thoughts, I dwelled on the collection of suspicious behavior reports that I had amassed in the previous months and determined that three were worthy of an upgrade to a mystery. To refresh your memory, the list follows:

The Mystery of Mom

Evidence: Motorbike vandalism, unmet dental appointments, hostility toward oldest son, unexplained absences.

The Mystery of David

Evidence: Drinking before noon, grooming standards declining, wife has skipped town, constantly agitated, appears guilty of something, disappearing to a yoga retreat.

The Mystery of John Brown

Evidence: First and last names are conveniently common. Cannot establish a true identity under that name; Subject has offered conflicting dates and places of birth; Subject has responded suspiciously to almost all identifying questions; Subject keeps a secure room in his home for no apparent reason; Subject has been observed having contact with two women who later disappeared. Subject deliberately set me up for a B&E arrest. Why?

*   *   *

The case of my father was solved, although it still needed to be revealed to my mom. On the mostly silent drive 'home' with Mom, I contemplated whether I should tell her. I was so lost in thought that I didn't notice Mom was not driving to 1799 Clay Street, but instead pulling up in front of my old apartment in the Avenues.

'Your suitcase is in the trunk,' Mom said. As I was trying to understand her intentions, she clarified. 'You can't stay at our house anymore. Please don't make me change the locks.'

'Mom, you're not serious.'

'You just lost the last twelve hours of your life in jail—'

'Technically it's called a holding cell—'

'—for breaking and entering. I don't know what to say to you.'

'Don't you want to know why?'

'I don't care. You could lose your license. He could file a civil suit against us. We'd be ruined.'

'I'm sorry, Mom. But *I know* he's doing something he shouldn't be doing. I just want to find out what it is. Maybe help some people.'

Mom unlocked the car door. 'Please let the police handle it. Listen, it's late. I'm tired. The disappearance took a lot out of me,' she said. 'Call if you need anything. But you cannot come by the house for at least the next few weeks, until we sort things out with Mr. Brown.'

'What about work?' I asked.

'Your only case is the Chandler job. Try to channel all your investigative energy into finding the thugs who admire your work so much.'

'I have no idea what you're talking about,' I replied without my usual conviction.

Mom shot me a hard look and popped the trunk. I hoisted my suitcase out of the car and left it on the curb. I walked back to the passenger window and leaned inside. I tried to think of something to say that might justify my actions, but Mom got in the last words.

'You're thirty years old,' she said, rolling up the

window. I stepped back onto the curb and watched her drive away. Her exit line stung more than you might imagine.

I lumbered up the stairs to my old apartment and knocked on the door just to be safe. A deep, male voice grumbled, 'It's open.'

Through a fog of cigar smoke, I spotted five older 'gentlemen' seated around a kitchen table littered with beer and pretzels, playing poker. Bernie's face lit up when he saw me.

'Hey, roomie,' he said, getting to his feet. 'Why don't you give your uncle Bernie a kiss?'

Bernie approached with his arms open for an embrace. I zigzagged past him in a move that resembled something a running back might do and grabbed a beer out of the refrigerator. I noticed the pot of chips on the table. This was no friendly game.

'I could call the cops and shut you down,' I said.

'Sweetheart,' said a sixty-something man with the most chips. 'We are the cops.'

Bernie sidled up next to me. 'What do you need, Izz?'

'I need to sleep,' I replied, almost in tears.

'Take the bed,' Bernie replied. 'Me casa is su casa.'

'Su casa used to actually be mi casa,' I said. 'How long is this game going on?'

'Who knows? As long as we can stay awake and no one's got all our dough.'

'Good-bye,' I said. After a night in a holding cell, I could not face a night with Bernie and four other drunken ex-cops.

My parents, while I was on the inside, had parked my car at Bernie's legal residence. I decided to stay at a motel that night to clear my head. Apart from solving three mysteries, I had to find a place to live in a city where the percentage of vacant apartments hovers around four percent.

I spent the night at a Days Inn in the Avenues. Mom packed my luggage with the care she might show a cheating husband that she's tossing from the house in a fit of anger. I threw on some flannel pajamas and crawled into bed.

My mental landscape made sleep almost impossible. There was something about my mother's disappointment that flattened me. Putting everything in perspective, John Brown's secrets were not worth the cost of my family or my career. At least, I understood that intellectually. Sleep only came in the early hours of the morning, when my mind could process no more information.

UNSTAGED DENTAL APPOINTMENT #7

Friday, March 24
1600 hrs

Rae phoned my cell the next afternoon to suggest I meet her at Daniel's office for a tête-à-tête [She actually used that word.] about the recent goings-on in the Spellman household. Since all I was doing was camping out in a café, drinking far too much coffee, and continuing my fruitless background check on Subject, I agreed to meet her.

The debriefing began in the examination room

before Daniel entered.

'Has Dad said anything to Mom about his meds?' I asked.

'I don't think so,' Rae replied. 'How sick is he?'

'Don't worry about it. He's fine. He just has to take care of himself. I'm going to give him a little more time to tell her.'

Daniel entered the examination room. He performed a double-take when he saw me leaning against the corner wall.

'Isabel. What a pleasant surprise.'

'Hi, Daniel,' I said, and then I kissed him on the cheek. 'I needed to discuss some matters with Rae and I'm forbidden in the Spellman home, so we thought we'd meet here.'

'Why are you forbidden . . . scratch that question,' Daniel said wisely. He'd had enough Spellman drama to last a lifetime and would not seek out any more. Daniel put the bib on Rae while I dug for more details.

'Have you witnessed anything unusual from Subject's residence?' I asked.

'Dad went to talk to him this morning,' Rae said.

'Open your mouth, Rae,' Daniel said, the buzz of the handpiece whirring in the background.

'What was he doing?' I asked.

'Ooing ings oer,' Rae said.

'What?'

'Smoothing things over,' Daniel translated.

'Did it work?'

'Ahh on oohh.'

'What?'

'I don't know,' Daniel translated. 'Rae, are you flossing?'

'Every day,' Rae replied.

'Liar!'

'So, how angry are Mom and Dad?'

'Rinse,' Daniel said to Rae.

Rae spit a couple times in the sink and started talking before Daniel could get the scaler and mirror back in her mouth.

'Mom's pretty mad, but I've noticed that she's looking at John Brown differently. Sometimes I catch her watching him from the living room window.'

'Is she still keeping odd hours?'

'Last night I heard her leave at like two A.M.'

'Ahem,' Daniel said, clearing his throat. 'Is this dental exam interfering with your conversation?'

'No,' I replied pleasantly. 'Rae, open your mouth.'

Daniel spoke before I could continue my Q&A.

'Rae, you are aware that you get only one set of adult teeth, right?'

After he removed the handpiece from her mouth and Rae spit, she said, 'Is that a rhetorical question?'

The exam ended with X-rays that revealed four new cavities. In a kind of dental *Scared Straight!* Daniel sat Rae down in his office and showed her photographs of what happens to people who never brush their teeth. Rae then reminded Daniel that these were photographs of people who never actually went to the dentist. Then Rae asked a probing question.

'So, like, whenever I get a filling that's another place on my tooth where I can no longer get a cavity, right?'

Daniel concurred, but he didn't like where her argument was taking them.

'So, like, the odds of me getting a cavity decrease every time I get a filling because it reduces the overall area that a cavity could strike?'

Daniel said to good-bye to Rae and told her to schedule an appointment the following week to have her cavities filled. While Rae talked with Mrs. Sanchez, the receptionist, Daniel pulled me aside.

'Did you get your invitation?' he asked.

'To what?'

'My wedding. I mailed it over a week ago.'

'I had my mail forwarded and I haven't checked it in a while.'

'It's Friday June twenty-third. Think you can make it?'

'Sure,' I said. 'As long as I'm not in jail.'

That was intended as a joke at the time.

CHANGE OF ADDRESS

PART-I

That evening, before I found a bed to stay in for the night, I went to the Philosopher's Club to contemplate my options. I caught Milo chuckling to himself about some Olympics-related joke he was perfecting in his mind. I shot him a glance so loaded with hostility, he decided against sharing his witty creation.

'Can I sleep in your office tonight?'

'No.'

'Please.'

'No.'

'Why not?'

'Because I run a bar, not a motel.'

'You've been cranky lately,' I said.

'I've got things on my mind, beyond not making the Olympic team.'

'Would you get off that?'

'For future reference, Isabel: Don't talk to a bartender about how you never lived up to your potential. Okay?'

'Sorry, but to correct you, my problem is that maybe I *have* lived up to my potential.'

Milo served me a Guinness and then poured himself a shot of whiskey and sat down on a stool behind the bar.

'So, how are you doing?' I asked, making small talk.

'I could be better,' Milo said.

I didn't ask him to elaborate since I assumed 'better' meant he could have a better job, more hair, and fewer bills to pay. Milo's comment was the sort of thing anyone could say. I didn't read it beyond the flat surface; I simply echoed its sentiment.

'Me too,' I replied.

I finished my beer and left. I sat in my car for five minutes calculating my options: go back to Bernie's; drive across the bridge and stay with Len and Christopher; motel; sleep in my car; go to David's place. The final option seemed the wisest and I made the ten-minute drive.

I had not yet plotted the precise elements that caused my brother's recent decline. I assumed it involved infidelity followed by profound regret. Knowing that David was still at his yoga retreat and Petra was still AWOL, I didn't see any harm in breaking into their home and sleeping there. No one in my family hides keys. If you lock yourself out, you call someone who has the key or you break in. You don't leave a key sitting around for someone who doesn't have B&E skills to use.

I circled David's house looking for an open window. Everything was secure, as I predicted. I pulled a flashlight from my car and grabbed my picking tools from the glove compartment. David's front and back door have two deadbolts each. However, there's a basement entrance with only a single lock, which is out of the view of most of the neighbors. Five minutes later, I was inside David's house.

I poured myself two fingers of his fancy bourbon and sat down in front of his fifty-six-inch flat-screen TV on his ten-thousand-dollar suede couch. David's excess always offended me, but there was an unmistakable thrill I got from using his space without his knowledge. I suspect David got his own thrill from his later knowledge that my entrance into his home set off a silent alarm. Fifteen minutes after I sat down on his offensively expensive couch, there was a knock at the door.

I answered the door, drink in hand. When the uniformed officer told me to keep my hands up, I spilled some of the bourbon down my arm.

The second officer (at this point I can't even bother with names, descriptions, or ranks) took the glass out of my hand, spun the hand around my back, and cuffed me in one slick move.

'There's been a mistake. I'm Isabel Spellman. David's sister.'

'Ma'am, a neighbor observed you picking a lock in the back of the house and you set off a silent alarm.'

'I'm allowed to pick David's lock. Call him and ask him.'

'Ma'am, we have to take you in.'

'Please stop calling me 'ma'am.' '

ARREST #2

My long-winded explanation of my friendly B&E took nine hours to verify. I waited until two hours in, hoping that David would return the call to the police department before I did any name-dropping. But the prospect of another twelve hours in lockup was more painful than the prospect of facing my father. At 2 A.M. the captain on duty phoned my dad, who didn't arrive at the station until five hours later. I attempted sleep on a soiled cot in a fully-lit holding cell. When Dad finally collected me, I couldn't contain my hostility.

'What took you so long?'

'I went back to sleep,' Dad replied.

'Nice. You can forget about a Father's Day gift this year.'

'So. I'll have to buy my own bottle of Old Spice now?'

'How could you leave me in there?'

'I thought that maybe a night in jail would remind you that breaking and entering is a crime.'

'All I did was break into David's place. He wasn't even there.'

'If you don't have a key and an alarm code to a home, you shouldn't be entering it uninvited. This

261

is basic human behavior, which I should not have to explain to you at this point in your life.'

Dad parked his car in David's driveway, right behind my Buick.

'I know your little secret,' I said.

'What?' Dad replied.

'I found the pills in the glove compartment. I asked a doctor and he said—'

Dad grabbed the collar of my jacket and gave me a threatening stare.

'Not another word,' he said in a slow, throaty whisper.

'I know,' I whispered back to him. I have no idea whether it was my actual plan to blackmail Dad with his own health condition, but my tough-guy delivery certainly implied that.

Dad leaned in and whispered in my ear. 'Don't you dare say anything to your mother.'

'Or what?' I replied, feeling the hostility burning in my cheeks.

'You don't want to fuck with me, Isabel. Remember, I know where you live.'

'Really?' I replied. 'Could you tell me?'

I got out of the car and didn't look back. The collection of loose facts knocking about my brain took on an unrestrained volume. I had other things on my agenda at the moment: 1) Take a shower. 2) Find a place to sleep.

I drove to Bernie's for the shower. He was out cold in the bedroom. Based on the sheer volume of beer bottles and cigar butts around, I knew he would remain unconscious for a few more hours. I showered and changed in peace and hid his beer in the closet (my sad attempt at playing *Gaslight*) and departed, leaving only the scent of some fruity shampoo behind me. Bernie would wake thinking he spent the night with a woman, but wouldn't recall her name or what she looked like.

It was ten A.M. by the time I left Bernie's place. Since my only job was the Chandler vandalism case and Easter wasn't for another few weeks, I had time to kill. I drove to the library and spent the day with other homeless people. I found a nice spot in the medieval history section and took a nap. A few hours later, I called Morty and asked him if he wanted to meet for lunch.

I arrived at our usual deli shortly after one P.M.

'Any chance I can stay with you and Ethel for a few days?' I asked, conjuring my best urchin stare.

'The grandkids are coming tonight,' Morty replied, spooning ice into his coffee. 'If you can handle the noise, you're welcome.'

'No. That's fine,' I replied. 'I'll find someplace else.'

'You sure?' Morty said, taking a sip of his coffee.

'I'm sure,' I said.

Two minutes later, Morty summoned the waitress to heat up his decaf again. Four hours later, I was on the Bay Bridge, visiting Len and Christopher.

When I arrived, they were rearranging their couches and chairs in a semicircle facing an empty space. Christopher served me tea and said, 'To what do we owe the pleasure of this visit? Is there a gang member you would like me to impersonate? Blood or Crip? I need to know to choose the proper wardrobe.'

'I was wondering if I could stay with you guys a few days. My apartment needs to be fumigated.' [In fact, not a lie.]

263

'Of course,' Len replied pleasantly. And then he explained the furniture arrangement. 'And you get to see our at-home production of *Waiting for Godot*. We'll be performing it all week long.'

Two hours later, I was sitting in the Philosopher's Club, asking Milo yet again for a place to sleep, albeit this time it was a different place.

'Any chance I can stay at your apartment? I'll sleep on the couch and make myself scarce in the morning.'

'Sorry, kid. Out of the question. There, uh—I got some construction going on in my apartment. I'm staying at a motel.'

'What kind of construction?'

'Painting. Just go home, Izzy. Say you're sorry and behave yourself. What are they gonna do?'

I contemplated my options for the next three hours at Milo's. At eleven P.M. I drove back to 1799 Clay Street and noticed that the lights were out. I parked three blocks away and walked back to the house. I circled around back and climbed up the fire escape into my old attic apartment. I was so exhausted after my prior night in jail that I just slipped off my sneakers, got under the covers, and fell fast asleep.

SUBJECT GOES FOR A LATE-NIGHT DRIVE . . .

Sunday, March 26
0315 hrs

I woke to the sound of things opening and closing: car doors, trunks, front doors, screen doors, etc. There was an attempt at quieting the sounds, but car doors won't latch without an accompanying slam. (I have often wondered why automobile manufacturers have never tried to correct this obvious glitch.) Keeping the attic apartment dim, I pulled up the blinds just a bit to peek outside. Subject's residence was partially lit. Subject was awake. As he moved through his flat, he appeared like an element in a flip book being shuffled.

The view, obscured by the limits of the window, revealed Subject moving from office to foyer a couple times and then from foyer to car, parked in the driveway of his residence. I moved out of the attic and tiptoed down the stairs, trying to catch a view of Subject as he exited his apartment. The Spellman office door was locked, so I moved into the living room and watched Subject from an awkward angle out of the bay window. Subject was packing his car full of boxes. I watched for the next ten or fifteen minutes, trying to decide what I would do if he moved. My car was parked three blocks away. It would not be possible to reach my car and return undetected while laying in wait for Subject to move.

My mother keeps an extra set of her car keys on

a hook by the refrigerator. I took the key, returned to my bunker behind the couch, and watched Subject as he brought two more loads of file boxes down to his car. My father descended the stairs just as Subject entered his vehicle.

'Izzy, what are you doing here?' Dad said. I was too preoccupied with Subject's movements to notice the overly hostile tone in my father's voice.

'I got to go,' I said, still watching Subject through the window. 'I'm taking Mom's car. Shouldn't be long.'

'Isabel, don't!'

'Relax. I'll be right back.'

Dad shouted after me, but I couldn't make out the words. I jumped into Mom's Honda and sped after Subject's dented Volkswagen.

I tailed the VW up California Street over two hills, and into the Avenues. At four A.M., I stayed one car back and hoped that my mother's nondescript Honda Accord had never registered on his radar.

*　　　*　　　*

Note to the reader regarding the events that happened next: When one is performing surveillance, one's attention is virtually 90 percent on the subject, and the other 10 percent is on abiding basic traffic laws. Noticing if someone were following you while you were being followed would be almost impossible. That's how I missed Dad's car tailing me in the distance and that is how Dad, driving in his car, had time to call the police and give them my precise coordinates.

*   *   *

I heard the siren first, and then the blinding flash of the lights glared at me through my rearview mirror. The officers pulled up alongside my (okay, not my) vehicle and motioned for me to pull over. I pulled over. One officer got out of his vehicle while the other hung back and spoke to my father. The first officer approached the car I was driving as I rolled down the window. He asked for my license and registration. I didn't even have shoes on, so the license part was out of the question. I pulled the registration from the glove compartment and explained that I was in a rush and forgot my license, but the man driving behind me could verify that I was the daughter of Olivia Spellman, owner of the vehicle I was driving.

My officer returned to his vehicle and had a very brief chat with his partner and my father. He then returned to me and asked me to get out of the car. I obliged.

My bare feet chilled against the rough asphalt.

'Turn around and face the vehicle,' the officer said.

'Huh?' was my reply. But the officer spun me around before I could register what was happening.

He snapped the cuffs on me and repeated words that were beginning to become all too familiar.

'You have the right to remain silent. Anything you say can and will be used against you in a court of law. You have the right to an attorney . . .'

ARREST #3

There are few places besides one's home where flannel pajamas and bare feet are appropriate attire. Off the top of my head, I can't think of any, but I'm certain that a holding cell on Bryant and Third Street is not one of those places.

I replayed the last hour of my night as I contemplated my options for posting bail. I turned to my father when the officer cuffed me and shouted his name.

'Dad! What are you doing?'

Dad couldn't make eye contact. He returned to his vehicle, shouting over his shoulder, 'Not your car!'

All things considered I opted against phoning Mom or Dad for bail. I would have tried Morty had it been a more reasonable hour, but a phone ringing in the early hours of the morning in the home of an eighty-something-year-old man who likes his pastrami didn't sound wise. David was at the yoga retreat. And Petra, she was still AWOL, as far as I knew. Not that she was returning any of my calls. My life would have been so much easier those past few weeks if she had been around.

I waited until early morning and phoned the only person I could think of. Forty-five minutes later, I was sitting in his car in awkward silence.

'That's an unfortunate outfit for a holding cell,' Henry said plainly. Unlike members of my family, Henry seemed to derive no thrill from mockery.

'I know,' I replied.

'Where am I taking you?' Henry asked.

'There's a bag at my parents' house. Some clothes, shoes, my wallet, car keys. I have to get that first.'

Ten minutes later, Henry pulled into the Spellman driveway.

'I can't go in there,' I said.

'Wait here,' Henry replied, as he got out of the car.

While Henry was presumably gathering my belongings and firmly suggesting to my father that he drop the felony auto theft charge, Subject peered down at me from his window. It was a stare fraught with hostility. Perhaps he spotted me earlier that night and was saved only by my father's careful manipulation. Or maybe his glance was fear shrouded in hostility. Maybe I was close to something. Maybe he was afraid of me. But sitting there, with three recent arrests under my belt, I couldn't consider Subject's crimes. I had my own to worry about.

As I returned my attention to the front door of 1799 Clay Street, I spotted Rae exiting the house, carrying a paper lunch bag and a commuter mug of coffee. She got in the driver's side of the car and sat down next to me, handing over her offerings.

'I thought you might be hungry,' she said.

My sister's gesture was so precisely what I needed (minus the Pop-Tarts inside the paper bag) that I wanted to kiss her. Instead I patted her on the head and drank my coffee, trying not to let tears whose source I couldn't identify fall down my face.

'I'll keep an eye on him for you,' Rae said.

'Don't do anything, Rae.'

'I won't. I'm just going to keep my eyes open.

That's all.'

Henry opened the car door and swapped places with Rae.

'I got an A on my geometry test,' Rae said to Henry.

'An A?' Henry questioned suspiciously.

Rae sighed. 'An A-minus. It's still an A.'

'Good job,' Henry replied.

'I need to tell you something private,' Rae then said, and leaned in and whispered something in Henry's ear. He nodded in apparent agreement and then Rae shut the car door and waved good-bye.

Henry double-parked next to my car.

'If you need a place to stay, I have a guest room,' Henry said.

I was surprised by the offer. But pride ordered my response.

'Thanks, but I think I'll just go back to Bernie's. He'll sleep on the couch if I ask nicely.'

*   *   *

As it turned out, I didn't have to ask nicely. Bernie was nowhere to be found. I settled onto the couch and watched television all evening. At eleven P.M, bracing for Bernie's return, I phoned his cell to gather his E.T.A.

'Hey, roomie,' Bernie said when he picked up the call. The background noise was the unmistakable chaos of a casino.

'Where are you?' I asked.

'Tahoe,' Bernie replied as if it were obvious.

'When are you coming back?'

'Why, do you miss me?'

'Not even a little,' I replied.

'Such a kidder,' Bernie said. 'I'll be here for a while. My luck is looking good. You back at the apartment?'

'Yes,' I replied. 'Do me a favor and give me a call before you plan on returning.'

'What? I didn't get that?'

'Nothing,' I replied, and hung up the phone.

That night I changed the sheets, took a shower without locking the door, and slept eight hours in what used to be my own bed.

For the next four days I barely left 'my' apartment, knowing that this brief window of privacy would not last. I caught up on much-needed rest, decontaminated the apartment and researched 'John Brown's on the internet, hoping to find the one I was looking for.

But all good things must come to an end. Thursday afternoon, without providing the previously-requested advance notice, Bernie arrived at the apartment with his overnight bag and groceries.

'Roomie,' he said pleasantly upon entering our home.

'Bernie,' I replied, trying not to cry. 'I thought you'd still be in Tahoe.'

'It was to take a breather. Stay, Izz. Like I said, Me casa is su casa.'

'Stop saying that,' I replied, snapping just a bit.

'Like I said before, Izz, this place is big enough for the two of us.'

'It's a one-bedroom.'

'In some countries families of eight share a one-bedroom apartment.'

I chose to discontinue this line of conversation.

Instead I grabbed a bag of potato chips and a beer out of Bernie's grocery bag.

'What's with all the snack food, Bernie?'

'Poker game tonight. Are you in?'

*　　　*　　　*

Four hours later I was down two hundred dollars and a watch, which I'd thought I could parlay into motel money for the week. Bernie had apparently figured out my 'tells' [Squinting and tapping on a bluff, and a 'look of disdain' on a winning hand.] and shared them with his buddies.

'I'm out,' I said after my fourth straight loss. 'It stinks in here.' I got up and cracked a window.

I sniffed my own shirt. 'I smell like a cigar.'

Bernie's friend Mac pulled a bottle of cologne from his satchel and sprayed me.

'Hey!'

'It covers up the cigar smell. You'll thank me later,' he said. [No, I didn't.]

'So, how long do you think this game will last?' I asked.

'Now that you're out?' Bernie replied. 'Until morning, probably.'

It wasn't just the cigar smoke and the cologne and the wasted potato chips on the table and the volumes of empty beer bottles invading the apartment, but I looked around and knew that I couldn't spend one more night under the same roof as Bernie.

'I got to get out of here,' I said, repacking my suitcase.

'See you later, kid,' Bernie replied, and then he went all in.

272

I didn't stick around long enough to see whether Bernie won the hand or lost everything.

CHANGE OF ADDRESS

PART-II

Thursday March 30
2300 hrs

'Is the offer still good?' I asked, standing in the foyer—looking humbled and forlorn, I'm sure.

Henry Stone nodded his head and opened the door for my entry. I brushed past him into his immaculate home.

'You smell like a cigar,' he said.

'And cheap cologne,' I added.

Henry showed me the guest room, emphasizing the shower. The guest room, like everything else in Henry's apartment, had that five-star-hotel spotlessness. After Bernie's place, there was something oddly satisfying about being in an uncontaminated environment. I showered and went straight to bed. I awoke, eight hours later, as Henry was leaving for work.

He poured me a cup of coffee when I entered the kitchen.

'Make yourself at home,' Henry said, although judging by appearances he didn't make *himself* at home.

'Thank you.'

'I have just one rule—'

'Are you sure it's just one? Because it looks like

273

you have many,' I said.

'If you get arrested again, I'm kicking you out.'

'Fair enough,' I replied.

'And I have a few requests: Stay away from my neighbors—they're clean, law-abiding citizens—and, uh, try to keep your snooping to a minimum. I don't have any dark secrets, but I don't like people going through my stuff.'

'When will you be home?' I asked.

Stone smiled. The question was not so innocent.

'I'll surprise you,' he said, and left.

I couldn't resist a tour of Stone's house in his absence; I can rarely resist unsupervised tours. My previous visits to his residence included a break-in almost two years ago. I had assumed (for reasons I won't get into) that he was involved in my sister's 'vacation,' and so I was searching for evidence. The remainder of my visits, approximately half a dozen, had been for Rae extractions, which occasionally include a beverage, but never have I actually had the chance for a leisurely search of the premises.

After three hours of uncovering well-folded linen, suits hung professionally in litmus-test order, a refrigerator devoid of any mold (other than the cheese variety), a collection of books that appeared to have been read, an assortment of CDs and vinyl that ranged from the Ramones to John Coltrane to Outkast, [I'm pretty sure this was a gift from my sister so she'd have some music to listen to at his place.] an office with one locked file cabinet that presumably held seven years of financial data, and a computer that, on careful scrutiny, had never visited a porn site, I made lunch. I even washed the dishes and put them in the dish rack.

I read the newspaper for the next hour and filed through Stone's limited cable selection for two hours after that. As you might have concluded already, I have problems with activities beyond investigation, drinking, and participating in bizarre and doomed courtships. I routinely ignore my own character flaws, because usually there's some suspicious behavior diverting my attention. But when everything is suspicious and I'm expected to fill my days the way a normal unemployed person might, there lies the problem.

DOCTOR WHO?

Friday, March 31
1630 hours

At three-thirty p.m. there was a knock at the door.

'Rae, what are you doing here?'

Rae pushed me aside and said, 'We don't have much time.'

She then walked right up to the television and opened a drawer beneath it that I had somehow missed in my earlier combing of the premises.

'Sit down,' Rae ordered me, and since I had nothing else to do, I obliged.

She popped a disc into the DVD player and sat down on the couch next to me.

'What are we watching?' I asked.

'_Doctor Who._'

'Weren't you watching that the other night?'

'I was watching an old one. It's the new ones I

want to watch.'

'What's the hurry?'

'Henry will be home soon and he doesn't let me watch it.'

'Why not?'

'I already told you. Because he says I can't watch the new *Dr. Who* series until I watch *all* the classic ones.'

'That kind of makes sense,' I said, thinking that I wouldn't start watching the fifth (and sadly final) season of *Get Smart* unless I had watched the previous four.

'No, it's just cruel. Do you realize that the first *Doctor Who* was on the air in 1963? They've gone through ten doctors to date and there are over seven hundred episodes, most of which are super old. The "classic"—Rae used sarcastic finger quotes—'series is so outdated. The special effects are a complete joke. You can't take it seriously.'

'What's the premise of the show?' I asked.

'There's a doctor—'

'What kind of doctor?'

'He's just *the doctor.*'

'But he has to be some kind of doctor.'

'If he is, they don't say. Anyway, so the doctor travels through time saving the world from destruction.'

'And it's the special effects you can't take seriously?'

'It's a really good show. At least the new one is.'

'Why do you have to watch it at Henry's house? Why don't you just rent the DVDs and watch at home?'

'I tried that, but then as soon as Dad hears the music, he comes into the room and watches with me. And you know how that goes.'

'I hear you.' [Dad's one of those people who think television is interactive. We have tried to cure him of this vile habit, to no avail.]

'Besides, only the first season is available on DVD for the new series, but Henry has bootlegs of the second season.'

We simultaneously heard a key in the front door. Rae promptly pressed Play and handed me the remote control. She stared straight at the television, ignoring Henry's entrance.

The theme music had an oddly familiar refrain, but I was distracted by the sidelong look Henry gave my sister. It was as if he was deciding whether to reprimand her. I thought few things could make a better peace offering to my mother than the Stone and Spellman show, so I grabbed my digital recorder, turned it on, and slipped it into my pocket.

Rae and I watched the first forty-five-minute episode of *Doctor Who* in complete silence, while Henry presumably cleaned up whatever invisible mess I had made. When the episode ended, Rae pressed the Stop button and I slipped my hand into my pocket and pressed Record.

THE STONE AND SPELLMAN SHOW—EPISODE 42

'THE READING RULE AND THE MUCOUS MYSTERY'

The transcript reads as follows:

RAE: That was so much better than the 'classic' episodes. [once again with the rude finger quotes] The special effects in those old episodes are so cheesy.

HENRY: You're supposed to use your imagination.

ISABEL: I want to watch the next episode.

[I reach for the remote.]

RAE: You can't.

ISABEL: I think I can. Just press Play.

[Rae shakes her head in sad disappointment.]

RAE: You can't. For every hour of television you watch in Henry's house, you have to read for one hour.

[Rae walks over to the bookshelf, grabs a copy of Charles Dicken's *Our Mutual Friend,* and opens it to the bookmark, approximately halfway through.]

ISABEL: Is this a joke?

RAE: I thought so at first, but no. You should choose a book on your own, before he decides for you.

ISABEL: Rae, I'm a grown-up. Henry can't enforce this rule with me.

HENRY: Rae, do your parents know you're here?

RAE: They've probably figured it out by now.

HENRY: Call them.

[Rae picks up the telephone and makes the call. I press *Play* on the remote control. Henry removes it from my hands and presses *Stop*.]

ISABEL: You can't be serious.

HENRY: I understand there are few things that divert an undisciplined mind like yours better than television—

ISABEL:—I think that was an insult.

HENRY:—but I need to maintain some rules in this house, or she would never leave.

[Henry picks up a copy of Dostoyevsky's *Crime and Punishment* from his bookshelf and hands it to me.]

HENRY: It's just an hour.

[Ten minutes later: Rae is sitting next to me on the couch with her book as Henry prepares dinner.]

RAE: [whispering] Today, I checked Mr. Peabody's snot drawer and all the tissues were gone. But then during class, he blew his nose again and put the tissue in the drawer.

ISABEL: [at full volume] Why are you whispering?

RAE: [whispering loudly] I can't talk to him about the snot.

ISABEL: Why?

RAE: Because he thinks all collecting is the same.

ISABEL: I doubt he thinks stamp collecting and mucous hoarding are the same.

RAE: Shhh. But he thinks it's the same if you keep extra cereal around and you keep your mucous around.

ISABEL: [loudly] Henry, do you actually think Mr. Peabody's vile habit of saving his own used tissues is really the same thing as stockpiling unusual quantities of cereal?

HENRY: Are you ever going to get off that subject?

RAE: What I do and what Mr. Peabody does are completely different things.

HENRY: I'm not suggesting they're in precisely the same classroom of abnormal behavior, but I do think they're in the same school.

RAE: [to Isabel] See, I can't talk to him about this.

HENRY: Isabel, are you recording this?

ISABEL: Yes.

HENRY: I'm going to confiscate the tape recorder.

[End of tape.]

*　　　*　　　*

After five pages of *Crime and Punishment* Rae pressed the Play button and we watched episode two of the first series [The first season of the new series. Technically, not the first.] of *Doctor Who* (2005, BBC), 'The End of the World.' [In this episode the doctor and his sidekick, Rose, travel to the year five billion to watch the sun swallow the earth. But the real trouble is that there is a murderer amongst the aliens who have convened for the big event.]

During a brief lull in the on-screen conversation, I said, 'This show makes me want to get stoned and watch every episode back-to-back.'

Henry cleared his throat at the 'get stoned' comment. He got two beers out of the refrigerator and handed me one.

'Perhaps this will do.'

'Thank you.'

'Try to keep the drug references to a minimum around a cop and a minor.'

'Sorry,' I said.

'Shhh,' Rae hissed, her eyes like lasers on the television.

'The End of the World' ended and Rae checked her cell phone for messages.

'Got to bail,' Rae said.

'Where are you going?' Henry asked.

'To Ashley's house. They're ordering pizza tonight.'

'Call your mother,' Henry said.

'I'm not telling her about the pizza,' Rae replied.

'I don't *care* about the pizza. Just let her know where you'll be.'

'Oh, right.'

'Call her *now.*'

'You are so prehistoric,' Rae said while picking up the receiver.

*   *   *

Two hours later, after a dinner of salmon, wild rice, and kale, I washed the dishes while Stone dried and inspected.

'You missed a spot,' he said for the third time in a row.

'I really think medication would help you,' I replied.

'It might help you as well,' he replied.

'You really are oddly clean.'

'I know,' he said, as if this were his dark secret.

'And organized. Your sock drawer is unbelievable.'

281

'You snooped, didn't you?'

'You even smell like soap.'

'No, I don't.'

'A very nice soap, but soap. Yes.'

Breathing in the smell of Stone's soapy essence, I felt kind of dizzy. I handed him the final dish and opened the space between us.

'Did you learn anything else about me today?' he asked.

'As far as I can tell you're not that into porn.'

'Are you sure?' Stone asked, sarcastically. 'Men have very good hiding places.'

'I know all the hiding places,' I replied.

'Wow. You've had a busy day,' Stone said, scanning his home for signs of invasion.

'Relax,' I said. 'I didn't look all that hard. You're just not the type.'

'What type am I?'

'I really don't know,' I said. 'You're kind of like some alien life form.'

The mention of aliens reminded Stone and me that hours of *Doctor Who* awaited us. Since Stone, like an unprepared babysitter, was happy for any form of diversion from my usual diverting habits, he popped in the DVD and refrained from enforcing his alternating reading rule.

Snippets of conversation emerged in the midst of a series of close calls with the end of civilization.

Doctor Who

Episode 3: 'The Unquiet Dead' [The doctor and his sidekick, Rose, travel back in time and meet Charles Dickens and some zombies.]

'I had no idea you were such a geek,' I said authoritatively.

'Now you know,' he replied.

'Clever how you got Rae reading Dickens.'

'Isn't it?'

Episode 4: 'Aliens of London' [During World War II, a spacecraft crashes on Earth, spreading matter into the air that alters human DNA and causes gas masks to adhere to people's faces, and then they roam the streets of London saying, 'Are you my mommy?' Hard to explain. You should probably just watch the episode. Warning: It's surprisingly scary.]

'I need you to do me a favor,' I said.

'Other than giving you a place to crash?'

'Yes,' I said, turning to Stone. 'The last time I followed John Brown, he parked in front of this building for about an hour. A woman came out to speak to him—'

'I thought you were done with this,' Stone said, pausing the alien image on the screen.

'I am done. But you're not.'

I handed Stone a slip of paper from my pocket. 'This is the address of where he was parked. The woman, Jennifer Davis, has since disappeared.'

Stone took the slip of paper. 'I'm sure the police are investigating this matter.'

'Look into it for me,' I said.

'Why can't you just let this go?'

'The same reason you can't leave a dirty dish in the sink. It's just who I am.'

THE EXPERIMENT

Saturday, April 1

I awoke sometime after ten A.M to find my host, still in his pajamas, reading a newspaper on his living room sofa.

'Happy Birthday,' [Yes, April 1st is an unfortunate date for a birthday. I'll spare you the historical details.] Henry said as he looked up from his newspaper. He then put his bare feet up on his coffee table. It was an awkward shift, as if he had never done it before. 'I made you a cake,' he continued, nodding toward the kitchen.

'How'd you know it was my birthday?' I asked, following his gaze.

There was a coffee cake on the kitchen counter. Next to it, fresh-brewed coffee. Next to that, a coffee ring where a mug used to rest. Next to that, a sink full of dishes, presumably from the cake making.

'I don't know who you are, sir. But tell me what you've done with Henry,' I said in mock desperation.

'Very funny,' he replied, not moving his eyes from the newspaper. 'Just eat your cake.'

I poured myself a cup of coffee, sliced a large square of the accompanying cake, and sat down on the couch next to Henry.

'This is *really* good,' I said. 'Did you make it from scratch?'

'Of course,' was his only reply.

'How'd you know it was my birthday?'

'Your parents called early this morning,' he said as he took the fork out of my hand and gave himself a bite of cake.

I felt his forehead with the back of my hand.

'Should I call a doctor?' I asked.

'People can change,' he said giving me back my fork.

'What game are you playing?' I asked suspiciously.

'I'll make you a deal,' Stone said. 'I'll cut back on the cleaning-and-control-issue type things if you avoid all forms of surveillance.'

'For how long?'

'Until Monday morning.'

'It's only a weekend.'

'It's a start.'

Like my sister, I enjoy a good negotiation. But I needed to enhance the sacrifice on Stone's end of the bargain.

'Cutting back on the cleaning isn't going to work for me,' I said.

'What's your counteroffer?' Stone replied.

'A complete moratorium on cleaning. If the sink gets too full, I'll wash the dishes and dry them. There will be no inspection. Also, you have to wear your pajamas into the afternoon.'

'What if I have to go out?'

'Not my problem. And, one shower a day only. No shaving.'

'Be reasonable, Isabel.'

'It's my birthday,' I said.

Stone mulled over the terms of our negotiation. 'Let me make my demands clear,' he said, spelling out his final counteroffer. 'You can't go near any computer. You may not leave the house, unless you're accompanied by an adult (or Rae), and you may not use your cell phone unless I am within earshot.'

'Where's the trust?'

'There is none.'

'So is this like a bet with winners and losers?'

'No,' Stone replied. 'It's just an experiment.'

LOST WEEKEND REDUX

A storm came through the Bay Area in the morning. Outside, thunder roared and lightning followed. With our usual pastimes off the table, Stone and I briefly debated how we could occupy ourselves.

'We could go to the museum.'

'Nah.'

'The library.'

'Why?'

'The aquarium.'

'The aquarium? Are you trying to educate me?' I asked.

'It was a thought,' Stone replied.

We chose television to numb our respective minds and opted to continue our *Doctor Who* marathon.

A surveillance report on Stone and me would read something like this.

Lost Weekend—Day 1
1110 hrs

Henry Stone (hereafter referred to as Subject #1)

and Isabel Spellman (hereafter referred to as Subject #2) are observed sitting on a couch. Subject #1 is wearing green-and-navy-blue checked pajamas. Subject #2 wears red-and-green flannel pajama bottoms and a hooded sweatshirt. Subject #1 puts a DVD into the player. Subjects lean back and watch the television screen.

Subjects remain on the couch for the next five hours.

1230 hrs

A young woman, approximately fifteen years of age (Subject #3), with sandy blonde hair, wearing jeans, a T-shirt, a sweater, and a raincoat, rings Subject #1's doorbell. Subject #3 is granted entrance into Subject #1's home.

* * *

The fault with surveillance reports is that they rarely provide the soundtrack. And the following events require a soundtrack. I'll have to recount the details from memory since Henry frisked me for a recording device the moment Rae arrived.

'Happy Birthday,' Rae said upon entering the apartment. She then passed me a plastic bag that contained a birthday card and a one pound bag of Peanut M&M's. The card was one of the Hallmark-humor variety. 'Hey, you don't look your age . . . I thought you were older.' A ten-dollar bill accompanied the insult.

'Thanks,' I replied. 'I think I'll use it to buy a quarter tank of gas.'

But Rae wasn't interested in my response. She

promptly spotted the dirty dishes in the sink, noted the coffee cake on the counter, and gawked at Stone in his PJs. I'm fairly certain she has never seen him in anything that didn't button up and tuck in.

'Do you have the flu?' Rae asked Henry.

'No,' Henry replied. 'I'm going to get dressed.'

'I don't think so,' I said, blocking Stone's entry into the bedroom.

'It's afternoon. The deal was I wear the pajamas through morning.'

'No, the deal was you wear them until afternoon. Rae, what is afternoon to you?'

'Three o'clock,' Rae said, and then she darted for the television and opened up the DVD player to find out which episode we were on.

'Did you skip ahead?' Rae asked, looking betrayed.

'No,' I replied, turning Henry around and pushing him back toward the couch.

'When did you watch all of these?' Rae asked, doing some internal calculations.

'Last night and this morning,' I said.

'There's no way you were reading, too.'

'Your sister and I are conducting an experiment.'

'Well, if the experiment involves a *Doctor Who* marathon then I want in. I can't believe you did this without me.'

Rae, with a look of determination unmatched in her entire history, swapped out DVDs and plopped herself down on the couch, clutching the cushions to secure her place there.

'You're going to have to wait until I catch up,' she said, after locating the remote and pressing *Play*. 'Oh, and I *won't* be reading any books today,' she said authoritatively.

'What time is it?' I asked.

'One forty-five,' Stone replied.

I opened the refrigerator and grabbed a beer.

'Isabel, it's one forty-five,' Stone said.

'I know. You just told me.'

I took another beer out of the refrigerator.

'You'll have one too.'

Henry nodded his head toward my sister, silently trying to convey that he did not wish to set such an example for a minor.

'Relax, Henry. She's seen people drink beer in the afternoon before.'

'Shhh,' Rae demanded, staring at the television with rapt attention.

'Got any board games?' I whispered.

'Scrabble,' Stone replied.

'Of course you have Scrabble,' I said sarcastically. 'Get it. We have time to kill.'

1630 hrs

Final Score in Scrabble: Henry: 14,876 points; Isabel: 5,234 points.

Beer Score: Henry: 2; Isabel: 4

Episodes of Doctor Who *watched by Rae:* 5

Rae, finally realizing that these hours of bliss would not be snatched from her in the immediate future, decided to take a break from her viewing pleasure and test the limitations of this 'experiment.' She got up from the couch and announced that she was going to the store.

'I'll come with you,' I said. 'We need more beer.'

I threw a raincoat over my pajamas and slipped

on Henry's rain boots, which were by the front door. The nearest corner shop was about two blocks away. Rae and I decided to walk in the cold, damp air. I tucked my pajama bottoms into the boots and stomped through the puddles on the way to the store.

'Would you stop that?' Rae demanded, as she dodged my splashes of water.

I didn't stop.

'Grow up, Isabel.'

I circled the next puddle and said, 'I'm going to let you in on a secret: People don't grow up like you think they do.'

Rae sighed and said, 'What are you talking about?'

'The whole grown-up thing is a myth. Whatever is wrong with you now will probably be wrong with you in twenty years.'

'There's nothing wrong with me now,' Rae replied.

'If people really grew up, there would be no crime, no divorce, no Civil War reenactors. Think about it. Was Uncle Ray a grown-up? Does Dad always behave like a grown-up? It's all bullshit. I can't tell you what Mom's been doing lately, but I will say, *not* grown-up.'

'I miss Uncle Ray,' my sister said.

'Me too,' I replied.

It had been a while since his name was mentioned. Silence washed over us as we reached the corner shop. I tried not to think of Uncle Ray as being gone forever. I just liked to imagine him on one really long Lost Weekend. I welcomed the distraction of choosing beer.

After Rae and I bought our provisions we strode

back to Henry's house on the rain-soaked sidewalk. I stomped in a puddle one more time to take Rae's mind off her uncle. I could read from her sober expression that tears might surface if she let them.

'I asked you to stop that,' Rae said, dodging the splash after the fact.

'Sorry, I forgot,' I lightly replied.

'Henry's a grown-up,' Rae said after a long pause.

I didn't have any evidence to the contrary, so I let that one slide. 'Maybe,' I said. 'But my point is it's not like you think it will be, that one day you'll wake up and realize that you've got things figured out. You never figure it out. Ever.'

'So is there any benefit to getting older?' Rae asked.

'Sure,' I said. 'You can buy your own beer.'

Five minutes later we were inside Henry's house, dropping our shoes and raincoats in the foyer. I scanned the room for signs of order, but it appeared Henry had left all items in their place, out of place. He did, however, dress while we were out. There was nothing overly formal about Stone's attire, but the tucked-in oxford shirt under the blue sweater looked a touch too college-lecturer for me.

'No shoes,' I said to Henry, looking down at his loafers.

'I don't recall our deal involving complete wardrobe control. Do you?'

'Untuck this,' I said, reaching under his sweater and pulling the tails out of his pants. Henry smacked my hands away.

'I got it,' he said, finishing the job.

'That's better.'

Rae unpacked her groceries and began melting butter in a saucepan.

'Rae, what are you doing?' Henry asked, looking concerned.

'There's only one conclusion to draw from these three ingredients,' my sister replied. 'Rice Krispies Treats.'

'Are you planning on cleaning up after yourself?' Henry asked, imagining pots and pans taking over his kitchen like an alien invasion.

My sister, accurately judging the temperature in the room, replied, 'Eventually.'

I won't bore you with a detailed retelling of the next twenty-four hours. Suffice it to say, it was more of the same. The following are the highlights, which can be illustrated with attributed bits of conversation.

1830 hrs

RAE: Izzy, want another square [shorthand for RKT]?
ISABEL: No, but Henry will have one.
HENRY: No, thank you.
ISABEL: I wasn't asking. I was telling.

1930 hrs

RAE: I *hate* the Slitheens. [Wormlike creatures that fit into human bodysuits as a disguise and are frightfully gassy.] I really, really hate them. They're so disgusting. Frankly, I prefer the Daleks. [Evil alien beings that resemble a cross between a bronze R2-D2 and a thimble, with a gooey squid center on the inside. They appear to pose the greatest risk of ending humanity.]

ISABEL: But the Slitheens aren't as big a threat as the Daleks.

RAE: The Daleks are really scary, but I don't hate them in the same way. Henry, who do you hate more?

HENRY: They're fiction. I don't *hate* either.
[Rae accidentally spills a bowl of pretzels onto the coffee table. Henry reaches to clean it up.]

ISABEL: Leave it.

HENRY: Are you going to clean it up?

ISABEL: Later.

2100 hrs

RAE: This is fun. We should do this every weekend.

HENRY: When will you do your homework?

RAE: You are so prehistoric.

ISABEL: I think I'll have another beer.

HENRY: Me too.

ISABEL: Really?

HENRY: Rae, how will you get home?

RAE: I thought I'd use the Tardis. [The aforementioned time-travel call box.]

HENRY: Call home. We can't drive you.

RAE: I'm not ready to go yet.

HENRY: Isabel, hand me the phone.

ISABEL: This is so great. The experiment is working. You're, like, totally lazy.
[I hand Henry the phone. He calls the Spellman house.]

HENRY: [into phone] Hi, Olivia. It's Henry. Rae's

293

going to need a ride home sometime this evening. I've had a couple beers and can't drive. Isabel can't drive either. Yes, she's here. I thought you knew that. Isabel, why didn't you tell your mother that you were here?

ISABEL: Because she had me arrested for grand larceny just because I borrowed her car.

HENRY: You heard that? Anyway, can you pick up Rae? She's been here about twelve hours already. [pause] We've been watching TV and eating Rice Krispies Treats. I'm fine. I'll see you later.

*　　*　　*

One hour later Henry's doorbell rang. I answered it to encourage Henry's slothfulness. My mother and father were standing in the foyer. Mom handed me a card which presumably contained an amusing insult about my age and a check for a not-insignificant amount of money.

'Happy Birthday, dear. This should keep you out of trouble for a while . . . I hope,' Mom said as she kissed me on the cheek.

Dad followed up with a hug and suggested we have dinner sometime next week.

Both parents brushed passed me and took in the spectacle of Henry's disordered home on their own.

'You know it still only requires one adult for a Rae extraction, right?' I said.

'We were worried,' my father replied.

'I'm fine, Dad.'

'Not about you,' Mom said. 'Henry.'

'Henry, is everything all right?' my dad asked the

294

new-and-improved Henry.

'Oh, yes. Everything's fine. Isabel and I just came to an understanding.'

Rae packed up her Rice Krispies Treats in plastic wrap.

'What kind of understanding?' Mom asked suspiciously.

'Olivia, it's nothing. We're fine. Rae just needed a ride home.'

'Ready?' Dad asked Rae.

'Yeah. I'll be back tomorrow. Ten A.M.' Rae said. '*Don't* even think about starting without me,' she added with the tone of a severe warning.

Mom and Dad shared a silent, baffled communication. Mom sat down on the couch next to Henry and whispered loud enough for me to hear. 'We can take Isabel away too. Just say the word.'

'We're fine. Isabel is fine. I'm fine.'

'You have my cell number,' Mom said. 'Call anytime. We're here for you, Henry.'

LOST WEEKEND REDUX

DAY-2

Sunday, April 2

Day two was almost an exact replica of day one, except Henry refused to drink any beer and Rae arrived an hour earlier. In the afternoon, when Stone was finally allowed to change out of his pajamas, Rae and I were alone on the couch. The conversation began innocently enough, but my Lost Weekend was simply a minor diversion from my primary focus, which I could not jar out of my head.

'I *love* the tenth doctor,' Rae said after we watched our sixth episode of *Doctor Who* that day. Interestingly, the actor playing the doctor had changed between the first season and the second. The transition was remarkably smooth. Still, I wasn't as convinced of the tenth doctor's superiority over the ninth as my sister was.

'You only like the new doctor because you think he's cuter than the first,' I said.

'He is cuter.'

'No, he's not,' I replied. 'In your opinion he's cuter. But it's not an absolute truth.'

'You like the ninth doctor better than the tenth doctor?' Rae asked in shock.

'Totally,' I replied.

'Okay. Let me rephrase the question: Do you think the ninth doctor is better looking than the tenth?'

'Yes, I do,' I replied.

'You can't be serious. Look at his ears.'

'Would you stop talking crap about *my* doctor?' I said in mock anger.

'Whatever,' Rae replied, turning back to the television. I pressed Pause and hoped to switch subjects briefly, while Henry was out of earshot.

'I need you to do me a favor,' I said in a whisper.

'What?' Rae whispered back.

'Are we using any of the GPS devices right now?'

'Mom might be using one, but the other is available,' Rae replied.

'I need you to sneak one on Subject's truck. Be

very careful. If anyone catches you, I am in big trouble.'

'What's in it for me?' Rae asked.

'Name your price.'

'Fifty.'

'Forty.'

'Deal.'

Henry entered the room and Rae covered like a professional. 'I can't believe you think the ninth doctor is cooler than the tenth.'

*   *   *

Judging by television and film, the life of the PI is filled with gadgets and high-tech devices worthy of top-secret organizations. We disabuse clients of this notion all the time. In truth, my job is far less *Mission: Impossible* than one might imagine, but modern invention has pushed a few tricks up our sleeve, and based on my recent arrests, I needed to resort to tricks.

My parents had recently acquired two GPS tracking devices. You're probably wondering why I hadn't used these sooner. While it might be fun and all to know where Subject is going, what I really want is to know what he does when he gets there. GPS systems are great for tracking individuals, but not for monitoring their activities.

THE PHILOSOPHER'S CLUB

Later that night, after Henry and I got Rae home safely, I insisted we drop by the Philosopher's Club. Henry and I sat down at the bar. Milo nodded pleasantly at Henry.

'What can I get you?'

'Club soda,' Henry replied.

'Whiskey for me. Isn't this great? I've always wanted a designated driver.'

Milo poured the club soda and whiskey and served the drinks. Then he leaned over the bar in front of me and made bored but direct eye contact.

'Izzy, tell me something,' Milo said. 'What does the sign outside say?'

' "We reserve the right to refuse service—" '

'The other sign.'

' "Use other door." '

'No, Izzy, the big fat neon sign out front.'

I stared at Milo quizzically, unsure what sign he was referring to.

'You mean the sign that says 'The Philosopher's Club'?'

'That one,' Milo said, pointing at me like I was a contestant on a game show.

'It actually says "he hilosop er's Clu,"' I corrected, having many a time mentioned the fading neon to my friend.

'But it does not say 'The United States Postal Service,' does it, Izz?'

'Not since I last checked,' I replied, finally following Milo's conversational thread.

Milo collected a pile of mail from behind the bar

and dropped the stack in front of me.

'You had your mail forwarded here?' Milo asked, even though the answer was plain as day.

'Thank you,' I said, looking through the collection. 'Sorry, I forgot to mention it.'

'What would possess you to have your mail forwarded to a bar?' Milo asked.

'I didn't want to go back to Bernie's and wasn't sure where I'd be staying. I usually drop by every few days. It was the logical choice.'

I separated the junk mail while Milo approached Henry for a chat.

'You seem like a nice guy,' Milo said. 'This one's trouble. You know that, right?'

'I do,' Henry replied nonchalantly.

'What is with you, Milo?' I asked, just as I spotted the unmistakable peach shade of a wedding invitation.

'Nothing,' Milo replied. 'Just making small talk. That's what we bartenders do. Oh, and deliver mail.'

Milo's bad mood prompted an early departure. On the car ride 'home' I played with the invitation, wondering how conveniently it could get 'lost' in the mail.

'Is your bartender always so hostile?' Henry asked.

'No,' I replied distractedly. When I thought about it, Milo had not been himself for weeks. I made a mental note to myself to ask him about that one of these days.

THE 'LAW OFFICES' OF MORT SCHILLING

Monday, April 24
1305 hrs

'My blood sugar is getting low,' Morty said, scanning the garage for something to eat.

Twenty minutes later, we were seated in a diner in the Sunset district. Morty wanted to skip the shop talk to aid his digestion, so his comments leaned in a more personal direction.

'You know who is a mensch?' Morty asked.

'*You* are,' I replied, thinking he was fishing.

'No, that cop fellow, the one that let you stay with him. He's a mensch.'

'I suppose he is.'

'You should give him your phone number.'

'He has my phone number.'

'You know what I'm talking about.'

'Yes, but I'm pretending I don't. Can we move on?'

'You're not so young anymore. And not all the fellas are comfortable with a woman with a record. Snatch that one up while you have the chance.'

'Morty, change the subject.'

Morty spooned ice cubes into his hot cocoa.

'That's enough,' I said, anticipating the upcoming act.

Morty looked like he was churning around some idea in his head.

'Why was your bartender angry at you?'

'He's not angry at me; he's just been cranky

lately.'

'For how long?'

'Like a month or two.'

'Has he gone through a cranky phase before?'

'Not that I recall.'

'Then why would he go through one now?'

'I don't know. He's getting older. He's tired.'

'You think we go along all happy and everything and then overnight we become rude because we're old?' Morty asked.

'I don't know. I didn't really think about it.'

'Remember, Izz, the world keeps spinning even when you're not around to witness it.'

'What's that supposed to mean?'

EIGHT BALL EASTER

Henry and my Lost Weekend ended on Monday morning when he shaved off two days of stubble; washed, dried, and carefully replaced every dish in its correct cabinet; and left the house, well-coiffed and tucked in, reminding me not to get arrested that day.

Another week passed in Henry's house without event. In fact, we fell into a routine that served me quite well. Henry would leave in the morning, while I perused the newspaper, pretending to be looking for apartment rentals. I would kill the day with various leisure activities—a trip to the coffee shop, a stroll in Golden Gate park, a few hours on the computer investigating John Brown, and even finishing that book I had started a week or so earlier. In the evening, when Henry returned home, he would cook me dinner and then clean up after me. I performed some token dish-drying, but he didn't like my method and firmly suggested I stop trying to help. At no point did Henry suggest that I was overstaying my welcome. So I stayed.

Tuesday, April 11

Based on anecdotal evidence the Copycat Vandals would strike any time between the night that Mrs. Chandler installed her tableaus and the date of the holiday for which they were intended.

Mrs. Chandler called me Tuesday afternoon to inform me that she had completed her latest installation, and that the surveillance should begin that evening.

Rae arrived at Henry's house later that afternoon.

'Is he here?' Rae asked conspiratorially.

'No,' I replied.

'I haven't had a chance to take care of that thing you wanted me to take care of.'

'He's not here, Rae. You can speak plainly.'

'Both of the GPSs Mom and Dad are using on jobs. One will be available tomorrow. So I'll get the device on Subject's car as soon as I can,' Rae said.

'The sooner the better,' I replied.

'I have to tell you something and it's a secret.'

'Shoot.'

'I've been checking his trash,' Rae said.

'For how long?'

'Since that first night we took his recycling. I've been grabbing it any chance I could get, thinking he might not always stay on top of it.'

'Do Mom and Dad know?'

'No; I sort through it, just to be sure, and then I put most of it out with our garbage the next day. He's usually pretty careful, but last night I found this.'

'What have you got there?' I asked.

Rae removed a plastic bag from her backpack. Inside it was a woman's blouse. Size medium. Blue with a ruffled collar. One of the buttons was missing.

'This is unusual,' I said, although what I was thinking was that it was unusual that Subject was careful for months and then slipped up like this.

My sister's discovery was intriguing, indeed, but so was her timing. I had to consider that I was being played.

'You found this last night in his regular trash?'

'Yes. Last night,' Rae replied, studying her shoes. 'I think you should probably resume your tail on him,' she continued.

Catching my sister in a lie is satisfying, but this lie would lead me to other lies, and I had to tread carefully so as not to alert her.

'I want you to keep an eye on Subject this evening. If he heads out, give me a call.'

'Where will you be?' Rae asked.

'Just a few blocks away at Mrs. Chandler's, so I should be able to catch him if he moves.'

My next question would solve one of the many mysteries that had plagued me in recent weeks.

'Rae, does your boyfriend have a motorbike?'

'How'd you know?'

'So, he has one?'

'Well, sort of. He has one, but someone's always messing with it, so it never works.'

I left Henry's place after eleven P.M., drove to Mrs. Chandler's and waited an hour and a half until Rae called as expected.

'He's on the move,' she said.

'Which direction?'

'He made a left on Polk Street.'

'I'm leaving,' I replied, although I didn't move an inch and I would have bet serious money on the fact that neither did Subject.

Ten minutes later, several young males drove up in a late-eighties-model Oldsmobile. They scanned the area for signs of witnesses and then proceeded to swap out Mrs. Chandler's basket of Easter eggs for eight-balls they had lugged in an old pillowcase.

The eight-ball swap was the simplest and least time-consuming of all the pranks on my résumé. The adolescent boys were done in five minutes and I followed their vehicle as two members of the three-person gang were dropped at their respective residences. The final member, Jason Rivers (Rae's mystery boyfriend), drove to his home in Noe Valley. Rivers stared longingly at the motorbike that would never work and entered his home.

MYSTERY!

Wednesday, April 12
1830 hrs

I chose to reveal my conclusions as they are unveiled in traditional drawing-room mysteries. I gathered the key players at Henry Stone's house the following evening, sat them all down on the couch, and allowed a pregnant pause to fill the room as I paced back and forth.

'Isabel, what's going on?' my father asked impatiently.

'I've solved the copycat vandalism case,' I said.

'Who did it?' Mom asked in anticipation.

'That's not how it's done,' I replied. 'Let me begin with the evidence. On Groundhog Day of this year, a series of adjustments to Mrs. Chandler's holiday tableaus began. The adjustments followed the same MO as a series of vandalisms that occurred during the nineteen-ninety-two-through-ninety-three season.

'While many individuals were aware of these capers, only members of this family and possibly Henry were privy to the details, which means there are only seven true suspects. Since I know I didn't do it, and let's face it, we know Henry didn't do it, that leaves only five suspects. Petra has been out of town for weeks now, which can be verified, so I know she didn't do it. That leaves me with four suspects: Mom, Dad, David, and Rae. Let's start with Dad . . .'

'Isabel, this is ridiculous. I was out of town over

St. Patrick's Day.'

'That was precisely the point I was going to make, although I was going to take my time doing it.'

'Can we move on?' my mother said.

'No,' I said sternly. 'We're going to do this my way.' I continued. 'Since Dad was out of town on St. Patrick's Day and Mom was out of town as well, I had to rule both of them out. Of course, David knew about the original vandalisms as well as anyone. But David was too depressed to have the follow-through and dedication required to commit these crimes. It's true he had no alibi, but I had to consider him innocent. The only suspect left was Rae.'

'I have an alibi,' Rae said.

'It's true,' I replied. 'I am your alibi. You were in the Spellman home the night of the leprechaun attack. But you're more clever than that, aren't you, Rae?'

'I don't know what you're talking about,' Rae casually replied.

I stared at my mother pointedly. 'Everyone in this room has something to hide,' I said shrewdly. 'I think it's time we reveal some of these secrets and then maybe we can all get on with our lives.'

'What are you talking about, Isabel?' Dad asked nervously.

'In good time,' I said, savoring the moment. 'You see, I had to solve another mystery to solve the case of the copycat vandals.'

'This is stupid,' Rae said. 'Can I watch TV?'

'No,' I said. 'Let's see, where should I begin? I guess I'll start with the evidence . . .

'Some time ago, I noticed that Mom was keeping

unusual hours. One night I decided to follow her, and when I did I found Mom doing the oddest thing. She was driving to Noe Valley and vandalizing a motorbike.'

Rae gawked in sudden comprehension. *'Oh my god!'* she shouted.

My father turned to my mother in confusion, and Henry Stone put his head in his hands and sighed.

'Dad, since you're the only person in the room who doesn't understand what's going on, let me clue you in. Rae has a boyfriend—'

'What?' my father said in disbelief.

'Let me finish. Rae has a boyfriend named Jason Rivers. She told Henry about this boyfriend four months ago when they started hanging out. As you know, she tells Henry everything. Henry didn't like having key information like this all to himself, so Henry told Mom, because he felt it was the kind of information a mother should have. But he also emphasized to Mom that he didn't want his broken confidence revealed.

'Mom, equipped with the boyfriend's name, got an address from the school directory and began an informal tail on the young man. Discovering that this young male had a motorbike, and not being able to discuss young male with daughter and tell daughter in no uncertain terms that she was not to ride on said motorbike, Mother let air out of the tires, siphoned gas, put gum in the ignition, and did anything she could think of so that motorbike would not work.

'I solved the copycat vandal mystery perhaps a week or two ago. But then yesterday, it was confirmed. The person responsible for the copycat vandalism is Rae Spellman.'

I paused for dramatic effect and then pointed at my sister.

'But you're my alibi,' Rae said in desperation.

'I'm not saying you committed the act, but you were the mastermind behind it.'

I turned to my mother and father and laid out all the facts that made my conclusion obvious.

'I caught three boys in the act last night. One of whom was Rae's boyfriend. Rae had heard about these pranks for years. It's safe to say she had the details memorized. The only problem was, when I got the job, Rae had to find a window of time when I wasn't on the case for her pawns to strike.

'On St. Patrick's Day, she waited until I was laid up in bed from a rib fracture. Then there was last night. I won't go into the details, but Rae tried to distract me with another job. I didn't bite. I stayed on the Chandler residence and that's when I found the boys in the act.

'Case closed,' I said, as my family and Henry stared at me in disbelief.

Rae stood up and held out her hand. 'Well done,' she conceded.

My mother turned to my sister and asked the obvious question: 'Why?'

'I don't know. Jason was talking about toilet-papering her yard after he saw her Christmas decorations and I thought that was so lame and boring. And then I told him about Isabel's pranks—'

'I have no idea what you're talking about,' I said.

'Would you stop that?' my dad snapped.

'The more I told them, the cooler the idea seemed,' Rae continued. 'It was kind of like an homage.'

'Good word,' Henry said, 'although I do *not* approve.'

Dad turned to Rae. 'Pumpkin, this crime will not go unpunished.'

'I wouldn't expect otherwise,' Rae stoically replied.

'Are we done here?' my mother asked.

'No,' I answered flatly. 'There is one more thing I need to get off my chest.

'Mom and Dad. You both hate the vacations. If you're doing them for each other, stop. I have the e-mails to prove that neither of you had good time on either of those trips.'

Rae groaned like she was the victim of a stabbing, knowing that her parent-free weekends might never come again.

My stunned family filed out of Henry's apartment in almost silence.

As Rae brushed past me, I whispered the obvious question: 'Did you really find that shirt in Subject's trash?'

Rae shook her hread in the negative and stared at her feet. 'Sorry,' she said. 'You gave me no choice.'

Dad was the last to leave, so I pulled him aside.

'You have twenty-four hours to tell Mom what I found in the glove compartment of your car. After that, I tell her.'

*   *   *

I presented the above episode of *Mystery*! in Technicolor because it was a case or a series of cases that I actually solved. I use the above episode to illustrate that I do have some skills of deduction that are perhaps better than average. Sometimes the evidence comes too quickly or one believes they've solved the mystery before all of the evidence is in. In those cases one might—meaning I might—take those new pieces of information and fit them into a theory that I've already imagined in my mind. This doesn't mean I'm lousy at my job, it simply means that even when I gather all the relevant facts, I might force them into a puzzle that looks right on the surface, but has a few pieces left in the box.

THE DAY AFTER

Thursday, April 13
1610 hrs

Rae knocked on the door to Henry Stone's apartment. When I unlocked the deadbolt, Rae pushed past me, grabbed the second-season DVD from beneath Stone's television console, and popped it into the player. Before she pressed the Play button on the remote, she said, 'I took care of that thing you wanted me to take care of.'

'You put the tracking device on Subject's car?' I asked.

'Yes,' she replied. 'You can put my payment in the outside pocket of my backpack.'

'Do Mom and Dad know you're here?'

'Shhh.'

'Have you told your boyfriend yet that the jig is up?'

'Shhh.'

'Are you planning on confessing to Mrs. Chandler or will I do that for you?'

'Shhh.'

Rae was clearly done talking. Only 'Can I get you a snack?' elicited any response.

'There are some Cheetos stashed behind the five-pound bag of brown rice in the pantry. And I'll take a glass of orange juice.'

Three episodes and two hours and fifteen minutes later, Henry arrived home. Rae ignored him, staring at the credits on the screen. Remember, Henry told Mom that Rae had a boyfriend—a fact that was conveyed in confidence. Rae's cold shoulder put a frost on the entire room.

Henry sat down on the couch next to Rae. She didn't even try to hide the bag of Cheetos or the bright orange dust that was settling on his couch and coffee table. Their brief conversation went like this.

'Rae.'

'Henry.'

'I can see you're upset.'

'You betrayed my trust,' Rae said, finally looking him in the eye.

'You ran me over,' Henry replied.

'Oh, right,' Rae said. 'Clean slate?'

'Deal,' said Henry, and then they shook on it.

Later, Henry explained to Rae that there were certain kinds of information of which he was uncomfortable being the sole recipient. In the future, he would give her the heads up if he planned on revealing any confidence.

*   *   *

The simplicity of their settlement struck me as beautiful. I counted all the relationships in my life and none were quite as perfect as this one. Henry loosened his already-loosened watchead rule and Rae spent the evening finishing the second season of *Dr. Who*.

'If you could time travel, where would you go?' Rae asked me.

'I'd go into the future and find out what Subject was up to. Then I'd go back in time and stop him.'

'You're so predictable,' Rae said.

'I know,' I replied.

*   *   *

On the drive back to the Spellman residence, Rae confirmed that our father had finally revealed his medical condition to Mom.

'How'd she take it?' I asked.

'She said if he even looked at a French fry the wrong way she'd file for divorce.'

With that incident settled to my satisfaction, I decided to pump Rae for information that was not as easy to come by.

'Remember when you were giving Henry his space?'

'Oh, I remember,' Rae said, as if it was a traumatic event she did not wish to revisit.

'Right before I told you to leave him alone, I caught him in my bar one night. He was upset about something but wouldn't tell me what it was. Do you know?'

'Yes,' Rae replied.

'So spill it.'

'I'm going to need some incentive,' Rae replied.

'What do you want?' I asked.

'Free reign on Henry's DVD collection . . .'

'Done.'

'And,' Rae continued, 'make sure I've got some snacks around for my after-school visits. You can hide them on the bottom shelf in the linen closet. He won't look there.'

'He will if he starts getting ants.'

'Those are my terms,' Rae replied as I pulled up in front of the Spellman home.

Rae and I shook on the deal and then Rae revealed her information: 'This is what happened. Henry's wife left him about two years ago. She moved to Boston or something. A couple months ago she came back hoping to reconcile. Henry needed some space to make the decision. Anyway, he decided he wanted a divorce. Which is a really good thing, because I hate her.'

'Have you met her?'

'No.'

'Henry told you all this?'

'Of course not,' Rae replied. 'Henry doesn't tell me anything.'

'So, how did you acquire this information?' I asked.

'Through my keen powers of deduction and a thorough search of his residence,' was Rae's cagey reply. 'Thanks for the ride.'

Dad exited the house as Rae got out of the car. He approached the driver's-side window, looking a little too serious for my liking.

'Isabel.'

'Dad.'

'I got John Brown to drop the B&E charge.'

'How?'

'I told him to file a restraining order instead.'

'Brilliant idea. Why didn't I think of that?'

'This gives you a second chance. Do *not* disappoint me.'

Dad handed me an envelope. 'You've been served,' he said.

THE DOT

Tuesday, April 18

Without a doubt the restraining order put a cramp in my investigation of Subject. I was reduced to surveillance from afar, following a dot on my computer screen. For the four days, I tracked Subject's whereabouts, hoping to find a break in his pattern that might lead me to the truth. But his pattern remained predictable. Other than his galaxy of community gardens and landscaping clients, Subject stayed within his usual stomping grounds. There was, however, one address across the Golden Gate Bridge that I found suspect. When I arrived at the site the day after observing the Dot, it seemed obvious that it was the home of a client, based on the quality of its surrounding garden.

That afternoon, I returned to Henry's house and tried a reverse directory search on the address. The chain of ownership was hard to follow and the records appeared to have been set up purely to confuse. My cell phone rang, interrupting my internal deliberation.

'Isabel?'

'Yes.'

'Why haven't you RSVP'd to my wedding invitation?'

'Who is this?' I said, even though the caller ID told me exactly who it was. I said it to buy time.

'Daniel.'

'Oh, Daniel. Right. We'll, it's just that I've gotten so many wedding invitations this month. It's hard to keep track of them all.'

'Sophia thinks you're short on manners.'

'I am, aren't I?'

'Yes,' Daniel replied. 'But there's no reason for her to know that. Please send back the card. Will you be bringing a date?'

'I'm not sure.'

'If you're not, then I have a few friends I'd like to introduce you to—'

'Yes.'

'Yes, what?' Daniel said.

'Yes. I'll be bringing a date.'

DISAPPEARANCE #3

Even after my sister's e-mail deceptions were exposed, she did not give up on pushing her disappearance agenda on my parents. Rather than play each side of the coin, she brought the two sides together and suggested they try something simpler. Rae went online and found a four-star spa resort in Big Sur, California. No planes, boats, or extended car rides required. They could arrive at their destination within two hours and live in the lap of luxury for three days. My parents agreed

315

and Rae booked the rooms for that weekend.

My parents, not to be outwitted by their almost-sixteen-year-old daughter, made certain that their disappearance did not have the beneficial by-product of an adult-free weekend for Rae. My mother, after discovering David's return to the city, insisted that he stay at the house for the weekend with his youngest sibling. David, still tormented by whatever he had done, welcomed the escape from his own home.

I phoned Petra yet again, and two days later the call was still unreturned. I then sent her another e-mail, which received an auto-reply that she would be out of communication for the next week. Had there been no other mysteries on my agenda, I would have flown to Arizona to track her down. When I questioned David on the subject, he claimed he had no idea of her whereabouts. His direct, but depressed, eye contact indicated that he was telling the truth.

MORE DIGGING

Thursday, April 20
1730 hrs

Perhaps it was all the dead ends that prompted the next phase of my investigation, but it occurred to me that Subject's profession might have provided him the ultimate cover-up. With dozens of gardens, soil, shovels, and acres of land in his evil but capable hands, how hard would it be to dispose of the bodies? Did I truly believe Subject was a murderer? I wasn't sure of anything, but I did know that women had disappeared. They had to be somewhere.

During the past week, I shadowed Subject after the fact, arriving at his gardens late at night with a flashlight and a shovel. I searched for areas of fresh soil that somehow appeared out of place in the landscape. Had I any actual knowledge of gardening, it probably would have been easier for me to spot the incongruities. That said, I probably dug up at least a dozen holes in half as many gardens over the next week.

When I returned to Henry's place, I would change clothes in the backseat of my car, which is something I'm oddly adept at. If Henry saw the dirt, he would be suspicious. Unfortunately, one night, Henry was returning home as I was in the middle of a car change. He approached the window as I was buttoning up my pants. I opened the door, just a crack.

'Can I have some privacy, please?' I shouted.

Henry backed away. I could tell from his expression that he was going to require an explanation. Sometimes in cases such as this, the simplest answer is the best, even if it doesn't make any sense.

'What were you doing in your backseat?' Henry asked, after I exited the vehicle.

'Changing my clothes.'

'Why?'

'I didn't like what I was wearing.'

A sigh, followed by silence. Henry unlocked the front door.

'Can you do me a favor?' he asked.

'Sure,' I replied, glad to have him off the subject

317

of my clothes.

'Please stop telling the neighbors that you're my life coach.'

'I had to tell them something. They were looking at me funny.'

'Now they're looking at me funny,' Henry said. 'Why don't you just tell them you're my friend?'

'I hadn't thought of that,' I replied. Sometimes the simplest truths escape me. Like the phone call that happened the following day. If I had really been paying attention, I would have realized it was not a friendly invitation.

Friday, April 21
1800 hrs

'Hello,' I answered on the third ring.

'Meet me at Twin Peaks in forty minutes.'

'Who is this?' I asked.

'I think you know,' Subject replied.

*   *   *

Thirty minutes later, I was winding up the foggy road to the highest point in the city. I stood where one can usually see the most spectacular view of San Francisco and the bay on a clear night. However, it was not a clear night. The fog had rolled in early and heavily and the visibility from the lookout point was no more than twenty feet.

I was alone in the dark. I could see green hills behind me and gray matter in front of me, blocking any view at all of the city lights. The sound of life was faraway. When Subject appeared out of what looked like a cloud, a rush of fear

318

came through me.

'I've got a lot of unhappy customers,' Subject said. His tone was casual. Too casual to be followed up by, say, murder, so my nerves eased.

'Why are they unhappy?' I asked.

'Someone's digging up their gardens in the middle of the night.'

'Sure it's not raccoons?'

'I'm sure.'

'Maybe some other kind of wildlife. I'm not really an expert on that sort of thing.'

'What are you looking for?'

'The bodies,' I said.

'Isabel, you are making a huge mistake.'

'I don't think so,' I replied.

'What will it take?'

'Huh?' I said.

'What will it take to get you to leave me alone?'

I heard the engine of a car pulling into a nearby parking space. The lights broke through the fog. I welcomed the company, whoever it was.

'The truth. That's all I need. And, of course, you would have to go to prison to answer for your crimes.'

'Isabel, you don't know what you're doing.'

'*I'm* not doing anything. I'm just trying to find out what you're doing.'

'Your father said you'd stop if I filed the restraining order.'

'My father doesn't know me as well as he thinks he does.'

'What do you want from me?' Subject asked.

'Your social security number.'

Subject picked up his cell phone and dialed. 'Okay,' he said into the receiver.

I watched him for a moment, trying to figure out the hand he was playing. But it was too late. Two men in suits also appeared out of thin air. Plain clothes, my ass. You can always spot a police officer.

'I'm going to make you pay for what you've done,' I said as I was handcuffed for the fourth time in two months.

'Isabel Spellman, you are under arrest for violating the TRO filed by Mr. John Brown.'

'That's not his name.'

Subject thanked the officers and departed without another word. The cuffs were cold from the night air. The plumper cop Mirandized me as he guided me over to the unmarked vehicle.

'You have the right to remain silent. Anything you say can and will be used against you in a court of law. You have the right to an attorney . . .'

IN THE MIDDLE . . .

Arrest #4

MOM: We're already on the road, dear. I'm not canceling our disappearance to bail you out of jail.

ME: Oh, I forgot about the disappearance.

MOM: You're on your own, sweetie.

ME: No, Mom! You've got to call someone to get me out of here. I don't want to spend the night in this place.

MOM: That might be a good idea. Remember *Scared Straight*!?

320

ME: Of course I remember it. You made me watch it at least ten times in high school.

MOM: A lot of good it did.

ME: Listen, call Morty again. Call until he picks up the phone. He's home. He just can't hear it.

MOM: I don't think he should be driving at night.

ME: Mom, please.

MOM: Or during the day, for that matter.

OFFICER LINDLEY: Spellman, can you hurry this up?

ME: I got to go. Just make sure someone gets me out of here.

MOM: I'll do my best. See you on Monday, Isabel.

ME: Have a nice disappearance.

2300 hrs

Morty drove me to Henry's house, where I assumed I was no longer welcome. We had a deal and I broke it. I also correctly assumed that my mother had already broken the news to him about my fourth arrest.

I reminded Morty to drive safely and we arranged to meet at the courthouse on Monday for my arraignment. As I got out of the car, Morty said, 'Izzila, let's make this your final arrest of the year.'

'Why not?' I replied unconvincingly.

I knocked on Henry's door, bracing myself for an onslaught of insults and reprimands. He stepped outside when he saw me and mumbled in my ear, 'Let me do the talking.'

'Okay,' I replied.

Henry took my arm and lightly shoved me into his house.

'Isabel, where have you been?' he said, sounding like an actor on a sitcom.

'In jail,' I replied, and then I saw her. My complete opposite sitting on Henry's couch, drinking what had to be herbal tea.

She was well groomed and pretty in that way that being excessively well groomed can make you pretty. She had figured out precisely what she had to do to herself to be attractive. Based on the highlights in her hair and the unmistakable hue of a spray-on tan, it came with a steep price tag. She smiled unconvincingly, got to her feet, and shook my hand while Henry made his inadequate introduction.

'Isabel, this is my ex-wife, Helen.'

'Technically, we're still married,' she replied.

'I just signed the papers,' Henry interjected.

'But they haven't been filed,' she retorted.

'Do you two need to talk in private?' I asked.

'No,' they both replied in unison.

Helen looked me up and down, an assessment to serve her own ego. It had been a long day, and even a few hours in a holding cell can land a week's worth of grime on your clothes. I'm sure it served her ego very well.

'So, Isabel, how is it that you and Henry know each other?'

I remembered Henry's 'let me do the talking' warning, but I ignored it. 'I'm Henry's life coach,' I said.

Henry put his arm around my waist and squeezed, rather hard. 'Always such a kidder.'

It was only then, with Henry's arm around my waist, that I realized he was trying to pass me off as his girlfriend.

322

'I need a drink,' I said, heading over to the refrigerator.

'Thanks for dropping by, Helen. If you don't mind, Isabel has had a very busy day and I would really like to hear about it.'

'Of course it's getting late,' Helen replied. She offered me a fake smile and said, 'Isabel, it has been a pleasure.'

'Sure you can't stay for a drink?' I asked, realizing that her departure would allow Henry to speak freely.

'No,' Henry interrupted. 'She has to go.'

Helen kissed Henry on the cheek, letting her hand linger suggestively on his.

'Be well,' she said theatrically. When she was finally out the door, Henry dropped his fake smile and glared at me.

'What was that, arrest number four?' he asked.

'I'm not counting two and three.'

'We had a deal.'

'Let me finish this beer and I'll get out of your hair.'

'Where will you go?'

'There's this bus bench around the corner that I've had my eye on.'

'You're not serious.'

'No. I might sneak into my parents' house, since they're out of town. Keep an eye on Rae.'

'David is staying there.'

'Oh, yeah,' I replied, internally calculating a different plan.

'Your mother wanted me to remind you to stay away from the neighborhood and the neighbor.'

'He entrapped me.'

'What?'

'The last arrest was a trap. He told me to meet him at Twin Peaks. He asked what it would take to get me to leave him alone. He had the cops on hand if he didn't like my answer. He didn't like my answer.'

'Why can't you stop?'

'Because innocent people don't keep secrets like that. They just don't. I'll pack my things.'

'No.'

'I agreed to your terms. Besides, I've already overstayed my welcome.'

'Forget my terms. I knew you wouldn't listen to me anyway. Just stay. At least when you're here, I have some idea what you're up to.'

I settled into his couch and transitioned the topic of conversation off of me. 'So, that was your wife,' I said.

'Ex-wife,' Henry replied, and I could tell from his tone that the discussion was over.

I fell asleep long after midnight, my mind twisting around the day's events. I drifted off to sleep with a certain resolve. This case wasn't over. I just wouldn't get caught again.

THE DAVID SPELLMAN PROBLEM

Saturday, April 22
1400 hrs.

'Where are you going?' I asked.

'Rae just called. There's some kind of emergency at your parents' house.'

'A 911 kind of emergency?'

'I doubt it,' Henry replied grumpily. 'It has something to do with David.'

'Sounds fun. Can I come?'

I took Henry's lack of response as a yes and accompanied him on the ride.

The 'emergency' my sister spoke of would never have been given that title in other households. But there is a certain level of predictability that all the Spellmans possess, and when one of us deviates entirely from our known patterns, well, this can be cause for alarm. David, arguably the most predictable of all of us, has essentially never strayed from his usual MO. Until recently, that is.

Seventy-two hours after David arrived at 1799 Clay Street, ostensibly to 'keep an eye on' his youngest sister, Rae called Henry in a panic. It turns out that in that full day's time my brother had put on a pair of pajamas and a bathrobe, sat down in front of the television, and not moved except for short bathroom breaks and trips to the pantry. Rae, finding this behavior in itself suspect, kept a watchful eye on her thirty-two-year-old brother and finally made the call to Henry after David ate an entire bag of Cheetos, half a pound of M&M's, and two packages of Twizzlers, depleting my sister's emergency snack food stash by 50 percent.

The phone call Rae made to Henry went something like this:

RAE: [whispering] Henry?
HENRY: Rae, why are you whispering?
RAE: You need to come over. There's something wrong with David.
HENRY: Is he breathing?

325

RAE: Dude, if he weren't breathing, I would call 911 and perform CPR.
HENRY: I really don't like being called 'dude.'
RAE: There's something seriously wrong with David.
HENRY: Be specific, Rae.
RAE: He's been watching TV all day.
HENRY: And?
RAE: He's only eating junk food. What time is it?
HENRY: Around one P.M.
RAE: He just opened a beer.
HENRY: I really don't think this is an emergency, Rae.
RAE: He's given me almost three hundred dollars since he arrived. Every time I ask for money, he forgets that he just gave me some. Henry, please hurry! Before it's too late!

My sister's hyperbolic response to David's behavior hinged on a number of factors: her genuine worry based on seriously atypical behavior; her desire to regain mastery of the remote control; her desire not to be relieved of her entire junk food supply; and, most importantly, her desire to have more quality time with Henry.

Henry, Rae, and I peered at David through the keyhole of the living room door. We studied him the way anthropologists observe gorillas. Each of us offered our own careful assessment.

'I think he's having a Lost Weekend,' Rae said.

'No,' Henry replied. 'He's not drunk enough.'

'Maybe he's having a MILFO,' Rae suggested.

'He's too young for that,' Henry replied.

'Then what's wrong with him? He doesn't shower or go to work. He drove over here in his bathrobe. Did I mention that?'

'I think he's just depressed,' said Henry.

'Maybe he's never watched a lot of TV before and now he realizes how fun it is,' Rae suggested.

'Wrong. He's guilt-ridden,' I interjected, and kicked the door open with my foot. I walked into the room and stood in front of the television.

'Move,' was David's only response.

'Make me,' I replied.

'I will,' David replied, his dull, glazed face flushing with anger.

I smacked the power button on the TV with the palm of my hand. David switched it back on with the remote. I smacked the power switch again. David responded in turn. I walked to the back of the television and pulled out the power cord.

'Why do you have to be such a bitch?' David asked.

'Because you're an asshole,' I replied. 'Did you think I was going to side with you just because you're my brother?'

'You don't know what you're talking about,' David said, seething.

I didn't realize how angry I was until he started talking back. I wanted to see guilt, despair. Instead, he wanted a fight. And I was ready for one.

'I should have warned her about you.'

'If you know what's good for you, Isabel, you'll shut up right now.'

I picked up the bowl of pretzels from the coffee table and began tossing each twist as a single punctuation mark.

'Are you threatening me?' Pretzel toss.

'Stop that.'

'No.' Pretzel toss.

'I'm warning you, Isabel.'

'You're warning me?' Pretzel toss.

'Get out of here. Now.'

'No.' Pretzel toss.

'Henry, can you do something about her?'

'Isabel, stop throwing pretzels at your brother,' said Henry, unsure of how involved he should be.

I'd like it to go on record that David struck the first blow. Actually, it wasn't a blow. It was a leap over the coffee table and an attack on the pretzel bowl, which he extracted from my tight grip and threw across the room.

'Everybody calm down,' Henry said, like a zookeeper at the wild animal park. But the pretzel pelts charged David's anger. He pushed me as I reached for his beer (it was my plan to keep this altercation purely in the food-fight category). The shove knocked me flat on my back. I felt a dull pain from my recent rib injury, but nothing that was incapacitating. I spun around and swiped the back of David's knees with my shin. David crumbled to the floor.

In the distance I heard Rae say to Henry, 'Ten bucks on Isabel.'

David put me in a loose choke hold. I bit his arm (not hard, just enough to loosen his grip) and freed myself.

'Psycho!' David shouted after I bit him.

'Okay, that's enough!' Henry said more loudly.

'Ten bucks on Isabel,' Rae said forcefully. 'Take the action now or the bet's off the table.'

'For one thing, Rae, that's a stupid bet. She's a girl and he's got about thirty pounds on her.'

'More like forty!' I shouted as I tried to twist

David's arm around his back.

'She fights different than he does,' Rae calmly said to Henry, by way of explanation.

'But he's bigger and stronger,' Henry replied. 'Both of you! That's enough.'

'You'll see,' my sister replied, practically on cue.

'Isabel, your ribs! The doctor told you not to do anything physical for six weeks!' [It had been only four weeks at this point; however, I was mostly healed.]

'Shut up, Henry!' I shouted. He was giving up my Achilles heel.

David, on cue, elbowed me in the ribs.

'Ouch!' I shouted, still trying to twist his arm behind his back.

Rae continued her color commentary: 'Izzy's injury will make the fight more interesting, but I don't think it will alter the ultimate outcome.'

*   *   *

David vs. Isabel: The Three Great Bouts

1987
The fight began when David ratted me out to the school principal for ditching class. I lay in wait for him outside the 7-Eleven he frequented for his after-school Slurpee. [A habit that died two years later when he read research on high-fructose corn syrup.] David won the bantam-weight championship with a headlock I couldn't escape from.

1990
David locked the window of the downstairs office,

so I couldn't sneak in after curfew. I rang the doorbell, woke my Dad, and was grounded for two weeks. The following morning I attacked my brother in the kitchen as he was making breakfast. Our amateur wrestling lasted about five minutes until I pulled out of his grasp and blinded him with my mother's breakfast smoothie. David conceded defeat and I was grounded for another week.

1992
David found my marijuana stash and flushed it down the toilet. I retaliated by turning off the hot water while he was in the shower. He then put chewing gum [Only half a stick of Dentyne, because fighting dirty isn't David's style. He fought back merely to hold his ground. His heart wasn't ever really in it.] in my hair while I slept. The next morning I woke him up by assaulting him with his entire library of history books (David was a bit of a World War II buff). When David launched himself out of bed to cease my attack, I caught his index finger and twisted it back behind his arm.

Unable to move because of the pain, the then nineteen-year-old David was at my mercy.

'Say uncle,' I said.

'Uncle.'

Score: Isabel—2; David—1

Which brings me to our final bout. I relied on the fact that David had yet to determine how dirty I would fight. I made him believe I was capable of anything, which gave me the edge on the psychological front. Rae's bet was a good one. David was physically stronger, but I fought without any sense of decency. However, my brother's memory was solid. He knew my tactics and kept

330

his fingers out of my grasp for as long as he could.

I yanked on his ear instead. When he reached to pull my hand away, I twisted his arm behind his back and stretched his index figure back until he screamed for help.

'Say uncle.'

'Help me!' David said, I think to Henry.

'Isabel, that's enough,' Henry shouted, quickly approaching.

'Stay out of this,' I responded, my voice in a Dirty Harry whisper.

'Apologize,' I said to David, pushing the limits of his joints.

'Ouch! She's going to break my finger.'

Henry grabbed my wrist and squeezed hard. 'Let go,' he said with his unique authoritative air. He *is* a cop. I released the grip on my brother and watched David roll onto his back and grab his hand in pain. David looked up at me and glared.

'Petra cheated on *me*,' he said, slowly getting to his feet. He then sat down on the couch and finished his beer in one giant swig.

My rage mutated first to sympathy and then to complete mind-blowing shame. All eyes in the room stared at me with blanket distaste. My brother's expression was one of cold disdain, Henry's spoke of disappointment, and Rae seemed to suddenly realize how fantastically flawed I really was.

I exited the room and went to the refrigerator. I removed two beers and returned to the living room, uncapping one and handing it to my brother as a flimsy peace offering. I sat down on the couch next to him and allowed the silence to hang in the air. An apology was in order, but the right words

331

wouldn't come to me. I phrased it in the form of a question.

'I'm a horrible person, aren't I?'

'Yes,' David replied, and we drank in silence.

Henry suggested to Rae that they give us some privacy to talk. They stole off into the kitchen, where Rae was treated to another unwelcome educational episode, this time a lesson in chess playing. I suspect Henry was hoping David and I would work out our differences. But this conflict was too complicated for either of us to know quite how to approach it. And so I plugged the TV back in and we stared at the screen, drinking in silence.

Ten minutes later, my cell phone rang.

'Hello.'

'Have we met?'

'Speak up. I can't hear you.'

'Who?'

David grabbed the phone out of my hands. 'Hi, Mom,' he said. 'Oh, sorry,' he continued, and handed the phone back to me. 'That wasn't Mom.'

'I never said it was,' I replied. 'Hi. I think the connection is bad. I can barely hear you. That's better. *Oh, Mrs. Chandler.* Hi. Actually, I do have some information for you. I can be there in fifteen minutes. Okay. Thank you. See you then.'

I got off the phone and turned to my brother. I finally saw how devastated this new bathrobe-wearing, cheese-puff-eating David was. Had I noted at the time how wrong I had been, I might have been able to prevent the further misinterpretations of evidence that would soon come. As it was, I simply tried to redeem myself with a collection of what I believed to be supportive, sisterly comments.

332

'You're my favorite brother. You know that, right?'

'Shut up,' he replied.

'I'm here for you, if you need to, like, cry or something.'

'Shut up.'

'Do you want me to talk to her?'

David, in a flash, grabbed me by the collar of my jacket and pulled me close.

'If you say one word to her, I will hurt you.'

'So, you don't want me to talk to her?' I casually replied.

'No,' David said firmly.

'You can let go of my collar now.'

More silence.

'So why was Mom mad at you?'

'Because she thought the same thing you thought. I had my suspicions, so I hired an investigator to follow her. Mom saw me one day meeting with the woman. She assumed the worst and I never convinced her otherwise.'

'Why not?'

'Because I didn't want Mom telling you; I didn't want you in the middle of it.'

More silence.

'What am I supposed to do?' I asked, hoping David would tell me what a normal sister might do under the same exact circumstances.

'I don't know. Let's talk about something else.'

Since I had another topic at the ready, I acquiesced. 'Sure,' I said. 'Have you noticed any unusual behavior next door?'

'I haven't been looking.'

'Has he had any visitors? Been removing garbage late at night? Gardening at odd hours?'

'You're pathetic, you know that, Isabel?'

'I call it wisely suspicious. If you want to call it pathetic, that's your choice.'

David returned to his somber beer consumption. I thought perhaps I'd cheer him up with the latest family gossip.

'Have you met Rae's boyfriend?'

'She has a boyfriend?'

'Yeah, you didn't hear?'

'What's he like?' David asked.

'He's an awful lot like Snuffleupagus.'

'Meaning?'

'Sightings of him are rare.'

'Who was that on the phone?' David asked.

'Mrs. Chandler.'

'The lady with the nativity scenes you used to vandalize?'

'I have no idea what you're talking about.'

'Why is she calling you?'

'She's been struck by copycat vandals since the beginning of the year. Same MO as the ninety-two-to-ninety-three season.'

'You're investigating?'

'I was. Case solved. Rae was the mastermind.'

On cue, Rae entered the room on Henry's coattails.

'Rae, I don't want to play checkers with you.'

'Pleeeease.'

'No. If you want another lesson in chess, fine. But I am *not* playing checkers.'

'Monopoly.'

'No.'

'Jenga.'

'No!'

'You are so prehistoric.'

334

I interrupted their classic spat to prep Rae for her confession.

'Put on a nice shirt,' I said.

'Why?' Rae replied, on guard.

'Because Mrs. Chandler might be easier on you if she doesn't think you are a slob.'

'Must we do this now?' Rae asked assertively.

'Yes,' I replied. 'I need to close this case once and for all.'

THE CONFESSION

Fifteen minutes later, Rae was standing in front of Mrs. Chandler explicitly stating the crimes for which she was guilty and, impressively, taking full responsibility. Unfortunately Mrs. Chandler wasn't buying the story that Rae was the lone gunman.

'Are you telling me,' Mrs. Chandler asked, 'that you alone managed to steal, buy, or borrow fifty eight-balls on your own, that you acquired over one hundred used cans of Guinness, that you made that crime scene out of the cherubs all on your own?'

'Yes,' Rae replied, not taking the bait.

'Dear, I find that very hard to believe,' Mrs. Chandler said, staring down my sister.

'Perhaps in a few days you'll find it easier to wrap your head around the idea.'

'I doubt it,' Mrs. Chandler coldly replied.

'I'm ready for my sentencing,' Rae said, like a contrite bank robber in a courtroom.

'Excuse me?' Mrs. Chandler replied.

'She'd like to know how to make restitution,' I

interjected.

'I'd like to know *why* she did it,' Mrs. Chandler said as she carefully observed my sister.

Rae shrugged her shoulders and repeated her previous evening's explanation. 'It was an homage.'

'I see,' Mrs. Chandler said, somewhat satisfied. 'In the future, I'd appreciate it if you could keep your homages off my yard.'

'Certainly,' Rae replied.

'And now I want the names of the boys who helped you,' Mrs. Chandler said, 'because they were not creating any homage. They were simply vandalizing something.'

'I'm willing to wash your car for a month or two,' said Rae.

'Names,' Mrs. Chandler repeated.

'I'd be happy to wash your windows . . .'

Mrs. Chandler took out a pen and pad of paper from her writing desk and placed them on the dining room table.

'Names,' she repeated more assertively. It occurred to me that if Mrs. Chandler had grown up in a different time she might have done quite well in law enforcement.

'I'd be happy to walk your dog,' said Rae.

'I don't think so, dear.'

'It would be no problem.'

'Names,' Mrs. Chandler repeated yet again. But Rae wouldn't crack.

I, however, did. 'I'll give you the name,' I said. 'I only have one of them, but I'm sure he'll crack and give you the rest.'

'No!' Rae shouted at me.

'Quiet,' I snapped, and wrote down Jason

Rivers's address and telephone number. I had kept it handy, knowing that Mrs. Chandler would want not only the mastermind but the pawns in this particular crime.

We departed with the understanding that Mrs. Chandler had time to consider reparative measures and she would get back to us.

Rae was brutally silent during the brief car ride home. Her hostility could not be subdued, so I ignored her and let her seethe. We returned to the Spellman house, where Henry and my brother appeared to be having a heart-to-heart. I tried to eavesdrop, hoping to learn something about appropriate sympathetic behavior, but David heard my footsteps outside the living room door and silenced the conversation.

On the car ride back to Stone's house, I grilled Henry for further information about my brother and advice on how I should deal with my own conflicting interests.

'Just be a human being,' Henry said, after he began tiring of my questions.

'Can you elaborate on that?'

I was arraigned Monday morning at the San Francisco county criminal court building. My preliminary hearing was scheduled for the following week. Morty and I took the rest of the morning to discuss my defense.

THE 'LAW OFFICES' OF MORT SCHILLING

Monday, April 24
1335 hrs

'Which brings us to today,' Morty said.

Over our usual deli fare, Morty reminded me what was at stake.

'Your job, your reputation.'

'Women are missing because of this man.'

'You have no evidence.'

'I have a little bit of evidence.'

Morty spooned ice cubes out of his water and dropped them in his coffee.

'You got lucky until now, Izz. The first three arrests went away. But now, it could go to trial. If they offer a plea, you'll take it.'

'We'll see.'

'Listen to me carefully, Izz. You'll take the deal or you'll find a new attorney.'

THE PHILOSOPHER'S CLUB

Sunday, April 30,
1730 hrs

Almost a week had passed since my parents returned from their disappearance. Under normal circumstances, Mom would have phoned me within hours of her return to give me the inside scoop, but I suspect she was giving me the silent treatment because of Arrest #4. Just as I was about to break down and call her myself, my cell phone rang. It was Milo.

'Your sister's off the wagon again,' he said, and quickly hung up the phone.

It had been three months since Rae's previous slip. Usually her bar etiquette is somber and introspective. This time, there was an undercurrent of anger. I entered *my* bar as Rae swigged another shot of ginger ale and slammed the cup on the counter.

'I'll have another,' she said, trying to conjure the toughness of a dive-bar regular.

'What's the magic word?' Milo replied, refusing to play along.

Rae rolled her eyes and said, 'Pleeeease.'

Milo poured another shot of ginger ale and made eye contact with me as I moseyed on up to the bar.

'Well, if it ain't the long-lost Olympian,' Milo commented sarcastically.

'Are you never going to let that one die out?' I snapped.

I sat down on the barstool next to Rae and scanned the emptier-than-usual room.

Rae took a tiny sip of her whiskey-colored beverage and said point blank, 'I'm not going anywhere until I finish my drink.'

The bar was empty, I needed a beer, and it looked like the newly rude Milo could use the business. I waited for his approval.

'You get out of here as soon as another customer shows. Got it?'

'Got it,' I replied.

'What'll you have?' Milo asked.

'Guinness,' I replied, and then I decided not to test his patience. 'Red Hook.'

While Milo poured my beer I returned my attention to Rae. She was staring into her drink as if there might be something interesting at the bottom of the glass.

'What's a nice underage girl like you doing in a place like this?' I asked her.

'Why do you do that?' Rae asked somberly.

'Do what?'

'Use cheap humor to deflect all real human interaction.'

'What adult fed you that line?'

'Forget it.'

'I want a name. Now.'

'It's not all about you,' Rae said.

Milo served me my beer and chimed in, 'She's right, you know.'

'If I knew there was going to be this kind of abuse, I would have gotten drunk *before* I got here.'

Dead silence.

'What's going on?' I asked my forlorn sibling and

340

my rude bartender.

'Nothing,' Rae said, still studying the depths of her alcohol-free beverage.

Milo refreshed Rae's drink and said, 'Talk to her. You need to get it off your chest.' Then Milo turned to me and said, 'Why don't you try a more subtle approach.'

'I demand you tell me your troubles,' I said to my sister.

'You're not as funny as you think you are,' Rae replied.

'Now that's the ginger ale talking.'

More contemplative silence followed. I decided not to push her. 'I'm here if you want to talk,' I said.

'I'm not blind,' Rae replied.

Ten minutes later Rae mumbled under her breath. 'He's a rat.'

'Excuse me?' I said.

'He's a rat.'

'Who?'

'Jason Rivers.'

'Your boyfriend?'

'Ex-boyfriend.'

'What did he do?' I asked.

'He let me take the fall on the Chandler job. He told his mom it was all my idea—'

'It was all your idea.'

'Actually, it was your idea.'

'I have no idea what you're talking about.'

'Whatever,' Rae responded. 'My point is he let me take the fall. He refused to share any of the blame. Sure, I drafted the plans, but he was my wingman. We were in it together and then he starts talking like a fish.'

341

'Your metaphors need to make a doctor's appointment.'

'He ratted me out to his mom. I could understand maybe if we were in a prison camp and he was being tortured, but his *mom* . . . I need another drink.'

Rae downed another ginger ale like a shot of whiskey. The quick slug down and the grimace that followed were pure Old West. I began to wonder what kind of late-night television she was consuming.

I threw a couple bills on the bar. 'Thanks, Milo,' I said. Milo nodded a somber and silent good-bye.

'Let's go,' I said to my sister. 'I think I know something that will make you feel better.'

An hour later I watched as my sister unloaded six dozen eggs on Jason's newly purchased, used four-door Datsun. Rae topped off our car casserole with half a bag of Cheetos, which she said was her 'calling card.' On the car ride home, I briefly regretted my lapse into my juvenile response system. But then I turned to Rae and the expression on her face was one of complete peace.

'You feel better?' I asked.

'Yes,' she replied, smiling and staring off into the distance.

I pulled the car in front of 1799 Clay Street.

'So did Mom and Dad enjoy their disappearance?'

Rae turned to me with a satisfied smile. 'They said it was the best one they ever had. They're going on another getaway over summer for at least a week.'

'Well played,' I responded.

'Do you want to come in and say hello?'

342

'No,' I said. 'I'll see them tomorrow in court.'

'Later, Isabel,' Rae said as she got out of the car. 'Oh, and you might want to go back to the Philosopher's Club and check on Milo.'

'What do you mean 'check on' him?' I asked.

'He's depressed.'

'How do you know that?'

'I'm assuming he's depressed.'

'Why are you assuming he's depressed?'

'Because he lost his house.'

'How did he lose it?'

'It's a figure of speech, Isabel. He knows exactly where it is. He just no longer owns it.'

'I get the reference. How did he lose his house, figuratively speaking?'

'He couldn't pay the mortgage, I guess.'

'Why not?'

'Because business is bad.'

'How do you know his business is bad?' I asked.

'Well, for one thing,' Rae said, 'look around. And another thing, I asked him how his business was and he told me it was lousy.'

'How do you know he lost his house?'

'Because he's been sleeping on a cot in his office.'

'I go there way more than you do. How did you notice this and I didn't?'

'I'm observant,' Rae said.

'So am I,' I snapped.

'You don't always see the big picture,' Rae replied. 'At least that's what Henry says.'

Fifteen minutes later, I entered the Philosopher's Club, stormed straight through the almost-empty bar, and went right into Milo's office in the back. The surprise was that there was no

343

surprise. Rae was dead-on. Clothes were strewn about the office. His record collection and turntable were stuffed in the corner. Luggage lined the walls, along with cardboard boxes stacked in a lopsided pyramid. Milo chased after me, trying to prevent my discovery of his not-so-secret secret.

'Can't you read?' Milo said, pointing at the DO NOT ENTER sign on his door.

'Why didn't you tell me?' I said, finding myself feeling more hurt than I first imagined.

'You never asked,' he replied.

*   *   *

I drank at the bar for the rest of the night, partly to give Milo some business, but mostly to dull my nerves about my impending day in court. My preliminary hearing was scheduled for 9 A.M. After three beers, I suggested to Milo that he and I find a place together. He stared at me for a full three seconds and said, 'You're taking a cab home.' I drank another beer and asked him if he would visit me in jail, if it came to that. Then he called Henry without my knowledge. Apparently Henry had given him his card. Another beer later, Henry came to pick me up.

'Don't you have court tomorrow?' Henry asked, even though he knew the answer.

'Yes,' I said. 'That's why I'm drinking.'

'You don't want to be hungover when you talk to the judge, Isabel.'

'How do you know?'

'Let's go. I'm tired.'

On the car ride back to Henry's house I began thinking about all the life lessons, educational

344

hours, and etiquette tutorials that Henry has bestowed upon my sister, and it occurred to me that there was a clear purpose to all of it.

'I just figured it out,' I said.

'The meaning of life?' Henry replied.

'No,' I said, slurring my words a bit. 'What you're teaching Rae.'

'I'm imparting some very basic life lessons.'

'That's not it.'

'What is it, then?' Henry said, as if he were simply humoring me.

'You're teaching her how to not be like me.'

Dead silence. I gathered Henry never looked at it like that. But he had to reconsider.

'Do you want her to be like you?'

'No,' I replied. 'But I'd rather it weren't such an obvious negative.'

MY DAY IN COURT

Monday, May 1
0845 hrs

Morty and I met in the foyer of the Bryant Street criminal court building. My ancient attorney reminded me that he would be doing all the talking. I reminded Morty to wear his hearing aid. Morty then gave my outfit—a tweed skirt and blazer with a white shirt buttoned almost to the top (a relic from days impersonating a schoolteacher) [For further information, please see the first document. (Now available in paperback!)] —a nod of approval.

345

'Why can't you dress like that all the time? You look like such a lady.'

'Are you implying that I look like a man the rest of the time?'

'Maybe you should save all your smart talk for prison life.'

'That's not funny.'

'You're right. It isn't.'

My mother and father showed up a few minutes later. Their presence there was purely for show. We thought my ex-cop dad and law-abiding/surprisingly attractive mother might unduly influence the judge in my favor.

'I heard you had a nice disappearance,' I said, hoping that small-talk would take their minds off the fact that I was facing criminal charges.

'We'll tell you all about it later,' Mom said dismissively. She then adjusted my collar and said, 'This is the kind of day a mother dreams of, watching her daughter face charges of violating a temporary restraining order. We're just so proud,' Mom said, gushing sarcastically.

'You should consider a career in comedy,' I replied.

'Just keep your mouth shut in there,' Dad said, not finding any humor in the situation.

*　　*　　*

Fortune was smiling on me that day—at least that's what my father said. Morty knew the prosecuting attorney. In fact, Morty gave the prosecuting attorney his first job thirty years ago.

Morty, my own personal shark, in a twenty-year-old suit, conferred with opposing counsel and laid

346

out the evidence that we were planning on showing in court. Morty presented an affidavit from my brother explaining the B&E arrest, another affidavit, under oath, from my father explaining that the call to 911 regarding my 'borrowing' of the car was a misguided attempt to teach me simple etiquette. Dad then further justified my erratic behavior with the explanation that I was only thirty years old, but I had been working for the family business over half my life. I was bred to be suspicious, he explained; it was not my fault. Morty, without my consultation, suggested I need clinical help, not probation or jail time.

My lawyer returned to the corner where my parents and I were waiting and explained the plea: court-ordered counseling for three months. If I didn't violate the restraining order again, the conviction would be expunged from my record. If I came in contact with Subject or failed to meet my counseling obligations, two months in prison.

'You mean I need to see a shrink?' I asked.

'She'll take the deal,' my dad said.

'Wait a second,' I interrupted, wanting to fully comprehend what I was getting myself into.

'Twelve sessions,' Morty said.

'She'll take the deal,' my mom said.

'Isn't it my decision?' I asked.

'Yes,' Morty replied, 'but you're taking the deal.'

My lawyer patted me on the cheek and crept back to the opposing counsel to finalize the offer.

The most unfortunate part of the morning was that I barely noticed my narrow escape from doing real time. All I could think about was Subject and where his dot was at that very moment.

MY LAST LINE OF DEFENSE

Friday, May 5

As if reading my thoughts, my parents suggested I take a break from all fieldwork. They assigned any job that could be accomplished from my laptop computer inside Henry Stone's apartment. They further gave me the assignment of finding myself a new apartment, citing the fact that my welcome had long since been overstayed.

Before I fully committed to an all-out apartment hunt, I had one more trick up my sleeve to facilitate Bernie's removal. I printed out a flier for a party and then made five hundred copies at Kinko's. I picked up Rae after school and paid her thirty bucks to help me staple the fliers around the San Francisco State, UC Berkeley, and University of San Francisco University campuses. We also left stacks of the fliers in an assortment of Mission District cafes.

Friday evening I dropped by Bernie's place to witness the outcome of my handiwork. Bernie, drinking a beer and holding court with at least forty twenty-somethings, waved at me cheerily when I entered the party zone.

'What's going on, Bernie?' I asked, although the edge in my voice was hard to conceal.

'Some crazy kid made up fliers for his party, but he got the address wrong.'

Then Bernie guided me over to the refrigerator. 'Would you look at all this beer?' he said. 'I'm in heaven.'

It was then I realized that my fatal flaw was putting the BYOB [Bring your own booze.] acronym on the flier. That night I accepted defeat. Bernie's place was mine no more. The next day, I trolled the streets of San Francisco, meeting with landlords and scoping out FOR RENT signs.

MY CLOSET

Other than Bernie Peterson's place and a brief stint in a dorm before I failed out of college, I had always lived in the attic apartment of my parents' home. What became unmistakably clear was that, because of my limited earning potential, [Unless I was running Spellman Investigations, I couldn't expect to make more than the high 30s per year. And that's a good year.] I would soon be required to move into a closet. The closet I found was in a five story walk-up on Larkin Street in the Tenderloin. Three hundred and fifty square feet with a shag rug once a shade of cream, I presume, but now an uneven gray from years of foot traffic and cigarette dust.

I bought a bed and a secondhand dresser and desk (which would double as a kitchen table). My mother invited herself over to help me 'unpack' and 'decorate.' She took one look at the place and said, 'I hope you've had all your vaccinations.'

My mother's version of decorating involved scrubbing the apartment from top to bottom. Sometime between the delousing (her word) of the shower and decontamination of the refrigerator, my mother got off her hands and knees and helped me reposition the bed, to find a setup that would allow the front door to open completely.

'Isabel, I need you to answer a question honestly,' Mom said as we rolled the bed across the rug.

'What?'

'Are you in love with Henry?'

The question was unexpected and so was my answer, which I blurted out minus my usual habit of censorship.

'Uh, yeah.'

'He doesn't know?' she asked.

I straightened up from my bed adjustment and looked my mother in the eye. 'I thought I'd wait two and a half years until he gets Rae off to college. Then I'll make my move.'

It was really quite simple. Rae needed Henry more than I needed him. My mother got the point in a moment. Her expression softened in an instant. For my money, she looked disturbed. I didn't like it.

'Stop looking at me like that.'

'Sorry. I just want to savor the moment,' Mom replied.

'What moment?' I asked.

'You're in first place,' she said, and then began washing the windows.

THE DOT CARRIES ON . . .

I convinced myself that the terms of my plea bargain only involved me keeping my physical distance from Subject. The fact remained that I believed he was a danger to society and I wanted to catch him in whatever evil act he was guilty of, mostly to protect society, but also to redeem myself.

Each day I kept careful track of Subject's whereabouts without actually coming in contact with him. He never veered from his usual hauntings. I decided that I would only strike when he ventured out of his comfort zone. Meanwhile there was another part of the investigation that I could follow up on without breaking my probationary confines.

I returned to the Davis residence to check in and see whether there had been any new developments in the disappearance of Jennifer Davis. This time around I tried a different tack. I concluded that Mr. Davis and I, in theory, should have the same agenda.

Mr. Davis recognized me the instant he opened the door.

'Looking for a book club?' he asked dully.

'No,' I replied. 'I'm afraid that was a ruse. I'm a private investigator,' I said, taking my card out of my pocket. Not the real card, the one that says IZZY ELLMANSPAY, PI and gives the address and phone number of the Philosopher's Club as the contact info. In general, business cards seem to work like a police officer's badge. Mr. Davis opened both his door and his home to me. I made a note to myself to suggest he not be so trusting in the future. A business card is as easy to come by as a sandwich.

The house was a mess, the way a house inhabited by a married man whose wife was missing would be a mess. After a brief explanation of my interest in the case (I was investigating a person of interest in his wife's disappearance) I cut to the salient questions.

'Any word on your wife? Any new developments in the case?' I asked.

'Nothing,' Mr. Davis replied. 'The police have checked. There's no activity on her credit card, nothing from her cell phone, she's made no contact to any of her friends or family.'

'Did you notice anything different about your wife prior to her disappearance? Did any of her habits change? Did she make any new friends or develop new interests?'

'She was going to this community garden sometimes.'

'Do you know which one?'

'I think it was in the East Bay.'

'Have you ever met a man named John Brown?' I asked.

'Maybe,' Mr. Davis replied. 'It's a common name.'

'I mean recently. Have you met a man named John Brown recently?'

'Not that I can recall. What's this about?'

'Did you notice any usual behavior from your wife prior to her disappearance?' I asked.

'Do you know something about my wife's disappearance?' Mr. Davis asked, becoming justifiably agitated.

'Probably not,' I replied. 'But your wife was in contact with a man prior to her disappearance. I've been investigating that man.'

'You think she left me for another guy?' Mr. Davis asked.

'Oh, no. Nothing like that,' I said, and then realized I had said way too much. 'It's probably coincidental. She could have been asking for directions. But I like to follow all leads.'

'Who is this man?' Mr. Davis asked more aggressively.

'No one,' I replied, already trying to figure out how to handle the situation. I was so preoccupied with my investigation of Subject that I didn't consider how a man whose wife had recently vanished would respond to someone offering a potential lead.

'Clearly he's someone if he was in contact with my wife prior to her disappearance.'

'Let's not get ahead of ourselves.'

'Why were you investigating him in the first place?'

This is where my quick-on-my-feet adolescence comes into play. Deceit requires a backup plan, a story you can turn to in case of emergency.

'I'm afraid, Mr. Davis, that I've done you a disservice. I don't want to get your hopes up when my investigation may have nothing to do with your wife's disappearance.'

'If you know anything, you need to tell me now,' Mr. Davis said more forcefully.

'This is what I know,' I said, as I formulated my lie. 'I was hired by two men to perform a 'round-the-clock surveillance of a man who goes by the name of John Brown.'

'Is "John Brown" an alias?' Mr. Davis asked.

'I believe so, but I can't be sure. The men who hired me I've never met. They communicate with me through mail or e-mail and I'm paid via wire transfer from an account that I cannot seem to trace. My job is very simple: Follow Mr. Brown, document his activities, and provide a cursory investigation of anyone he comes in contact with. That's all. One day while I was following Mr. Brown he was parked on this street and had a one-minute conversation with your wife. It is my belief that your wife does not know this man, that their brief encounter was simply a coincidence. But, you understand, I needed to follow up.'

'I don't understand any of this,' Mr. Davis replied.

I stood to leave, deciding that it was time to implement an exit strategy. I handed Mr. Davis my un-card.

'If you think of anything else,' I said.

'Wait,' Mr. Davis said, 'I need you to explain to me who this Mr. Brown is.'

'Unfortunately, that's the problem. I don't know,' I replied, trying to come across as enigmatic rather than suspicious. This was a mistake, bringing an outsider into my own warped investigation. It was a mistake bringing a man who had no leads a lead that would probably go nowhere, a lead that I was on probation for investigating.

'I'll be in touch,' I said as I made my way to the door. 'I promise I'll contact you if any new developments arise,' I added and exited without looking back. I could feel Mr. Davis's eyes on me as I strode over to my vehicle. I hoped his eyes would not be able to make out the license plate number on my car. I further hoped he would not call the police and provide my license plate number. This whole thing would be hard to explain.

NOT-SO-SWEET SIXTEEN

Saturday, May 20
1200 hours

Henry Stone stayed true to his word after 'the incident,' as Rae called it, or 'the almost-vehicular-manslaughter' as Henry called it: He never gave my sister another driving lesson. My parents' recent disappearances, and work catch-up after their disappearances, offered little time for further driving instruction. Moreover, they asked me *not* to give Rae any driving lessons, since they 'didn't want me to ingrain in her any bad habits.' So, other than the school driving lessons and the rare supplement from my parents, Rae's sole practice came during my brother's depression when he let her drive his BMW.

We later discovered that while Rae drove David around on errands like his own mini chauffeur, David offered no element of instruction. He would stare out the window in a state of melancholy and not notice when Rae merely slowed down at a stop sign or failed to use her turn signal or exceeded the speed limit in a school zone. He failed to comment on the car's three-foot distance from the curb when Rae would parallel park. On occasion he would correct it himself, but mostly Rae simply pulled into driveways, which, to her credit, she had mastered.

That said, the day Rae turned sixteen my parents agreed to let her take her driving test, even though she was under suspicion at her school for spray painting the word 'Rat' on Jason Rivers's locker. They arranged a small party for after the driving test, which would include the usual suspects— Henry Stone, Mom, Dad, me, and Rae's single age-appropriate friend from school: Ashley Grayson.

The celebratory spirit vacated the room the moment Rae stormed into the house, disparaging her driving test proctor.

'Bastard.'

'Pumpkin, calm down,' interrupted my father, who had accompanied her to the DMV.

'Rat bastard.'

'Rae, stop that.'

'Stinking rat bastard.'

'That's enough!' my father said as he guided Rae to the couch for a brief chat.

'When you fail,' my father began, 'it is your fault alone, not somebody else's.'

'We have a driveway. I don't need to parallel park.'

'Actually you do, because you won't always have a driveway to pull into.'

'I can learn that later.'

'You also need to stop at stop signs. That's why they say "stop."'

'I did stop.'

'You slowed down.'

356

'Enough to see that no one was coming in either direction.'

'The sign says 'stop.' '

'Whatever,' said Rae, who then turned to and on Henry. 'This wouldn't have happened if you kept giving me driving lessons.'

'You're probably correct,' Henry replied. 'And I would have continued to offer driving instruction if you hadn't run me over.'

'I don't know how many times I can say I'm sorry,' Rae replied.

'I've forgiven you, Rae. But, seriously, you need to take responsibility for your actions. Today is your birthday; why don't you forget about the driving test. You can take it again when you're better prepared. There's cake to eat and presents to open. *Shake it off,*' Henry said assertively. And, miraculously, she did.

My mother then turned to my father and whispered, 'Maybe we should just let her move in with him for the next few years. We can take her back when she's completely house-trained.'

'Fine by me,' my dad replied.

Ashley Pierce arrived fashionably late, with her mother. Apparently my sister's recent antics had gotten around the school and up the ladder to the PTA. The Pierce mom decided that this would be a supervised visit. Rae introduced her school friend's mother to 'Henry' as a friend of the family, sensing the mother was a judgmental type. The room took notice and saw Rae's improving social radar as a sign of good things to come.

David was sitting in the corner, wearing a wrinkled shirt, eating a slice of cake, and drinking a beer, surefire evidence that he was still in a serious funk. I sat down next to him and tried to impersonate a warm and approachable sibling.

'How are you doing?' I asked, trying to keep the conversation casual and unforced. The night before I had called Henry and asked him to give me a list of safe conversation-starters for my brother. (See Appendix for full list). I was trying to avoid peeking at my cheat sheet for the rest. Fortunately David carried the conversation in an entirely new direction. David watched as Rae picked up her first present and tore through the wrapping paper before reading the card. Henry corrected her and Rae promptly rectified the situation. She hunted for the card, opened it in a flash, smiled politely, and then continued the attack on her gift.

David observed the scene with a sense of detached bemusement. 'I can't figure those two out,' he said. 'I questioned her about it not too long ago. I asked her what it was about him she liked so much.'

'What did she say?'

'She said the strangest thing. She said, 'Because he's better than us.' What does that mean?'

'I don't know,' I replied, 'but she's right.'

More silence hung in the air. I recalled a few more Henry-approved questions and decided to go for it.

'Seen any good movies lately?'

'Nope.'

'How's work?'

'I've been out since I left for the yoga retreat.'

'How was that, by the way?'

'I was only there two days.'

'Why?'

358

'Because they really frown on lying in bed and drinking bourbon.'

'I see,' I replied, without any kind of snappy retort, you might notice. 'You were gone for a week. Where did you go?'

'I checked into a five-star hotel just a few miles away.'

'What did you do there?' I asked.

'Lay in bed and drank bourbon,' David replied as if it were the most obvious of answers.

More silence, and then David offered the information I was subconsciously fishing for.

'She's coming back.'

'When?'

'Today or tomorrow.'

'Are you going to try to work things out?'

'I don't know,' he replied.

'You should go home and shower and bathe and stuff, so you don't look pathetic.'

'Thanks for the advice.'

'I'm sorry,' I said. 'I don't know what else to say.'

'Finally,' David replied.

I got David another slice of cake and a beer and left him to wallow, since that was clearly what he needed to do.

*   *   *

While Rae was opening her presents, I managed to slip out of the room and steal away to the attic apartment. The binoculars were right where I left them—under the bed. I pulled them out, parted the curtains, and viewed Subject's residence for any signs of life or death. I suspect, in my absence, Subject had once again developed some confidence in his own privacy. The shades were drawn, a few windows were open, and there were no signs that he was attempting to hide from me or anyone else.

Subject appeared to be packing. I came to this conclusion after I watched him fill cardboard boxes with items from his apartment and tape them up. I watched Subject repeat the same task for the next five to ten minutes. Then I observed Subject carrying—*you won't believe this*—a rolled-up rug down to his truck. He carefully placed it on the bed, looked around nervously, and then got into the truck and drove away. I was so engrossed in Subject's activity that I didn't notice a door open and close behind me.

'Sometimes a rolled up rug is just a rolled-up rug,' Henry said.

'But sometimes a rolled up rug is a crime scene,' I replied.

'If you make one move to leave,' Henry said, 'I'll tell your parents.'

'You are so prehistoric,' I said, checking my watch. The fact was, I had no plans to leave. With my tracking device on the car, I could calculate Subject's whereabouts and estimate where he dumped the rug and/or body.

I returned downstairs with Henry right behind me.

Rae was mauling the last of her presents.(She's not the kind of girl to save the gift wrap.) Her final acquisition, from months of unsubtle persuasion was from Henry. The entire *Dr. Who* collection on DVD. All of the newer unreleased series burned to disc, which, I pointed out to Henry, might be construed as illegal.

'How did you know this is *exactly* what I wanted?' Rae asked, playing the part of a surprised birthday girl.

'If you were less subtle,' Henry replied, 'I would be back in the hospital.'

I departed while Dad tried to convince Rae that he could watch television without talking to the TV. My mom eyed me suspiciously as I left. I returned to my closet to observe Subject's moves from my computer screen.

THE CARPET CAPER

1400 hrs

Subject drove from adjacent residence at Clay Street to the intersection of Van Ness, Market, and Eleventh Street, where he remained for ten minutes. Then Subject drove to the intersection of Market and Castro and returned home at precisely 1530 hrs, and seemed to remain in for the night. I got in my car, when I assumed Subject was home, to check the locations that he visited earlier in the day. The Eleventh Street location was a Goodwill store. Could it be that he donated his carpet, to dispose of the evidence? A dump site would be more reliable, but perhaps more suspicious. The second location had too many establishments to predict which one Subject entered.

I returned to the Goodwill Store that sits in an awkward triple intersection of Market, Van Ness, and Eleventh Street. I scanned the store for a rolled-up Oriental rug, but it seemed obvious that the item hadn't gone through processing yet. I found the foreman, who accepts deliveries, in the back of the store and provided a simple explanation for my query:

'So, my boyfriend and I just broke up and he got the rug in the settlement—but he didn't really want the rug, he just wanted to keep me from having it. Anyway, I'm pretty sure he donated it to you guys this morning. Could you check around for it? I'm happy to pay whatever you think is fair, but I really need to have that rug back. It has a lot of sentimental value.'

Twenty minutes later, the foreman was helping me load the rug into my car, not without some protest.

'There's no way this is going to fit,' he said.

There was also no way I was going to leave this evidence unattended. We stretched the rug through the trunk of the Buick, across the flattened backseat, into the front seat, and out the passenger window.

'You must really love that rug,' the foreman said as I was getting into the car to drive off.

'You have no idea,' I replied convincingly.

As soon as I exited the parking lot of the Goodwill store, I realized that the size of the rug and the experiment I needed to do on it presented a problem.

First things first; I phoned Henry. 'Where can I get Luminol on a Saturday afternoon?'

Sigh.

'Henry, are you there?'

'Why do you need Luminol?' he asked.

I lied because that's really what he wanted me to do. 'There's this stain on my carpet. I'd feel a

362

whole lot better about living here if I knew for sure it wasn't blood.'

'You took his rug, didn't you?'

'No. I need it to check the stain on my carpet, like I just said. Can you hook me up?'

'No, Isabel.'

'You could if you wanted to.'

'I'm not going to argue the point.'

'So you don't know where I can get some?'

'I can't help you,' Stone replied, and I hung up the phone.

* * *

You might think it's odd that a private investigator would have trouble finding a solution that's used on every major television crime show. But the truth is crime scenes are surveyed by cops, not PIs. At best, we might see a picture of one or witness a courtroom reenactment, but we don't investigate murders. I have never had cause to use Luminol before in my entire career. Therefore, I had no idea how to get my hands on it.

I called the only person who might know and might keep her mouth shut about the conversation.

'Rae Spellman's phone,' Rae said as she picked up on her personal line.

'Why don't you just say hello?' I said.

'Because if I just say hello it implies that the person has reached me and I can't get out of talking to him her it.'

'But you have caller ID.'

'Some people block their identities.'

'I don't.'

363

'Did you call for a reason?'

'Do you know where I can get Luminol?'

'Oh my god, you found a crime scene. I want to see it,' Rae said like a five-year-old begging for ice cream.

'No.'

'Please.'

'Where can I get Luminol?'

'There are tons of laboratory supply places online.'

'There's no time for that.'

'You could try the Spy Shop.'

'I hate that place. It's so tacky.'

'You just have to weigh your dignity against your desire to know the truth,' Rae said, and I hung up the phone once again.

*   *   *

Within ten minutes I was in the financial district, circling the block outside of the Metreon Center. I parked in a loading zone and entered the Spy Shop. As predicted, Luminol was for sale in overpriced metallic containers that looked sleek and television friendly. My transaction took under three minutes. I exited the shop and got on the bridge with my oversized companion—the Oriental rug.

*   *   *

When I arrived at Len and Christopher's apartment, I debated how to play out my little charade. In the car ride it was my plan to offer the gift, bring it inside, and spray the Luminol while I

364

had my polite hosts preparing tea and scones. However, there was something decidedly tasteless about this scenario, and since I was already on shaky ground with my actor chums, I decided to come clean.

'I need to do an experiment in your loft,' I explained when Len opened the door.

'That's a new one,' Len wearily replied.

After a cursory explanation of my 'case' and the recent trouble it had landed me in, my friends decided to oblige, since they know how my own brand of tunnel vision works.

Len, Christopher, and I lugged the hundred-pound carpet into their spacious loft and spread it out over the wide space of their twenty-by-thirty-foot concrete floor.

'If I don't find any blood on it, it's yours,' I said, hoping the offer of a potential gift might make my hosts less grumpy.

The rug, worn in various places, didn't show any signs of foul play to the naked eye, but that's what the Luminol is for. As much as I was looking forward to administering the spray myself, my actor friends wanted to live out their CSI fantasies and insisted that I let them do the inspection. Since I had invaded their home with a potentially blood-soaked item, I thought etiquette insisted I let them have their fun.

Christopher sprayed the Luminol first, crouching over the rug, studying it with the air of one who does this for a living.

'My turn,' Len said, reaching for the spray bottle.

'I'm not done yet,' Christopher replied, like a schoolboy not yet ready to relinquish his toy.

'One more spray and then it's mine.'

'Fine.'

Christopher sprayed once, then twice. Len turned to me to intervene. 'Isabel, make him give it to me.'

'Christopher, I believe it is Len's turn,' I said diplomatically, although I had already come to the conclusion that no blood would be found on the carpet.

Len took over the Luminol spray and doused the rest of the carpet in the solution. Nothing showed up. Then Christopher left he room and came back with an altogether different spray.

'It reveals urine and sperm,'

'Eew. That's disgusting.'

'I picked it up when we were dog-sitting that time, remember, Len?'

'Oh, I remember,' Len said, rolling his eyes.

The green light revealed a stain in the corner.

'You think he peed on his own rug?' Christopher asked.

'No, I think somebody's dog or cat peed on it and maybe he couldn't get the smell out. This is why *I'm* the detective. So, do you want the rug?'

Fifteen minutes later, the rug and I were heading back across the bridge. I returned to the Goodwill store to re-donate it.

The foreman was, as one might expect, confused.

'You've got to be kidding.' he said.

'I'm sorry,' I replied. 'I realized that it would be healthier for me if I just moved on. Shouldn't hang on to the past, that sort of thing. Clean slate, new carpet.'

On my way back to my closet, my cell phone rang.

'Izzy, it's your good friend Bernie.'

'I think of you more as my enemy,' I replied.

'Always a kidder.'

'Deadly serious.'

'I have some great news, kid.'

'Shoot.'

'Daisy and I are back together.'

'That's really just great news for you and Daisy. I don't see how the rest of the world might benefit.'

'Kid, the apartment. It's yours again. I had it scrubbed from top to bottom and I even cleared some more closet space.'

'I got an apartment, Bernie.'

'I thought you were living with your parents.'

'I had to move because of the restraining order.' [Note to self: End casual mentioning of restraining order.]

'So you don't need my place anymore?'

'Nope,' I said, but then I remembered something. 'Bernie, I'll call you back in a half hour.'

THE PHILOSOPHER'S CLUB

1700 hrs

The bar, as usual, was empty except for one 'on tab' customer nursing a drink and reading the newspapers in the back. Milo was wiping glasses just for show. It's not like he has to clean any.

I sat down at the bar and waited for a grumpy welcome.

'What can I get you?' Milo asked, without too much attitude.

'Can you afford seven hundred bucks a month rent?'

'First, last, security?'

'No. Just seven hundred. This month would be prorated.'

'Yeah, I could swing that,' Milo replied.

I pulled the key off the chain and wrote down the address.

'It's a sublet. The guy, Bernie, is there now. I'll watch the bar 'til you get back.'

'You sure you can handle it?' Milo asked.

I scanned the empty room and said, 'Don't make me say something rude.'

Milo departed and I pulled my computer from my bag and kept tabs on Subject. I also treated myself to the most expensive scotch in the bar. While I stared at the Dot on the computer screen, which remained parked at 1797 Clay Street, my sister entered the bar.

'What are you doing here?' she asked, although she didn't seem all that surprised.

'I'm over twenty-one,' I replied, 'so the real question is, what are *you* doing here?'

'It's still my birthday, so I thought I'd take myself out for a drink. Besides, I needed a break from the unit. Where's Milo?'

'Apartment hunting,' I vaguely replied.

'The usual,' Rae said, pointing at the ginger ale tap.

Since it was indeed her birthday and the bar was empty, I decided to let the rules slide for a day. I poured Rae a shot of her favorite beverage and tried to pump her for information.

'Have you noticed any more unusual behavior from Subject?'

'I overheard him talking with Mr. Freeman. He's definitely moving, although I couldn't tell you where. But I think he's vacating on the thirty-first.'

'That's in two days,' I said, thinking to myself.

'FYI, you better get the tracking device back before he goes. Mom's been looking for it. She's onto you.'

'Thanks for the info,' I said.

'What are you going to do?'

'Don't know,' I replied, although my mind was sorting through some interesting ideas.

'One more for the road?' Rae asked, pointing at her drink.

I squirted another shot of ginger ale and told Rae to drink fast. I wanted her out of the bar before Milo returned. Rae swallowed her shot and put two dollars on the counter, which I slid back to her.

'It's on me. Happy birthday.'

'Later, Izzy.'

Milo returned an hour later, his sour mood neutralized just a touch.

'You're a good kid,' Milo said, pinching my cheek. 'Deep down,' he continued. 'Deep, deep down.'

*   *   *

The following night, upon learning that Petra had indeed returned, I performed what I told myself would be my final act of vandalism in my adult life. I drove by David's place, found Petra's car parked in the driveway, and let all the air out of her tires.

I then left a message on her voice mail: 'It was me, in case you were wondering.'

369

I returned to my closet and drank two whiskeys as I watched the John Brown dot on my computer screen. I don't recall in all my thirty years feeling quite so pathetic.

My mother called later that night as I tried to formulate one final plan to expose Subject for what he really was.

'Isabel, do you have any idea how expensive those GPS tracking devices are?'

'Uh, yes.' [Around $400 retail.]

'If you don't return them [I only took one. Where was the other?] within forty-eight hours, I will dock your pay to cover the cost of replacement.'

'I have no idea what you're talking about,' I replied, and hung up the phone.

Clearly there was another covert investigation happening in the family. But I couldn't concern myself with that. I had the Dot to worry about, and the Dot was moving.

'THE DOT MOVES OUT OF 1797 CLAY STREET . . .'

Saturday, May 27
1140 hrs

Subject remained at 1797 Clay Street throughout the morning. I kept an eye on the Dot for signs of movement. If he was going to dump his car, this would be the time to do it. If I was going to continue my hunt, this was the point of no return.

1205 hrs

My phone rang. Milo, having just arrived at the bar, had checked his messages.

'Isabel.'

'Milo.'

'Do you have business cards with the bar's phone number on them?'

'Maybe a dozen or so.'

'Under the name Izzy Ellmanspay?'

'I almost never give them out.'

'Ellmanspay is pig Latin for Spellman?'

'You are so sharp.'

'That is so juvenile.'

'Got a message for me?'

'A guy name Davis is looking for you.'

'Thanks.'

'Maybe I'm nitpicking here, Izzy, but if you're gonna use the bar as your own personal storefront, how about giving me a heads-up?'

'Sorry, Milo. You know I'm etiquettely challenged.'

'You got some mail here too.'

'I'll be by later. Thank you, Milo,' I said more politely than usual.

1230 hrs

Rae called.

'Subject's on the move,' she said, and hung up the phone. Sometimes my sister enjoys the cryptic communications common in spy films.

The Dot got on the Bay Bridge and took I-80 to 580 east I concluded the Dot was taking I-5. From I-5 the Dot could go anywhere. I had to follow the Dot now or accept that I would never know the truth, and also I really had to get that tracking device back before the Dot moved out of the state. But the Dot knows my car, and so I decided to solicit help from the one person who had more at stake than I did.

1245 hrs

I arrived at Mr. Davis's home; he seemed to be expecting me. I explained my intentions quickly, providing just the brushstrokes, so that we could get on the road and make up for lost time. Subject was an hour ahead of us, but he wasn't shattering the speed limit, so there was time to catch up.

1300 hrs

The interior of Mr. Davis's four-wheel-drive Range Rover was spotless. I sat in the passenger seat with my computer open, shifting my focus between the Dot on the screen and the SUV's speedometer. I fought motion sickness by leaning out the window and taking in intermittent gasps of cold, fresh air.

'If you maintain a speed of seventy-five miles an hour, we should be able to catch up within the hour.'

'Now that I'm a captive audience, tell me what you know,' Mr. Davis said. His previously rational tone seemed to have grown more agitated in the last few minutes.

'In the interest of full disclosure, I have to be honest. I think Subject—I mean, Mr. Brown— knows something about your wife's disappearance, but I have no real evidence and I can't promise

372

you that we'll find anything.'

'What makes you think he has anything to do with my wife's disappearance?'

'It's a hunch, and that's all it is. I have to be honest. But he met with her briefly before she disappeared and I know that he has been connected to at least one other missing woman in the last five years. Anyone would tell you my theory is thin, but it's all we've got.'

My cell phone rang.

'Hello.'

'Isabel, it's Henry.'

'Oh, hello,' I said, trying to sound casual and not guilty.

'Don't talk. Just listen and answer my questions with simple yes or no answers. Do you understand me?'

'Yes.'

'Do you have your earpiece?'

'Huh?'

'The earpiece for your cell phone. Do you have it with you?'

'Yes.'

'Put it on so I can't be overheard.'

'Hang on,' I said, and then searched for the earpiece in my purse. I connected the device.

'Is it in?'

'Yes.'

'Are you in Mr. Davis's Range Rover right now?'

'Uh, how did you know that?'

'What did I just say? Yes or no answers only. Got it?'

'Yes.'

'Isabel, I want you to say, 'Hold on a second, I need to look that up.' '

'Huh?'

'Say it.'

'But that goes against your previous statement.'

'Don't make me ask you again,' Henry said, in a voice so loaded with irritation, I had to acquiesce.

'Hold on a second. I need to look that up,' I said.

'Is the tracking device up on your computer screen?' Henry asked.

'Yes.'

'Close it and pull up a bill and read me the balance on the bill.'

'I don't get it.'

'Just follow my instructions. Please, Isabel.'

I followed Henry's instructions, although I was slowly becoming convinced that his recent incessant contact with the Spellman clan had caused him to lose his mind.

'The balance is fourteen hundred dollars and eleven cents.'

'Leave the bill on the computer screen. Okay?'

'Yes.'

'I need to explain this as briefly as possible so Mr. Davis does not get suspicious. There won't be time for questions. You just have to trust me. Do you trust me, Isabel?'

'Of course,' I replied.

'Good. The man you're following. John Brown. He's not what you think he is.'

'I know that. That's the point.'

'Yes or no only!'

I decided silence was the best way to go.

'John Brown is good, not evil,' Henry said, and then there was more silence because yes or no would not suffice as a response.

'Did you hear me?' Henry asked.

'Yes.'

'As for Mr. Davis, the man you are currently in the car with . . .'

'Yes?'

'He's evil. Not good.'

I turned to my driver and smiled, hoping I hadn't tipped my hand. 'Annoying client' I mouthed.

'I'm gonna need more than that,' I said to Henry.

'In time. Right now, you need to redirect Mr. Davis south back to the city. Pretend you've hung up the phone, but leave it on. I'll explain while you're driving. You keep me posted of your current coordinates. Got it?'

'Yes.'

'Now say 'good-bye.' But don't disconnect.'

'A pleasure, as always, Mr. Peabody,' I said, just to annoy Henry.

In a state of utter bafflement, I followed Henry's instructions. I kept my sidelong glances to a minimum and focused on the computer screen. I pulled up a map of the city that could stand in for the previous GPS tracking program.

'He's turning around,' I said to Mr. Davis. 'He's coming back in our direction.'

'Why would he do that?' Mr. Davis asked.

'I don't know,' I replied. 'Let's keep driving until he's closed the distance. Then we'll turn around.'

1400 hrs

Davis was growing suspicious, I suspected. His patience with me was wearing thin.

'So, how was your marriage? Were you having any difficulties?' I asked.

'Don't ask any questions,' Henry said on the

other end of the line.

'We had our troubles just like anybody else, but we were working on them,' Davis replied.

'I just wish I knew what was going on,' I said.

'Me too,' Davis said.

'Why can't you just do this the easy way?' Henry asked.

'It's a mystery,' I replied.

Davis probably thought I was rambling like those people who can't stand long silences do. He ignored me, although I sensed his agitation was growing. What I wanted was for Henry to spill the dirt. I wanted to know who this man was that I was sharing a car with, this man who was apparently evil.

Henry decided to enlighten me: 'You left clues about your investigation all along. I won't go into the details now, but I had enough evidence to look at it with fresh eyes. Rae told me when the GPS device went missing. I figured you were tracking Brown since surveillance had become too risky. Rae also told me about the man you visited in the Excelsior district. Might I remind you that including a minor in an unsanctioned job involving knocking on the door of a complete stranger is irresponsible and potentially very dangerous?'

I cleared my throat to acknowledge my fault.

'I checked out the case,' Henry continued. 'The whole case. Not just the fact that Brown met a woman who later disappeared; I looked into her background, her husband's background. You wrote down an address of a location Brown visited more than once. You left it on a Post-it in my house. The address looked familiar, so I did some digging. It's a shelter for battered women. In the last ten years of her life, Mrs. Davis has been hospitalized over a dozen times for brutal assaults. She's pressed charges against her husband twice, only to drop those charges later. Now you're probably wondering what John Brown has to do with all of this. Say something casual to Mr. Davis so he doesn't grow suspicious.'

'I'm getting hungry. Are you?'

Davis eyed me quizzically. It wasn't my best material, I'll say that. I realized that my color was probably whitening as I stared at my companion, seeing him in an entirely new light. As my heart started racing, Henry continued his story.

'Here's what you need to know about John Brown. That is indeed his name, but he's working under a different social security number, not to hide his past but to protect those who contact him. I'm sure he gave you a phony DOB. What he does is provide new identities to women who are trying to escape abusive relationships. It's a last resort for some women who can't find protection under the law. They simply disappear and start a new life someplace else. Brown has cultivated connections with law enforcement and the Social Security Administration so there is no evidence of the woman's previous life. Jennifer Davis is alive and well and living thousands of miles away. Tell Mr. Davis to take the next exit and head back south. Tell him Brown's car has just passed you in the other direction.'

'We need to turn around,' I said. 'Subject has just passed us in the opposite direction.'

'That was fast,' Davis remarked.

'I think my screen froze for a minute. Sometimes there's a glitch in the device. He appears to be moving again. We have to turn around.'

'What do you think he's doing?' Davis asked.

'I don't know,' I replied, as I tried to figure out Henry's plan.

'This won't make sense now,' Henry said into my ear, 'but you need to mention money. You must somehow bring up that you will be charging him for your services. Tell him your per diem.'

Silence. I wasn't sure what Henry was getting at.

'Isabel, tell him right now your investigative services run two hundred dollars a day plus expenses.' Henry sounded pretty adamant, so I obliged.

'Mr. Davis, I hate to bring this up right now, but I feel I should mention that I-um-my investigative services cost two hundred dollars a day, plus expenses. We can, of course, negotiate a payment plan, but I just thought that in the interest of full disclosure I should mention that.'

'If you can get my wife back, I don't care what it costs.'

'Good,' Henry replied. 'Now figure out a casual way to tell me your current location.'

'Subject is currently on 580 westbound, nearing the 680 interchange. We're approximately three miles behind him,' I said, observing the upcoming exit signs.

'Good,' Henry replied. 'The Range Rover is black, right?'

'Yes,' I said. 'We're three miles behind Subject,' I added to avoid suspicion.

'We should be able to catch up with you in about fifteen minutes. You don't know me,' Henry said. 'And I'll do all the talking. And I mean it this time.'

'Yes. Stay at this speed, Mr. Davis, and we

should catch him shortly.'

'I know you're scared,' Henry said. 'But it will be fine. I'm going to hang up now,' Henry said, and the line went dead.

In the intervening ten minutes, my mind raced with the new slant on the facts of the case, facts I had misread or ignored, oversights in an investigation that were unforgivable. It never occurred to me to follow up on the missing woman's husband. It never occurred to me that Subject's insistence on privacy was to protect the innocent, not the guilty. My error in judgment left me alone in a car with a man who was probably capable of murder, and I was about to lead him to his next victim. Talk about screwups. I'd never live this one down.

1415 hrs

A siren flashed behind the Range Rover. Davis turned to me and said, 'Was I speeding?'

'Everyone is speeding,' I replied. 'But you better pull over.'

Davis pulled the car onto the shoulder of the road. The unmarked police vehicle pulled up right behind us. Henry Stone got out of the car and walked over to the passenger side of the vehicle. Davis rolled down the window.

'Is there a problem, officer?' he said, on guard.

Henry ignored the question and opened the passenger door. 'Izzy Ellmanspay, I have a warrant for your arrest. Please keep your hands where I can see them and step out of the vehicle.'

I followed Henry's instructions and got out of the car. He then spun me around and told me to keep my hands on the hood of the vehicle. He frisked me and then cuffed my hands behind my back.

Davis exited the car and circled to the other side.

'What's going on here?' Davis asked.

'Ms. Ellmanspay,' Henry said, 'is under arrest for fraud.'

'Fraud?' Davis asked, his face a collage of confusion.

'Yes,' Henry continued with pitch-perfect delivery. 'We've been after her for quite some time. Her MO is impersonating an investigator and preying on the families of missing individuals. She claims there's a man who has been seen with the individual shortly before his or her disappearance. She takes her victims on a phony chase where they eventually lose the trail. Once she's got their trust and their hopes up, she mentions her fee. I have to ask,' Henry said to Mr. Davis. 'Have you given her any money?'

'No. Not yet,' the stunned Mr. Davis replied.

'Good,' Henry said. 'You're one of the lucky ones. Sir, I suggest you go home and forget about this. I understand that your wife has recently disappeared. I'm sorry. But this woman does not know anything about her current whereabouts.'

'She was conning me?' Davis asked, looking truly lost.

'It's what she does. I'm sorry,' Henry said. 'Go home. Sit by the phone. I'm sure the police are doing everything they can. But this woman here, she can't help you.'

Davis studied me in a new light. Anger hadn't the time to surface. He remained baffled. 'I thought there was something unstable about her,'

Davis said.

Henry continued his performance: 'Your instincts were correct. Take off yourself, Mr. Davis,' he replied, and then guided me toward his car. 'You have the right to remain silent. Anything you say can and will be used against you in a court of law . . .'

AFTERMATH

After Henry placed me in the backseat of his car, he waited for Davis to pull back onto the highway. My sister popped up from her hiding place in the front seat and crawled next to me in the back.

'That was so cool,' Rae said, taking the key to unlock my cuffs.

'What is she doing here?' I asked Henry.

'She's been shadowing your investigation all along. She put a GPS device on your car so she could keep up with the investigation.'

'I was wondering who took the other device.'

'Don't feel bad,' Rae said. 'I thought Subject was evil too until I started looking into Mr. Davis.'

'What is she doing *here*?' I asked again with a different word emphasis.

'It was only yesterday,' Henry said, 'that I was able to follow up on Brown and Davis. I have a contact at women's shelter who was familiar with him. For years his older sister was a victim of spousal abuse. After working within the law to protect her, he gave up and helped her find a new identity. Over the years he's cultivated more and more resources and now it's just what he does—

that and gardening, of course. If you think about all your evidence—the credit cards, the equipment for making phony IDs. It all adds up.'

'Why didn't he just tell me?'

'The only reason he's lasted as long as he has doing this is that only a handful of people know. You went on a few dates with him and spent most of that time searching his apartment. I hardly think that encourages trust.'

'I need a drink,' I said.

'I was about to find you at your apartment,' Henry continued, 'when Rae came over and told me you had gone to the Davis residence.'

'But why did you let her come along for this sting operation?' I asked.

'Because,' Henry said with great hostility, 'she stole my car keys and then refused to get out of the car. I had already lost enough time. I had to get on the road so I could catch up with you.'

'It was only fair,' Rae said. 'I was the person who discovered that Davis was evil. Just a simple criminal check, Izzy. I can't believe you didn't do that,' Rae said, pouring salt on the wound. 'Mom says you have tunnel vision.'

'The phony arrest. What was that about?' I asked.

'Henry was the mastermind behind that,' Rae said.

'We had to convince him,' Henry explained, 'that you knew nothing. Otherwise he would have come after you and he wouldn't have stopped until he got the information he wanted. He needed to see you as a dead end. It was the only way I could think of.'

I had turned on my digital recorder in the car

382

with Davis, shortly after Henry called. I figured if things went bad, really bad, at least on my dead body the police might find some evidence to incriminate Mr. Davis. Fortunately, it never came to that. But I give to you now, ladies and gentlemen, the last known recording of *The Stone and Spellman Show*. After everything this man had done for me, I decided I could abide by his one recurring request.

THE STONE AND SPELLMAN SHOW—EPISODE 48

'THE-FAREWELL-EPISODE'

Setting: Davis pulled his car onto the road and disappeared in the distance. Rae climbed into the front seat.

RAE: Shotgun!
HENRY: Buckle up.
　　[Henry pulls the car onto the highway and we head back to the city.]
RAE: Your plan to throw Davis off the scent really was brilliant.
HENRY: Thank you.
ISABEL: Yes. Thank you.
RAE: You know what, Henry?
HENRY: What?
RAE: When I grow up I want to be just like you.
HENRY: You are too kind.
RAE: Minus all the rules.
HENRY: Of course.

RAE: And your fear of junk food.

HENRY: It's not a phobia.

RAE: And I probably won't make people read for every hour they watch TV.

HENRY: You don't have to decide right now.

RAE: And, of course, minus the whole being a man thing.

HENRY: I get the point, Rae.

[End of tape.]

At the time, I barely registered the above episode. As the landscape passed by at seventy miles an hour, I had only my own crimes occupying my thoughts. I have made many mistakes in my life, but I don't know of any one that paralleled this months-long error in judgment. To say it had me rethinking my future was an understatement. I was rethinking my whole life.

Epilogue

Epilogue

FOUR APOLOGIES
AND A WEDDING

June

A few weeks after the 'rescue operation,' as Rae would later call it, my father and I agreed that I should take some time off work. We also agreed that I owed a number of apologies. I asked my Dad what number he was thinking of and he said four. We never discussed which four people those numbers were to represent, so I decided on my own.

But first there was an apology that I did not have to give. Two weeks after Petra's return from Arizona and at least five unanswered phone calls later, David told me they had separated and were planning to divorce. Two more unanswered phone calls after that, I gave up trying to make contact and decided to wait for her to come to me. One month after Petra's return from Arizona, she knocked on my closet door.

'I'm a coward,' she said.

'I know that,' I replied.

'This is between me and your brother. I hope that one day it will be less awkward.'

'What happened?' I had to ask. She was still standing in the foyer.

'Everything happened so quickly. David started talking about having children and I thought, when did this happen? When did I suddenly grow up? I wasn't ready. One day I'm trying to decide where to go for happy hour and then the next thing I

387

know, I'm hosting dinner parties for the partners at his law firm. I woke up one day married to a respectable lawyer and I wasn't ready for it.'

'Have you seen him lately? He's not all that respectable.'

'He'll be fine,' Petra said. 'You know that, right?'

'But why did you disappear like that?'

'I was afraid of you and your family. I couldn't face any of you. And, frankly, I didn't know what you all would do. It was terrifying.'

This fear of hers was not unwarranted; I softened my stance just a bit. 'He actually tried to protect you from us,' I said.

'I know that now, but at the time I didn't,' she replied, nervously dragging her sleeves over her hands. Her hesitant eye contact was making me nervous. Petra had always been the more poised of the two of us. But the woman staring back at me from the hallway of my grungy building I could hardly recognize.

'You think you might forgive me?' she asked.

What made the question so hard was the fact that if she weren't married to my brother, I wouldn't really have cared that she betrayed her husband. But what Petra's vanishing act made me realize was that she was David's wife (or soon-to-be-ex-wife) more than she was my best friend. This role switch happened without my knowing it. The best friend would never have vanished on me. That was the crime I couldn't really forgive. I would eventually, but not in that moment.

'Maybe,' I replied. 'But not right now. He's my brother. I have to side with him, even if it's just for show.'

'Is it just for show?'

'Nah. You fucked up.'

'I know. Well, you know where to find me,' Petra said, and left.

Actually, I didn't. She had moved out of their house and didn't leave a forwarding address. But we could find that out easily enough. I watched her vanish once again down the hallway, and for a very brief moment I tried to imagine what she was going through.

It had probably taken her weeks to build up the courage to offer that apology. The delay made it even harder to receive. I decided then that I would wait no longer to deliver my own quartet of apologies. That bandage would be removed with a quick snap.

Apology #1: Mrs. Chandler

It was time to come clean with Mrs. Chandler.

We sat in her kitchen sipping an herbal tea concoction that I considered might be illegal in some states.

'I'm not sure if you're aware of this, Mrs. Chandler, but I was the person responsible for the first wave of attacks on your front lawn. Almost fifteen years ago now.'

'Dear, everyone knew you did it.'

'Really?'

'Yes.'

'Well, it's time I apologized. I'm very sorry for whatever pain I caused you.'

'Apology accepted.'

'Thank you,' I said, thinking this apologizing business was easier than I thought.

'Under one condition,' Mrs. Chandler added.

'Name it,' I replied, thinking I owed it to her.

'You'll assist me with my Fourth of July installation. I feel, in these difficult times, what our country needs most is a reminder to give peace a chance.'

I agreed to Mrs. Chandler's terms, although I was suddenly reminded why I began making 'adjustments' to her tableaus to begin with.

Apology #2: Milo

My apology to Milo was decidedly simpler. I sat down at the bar and ordered a whiskey neat.

I said, 'I'm a terrible, insensitive person. Sometimes all I think about is myself. Forgive me?'

'Eahh,' Milo said, waving his hand.

Apology #3: David Spellman

I announced my intentions at the front door. David's patience with me had reached an all-time low in recent weeks, which was not alleviated when he learned I had vandalized his future ex-wife's vehicle.

'I'm here to apologize,' I said. 'Please invite me inside and offer me an alcoholic beverage. I'm going to need some help getting through this.'

You see, as far as I could recall, this was the first time I had ever attempted an apology to my brother. David's agonizing perfection was always a barrier to any real apology. My brother walked over to his bar and poured us both a drink.

'Your godlike perfection has infuriated me for years. I've watched your playboy antics with women for close to a decade and I found you to be

390

offensive.'

'*This* is an apology?' David asked.

'I'm getting to it,' I said.

'Hurry.'

'I assumed that it was your fault because you had done it before.'

'I wasn't married before.'

'I used to think I got a raw deal having you as a brother, but let's face it, you were the one that got shortchanged.'

'You're not that bad, Isabel.'

'True. I could be a whole lot worse.'

'Don't remind me.'

'I really am sorry, David.'

'Okay.'

Apology #4: John Brown

Another thing I learned about apologies is that it's important to consider the needs of the person who is on the receiving end of the apology. Personally, I would have preferred to provide John Brown with a lengthy explanation of my recent behavior, but Henry Stone, after retrieving the tracking device from Subject's vehicle, suggested I keep it much simpler. I wrote him a very short letter, and mailed it to a P.O. box address that Henry tracked down for me.

Dear John,
I'm sorry.
Best Wishes,
—Isabel.

And Now . . . the Wedding

Daniel Castillo (Ex-boyfriend #9) did indeed marry his ex-Olympian sweetheart in a surprisingly ostentatious ceremony held at Grace Cathedral. The three-hundred-person reception took place at the Mark Hopkins hotel. Henry Stone accompanied me as my date. This was arranged by Rae, who told him I had no other options and that if I went with a relative or alone it would simply be 'pathetic.'

Henry and I shared a cab home, both having decided ahead of time that this was an event requiring large quantities of alcohol. By the end of the evening my date and I had introduced ourselves as a wide range of dignitaries and low-level royalty. (Henry was 167th in line for the throne and I was 169th). [We realized after the fact that this would make us related, and we determined to widen the number gap if we were to do a repeat performance.]

'I've never met so many Olympians in my entire life,' I said.

'We only met two: the Guatemalan wrestler and the bride.'

'Still, my previous statement is correct.'

'Did I ever tell you I was in the Olympics?' Henry said with a delightful slur in his voice.

'The Academic Olympics don't count,' I replied.

As the noise and sparkle of the evening gave way to the quiet of the San Francisco streets early in the morning of a Saturday night, Henry and I sat in comfortable silence. A night that I was convinced would be unbearable had turned out perfect. The liquor loosened my tongue and I spoke.

'We don't deserve you, Henry,' I said, echoing my mother's common refrain.

But luck was shining on me that night. Henry was out cold. Certainly a thank-you was in order, but there was no need to give him any ideas. The Spellmans needed Henry far more than he needed the Spellmans.

THE PHILOSOPHER'S CLUB

I decided to take an indefinite break from the family business and went to work for Milo at the Philosopher's Club. We thought a minor redecoration followed by a 'grand opening' might put a spark back into the bar. I contacted every person I ever shared a beverage with and eventually drew in a crowd. Soon business picked up and I was working five nights a week, making more money than I ever had as an employee of Spellman Investigations. I wasn't planning on remaining a bartender forever, but if I did decide to go back, at least I had some bargaining power.

My regular presence at the bar drew in a never-ending parade of familiar faces. About two weeks after I started, Rae dropped by the bar, ordered herself a celebratory ginger ale, and revealed to me that she had finally solved the Mucous Mystery. From the start, Rae had never accepted Henry's hoarding theory and was constantly trying to come up with another plausible explanation. Eventually she decided to ask Mr. Peabody point-blank:

'Why do you keep used tissue in your desk drawer?'

Peabody, it turns out, had some disagreement with the janitorial staff about the recycling of used tissue. The janitors believed that it was trash. Mr. Peabody believed that since bodily waste is biodegradable there was no good reason not to recycle the used tissue. To avoid any further conflict, Peterson would collect the tissues and dispose of them in the recycling bin himself. Rae thoroughly enjoyed her brief victory of logic over Henry Stone.

Morty liked to swing by on Thursday afternoons, formerly our standing lunch date. He would bring a sandwich and order a coffee, which I would spike with a bit of whiskey. We discovered that the room-temperature warmth of Milo's brew required no further adjustments on Morty's part.

I was given six months to complete my twelve obligatory sessions of court-ordered therapy. At one session a week, doing the math, I still had at least three months until I absolutely had to schedule an appointment. Not looking forward to weekly explorations of my mental landscape, I continued to procrastinate. My mother, in turn, continued to drop by the bar to see whether my therapy had, in fact, begun. She would study me in a mock-scientific fashion and then say with an authoritative air, 'Nope. You're definitely not seeing a shrink.'

She stopped once I pointed to the sign on the door that said WE HAVE THE RIGHT TO REFUSE SERVICE TO ANYONE. In my mother's defense, however, she had kept the secret I had told her to herself. The engagement ring was returned to her jewelry box. Child Protective Services would never make another house call.

As for other Spellman news: Dad had given me a deadline to figure out where I stood with the family business. That deadline was closing in. My father's un-REAFO, now exposed to my mother as a serious health concern, at first drew conflict into the unit, but now it united them. Brisk morning walks and afternoon yoga classes became staples of their daily activities. My dad no longer grumbled about the absence of red flesh at the dinner table, even coming up with 'interesting' ways to consume tofu. Of course, the new menu did curb my visits to the Spellman dinner table, but I don't think anyone noticed. On my Dad's follow-up visit to his doctor, his cholesterol had dropped eighty points and his physician agreed that surgery was no longer a necessity. My parents discovered that weekend getaways were just what they needed. Neither recognized or cared how they had been played by their youngest daughter. Within weeks Rae would get exactly what she wanted: an unsupervised weekend in the Spellman household.

As for other Spellman news: David and Petra did indeed separate, although to date neither has filed for divorce. David began showering, exercising, and working eighty-hour weeks again. The last time Rae visited his office, he made it perfectly clear that the cash machine was closed once and for all.

Rae, after the disappointment of her first driver's-test failure, devoted all her free time to manipulating family members into providing instruction. Henry continued his boycott of driving lessons, but the rest of the family (and Milo) could not escape her determination. Within two months of failing her first test, Rae retook the road test and scored 92 percent. My parents realized that a new era awaited them.

The last time Henry called me for a Rae extraction, I had to explain that now that she was driving, he would have to figure out other methods of facilitating her departure. It occurred to me that I might never see Henry now that my extractions were no longer required. But then Henry showed up at the bar on my dead Monday evening shift, and he showed up the following Monday and the Monday after that.

It seems that sometime between Arrest #1 and Arrest #4, Henry and I had become friends. [Although I never stopped introducing myself as his life coach.] It just took me longer to notice than most people.

As for non-Spellman news: Bernie sent me a postcard from Jamaica, where he and Daisy had traveled to reignite the spark in their marriage. I don't care to provide any more details, although details Bernie did provide.

*   *   *

Weeks after I had settled into my new job, Subject entered the establishment. He had received my apology in the mail and contacted my parents to find out where to reach me. Apparently, after you've harassed a person for three straight months, a simple apology is not enough.

Subject sat down at the bar and ordered a drink. He reached into his pocket to pay, but I told him it was on the house.

'You owe me,' he said.

I couldn't disagree with that.

'In the future, if I need your help, you'll give it to me. Right?' he asked, although it wasn't a question.

'Right,' I replied.

Subject finished his drink and disappeared.

*   *   *

On Friday, June 2, at 3:00 P.M., Dad dropped by the Philosopher's Club to find out if I saw my future with Spellman Investigations.

'Have you got anything to say to me?' he asked.

'You better take care of yourself, Dad, because I'm not ready to decide my future. I'm just not.'

Dad sipped his wine (the only alcoholic beverage Mom allowed me to serve him) and contemplated my response.

'Okay, Isabel. You've bought yourself more time. But you have to make a decision eventually. We all have to grow up sometime.'

'Fine, Dad. Just, you go first.'

'Very amusing. So what will you do in the meantime?' Dad asked.

'I think I need a disappearance,' I said.

'That sounds like a good idea. You could use the rest.'

APPENDIX

List of Ex-boyfriends

Ex-boyfriend #1

Name:	Goldstein, Max
Age:	14
Occupation:	Ninth grader, Presidio Middle School
Hobby:	Skateboarding
Duration:	1 month
Last Words:	'Dude, my mom doesn't want me hanging out with you anymore.'

Ex-boyfriend #2:

Name:	Slater, Henry
Age:	18
Occupation:	Freshman, UC Berkeley
Hobby:	Poetry
Duration:	7 months
Last Words:	'You've never heard of Robert Pinsky?'

Ex-boyfriend #3:

Name:	Flannagan, Sean
Age:	23
Occupation:	Bartender at O'Reilly's
Hobbies:	Being Irish; drinking
Duration:	2.5 months
Last Words:	'Oder dan Guinness, we don' haf much in common.'

Ex-boyfriend #4:

Name: Collier, Professor Michael
Age: 47 (me: 21)
Occupation: Professor of philosophy
Hobby: Sleeping with students
Duration: 1 semester
Last Words: 'This is wrong. I need to stop doing this.'

Ex-boyfriend #5:

Name: Fuller, Joshua
Age: 25
Occupation: Web designer
Hobby: Alcoholics Anonymous
Duration: 3 months
Last Words: 'Our relationship is a threat to my sobriety.'

Ex-boyfriend #6:

Name: Ryan, Sean
Age: 29
Occupation: Bartender
Hobbies: Porn, aspiring novelist
Duration: 2 months
Last Words:[1] 'I don't think we have enough in common.'
[[1] This time uttered by me.]

Ex-boyfriend #7:

Name: Greenberg, Zack
Age: 29
Occupation: Owner of web design firm
Hobby: Soccer
Duration: 1.5 months
Last Words: 'You ran a credit check on my
                brother?'

Ex-boyfriend #8:

Name: Martin, Greg
Age: 29
Occupation: Graphic designer
Hobby: Triathlons
Duration: 4 months
Last Words: 'If I have to answer one more
                fucking question, I'm going to kill
                myself.'

Ex-boyfriend #9:

Name: Castillo, Daniel
Age: 38
Occupation: Dentist
Hobby: Tennis
Duration: 3 months
Last Words: 'It was over after the fake drug
                deal.'

Ex-boyfriend #10:

Name: Larson, Greg
Age: 38
Occupation: Sheriff
Hobby: Never found one
Duration: 6 weeks
Last Word: 'Nope.'

Mark Twain's Reputed Quote: 'The coldest winter I ever spent was my summer in San Francisco.'

First of all, Twain never said this. Second, while it is true that San Francisco summers are mild compared to the rest of the country, in this climate of global warming, it sometimes gets downright hot, and unless you live in the Sunset or Richmond districts, it does not feel like winter. This is the most overused quote regarding San Francisco. It is my great hope in life that I never hear it again. And while I'm on the topic of my city, do not, under any circumstances, call it 'Frisco.' You will immediately tag yourself as a tourist and be taken advantage of by the locals.

Checklist for potential dates (Mom used this as a stocking-stuffer one Christmas)

- Should be able to verify his existence (i.e. social security number, DOB)
- He should have a complete set of teeth.
- He should have an address and phone number.
- He should speak at least one language fluently.
- You should not be able to smell him from over three feet away.
- All his vaccinations should be up to date.
- He should have at least one friend and one family member to vouch for him.
- He should have a job or a reasonable excuse why he does not.

(The list was actually three pages long, but I think you get the point.)

Memorandum
To: All concerned
From: Isabel Spellman
Date: 5/17/1998
Re: MILFO renaming.
MILFOs are now called REAFOS

Please note that since Albert Spellman has reached the age of 60, we no longer think it is appropriate to use the term MILFO for his midlife-crisis-resembling events. The new name for this phenomenon will be REAFO, which stands for Retirement-age freak-out. We think this is a superior acronym and hope you agree.

The change will take place immediately.

List of Henry-approved Conversation Starters
1. How's it going?
2. How's work?
3. What's new?
4. You doing okay?
5. If you need anything, I'm here.
6. Can I get you a beer?
7. Can I get you another beer?
8. How about one more beer?
9. Whiskey?
10. Nice shirt.
11. Nice shoes.

(Please note: Starters #6–11 I came up with on my own.)

4	4/10